HOUSE OF NO WHEN

HOUSE OF NO WHEN

MARIE Q ROGERS

Namai Press

Published by Namai Press

ISBN 978-1-7342413-3-4

Typesetting services by BOOKOW.COM

I dedicate this novel to my forebears who were carpenters and craftsmen, especially my grandfather, Charles E. Rogers, and my father, Russell G. Rogers. Growing up exposed to their work gave me the background to portray the characters and events in the story.

Acknowledgments

I could not have completed this novel without the guidance of the members of my critique pod: Allison Durham, Art Crummer, Bonnie Ogle, Catherine Puckett, Fran Sweeney, Jess Elliott, Ken Campbell, Kimberley Mullins, Richard Gartee, and Skipper Hammond. They helped me navigate the complexities of the plot and set me straight whenever I lost my way.

To the Reader

If you enjoyed this story, please leave a review on Amazon and Goodreads. Reviews not only help sell books, they encourage the writer to create new adventures.

I am available for readings and talks related to my writing. You can contact me through my website, marieqrogers.com.

EDITOR'S NOTE

The handwritten notebooks were transcribed without correcting spelling errors or abbreviations, except where clarification was necessary for readability.

THE WILSON HOUSE

Rick parked his truck across the street and studied the façade of the old house. A tall privacy fence obscured the ground floor, but the upper level peered at him through scrub trees that had grown unchecked for decades. It was a classic Queen Anne style home, complete with an octagonal turret. Once a handsome residence, the weathered siding had long ago shed its paint. Little remained of the fancy gingerbread trim.

The last time Rick had been in this part of town was the night he and Amy celebrated their thirty-fifth anniversary. Two years ago? Three? She'd been gone almost a year. He buried his grief behind a mask of memory.

They had driven by at twilight. Streetlights reflected off the bright colors of surrounding buildings, but the Wilson House brooded in shadow. He remembered Amy's laugh. "That house belongs in a scary movie!"

He'd laughed with her. "Yeah. Perfect for a ghost story. It's a shame no one ever fixed 'er up."

Rick had spent his life building new homes, but old houses always fascinated him. Today he'd come to assess whether this one was indeed worth fixing up.

He slipped the keys Bob had given him into his pocket and grabbed a flashlight. Sunday mornings saw little traffic in this college town. He walked up and down the block to get a better view of the structure. The turret roof still sported its original slate shingles. Cheap asphalt roofing covered the rest. Rick detected no sagging in the roof line. The chimney stood tall and proud. A few windows had been pierced by BB shot, but the attic window in the front gable appeared intact. Panes of colored glass formed a large "W" for Wilson, the original owner.

He crossed the street. The breath of late November, heavy with Florida humidity, stirred debris along the curb and troubled the leaves that still clung to trees. Yesterday had been sunny and nearly eighty degrees, but a cold front overnight had dropped the temperature into the forties. Rick shivered. The cold didn't use to bother him like this.

At the gate, Rick tried several keys before he found one that opened the padlock. The gate sagged to the ground and resisted opening. He set his shoulder to it and heaved. It yielded enough for him to squeeze through the gap. A veritable jungle confronted him.

Bob had told him, "I had termite and structural inspections done, so I know it's basically sound, but I want your opinion about whether I should spend money on renovation. The materials are worth something if I demolish it. And it sits on a prime business lot."

Whoever inspected the place had left no trace. Rick hooked the padlock over the gate's hasp and fought his way through the thicket until he could see the lower story more clearly. Many windows were boarded over, including the generous bay window. Plywood covered the front door. Its transom and sidelights were badly cracked. Nevertheless, the house stood defiant of time and neglect.

His plan to walk around the perimeter was thwarted by a tangle of weeds and vines that caught his jeans. *Need to come back with a machete.* He tried to avoid the little white blossoms of Spanish needles, but their seeds covered his clothing by the time he reached the front stoop. No steps, only a few cement blocks. The building had been moved here, set on piers with no foundation, and ignored for half a century.

Rick surveyed the porch roof and saw no sign of imminent collapse. The decking felt solid beneath his feet. Another padlock secured the front door. The door opened easily but scraped against shards of colored glass, the remains of a decorative glass panel. *What a shame.*

Odors of mold and cockroach assaulted him, so he left the door open for fresh air. The dark foyer stretched ahead. Doorways opened on either side and a staircase swept up into the gloom. Vertical sheets of dust motes hung in the few rays of light that slipped through gaps in the boards covering the windows. A puff of air brought them alive in a phantom dance.

Rick switched on his flashlight and entered the first room on his right. Something rustled behind him. He spun around. A rat scurried across the foyer. "Need pest control," he muttered. The flashlight beam revealed walls lined with empty shelves. Perhaps this room had been a library.

He crossed the foyer to the other front room, which was spacious, with a bay window and a fireplace. He moved down the hall, past the staircase, where two more doorways opened. The room on the right must have been the dining room. Ahead was the kitchen, identifiable by a chipped ceramic sink. As he approached the back door, Rick found a second staircase. "Wow! This house is fancier than I thought. The Wilsons probably had servants."

Beneath the back stairs was yet another door. The knob was missing but Rick managed to open it, expecting to find a closet or pantry. But —he stared down—no floor, just a few steps descending to nowhere, to the ground beneath the house. "Huh! It must have had a cellar once."

Opposite the dining room was a bedroom with a modern bathroom which reeked of human waste. In every room, floors were covered by trash, but Rick found no major damage. The staircase banister was remarkably intact, but some of the steps creaked. Halfway up, he had to pause to catch his breath. *I should exercise more.*

On the spacious landing, open doorways admitted light from the bedroom windows. Rick checked the ceilings and around windows for possible leaks. One large bedroom had its own bath. Where the back stairs emerged was another bathroom. Rick inspected two additional bedrooms.

The only sign of damage was a water stain above a door which led to a small octagonal room surrounded by windows—the turret room. No stain was visible on the ceiling. The leak appeared to be contained in the closet, under the valley between the turret and main roof. He shined his flashlight up into the closet but a shelf blocked his view. An overturned nightstand lay nearby. Rick set it upright, hoping it would support him, and climbed up to look at the closet ceiling. With his pocket knife, he poked a few boards to check for rot.

Whump! Something hit his arm. Rick nearly fell, grabbing at air to regain balance. It was only a board that had come loose from the wall above the shelf. He pushed it aside and peered into the space beyond. Inside lay a pile of dusty spiral notebooks. Cautiously, he pulled them out and laid them on the shelf. As he puzzled over who might have hidden them there and why, the nightstand collapsed beneath him.

"Oh, shit!" Rick tumbled to the floor. His phone, an old flip-phone, flew out of his pocket and lay across the room in pieces. *I am here alone. Bob is out of town. No one knows I'm here.* He checked for injuries. Nothing broken. Climbing to his feet, he picked up the remains of his phone and tried to put it together, but his hands shook. He stuffed the fragments into his pocket.

A corner of notebook peeked over the shelf. Rick pulled them all down and shook off the dust. He flipped one open. The word "cellar" leaped out.

Suddenly, the hackles rose on the back of his neck. Did a stair creak? Was someone in the house?

Shifting from alarm to anger, he stomped out of the room yelling, "Hey! You're not supposed to be in here!" He glared into each bedroom and down the back staircase. No one. Shouting, "You better get out!" he pounded down the main stairs and rushed through the first floor. Silence filled the house. He felt foolish, yelling at nothing. If anyone *had* been here, they likely escaped through the front door. He closed it.

His hand still clutched the notebooks. He set them down and returned to his inspection. In the attic, the only leak was the one by the turret, and the only debris was the remains of an antique radio. Its heavy oak cabinet lay in pieces, its tubes scattered across the floor. What a shame, he thought. Why would anyone destroy something like this?

After he finished, Rick carried the notebooks to his truck, wrapped them in a section of the morning's newspaper, and laid them on the floorboard. He brushed grime and beggar seeds from his clothing, then glanced up at the Wilson House with a grin. "Don't worry, old girl. Bob's gonna fix you up."

* * *

After supper, Rick took out the pieces of his cell phone and put them together. It still worked, but the battery cover was broken. He secured it with duct tape. *How do I go about getting it repaired?* He used to have a secretary who attended to such things. Or Amy would.

He tried to call Bob, who should have been home by now, but no one answered. Bob's cell phone went straight to voice mail. Rick left a message.

Then he remembered the notebooks. He finished cleaning them before bringing them inside. What were they and why were they hidden in the wall? He spread them on the kitchen table and hunted for his reading glasses. The front cover and first few pages of one had suffered water damage. He set it aside. On the first line of the next one, LVIII was written in the margin. A code? No, Roman numerals.

Time had yellowed the page, but the writing, in good feminine cursive, was legible. He read a few sentences before realizing they were some sort of diary. Why Roman numerals instead of dates? Another notebook began, "CLX. Today I went down to the cellar to check on Hugh." If they pertained to the Wilson House, they must have been written before it was moved. Yes, they were quite old—beige cardboard covers bound by rusty metal spirals. He hadn't seen their like since high school.

Rick closed his eyes and hunted through the recesses of his mind for the meaning of the Roman numerals. X was ten, C one hundred, L must be fifty, and V and I were five and one. If a smaller numeral preceded a larger one, you subtracted. The next notebook started with "I" in the margin. He began to read:

THE FIRST NOTEBOOK

I. Well, here I am in this little roundish room again. I seem to always end up here. The first time, I found an ashtray with an unopened pack of Salem cigs. on the bedside stand. I'm the only one here who smokes Salems. Every time I come in, the ashtray is clean, w/ a fresh pack of Salems. I have no idea who cleans & replaces things.

I wish I had someone I could talk to. Really talk to. I get tired of the others' moaning & groaning. On my way up here, I thought about my old journals. Back in real life, my journal was my comfort, my companion. I'd unload my thoughts & feelings & feel better afterward. I wished I had my old journals. Of course I didn't get them, but I got this notebook & pen.

I was destined for this room. Or it for me. The only thing I don't like is all those "windows." In the real world, they probably look out on the whole neighborhood, but I can't see a thing, so I keep the curtains closed. I pretend it's nighttime. Otherwise, I couldn't bear it.

I used to write the date in my journals, but I don't know what day it is. I thought about calling this January 1st, but that implies a new beginning & this is a crappy beginning. So I decided to use Roman numerals instead.

* * *

How odd, Rick thought. The phone rang.

It was Bob. "Well, what d'ya think? Should I fix 'er up? Or what?"

Rick cringed at the "Or what?" "Definitely fix 'er up. She's in better shape than you'd expect. I found only one leak in the roof. Renovation will cost a lot, but you'll end up with a real gem."

"I thought it was a good investment."

"How long has it been empty?"

"I'm not sure. They moved it forty-some years ago, and before that, I don't know how long since anybody lived in it."

"The wiring and plumbing need to be redone."

"I know."

"And the lead-based paint requires special handling."

"Umm."

"Did you notice those cellar stairs?"

"Yeah! I wasn't expecting that. A cellar in Florida! The house used to be on that little hill where they built the courthouse. Anywhere else, the water table's too high."

"Right."

After a long pause, Bob cleared his throat. "Well, you seem to have a handle on what needs to be done."

"What do you mean?"

"I want you to oversee the work for me. I'll make it worth your while."

"Whoa! I'm retired, remember?"

"Yeah, you're retired. You got time on your hands."

"I stay busy."

"Doing what?"

Rick sighed. "I do the work of two people. Keep the house up to Amy's standards, work in my yard..."

Bob laughed. "That doesn't take all your time. I'm not talking about an eight to five job. All you need to do is hire the best people, make sure they do it right, and send me the bill."

Rick shook his head. "You could do that yourself."

"In case you don't recall, I still work full-time. Besides, I don't have your expertise. Just think about it, will you?"

"I don't need to. I'm not interested."

"Not to change the subject, but are you still comin' over Saturday?"

Rick grinned. "Wouldn't miss it for the world."

After he hung up, Rick realized he hadn't mentioned the notebooks. Oh, well, he'd take them over Saturday. Settling into his chair, he turned the page.

II. When I went downstairs, Julio winked at me & said, "Hey, Red." I hate that. I didn't ask to be born with red hair. Besides, that's not my name. At 1ˢᵗ, I was attracted to Julio. Tall, dark & handsome, Latin charm. He came to the party dressed as Count Dracula. But the next day, after we tried everything we could think of to get out, I started crying. Julio put his arms around me. I thought he was just trying to comfort me, until his hands started roaming. Why is it, that's the first thing guys do! Doreen distracted him by sweetly asking him to open a wine bottle. She wasn't trying to save me, she was trying to get into his bed.

The first time I holed up my little room, I had a fifth of Scotch & drank most of it before I passed out. When I woke up—no hangover! That much booze should've killed me.

Maybe I'm already dead. I don't remember dying. I haven't been sick or in an accident, or anything. I just went to a damned Halloween party! I rode over with Virgil & a few others. I didn't take any drugs at the party, just Scotch, & not all that much. What happened?

Some of the others have wondered if they're dead, too. Linda said maybe we're in Hell. I'm no angel, but I don't deserve Hell. Julio said no, not Hell, maybe Purgatory. But isn't Purgatory supposed to cleanse you for Heaven? How is this cleansing?

Besides, I don't feel dead. I get hungry & thirsty. When I eat, I get full. When I drink, I get high. If I stub my toe, it hurts. If somebody tells a joke, I laugh, if I'm in the mood. When I get tired, I come to my room & sleep. With the light on. I didn't used to be afraid of the dark.

* * *

Well, this is rather bizarre, Rick thought. The writer described the little turret room where he'd found the hidden notebooks, but why couldn't she see out her windows? He looked down at the notebook. What was the story behind this? He was intrigued enough to keep reading, hoping to get an answer.

III. Where do I begin? Where my last journal left off? Before I came here? I'd just had my once-every-6-months-or-so phone conversation with that female called Mother & it ended as always. I can't please her. When I call, she's busy & will "call back." Never does. After 6 months or so she complains I don't call more often. This time she whined b/ c I didn't send her a birthday card. I reminded her that last year she complained about the card I sent, said it was cruel. She'd turned 50 & I knew she'd be depressed so I sent a funny card, one I chose carefully, one I thought wouldn't offend her. But it backfired. Of course.

Enough of that. Blaming her does no good. Nor does blaming myself. I've had enough therapy to know that. One therapist told me I shouldn't hold my anger in, I should let it out. But when I do, I get in trouble. If I don't stand up for myself, people walk all over me. If I do, no one likes me. And when I don't let the anger out, it just boils round & round inside.

Another therapist suggested I write a journal about my feelings. I stopped paying for therapists when I realized writing makes me feel better. And it's cheaper. Those negative emotions turn into paper & ink. Then they don't hurt so much.

IV. I wish I knew today's date. It must be sometime in Nov. We came here on Halloween & it was Nov 1ˢᵗ when we discovered we couldn't leave. Linda tried keeping track for awhile. She couldn't find a calendar so she took a sheet of paper & made one. Every time she slept & woke up she figured it was the next "morning." She asked what date Thanksgiving falls on this year. Not that we plan to celebrate.

Hugh pointed out that she doesn't always sleep 8 hours, just naps. She yelled, "How would you know? You sleep all the time!" Hugh shut his mouth, but Louie had to open his: "That's true." Then she started screeching. (She came to the party dressed as a witch. Was it really a disguise?)

When her voice gave out, she put her hands over her face & cried. Hugh tried to put his arms around her, but she bopped him in the head & shrieked, "Leave me alone!" So he did. She kept on boo-hoo-ing, snot all over her face. Nobody else tried to comfort her. Finally, she screamed, wadded up her calendar, threw it at Louie & stomped off to the bathroom. I can still hear her sobbing.

Louie laughed & said crying won't help. He didn't dare say that to her face! The rest of us gave him dirty looks. He sniffed & went upstairs.

I know what Linda was trying to do—use her calendar to hold onto some semblance of reality. Can't blame her for that. We have no way to keep track of time. She & Louie wore watches to the party, but they stopped working when the grandfather clock chimed midnight.

* * *

Rick held the notebook at arms' length. What was this all about? Was it written by a teenager? A mental patient? Why wouldn't she know the date? What connection was there between a clock chiming and watches not working?

V. Louie's such a prick. Linda practically lives in the downstairs bathroom. She should be all dried up by now, but the tears keep coming. I had to pee, but somebody was in the main bathroom, so I used the one in the master bedroom. Now I know what Louie does when he disappears. On the sink was a little hand mirror w/ white powder, a razor blade & a straw.

When I came out of the bathroom, he was standing by the bed staring at the curtains like he was looking out the window. He said, "This is my room. Get out!" I was too stunned to say anything. He didn't look at me, just went into his bathroom & shut the door.

It's just like him to claim the master suite. It has antique furniture, a brass bed & wallpaper with a peacock pattern. The bathroom fixtures must be original, especially the claw-foot tub. I always wanted one of those. When I was a kid, a neighbor renovated his bathroom & threw out a tub just like that. I wanted it, but nobody listened to me. It probably went to the dump.

To think I had a crush on Louie when we came to the party! He's tall & handsome, blue eyes, blonde hair, perfect skin, a true Aryan, a member of the Master Race. (That makes the rest of us mere peons.) I'd never met anyone like him before. He came to the party dressed like Louis XIV. He rode with us in Virgil's VW bus b/c his Karmann Ghia was in the shop, so he said.

When we got here, before we came inside, Louie expounded on Victorian architecture & the history of these houses. He pointed out the big green W in the gable window, backlit by a light in the attic. He said a man named Wilson built this house. One of the girls asked, "Are you an architect?" Louie looked down his nose & said, "No. I am a student." She asked, "Of what?" Louie had to think a minute before he came up with, "The Arts."

Can you believe he's still wearing his costume?

VI. At last somebody's done something constructive. Actually, destructive, but constructively so. Linda finally stopped crying & took action. Those Jack o' lanterns from the night of the party had kept burning all this non-time. I'm not sure if the candles get replaced when no one's looking or just don't burn out. The pumpkins should have rotted by now, but they're as fresh as when they were carved, as tho' no time passed.

Linda was mad at Hugh. Don't ask me why. She's always mad at Hugh. He's such a nothing. You could see him in a crowd & never know he was there. Neither short nor tall, not overweight enough to stand out, limp hair, eyes of no particular color. He was dressed as a hobo for Halloween. Did Linda pick him up off the side of the road?

This time, instead of hitting Hugh, Linda brought her fist down on a pumpkin hard enough to smash it. Instead of leaving the mess, she carried the pieces to the kitchen & put them down the garbage disposal. I helped. Then she went around the house smashing pumpkins. We all helped. We picked up the pieces & ground them down the disposal, not leaving so much as a candle. All the juice & goo got cleaned up when we left the room. And those pumpkins didn't come back.

In a way, it's a shame. Those Jack o' lanterns were works of art, carved by someone or something with skill. Each had a different expression. The pumpkin in the library by the wine bottles wore an expression of smooth satisfaction. The one on the dining room table seemed to invite us to taste its snacks. The Jack o' lantern on the keg of beer in the kitchen looked drunk. On the bar in the parlour was one with a goofy face. Upstairs were a few that looked sinister.

But I got tired of looking at them. Or them looking at me. There weren't any in the cellar & we couldn't get to the one on the front porch. If it's still there. If it ever was. It was the head of a scarecrow sitting on a rocking chair, with a friendly, welcoming smile. (Come into my parlour, said the spider to the fly.) My nerves crawled when I saw it, but I didn't know why. I do now.

* * *

Rick laid the notebook aside and rubbed his eyes. What was the story behind this journal? Some unknown red-headed woman wrote these entries and hid the notebooks inside the wall of her closet. Why?

Rick was struck by the spelling of "parlour." Amy used to do that. He recalled how frustrated she'd get with the spell check on her computer. "Now, I know that's spelled right! Oh. Darn, I used the British again." She wasn't British, but she taught high school English, and British literature was her passion.

He looked again at the penmanship. Clear and legible, it reminded him of Amy's, but she wrote left handed, with a hint of a slant. He glanced across the room at a neat stack of papers. He wasn't able to throw away anything with her writing on it, no matter how insignificant.

THANKSGIVING

The following evening, Rick's son Kyle called. "Just want to touch base. What time're you coming over Thursday?"

"Thursday?" Oh, right—Thanksgiving. Last year, despite her illness, Amy had insisted on hosting the feast. Kristie even brought her family down from Knoxville. That night he'd found Amy in tears. "I'm okay," she insisted. "This was the best Thanksgiving ever." And her last.

"Dad? You still there?"

He cleared his throat. "Sorry. No, I just don't feel up to it." He started to hang up, but Kyle put Allison on the line.

"Dad, do we have to come over and hog-tie you? The kids want you to come early and watch the Macy's parade with them."

"Aren't they getting too old for that?"

"Not Judy. She's lookin' forward to it."

When Kyle and Kristie were small, the family watched the parade together every year. The kids told their children what the tradition meant to Amy. Last year, all five grandchildren had piled on the couch with Grandma. He wasn't sure he could watch the parade without her. "I'll think about it."

Little Judy came on the phone. "Grandpa, can you make Grandma's oyster casserole for Thanksgiving?"

Rick couldn't help smiling through tears. "Of course."

After they hung up, he took out Amy's recipe box. He couldn't find the recipe under "O." He tried "C" for casserole. No luck. He rifled through the box until he came to "Scalloped Oysters." Ingredients were listed, but no directions. He called Allison back. "Do you know how to put this thing together? I don't even know how hot to set the oven."

"Yeah, I know how to make it. I just didn't remember all the ingredients. You dice the oysters and crush the crackers, then layer them…"

"Tell you what. I'll get the ingredients and bring them over Thursday. We'll put it together at your house."

Publix was out of canned oysters. The service desk called other stores for him. Main Street had a few and would hold them until he drove across town.

The duct tape on his cell phone began to unravel and stick to everything. He passed a Verizon store on his way home and decided to end that annoyance. A pretty young lady greeted him.

"I need a new battery cover." He handed her the phone.

The girl took the phone with two fingers, avoiding the tape. "It's a flip phone." She set it down and called, "Jake!"

A handsome, dark-skinned youth joined them and removed the tape. "We don't sell this piece. Maybe you could order it."

"How much?"

Jake's fingers danced over a keyboard. He shook his head. "They don't make this phone anymore. You can get a rebate on a new one. Jennifer?"

The girl picked a device off a display rack. "This one's on sale."

The screen came alive with patches of color. Rick couldn't make out the details on the screen without reading glasses. "All I want is a phone."

Jennifer reluctantly produced a flip phone similar to his old one.

* * *

Thursday dawned sunny and warm. Rick hated to be indoors, but he had promised. During the parade, Judy sat on his lap, David and Rusty on either side. Last year, the couch had been agreeably crowded. Now it was too roomy. Halfway through the parade, Judy curled up and buried her face in Rick's chest. "I miss Grandma."

Rick knew if he said anything, he'd lose control. He hugged Judy and kissed the top of her head. Neither of the boys spoke, but Rusty cuddled beside Rick and David scooted closer.

At last, the parade was over. A medley of aromas drifted from the kitchen. The children jumped up and ran to their rooms. Kyle said, "Dad, can I get you anything?"

"No thanks. Allison, isn't it about time to fix that casserole?"

"It'll be a few minutes before I'll have room in the oven."

"What else can I help you with?" Rick surveyed the kitchen. Pumpkin pie, apple pie, a cheesecake, plus whatever was in the oven. Allison and Kyle had duplicated last year's feast.

The boys bustled out the back door with a basketball. Judy came in and tugged on her mother. "Can I make Grandma's oyster casserole?"

"Of course."

"Dad, we got this," Kyle said. "Why don't you go out and shoot some hoops with the boys?"

Rick was glad to get out in the sunshine. His grandsons were faster, but he was taller.

"You're better at this than Dad is," David said.

By the time Allison called them for dinner, Rick was thoroughly winded and very hungry.

Allison had proudly set the table with china that had been a wedding gift to Rick and Amy. They'd used it last year for Thanksgiving, and Amy had bequeathed it to Kyle and Allison. Amy's menu. Amy's plates.

Once the blessing was given, Kyle asked, "Dad, what have you been doing with yourself lately?"

What had he been doing with himself? Rick sipped iced tea while he thought of something to say. "Oh. You know that old empty house on East University Avenue? Bob bought it. He asked me to check it out for him."

Kyle set his fork down. "The one with the tall fence around it?"

"Yeah. I went by Sunday."

Kyle frowned at him. "Did you go inside?"

"Of course. How else could I check it out?"

Kyle shook his head. "Why would Bob want to fix up an old haunted house?"

That got Rusty's attention. "Haunted?"

Rick smiled. "I didn't know it was haunted."

"You didn't?" Kyle said. "I thought everybody knew that."

"Just because it's empty and run down doesn't mean it's haunted."

Rusty mounded mashed potatoes on his fork and dangled it in front of his sister's face. "Wooo—a ghost!"

Judy squealed, "Don't!"

"Rusty, stop. I hope you didn't go in there alone."

"Did you see any ghosts?" David asked.

Rick shook his head. "Don't be silly. There's no such thing." He took a bite of oyster casserole. It tasted just like Amy's. "Why shouldn't I go in there alone? What do you know about the place, anyway?"

Kyle swallowed. "Back in college, me and a couple a' guys went in."

"What'd you do, break in?"

"It wasn't locked."

The boys stopped eating and looked from father to grandfather.

Rick frowned. "Just why did you go there?"

Kyle hesitated. "Hank and Willie'd heard stories and wanted to check it out. I thought we should go in at night—you know, for atmosphere, but they were dead set against that. So we went one afternoon. In broad daylight."

"Did you see any ghosts?" David asked.

"No. We didn't *see* anything." He addressed his father. "It was what we could feel. There was a coldness about the place. I don't mean temperature." He shrugged. "Hard to describe. I felt almost like... like an icy fist was squeezing my heart. It was weird. Really spooked us. We couldn't get out of there fast enough."

Rusty's eyes got big. "Did anybody get killed?"

"No." Kyle chuckled. "Hank tripped over his own feet and fell halfway down the stairs. He was too scared to get hurt. Too much adrenaline, I guess."

"What's a drenulin?" Rusty asked.

Kyle ignored his son. "Willie turned as white as the rest of us." He lowered his voice, and the boys leaned in to listen. "After we got out of there, we compared notes. The other guys described something kinda like what I felt. We were sure glad we didn't go in at night."

Rick laughed. "So, you felt something cold squeeze your heart. You boys did one heck of a job psyching yourselves up."

"Not me. I didn't believe any of those stories. Not before we went in, anyway. Now I don't know what to believe. I tell you one thing, though, I wouldn't want to go back."

"I want to! I want to!" chimed the boys.

Rick smiled. "Just what were those stories?"

"Well, Hank's aunt used to work next door for those lawyers. Secretary or something. She'd hear noises coming from the house, like banging and scraping, people screaming and crying. She told her boss, but he thought she was nuts. She actually had a nervous breakdown and had to quit her job."

Rick leaned back in his chair. "So, a crazy woman heard noises."

"No, she wasn't crazy, at least before she went to work there. Hank said the family never understood what happened. She got treatment, then she was fine, no more problems."

Rick tried the sweet potatoes. Delicious. "That's one story."

"You know Willie's dad's a cop. Willie was eavesdropping on a conversation between his parents. His dad told about one night when he and his partner were on patrol, this crack-head flagged them down, said his friend was cut real bad and needed a doctor, so they called an ambulance. The crack-head said they'd been in the house smoking, and something started bonging right over their heads. It was a grandfather clock. It just appeared, hadn't been there a few minutes before. They were so scared they jumped out a window. His friend got cut on the broken glass.

"Willie's dad suspected one crack-head had stabbed the other, so they put him in the patrol car—the one who wasn't hurt. Then they went inside to look around. Couldn't find any weapons, and they didn't see any blood, except on the broken window. And outside on the ground. They looked for a grandfather clock, but there wasn't one. Afterwards, they questioned the injured man at the hospital, and he told the same story."

"I'm sure Willie's father didn't put much stock in what a crack-head told him."

"Probably not. Willie asked if the house was haunted. His dad said no, but he told Willie to stay away from there, anyway. Of course, Willie didn't listen, but he didn't want to go in alone."

"Can we go with you next time?" David asked Rick.

Kyle gave his sons a hard look. "No. I don't want you anywhere near that place."

Rick thought about the clock mentioned in the journal. Did the writer say it was a grandfather clock?

"Dad, please be careful if you go back there, okay? Don't go alone."

"I've got no reason to go back. I checked the house out for Bob. That's it."

* * *

Friday, when Rick climbed out of bed, his whole body complained. He stretched his stiff limbs and arched his back, trying to find a square inch that didn't hurt. He'd tried too hard to impress his grandsons with his athletic prowess, and now he was paying for it. He took aspirin and regretted not taking some last night.

The morning newspaper was as thick as the humidity. Of course—the day after Thanksgiving. All those advertisements. Rick took the paper straight to his recycling bin and emptied the ads. Over his first cup of coffee, he thumbed through the news. As he poured his second cup, he looked out the window. It promised to be another warm day. A good day for yard work, if he didn't ache so badly.

The notebook he'd been reading a few days ago lay on the corner of his desk. He picked it up.

VII. I woke up to hollering & cussing right outside my door. The other girls were arguing with Louie about his bedroom. Linda insisted the room was big enough for 2 people, so she & Hugh should have it. Doreen & Rhoda said, "We're women. We need that bathroom more than you do."

Louie put his back to the door & stood up straight, a head taller than anyone else. His eyes went cold, his nostrils quivered, & his mouth pinched in at the sides. Cast him in a movie as a Nazi—he was made for the part. When he looks down his nose like that, anyone would back down. Even Linda.

Hugh was just sitting there, so she turned to him & screamed, "Why don't you do something? Why don't you speak up? Why do you just sit there like a lump of nothing?" Now Hugh is not a small man, but he seemed to shrink. His arms folded into his sides like the wings of a butchered chicken. His head seemed to sink into his shoulders like a turtle, & his eyes looked up at her like a scolded puppy.

Linda screamed, "You filthy piece of shit!" She kicked Hugh in the shins a few times, then stomped down the stairs, cussing all the way. I heard one door slam, then another. She must have gone to the downstairs bathroom. Hugh didn't move, only withdrew more into his shell.

Rhoda & Doreen were laughing. They turned to Louie and Doreen opened her mouth, but before she could say anything, Louie slipped back into his room & locked the door. They just shrugged & went into another bedroom.

I guess they're sharing a room. They're such an odd pair— Rhoda is pretty & petite. Doreen is a hippy, not all that attractive, boring brown hair & eyes. I don't know what Julio sees in her. Maybe he keeps his eyes closed.

VIII. I'm glad Linda got rid of those pumpkins. The place looks more normal without them. Now how can we get rid of those hors d'oeuvres?

Flush them down the garbage disposal? I'm in the mood for some real food but all we have is snacks. We'll finish off a tray of hors d'oeuvres, then when we're not looking, they come back. (I think I'm spelling hors d'oeuvres right. My 12th grade English teacher pounded the spelling into my brain.) Wendel can put away a bushel of them at a sitting. No wonder he's so chubby. But we never run out.

Wendel seems nice, but he doesn't talk much. Maybe b/c he's the only black person here. He must be lonely. Seems like every time I go into the parlour, Wendel's sleeping on the couch. He's almost as bad as Hugh about lying around doing nothing. At least he doesn't get in anyone's way. Neither does Hugh, but Linda does.

IX. If you want something better than hors d'oeuvres, you have to make a specific request, not just for "real food." Apparently Wendel wished for pizza. I could smell it from upstairs. Doreen said, "Let's have a party!" Julio got beer mugs out of the cupboard & Wendel filled them. We pushed aside the snacks on the dining room table & sat around eating & talking. The more we drank, the more maudlin we got. We started talking about our situation again. Nobody had any new ideas, but it got me thinking. Where did I go wrong?

It was an ordinary day at work. No one dressed up for Halloween because our boss said it was unprofessional. I had no plans that night, just go home, eat supper, watch TV. Then Gus tells about this Halloween party some guy named Virgil invited him to & said bring friends, the more the merrier. Some of my coworkers were going. Gus said be at his house at 7:30 & he'd take us over.

I had no costume, but my peasant blouse & a skirt did OK for a gypsy get-up. I wrapped a gaudy scarf around my head & donned all my beads & bangles. Then I found a mask, a little one that goes around the eyes, & I was good to go. I couldn't wear my glasses with the mask, but I had pockets.

When I got to Gus' apt., they were forming carpools b/c there wouldn't be much room to park at the party. Then this VW bus drives up—the old kind w/ the V front, & a big black dude gets out. Virgil.

He was dressed like he was going to the opera—top hat, cape, polished knee-high boots, even a walking stick with a big fake diamond! He swung open the passenger doors and bowed deeply. Something about him made my nerves rumble. I think that's where I went wrong, not listening to my intuition.

X. Isn't it amazing how 3 bathrooms aren't enough? I never lived in a house with more than 1 & we always managed. I woke up w/ a full bladder & headed to the bathroom. Rhoda came out of Julio's room, (So she's sleeping with him, too!) and beat me to the bathroom. I gave her a few minutes, then knocked on the door. No response. I heard water running—she was taking a damn bath! I pounded on the door & hollered. She told me to go somewhere else, then turned on the bathroom fan to drown me out. The door was locked. I didn't mind pounding & yelling all day but I couldn't wait. Fortunately, Louie's door wasn't locked. I went in & used his toilet.

XI. Bathroom problems again. I was downstairs & had to pee, so I headed for the study. The door was locked. I knocked. Linda said, "Go away. I'm trying to sleep." I told her I had to use the bathroom. She said go upstairs. Instead, I pounded on the door.

Hugh opened the door just enough—Linda was lying on the couch & there were blankets & a pillow on the floor. That's why she wanted Louie's room. It has both a bathroom & a double bed. And not only did she make Hugh sleep on the floor, she made him get up to answer the door!

He whispered, "Please, Linda won't let you in. Use the one upstairs. Please."

I don't feel sorry for someone who won't stick up for himself, but I weighed the inconveniences: go upstairs or argue with Linda. It was easier to go upstairs.

XII. Neither the TV nor radio work, but thank goodness the record player does. At least we can listen to music. Today we were sitting in the parlour listening. (I say "today" b/c I don't know what else to call it. I think of it as "yesterday" before I go to sleep & "today" after I wake up.

Just like Linda. It's frustrating to be lost in both time & space.) I'd had a few drinks, so did everyone else. Doreen was smoking pot. I don't know where she got it.

Wendel put on an album. Wicked Pickett. He likes black artists. The first song was "Mustang Sally." I couldn't listen to that. I came up to my room before I cried in front of everybody. I like the song, but it reminds me of my Mustang.

I loved my car. On the night of the party I left my Mustang on the street in front of Gus' apt. Didn't he wonder why it was still there the next morning? Did he even notice? Then what? I'm sure the city had my car towed. I hope they auctioned it off, didn't just scrap it. At least it'd get used, maybe even loved. It was the only thing of value I owned.

* * *

Rick cleaned his reading glasses. Why did she abandon her car? Did she get arrested? Why was she living in the house? Was it some kind of halfway house? But why would they give them pot & alcohol? Why didn't the TV or radio work?

He leaned back and closed his eyes. Amy had a Mustang when he met her. A high school graduation present from her parents. After they married, the Mustang kept breaking down, so they bought a new car, and he drove the Mustang. Eventually, they traded it for a Chevy pickup with a standard transmission. Amy drove his truck a few times when she had to, but she struggled. The gear shift required two good hands. She was safer with automatic.

XIII. Louie was in the library, reading. I wanted something to read and looked at the bookshelves, but I couldn't focus. Too many books. Too overwhelming. So I took a bottle up to my room. Guess what? A cheap romance novel lay on the bedside stand! I don't need a lot of functioning brain cells to read that stuff. I picked up the book, lit a cigarette, & read & drank & smoked until the letters wandered all over the page. Woke with no hangover, as usual, & didn't catch the bed on fire.

XIV. Awhile ago, I went down to look for something to eat. I heard a footstep behind me—Julio. I ignored him & continued rummaging through the cupboards. When I stood on tiptoe for a box of cookies, Julio reached over me & set them on the counter. I hate it when people think they need to help me, so I didn't bother to thank him.

Before I knew it, Julio's arms were twining around mine, his hands on my hands. Both hands. His touch was so tender, I couldn't resist. I leaned back against him. He slowly turned me around & started kissing me. It's been forever since I was in a man's arms. "You have the most beautiful blue eyes," he said.

I let him maneuver me across the room. When we reached the table & he started to back me over it, I realized he wanted to do it right there in the kitchen! I pushed him away. He asked what was wrong. "What's wrong?" I said. "You're screwing every girl in the house, that's what!"

"So? You'll like it. Let's go up to your room."

I wanted to. I really did. But we'd have to sneak past Rhoda & Doreen. Then once wouldn't be enough. There'd be more sneaking & I'd have to wait my turn. There'd be fights. And Julio goes from one girl to another without washing. Yuk! It just wasn't worth it.

I told him to leave me alone. He clenched his jaw & his eyes blazed. I didn't care. He walked away mumbling, "Frigid little bitch."

That's not true. I like it as much as anybody. But you have to deal with a guy's emotions, compete with his sainted mother. Or his pity. Or they give you something you don't want. The last guy I dated was 2 timing me. The other girl called & said I needed to get checked for VD. I didn't know if she was lying or not, but I took no chances. It's embarrassing to go to a dr. for something like that. I didn't catch anything, but I dropped him like a lead balloon & that cooled my taste for men.

XV. Today when I went out to the lounge, I smelled shit. Wendel was cringing by the bathroom door. I asked him what on earth was going on? "Somebody's hogging the bathroom. I can't get in." I told him to go to his room. He said, "I don't have one." I'd seen him sleeping in the parlour, but I thought he just wanted to stay close to the food. I held my nose & ran downstairs. When I returned, Wendel was gone, & so was his mess.

I can't say much about him stinking. I haven't bathed since I've been here. I wash my face when I wake up. Sometimes. If I feel like it. And I wash my hands after I use the bathroom, out of habit. Why bathe? I have no clean clothes to change into. It's not like I take overnight bags to Halloween parties.

I'm not the only one who neglects their hygiene. Louie probably bathes, but then he puts on the same clothes, the costume he wore to the party. I don't usually get close enough to smell anyone's odor, but I couldn't miss Wendel's. I wonder how he got his underwear clean.

XVI. Today I asked Wendel why he didn't take the cellar room. He said, "I don't like going down there." I don't blame him. It's creepy. Why didn't he room with Julio? I knew better than suggest Louie. Wendel just looked at his feet & shuffled one back & forth on the floor in front of him. I got it. Nobody wants to room w/ him.

XVII. Somebody just put on an Eagles album, "Hotel California." I can hear it through my door. The night of the party, that song was playing when I first stepped into this house. It should have been a warning, but I ignored it. I stood inside the front door, half-listening. Someone bumped against me trying to get in, so I moved aside. After the record ended, I could hear the radio upstairs playing Halloween songs. "Don't Fear the Reaper." Then somebody else came in behind me, swishing his cape. Virgil. I felt a draft when he shut the door. That was my last breath of fresh air.

* * *

Rick adjusted his glasses. Last breath of fresh air? Literally or figuratively? What happened at the party? All those references to magical things—was the journal writer schizophrenic?

Something else—the music. If he remembered correctly, the Eagles was a 70's band. When was the house moved? Forty-some years ago, Bob said, but it had been empty long before that. Things didn't add up.

A beam of sunlight slanted through a south window and interrupted Rick's thoughts. He sipped the last of his coffee and took the cup to the sink. As he rinsed it, he glanced out at the fine day. The aspirin had taken effect. Maybe he could get some yard work done after all.

He set the notebook on his desk. He'd take them to Bob tomorrow when he went over to watch the game.

THE GAME

Saturday evening, Bob greeted Rick with, "Are you ready for a thorough trouncing?"

"Are *you*?"

They settled in front of the TV with beer and chips, ignoring the talking heads' debate on how well Florida and Florida State would play.

Bob popped open his beer. "Well, are you going to renovate the Wilson House for me?"

Rick groaned. "I'm not looking for work. I'm supposed to be retired."

"It would really help me out. I don't know enough about this stuff. You do."

"I'll find you someone I trust. You depend too much on me. I need to cut the umbilical cord."

"Do I ever complain? Didn't I pay top dollar when you renovated my bathroom?"

The TV grabbed their attention. The Seminoles won the coin toss and deferred to the second half. As the Gators lined up to receive the ball, Bob lifted his beer, "Let's make this interesting. If the Gators lose, you fix the house for me."

"You don't want it fixed too badly."

When his team scored on their first possession, Rick allowed himself to gloat. A few minutes later, the score was tied. Bob smirked.

At the end of the first quarter, Bob brought Rick another beer and inhaled the aroma of his. "Mmm. I already envision what that house is gonna look like."

"You're crazy!" Rick said. "We're in the red zone. We're about to score."

"Naw. Get ready to watch some de-fense."

Bob was wrong. Florida made two more touchdowns. Each time, Bob handed Rick another beer. The Gators' last possession of the half resulted in a field goal. As Bob handed his friend yet another beer, he said, "Runnin' out of steam, are we?"

"We're kickin' your ass!"

"Game's not over yet. We'll rally after half-time."

They adjourned to the kitchen. Bob's wife always abandoned him on game night, but she left them a taco salad. It was too spicy for Rick. He washed it down with beer.

Bob asked, "What do you do with yourself all day, anyway? Sit around and mope?"

"I stay busy. I clean house and work in the yard. I try to keep Amy's plants the way she liked them."

"Bullshit."

Rick refused to admit Bob was right. He *did* spend too much time moping.

"You weren't ready to retire and you know it. You loved your work. You only stopped to take care of Amy. That was commendable, but what would she want you to do now? I tell you what—she'd want you to be happy. With what I'd pay you, you could hire a yard man and a housekeeper. Think about it."

At the beginning of the third quarter, the Seminoles struggled to make a field goal. Bob brought out two more beers. When the Gators made another touchdown, Rick jeered, "Still think the tide of the game is changing?"

The Seminoles answered with one of their own. "We're catchin' up!" Bob said.

"You need three touchdowns to beat us!"

At the end of the third quarter, when Rick stood up to sing, "We are the boys of old Florida...," he struggled to maintain balance. Yet, when

Bob handed him another beer, he took it. As the teams lined up, Rick grinned. "Tell you whatsh. If we *win* the game, then I'll fix yer house."

Bob grumbled, "Small consolation."

Halfway through the fourth quarter, Florida State missed a field goal. When Rick jumped up to cheer, his bravado collapsed back into his chair. *I think I'm in trouble.* What had he promised Bob at the beginning of the quarter?

At the end of the game, a sea of blue uniforms jubilantly swarmed the field. Bob grumbled, "At least I get my house fixed."

Rick looked at the pile of empty bottles beside his chair. "You tricked me! You know I don't drink much."

Bob grinned. "If I was a psychologist, I'd say deep down you want the project."

Rick had to sober up before he could drive. They finished the taco salad. Over leftover pumpkin pie and coffee, they discussed the Wilson House.

Despite himself, Rick's excitement began to build. "Have you decided what you want to do with the place when it's finished?"

"Sell it."

"As a business or a residence?"

"Probably a business."

"We need a game plan." Rick fetched paper and pencil from Bob's study. "First, we hire someone to clear trash and underbrush from around the house. Two, clean the garbage out of the house." A few bars of music flashed through Rick's head, reminding him of Bob's interest in vintage radios. "By the way, did you go up in the attic?"

"No."

"I found an antique radio there. Rather, what's left of one."

"Really? Can it be repaired?"

Rick shook his head. "It's all in pieces. Maybe some of the tubes could be salvaged."

"Bring the whole thing to me. I'll see what I can do."

"Sure." Rick returned to his list. "Three, we need to lift the house and have a foundation built. Perhaps a house moving company. After that, we'll replace the roofing. It originally had a slate roof…"

"What about tin?"

"That'd be less expensive. And cooler. I'll explore both options."

They talked for over an hour. Rick looked at Bob. "All this will cost you."

"I know. Maybe I can get a grant, from the historical society or something."

The notebooks he'd left on his desk popped into Rick's mind. "By the way, I meant to bring you something I found in the house."

"Don't worry. You can bring it another time."

"Do you know when, exactly, the house was moved?"

"Sometime back in the '70s."

"Did anyone still live there?"

"No. It was abandoned years before." A dreamy expression drifted across Bob's face. "I remember the neighborhood. There was a hardware store on the next block. When I was a kid, I'd go there with my dad. We'd ride by the old houses—they were all empty at the time. I wanted to explore them, but he wouldn't let me. He said they were unsafe, condemned." Bob smiled. "I distinctly remember the Wilson House because of the W in the gable. I liked that one best."

Rick made a mental note to research the history of the Wilson House. Maybe more information would solve the mystery of the journal. When he stood up to leave, his head was still swimming. "I don't think I should drive."

"I'll take you home."

"No! You drank more than I did. I'll call an Uber."

The next day, Rick reviewed his notes. They'd agreed to restore the building as close to original as possible. Since the notebooks contained hints of the house's appearance before it was abandoned, he decided to finish reading them before he gave them to Bob.

XVIII. It's uncanny that the 8 of us are the only ones trapped here. What happened to the other people at the party? Virgil brought us here. I didn't really want to ride with him because he gave me the heebie-jeebies, but I didn't want to offend him, so I ignored my gut feeling & put on my mask. As if that would protect me.

Virgil had other passengers, Louie XIV in the front seat & a hippie & a China doll (Doreen & Rhoda) in the middle. Gus ushered me into the back seat & started to climb in beside me, but more people drove up. Gus said he'd ride with them & show them where to go.

That was the last I saw of Gus.

Virgil drove us to Porter's Quarters. One of the girls must have said something about the neighborhood. Virgil turned around with a grin & said, "Oh, you're perfectly safe with me." He picked up a monk who got in the back with me. I was thinking, whoever heard of a black monk? Oh, well, whoever heard of a red-headed gypsy? The monk mumbled his name, Wendel. He didn't creep me out the way Virgil did.

Next, we were in the SE part of town. Virgil got out to talk to a witch & a hobo, Linda & Hugh. They argued w/ Virgil, got in their car & followed. Then to a garage apartment in the NE side. Dracula/Julio emerged from a shadow. After arguing with Linda, he followed us in his car.

Virgil pulled up in front of this beautiful Victorian house on University Ave & the others parked behind him. Now, I'd been told there'd be no room to park but we found 3 spaces right in front. A crowd of people were streaming across the lawn & into the front door. I wonder what became of them? In the end, it was only us.

Virgil opened the VW's doors with a grand flourish. I got out & admired the house. It was white with green trim. Every light was on, even the attic, shining thru a colored glass window w/ a big green W.

* * *

Wait a minute! That sounded like the Wilson House in its prime, but she placed it in its present location, on University Avenue. And the lights were on. No way! Utilities hadn't been connected after it was moved. Nor had it been painted. When had Rick first noticed the Wilson House? In college, before he and Amy were married. Through the years, the only changes he'd seen were for the worse.

Also, earlier references to a cellar—the Wilson House didn't have a cellar in its present location. No one would put a cellar in that low-lying neighborhood. It would flood. Did the party take place in a different house? No, the notebook clearly described the Wilson House. He resumed reading entry XVIII:

Louie said this house & 3 others were going to be torn down so they could build the new courthouse. He bragged about how the Historical Society, of which his mother is a member, saved them from demolition & paid to have them moved. The house on the far left had been painted rose color with lavender trim. The next one was light blue with white trim. The other was green.

Virgil joined us with a sweep of his arms, "Enter & enjoooy. This is a party you'll never forget."

Understatement of the century.

Strings of Halloween lights festooned the length of the front porch. Beside the door, a scarecrow with a Jack o' lantern head sat on a rocking chair, inviting us. We went in.

* * *

Rick scratched his head. That was an accurate description of the neighborhood, except, to his knowledge, the Wilson House had never been renovated. He read on:

XIX. Louie brags about his mother's Historical Register house. Today he & Rhoda were parading thru the house together. He'd point to a piece of furniture & say something like, "Colonial" or "Chippendale." Rhoda just ate it up. Someone giggled—Doreen was eavesdropping.

"I thought Chippendales were male strippers!" she said. They ignored her & marched upstairs. I asked, "Does Louie know how ridiculous he looks?" Doreen sniggered. "He hasn't a clue." I laughed. It felt good to laugh.

I looked around the parlour with fresh eyes, much as I did the night of the party. My first impression of the house had been—magnificent! It looked new, like I'd gone back 100 years to when it was 1st built. Wainscoting & wallpaper, a chandelier in the foyer with prisms hanging from it, others like it in the library & dining room, 2 in the parlour. Elaborate plasterwork on the ceilings. I couldn't believe it was one of those run-down places they moved instead of tearing down.

I'd never been in such a fancy house before. I felt shabby in my gypsy outfit. This house called for a full-dress affair, not a tacky Halloween party. I imagined myself in a formal gown on the arm of a guy in a tuxedo. One can always dream.

Most people decorate for Halloween with spooky stuff & keep the rooms dark, but this place didn't *look* spooky. The night was chilly & I hadn't brought a sweater but the parlour had a well-stocked bar & a cozy fireplace. I remember helping myself to a Scotch (they had Johnny Walker Black!) & warming myself by the fire. Come to think of it, I haven't felt cold since. The temperature is always perfect.

* * *

Rick was pleased with the descriptions of the décor, even though he couldn't resolve the conundrum of the dilapidated house that had been moved, never renovated, but appeared in its 1890's splendor. Temperature always perfect? Another odd remark.

XX. Someone put on a Bee Gees album. Probably Julio. For me, the jury's still out on disco, but I love that one, as long as I don't pay attention to the words. We're staying alive here, I guess, but our lives aren't going anywhere.

Disco was playing on the stereo the night of the party. People were trying to dance even tho it was crowded. One weird thing I remember— a couple dancing in the middle of the foyer, a southern belle in hoop skirts & a guy in a fake-leather frontier outfit complete with coonskin cap. Linda was trying to get thru the crowd with a plate of food. The couple went into a spin & the belle's skirts slapped into everybody, including Linda. Her dish & witch's hat went flying. Davy Crockett picked up Linda's hat, but his girlfriend only giggled. Linda said, "Excuse me!" in a tone that meant, "You idiots." She didn't bother to pick up the food she'd spilled.

No one else did, either. That's where it got really weird. The couple continued to dance, stepping on all those goodies like they didn't exist. I was buzzed from Scotch & thought maybe I wasn't seeing straight. Then I noticed how neat & clean the whole place was. There should have been empty glasses, used napkins, crumbs everywhere, but there weren't. Like invisible maids or butlers were slinking around, cleaning behind everyone. I thought that was odd, but unfortunately it wasn't odd enough to alarm me. The next time I went through the foyer, the floor was clean.

Sometimes I look at the place where Linda dropped her snacks. The image jumps into my mind—those people dancing, paying no attention to the food on the floor. What had I actually seen? Did I see their feet grind the food into the floor? Or did their feet pass thru it as if the food, or their feet, didn't exist?

* * *

Rick shivered. Had it grown cold in the house? A fire would take the chill off the air. Carrying firewood warmed him.

He poured another cup of coffee, settled down, and looked over those last two paragraphs, mulling over the surreal image of people dancing through food. The journal writer seemed to have a tenuous grip on reality, yet the writing itself was lucid. Only the events were bizarre.

That aside, why should the cleanliness of the place alarm her? He wouldn't have noticed such a detail, but Amy might have. So often he wished he could chat with her again. In the hope that things in the journal would start to make sense, Rick decided to read on:

XXI. I thought I was done writing about the party, but my brain won't rest. If I put everything down on paper, will it go away?

Sometime that evening, I returned to the bar for another drink. Virgil came in. I donned my mask. The crowd seemed to part as he approached. He saluted me with his walking stick. "Enjo-o-oy yourself. There are more delights upstairs." I asked if this was his house. "No-o-o." Every word he spoke was accompanied by a grand gesture. He said the house belonged to a good friend of his who just "lo-o-oves" to entertain. But whoever our host was, he failed to materialize.

Virgil strode away, boot heels clicking on the hardwood floor. I put my glasses back on & went upstairs. Rock music blasted on the radio, the dismal beat of "Boris the Spider." People sat around like they were stoned. I smelled pot smoke coming from a bedroom. The next had black lights. I suspect they were tripping in there. Another was dark, w/ little rustling noises. I stayed out. At the end of the hall, a door stood ajar. I peeked thru—another set of stairs led down to the kitchen! I'd never been in a house with back stairs before.

I returned to the parlour, refreshed my Scotch, & sat by the fire to smoke a cigarette & watch the costume parade. Linda & Hugh joined me. Her witch costume was homemade, but she probably bought the hat. Hugh's hobo get-up was just old clothes & he'd charcoaled his face. Julio came in with a glass of wine & some cheese. When he tried to chew, the cheese stuck to his vampire teeth & made them clack. When I got up to replenish my drink, Rhoda took my seat. Her Chinese outfit appeared genuine. She wore white face-paint & black eye makeup. While I looked for another place to sit, Doreen came in twirling her love beads. "Hey, have y'all seen the cellar? It's cool." I'd never seen a house with a cellar before. Not in Florida.

At the time, I wanted to see this cellar. Would things have turned out differently if I hadn't gone down there?

We all got up except Hugh, & Linda made him get up. Louie asked where we were going. Julio told him & he joined us. So our company was complete.

From the top of the cellar stairs, I could see Virgil. I started to put on my mask, but must have left it in the parlour. Going back for it was too much trouble. I never saw my mask again. It probably got cleaned up with the rest of the party mess.

Virgil tipped his hat. "Come on down. The weather's fine." The cellar was nothing like I expected, not dark & damp, no washing machine or furnace or rats or roaches, just one small room. Shag carpet covered everything, even the ceiling. Yellow shag carpet, of all things! There was no furniture, only cushions on the floor & lava lamps & ashtrays in the corners. A large lazy Susan full of food took up the middle of the room.

Virgil had a tray with a bottle of champagne & 9 glasses. Exactly the right number. The thought—how odd?—flitted through my mind. Still wearing his white gloves, Virgil poured each of us a glass & toasted to "Friendship!" I lifted mine to be sociable, then set it down. I'd learned the hard way never to mix Scotch with champagne. Major headache guaranteed. Doreen asked, "Aren't you going to drink that?" I gave it to her. When the bottle was empty, Virgil swooped upstairs. I thought he was going for more wine, but he never came back.

* * *

"This is impossible!" Rick announced to his empty room. "There is no cellar under the Wilson House and hasn't been since they moved it to University Avenue. What is going on here?" He tossed the notebook onto his desk.

RETURN TO THE WILSON HOUSE

Rick finished his coffee and paged through the Sunday paper. Then he wandered through the house. He didn't feel like reading or watching TV, and he wasn't up to cleaning. Despite his promise to Amy, he hadn't gone to church since her funeral. Finally, he grabbed his jacket and clipboard and drove over to the Wilson House.

He parked in the empty lot of the law firm next door. As the journal described, this building was blue with white trim. Next to it, The Inn, a bed and breakfast, was indeed rose colored. The latter had a turret, but neither house had a "W" in the gable. The fourth house could have been green once. More rundown than the Wilson House, it looked deserted except for a lamp burning in a window. The turret roof was missing, replaced by a shed roof covered with tar paper. The gable window had no "W".

He inspected the exterior of the Wilson House. The siding was weathered gray with spots of paint that once may have been white.

Rick had brought a machete to hack through the weeds and brambles, but it was barely effective. Vines drooped from trees and trailed along the ground. Something clutched his ankle. He stumbled and the clipboard flew out of his hand. He grabbed at something to check his fall—a smilax vine! The thorns tore into his flesh and blood dripped from his palm. Okay, enough! He'd have the yard cleared before he made any more excursions through this jungle. He wrapped his handkerchief around his hand, tucked the clipboard under his arm, and twisted his way through the brush to the west side of the house.

Wild grapevines shrouded this side of the porch. He went around front, climbed the concrete blocks, and explored the west porch. Some of the railings were rotten. He disturbed a loose post which fell toward him and a rusty nail snagged the knee of his jeans. Drops of blood oozed out. *When did I have my last tetanus shot?* He proceeded more cautiously and moved to the east side. Here, the porch roof had caved in and he could proceed no further. He took out the clipboard and started a list.

The original decorative glass door was a total loss and the transom and sidelights needed to be replaced. Where could he find anything authentic? Rick made a note to check antique stores and architectural salvage yards. He unlocked the door and switched on his flashlight. This time he wouldn't give anyone an opportunity to intrude. He closed the door tightly. Was every window on the first floor broken? Almost all were boarded over. He let his eyes adjust to the dimness.

Picking his way among crumbled hamburger wrappers, beer cans, and less identifiable trash, Rick explored the rooms. Every wall was paneled with wainscoting up to the chair rail. Above this was tattered wallpaper, but his practiced eye discerned the quality of the workmanship. A magnificent home at one time, it could be again, given love enough, and money.

Chunks of plaster lay on the floor. Above, remains of an intricate medallion clung to the ceiling. Once it had framed a chandelier, but all that was left was an electrical wire dangling from the center. Could he salvage enough pieces to recreate the pattern? Similar remnants clung to the ceilings of other rooms.

A few interior doors were missing, but ceilings and walls showed no water stains and the floors felt solid. In the dining room, the door that once led to that side of the porch was covered by boards and nailed shut. He followed the other doorway into the kitchen.

Judging by the style of the cabinets, Rick estimated the kitchen had been renovated in the forties or fifties. He shone his flashlight into the sink. What was this? Human vomit? He turned away in disgust and moved on. The bathroom fixtures would need to be replaced.

Returning through the dim hallway, Rick reentered the "parlour." The fireplace was choked with ashes. Rick frowned. How safe was it? The door to the east porch was blocked by the collapsed roof. When he kicked aside a pile of rags to expose a patch of hardwood floor, he disturbed a nest of roaches and a used condom. A rectangular hole by the wall, almost filled with debris, told him the house originally had a heating system. That made sense. They couldn't rely on only one fireplace. He added vent covers to his antique wish list.

Upstairs, only the landing and turret room had wainscoting. A stenciled border decorated the top of the walls. This border was absent on the wall between the two rooms. Rick decided the wall and closet had been built later to create the additional bedroom. He examined the water stain on the ceiling and glanced up into the closet. Where was the hidey hole? Covered by the loose board again. He didn't recall replacing it.

He paused to look out the bay windows of the turret room. He could see much of the neighborhood. Most of the buildings were Victorian era houses which had stood here for over a century. West toward the center of town, he could see the courthouse on its little hill. Why did the diarist say she couldn't see out her windows?

The steep attic stairs lacked a banister. Clipboard in one hand and flashlight in the other, he ascended cautiously. The gable windows admitted little light. His flashlight revealed no change from his last visit.

Downstairs again, Rick opened the door that once led to a cellar. Yes, a few steps descended to nothing but the funnel-shaped holes of ant lions. What was this? A scrap of green on the top step caught his eye. He bent down to retrieve it—a piece of thin cardboard with an oval-shaped opening in the center. Rick turned it over in his hand. It was the remains of a half mask. His memory tried to nudge him. When had something like this come up recently?

A scurrying sound—he looked up. There it was again, probably another rat. He dropped the mask fragment and wrote "rat traps" on his list before gently closing the cellar door.

As he was leaving, he thought he heard music upstairs, a hauntingly familiar tune he couldn't place. His eyes ran up the staircase. Then a car passed by, its sound system on full blast. That's probably where it came from. Before he closed the door, he listened carefully, but the house was quiet.

On his drive home, Rick thought about the notebooks. The paradox—she had described the house as it might have appeared when newly built, but with modern renovations, as though the house in the journal incorporated all time periods at once. No doubt the writer was intimately familiar with the Wilson House. Could she have been one of the vagrants who sheltered there?

At home, he called Bob. "Have you recovered from yesterday?"

"Let's not talk about it."

"Are you up to talking about the Wilson House? I went over there today."

"Sure. Tell me."

Rick went over his notes. "The floors are quarter-sawn lumber. They're badly stained, but I think they can be refinished. High quality material and workmanship went into this place."

"I know."

"With winter coming, we'll have to be careful to keep the homeless out."

"Right."

"By the way, did you know the house is haunted?"

A cold silence followed. Bob forced a laugh. "Why, did you see a ghost?"

"Of course not. Kyle told me it has that reputation."

"Oh." Bob cleared his throat. "Do you think it is?"

Rick laughed. "It's a good candidate, if there was such a thing."

"Yeah. I guess so."

After they hung up, Rick realized he had again forgotten to mention the notebooks. He fixed a light supper and settled down to read:

XXII. Halloween night, we stayed in the cellar for quite some time. We sat around on the cushions, talking & smoking & snacking on cheese & crackers. Julio took out his vampire teeth. Our conversation wasn't very stimulating, but at least Virgil was no longer with us. I assumed he was still upstairs.

After we ran out of things to talk about, a loud "Bong!" shattered the stillness of the cellar. Everyone jumped. Wendel & Julio looked at the ceiling. Another bong rang out. Louie laughed. "It's only the grandfather clock." We counted 10 more bongs—midnight.

As though he didn't trust his ears, Louie checked his watch. I was supposed to work the next day, so I stood up & headed toward the stairs. The others followed. The crowd had thinned out. I looked for my ride, Virgil, but couldn't find him, & I could have spotted his pomposity in the dark. I didn't think to go outside to see if his van was still there. Would that have saved me? Probably not.

No money for a cab. Too far to walk. I tried to think of anyone I could call. I found Rhoda & Doreen. They said Julio agreed to take them home, but he was taking Louie, too, so there wouldn't be room for me. In the parlour, Linda was yelling at Hugh, who'd lost their keys. I offered to help if they'd give me a lift. They'd already searched the parlour, so I offered to check the cellar. I hesitated at the top of the steps. I didn't really want to go down there alone, but I needed a ride. I turned over every cushion and looked under every lamp, even the lazy Susan. No keys.

Back upstairs, I looked for someone to beg a ride from, even a stranger. That's when I realized we were the only ones left in the house.

Heavy footsteps descended the staircase. Louie. He no longer appeared royal. His wig was askew, his ruffles drooped, & the "mole" on his face was a black smear. His lips were so pale I thought he'd faint. When he reached the foot of the staircase, he turned in slow motion, staring at nothing. In a cadaverous voice he said, "I cannot find my way out." I laughed and wondered what he was on. But to my dying day, I will not forget the spectacle he made, & his words still echo through my soul.

* * *

Rick shuddered. He laid the notebook on the arm of his chair and mulled over what he'd just read. Where was this leading? He recalled Kyle's story about the crack-heads who were frightened by the chiming of a non-existent grandfather clock. Then there was the puzzle of the cellar and the impossibility that this party took place after the house was moved.

He read on:

XXIII. I'm still struggling to get things straight in my mind. I try not to think about it, but it won't let me be. If I write it down, will it stop haunting me?

At the Halloween party, one minute all those other people were here, then they weren't. When we went down to the cellar w/ Virgil, the party was in full swing. When I searched for Virgil, did I not sift through a crowd of dawdlers? Although phantoms of party-goers drift through my mind, I cannot recall any specific person, any particular costume. Was it only the eight of us? One minute the house was crowded. Then—just us.

I figured we could squeeze one more into Julio's car. I found him in the library & asked for a ride. He said yes. Then he poured himself another glass of wine. I asked for his keys. Instead, he gave me a sly smile & said, "What will you give me for them?" I gave him what I hoped was a withering look. Doreen & Rhoda had followed me. They also didn't think he should drive & tried to cajole him. When Julio dangled the keys in their faces, inches out of reach, I snuck up beside him & snatched them with my left hand. He didn't expect that.

Nobody expected what came next.

I made a beeline to the front door, grabbed the knob, & pulled the door open.

Then—it was as tho someone hit me in the head with a sledgehammer. My eyes & brains went swimming around, all loose in a stormy sea, & I was all too aware of the depths below, waiting to swallow me.

The world I knew no longer existed.

Instead of the porch & the sidewalk & the street, I was looking into the kitchen!

* * *

Rick dropped the notebook, adjusted his reading glasses, picked it up again, and looked at the last few sentences: "The world I knew no longer existed. Instead of the porch & the sidewalk & the street, I was looking into the kitchen!" He tried to wrap his mind around this.

Then he slapped the notebook down, threw his head back, and laughed. "I get it now—this is fiction!" But why did the author write this as a journal rather than straight narrative? And why did she hide it in the closet wall?

XXIV. Every time I think about that moment, I relive it. I slammed the door. Hard. I turned around. The others huddled in the foyer, staring at me, staring at the door.

My first thought—I was really, really drunk. I staggered down the hall toward the kitchen, reminding myself that the front door & kitchen are at opposite ends of the house. The others followed. Wendel was passed out on the floor. Louie stood facing the back door, his mouth gaping. Julio came up behind me, grabbed his keys, & snatched the kitchen door open.

Where the back porch should have been, was the foyer, the front stairs, the grandfather clock, & beyond, down the hall, the kitchen. The back door stood open, showing the foyer, the front stairs, the grandfather clock, the hall, the kitchen.

I don't know why I didn't faint.

The others crowded around, shocked to silence. Louie croaked, "You can't get out." He stepped around Julio. Then, as tho drawn by some inconceivable force, he receded through that kitchen doorway, into the foyer. There was no way I'd go near that door!

I turned around & looked back through the kitchen, down the hallway toward the front. There stood Louie in the foyer, looking at me. You know the feeling you get when you're on a carnival ride that drops suddenly & you're suspended in the air for half a second before you fall? But a carnival ride will end. And you choose whether to get on. I wasn't given a choice.

Behind Louie, thru that open front door, I could see into the kitchen where the others bunched together staring at the open kitchen door. I watched them slowly turn around. I saw the backs of their heads as they looked at the back of my head & beyond me, through the house, to Louie in the foyer.

Doreen screamed. Rhoda fainted. Linda threw herself into Hugh's arms & he was so pale I thought he'd faint, too. Julio slammed the door. Wendel stirred & shouted, "No!" Julio said, "Wait, there's a door in the dining room." He nearly knocked me over to get there. But that door opened into the parlour! I ran to the parlour & there was Julio, facing me thru that open door. "This is not possible," he said & shut the door. We ran from one door to another, opening & closing them. Each time it was the same. Every door opened to the opposite side of the house.

What do you do when confronted by such an impossibility? Accept it? Hell, no! How can anyone accept something like that?

Rhoda tried the phone. I heard her clicking the hook. I was standing close enough I should have heard a dial tone. None. She dialed anyway. I watched her finger poke into the dial, drag it around & release it. Another number, poke, drag around, release. Poke, drag, release. Seven times. Each took an eternity. Nothing. Rhoda clicked again and dialed "o" for operator. Silence. Then she collapsed into the chair at the phone table & cried, smearing face paint everywhere. Wendell checked the telephone wire. It hadn't been cut. Not from the inside.

Then, as if someone had shot a starter's pistol, we all bolted for the windows. We tried to open them. Linda pounded on one hard enough to break it, but only bruised her fist. Julio grabbed a poker from the fireplace & tried to pry one open. The poker bent. He tried smashing the window with the poker. It bent further. Louie broke a fingernail trying to open a window. Then he sat down & whimpered. He had a diamond pinkie ring. Julio convinced him to use it to cut a window pane. Not even a scratch.

I stood in the parlour at the bay window, cupped my hand around my eyes, & tried to look out. The antique glass was rippled & distorted. Thru one of the center windows, I had a hazy view of the kitchen. The left window gave me a glimpse of the dining room. Through the right window, I saw into the parlour about 10 feet from where I stood. My belly quavered. I didn't try another window. I closed the curtains. Besides being impregnable, no light shines through those windows. Not even darkness. When curtains are open they don't even reflect light. Just—nothing.

* * *

Rick glanced at the clock. A working man again, he should go to bed at a reasonable hour. Besides, why was he bothering with this? He enjoyed reading anything practical but saw no sense in wasting time on something made up. When he thought the writer was describing the house in its prime, he had a reason to read it. But now—oh, it was interesting, but useless.

In the darkened bedroom, his mind raced through plans for tomorrow. He flopped over, but his arm found only empty mattress. Even after these many months, he reached for comfort that was no longer there. He rolled onto his back and clenched his eyes against tears. No use. He might as well get up. He used to sleep like a baby.

Amy had suffered from insomnia due to the stress of her job. Whenever her restlessness woke him, he'd fix her warm milk with honey. Now her absence reminded him to do this for himself. But he overheated the milk and had to let it cool. The notebook lay on the arm of his chair. He returned to it:

XXV. I got so upset reliving that, I got drunk. Really drunk. I tried to finish a 5th of Scotch. I put a big dent in it, but still couldn't get that night out of my mind.

When we'd exhausted all possibility of escape, we collapsed in the parlour. I sat by the bar. I wanted another drink but couldn't lift an arm to fix one. Wendel suggested we go back down to the cellar. Since the weirdness started when we were there, maybe something would happen to break the spell. No one had a better idea.

In the cellar, the food had been replenished & the mess, including the champagne glasses, cleaned up. How could anyone have done this w/ out our knowing? Did they pass through the walls? I took off my gypsy scarves & beads & bangles. I was done w/ Halloween. Linda removed her witch's hat & Julio took off his vampire cape. I'd smoked my last cigarette. Altho I don't like Marlboros, I was desperate enough to bum one from Julio.

Louie's watch still showed midnight.

Doreen said we were only hallucinating, that we'd be ok when we came down. But why should I hallucinate? I didn't take any drugs. Were the drinks spiked? They couldn't all be. Rhoda said it was the champagne, but I hadn't touched it. What about the food? Everyone else at the party ate & drank, too—where were they? That "Twilight Zone" stuff was only stories, right? W/ no better explanation, we settled on mass hallucination & decided to sleep it off. I hoped to wake up & discover it was only a bad dream. The owner of the house would find us & throw us out.

Linda turned out the light. We lay down on the cushions. Louie hogged 3, which didn't leave enough for everybody, but I was too tired to care. I grabbed one, but the prospect of sleep brought a cold feeling to my gut. I wanted to wake from this bad dream, but what if sleep brought more nightmares? Exhaustion grappled with unseen demons and finally won out.

* * *

Rick finished his milk and returned to bed. This time he successfully fell asleep.

BRING A MACHETE

The next morning, Rick called Carlos, a yard man he often hired. They agreed to meet at the Wilson House after lunch. "Bring a machete," Rick advised.

Then he called Bob and invited him to join them.

"Not today. I can't get away from work."

That afternoon, neighborhood businesses were open, parking lots full. There was no street-side parking. The yard of the residence next door was empty. He thought of asking to park there, but hesitated, and drove his truck onto the sidewalk in front of the Wilson House fence. Carlos arrived and brazenly pulled into the neighbor's yard. As Rick walked over to greet him, a face scowled at them through a filthy window pane. "Help me take down a section of fence," Rick said, "so we can park on the property."

Carlos took one look at the yard and whistled. "You're gonna need more than a lawn mower here. I'll bring a bush hog." Before they could move the fence, they had to chop their way through weeds and brush. The day was unseasonably warm. Soon Rick was drenched in sweat.

His cell phone rang. By the time he fumbled out of his gloves to answer, the call had gone to voicemail. It was Kristie. "Nothing important, Dad. I'll call you another time." To give himself time to catch his breath, he pretended to call back. By then, Carlos was ready to pry lose a fence section. Once they had an opening, Rick pulled his truck off the sidewalk and into the yard. He winced at the shriek of a branch scraping his door. Carlos didn't seem to mind scratching his truck. It was old.

They hacked their way to a narrow trail that snaked around the west side of the yard. It led to a young live oak near the back fence. Under its shade, something poked up out of the leaf litter. Rick lifted a corner with his machete. It was the remains of a small tent. Nearby, a ring of broken cement blocks encircled a pile of charred wood. Something crunched under Rick's boot—the shards of a wine bottle. He warned Carlos, "Be careful where you step." Rusted cans and disintegrating grocery bags surrounded the campsite.

Something brushed against Rick's head. A frayed rope dangled from a branch of the tree. At his feet was a broken flower pot. From it trailed a small vine with heart-shaped leaves. Amy had a plant like this. When she became unable to care for her houseplants, she'd entrusted them to his care. Some had died with her, but this particular variety, whose name he couldn't recall, had managed to survive.

Carlos said. "I wonder why they'd they camp out here instead a stayin' in the house?"

Rick shook his head. Why would a homeless person have a house-plant?

Another path led back to the house. Curiously, it seemed to disappear under the building. "Could this be an animal trail?" Rick asked.

Carlos shrugged.

Now Rick got a good look at the rear of the building. The back porch was nearly detached. Warped plywood covered the back door.

They pushed their way around the building. The collapsed porch on the east side was engulfed by many years' growth of grape vines. Tree seedlings grew in the accumulated leaf litter on what was once its roof.

Using plastic tape, they marked which trees and shrubs to keep. Carlos promised to bring his crew over Wednesday.

After Carlos left, Rick entered the house. A tinkle of music made him pause. Someone was playing a piano. He stepped back onto the porch but was unable to determine where the sound came from. Certainly not the Wilson House. But the approaching evening made the interior more gloomy than usual. *There's no way we can work in here with these windows boarded over.* He locked the door and went home.

That evening, he called to update Bob. "Why don't you come by Wednesday? You can get a better look at the place."

"Naw, I gotta go out of town."

Rick shook his head. Bob always had an excuse not to come to the Wilson House. The notebooks lay by the phone on his desk. Why did he keep forgetting to mention them? He took the one he'd been reading and resumed:

XXVI. The next morning, Louie got up & tripped over Wendel. Wendel hollered & Louie cussed. That woke everybody. Then he turned on the light. The lazy Susan had been restocked! How? Everyone denied knowing anything. Wendel said no one came into the cellar. He slept at the foot of the steps. Nobody could have gotten by him.

Someone asked Louie what time it was. His watch still said 12. He tried to wind it, but couldn't get it to work. Linda's watch was also stuck at 12. No one complained about being achy even tho we'd slept on the floor. Julio said he'd die for a cup of coffee. As if in answer, the aroma of fresh brew drifted down from the kitchen. Who made it?

In the parlour, I found an ashtray with a new pack of Salems. The disorder from the party had been cleaned up & the food & drink replenished. How? I tried to look thru the fancy glass in the front door. All I could see were vague shapes. I took a deep breath & opened the door just a crack. The kitchen. I wasn't about to go thru that door.

The coffee was good. Even Louie said so. We searched the house again, upstairs & down, including the attic, the cupboards & closets. We stationed one of us at the bottom of each staircase & another at the top so nobody could get by. We found no one. Again, we tried doors & windows. We banged on walls, looking for hidden doors & secret passages. The walls are as impregnable as the windows, or we'd have broken thru them. The phone was still dead & there was no TV. The radio was silent. Not even static. We were cut off from the outside world. No radio or phone, yet we had electricity. How?

The fire in the parlour still burned. Julio & Wendel tried to put it out to look up the chimney. They doused it with water but it barely sputtered. They took cushions off the couch & laid them over the fire. Even tho flames licked up from underneath the cushions, they didn't burn. Julio braved the heat, lay on the cushions, & poked his head up the chimney. Then he shouted for Linda's broomstick & more water. Wendel poured water on the cushions & Julio poked the broomstick up the flue as far as he could reach. Then he dropped it & backed out of the fireplace. Linda made Hugh take the cushions off the fire. They weren't even scorched. Julio started to brush himself off, but there was no soot on him.

I thought Julio was going to cry. He said he couldn't find an opening with the broom. He couldn't even find the sides of the chimney, like it absorbed anything that goes up there. In an ordinary house, you could glimpse daylight at the top, but this is what Julio saw: "It looked like a fire was burning where the top of the chimney should be." He pointed at the fireplace. "That fire." Wendel tried to console him. "There wouldn't be enough room to climb out anyway." Julio shook his head and said, "At least it would be *something*."

I felt like that non-chimney—empty, no border to define me, swallowed by nothingness.

XXVII. Those 1st few "days" we clung to each other like there was safety in numbers. If one of us got up to leave the room, we all followed. Whenever we got tired, we'd just crash on the nearest couch or chair or carpet. We were so listless we could barely do anything for ourselves.

Every "morning" I wake up hoping the nightmare is over. Can you fall asleep in a nightmare? Every "day" the "outside" doors still open to the opposite side of the house, like it's been turned inside out. The windows are still impregnable & if you peer thru them closely you see other rooms. We are totally cut off from the outside world. There are books & records for entertainment, electricity & running water. Where they come from is anyone's guess. The toilets flush & the sinks drain, where to, we don't know. Tho time & life stand still, we still eat & drink & pee & shit.

XXVIII. Today we made the upstairs hallway into a lounge. (Louie calls it a landing. Whatever.) It's as big as any room, big enough for all of us to sit & listen to music. But we could hardly hear the record player when it was down in the parlour, so Julio suggested we bring it up here. Why not? The radio hasn't worked since the night of the party. Julio & Wendel hauled it up to the attic & the rest of us brought up the stereo & records.

There aren't enough chairs for everyone. The carpet is soft enough to sit on, but Doreen suggested getting the cushions from the cellar. Everyone thought this was a good idea & we all pitched in. We also brought up the lava lamps & lazy Susan. Even tho no one's been going down to the cellar to eat from it, the food was fresh, as tho someone replenished it every day.

The cushions are bulky. Most of us could carry only one at time, so we had to make several trips. I'm not used to stairs & my legs started to ache. When I stopped to rest, I noticed Hugh sitting in the kitchen with a cushion. I hadn't seen him upstairs. I asked if that was his first cushion. He nodded. When I told him to take it upstairs, he looked up w/ those washed-out eyes & said he was tired. After one trip to the cellar? I told him to get off his lazy butt & take the cushion up. He shifted his weight & seemed to almost roll into a standing position. He picked up the cushion as tho it weighed a ton & made it as far as the foot of the stairs. Then he dropped it & walked off. I asked where the hell was he going? "To the bathroom," he said.

I returned to the cellar for a lava lamp. On my way back, I stumbled over Hugh's cushion. It doesn't take a guy that long to use the bathroom. Guess where I found him—in his room on the couch! Just sitting there! He was going to carry that cushion up if I had to kill him. I don't know what came over me, but when he wouldn't move, I lost it. I swung that lava lamp & hit him upside the head. The glass broke & all that goo went flying. That got him moving. He shuffled out to the foot of the stairs, got his cushion, carried it up & sat on it.

I followed him. The side of his face was bleeding. That scared me. I've always had an anger problem, but I seldom get violent. I was afraid I'd injured him. He let me clean off the blood with a wet washrag. Only a scratch, thank goodness. I told him I was sorry & asked if he wanted a band-aid. He shook his head & said it was alright. I worried what Linda would do to me. She doesn't let anyone else be mean to Hugh.

XXIX. Rhoda moved in with Julio, & Doreen's happy to have her own room. Wendel finally moved up to the attic. I don't know where he got the bed. It probably just appeared, like things do. Conversely, most things we don't pay attention to, don't want, eventually go away. I left my do-dads in the cellar & haven't seen them since. They weren't there when we fixed up the lounge. Nor were other things we left there— Julio's vampire cape, Linda's hat, Wendel's monk habit. Only those hors d'oeuvres.

I like the lounge b/c there aren't any windows, so I can imagine I'm in a real house. The lazy Susan is always filled with snacks. If we make a mess it gets cleaned up. It is nice to have the record player up here. We all agreed not to play it too loud when someone's sleeping.

I still feel bad about hitting Hugh. He must not have told Linda or surely I'd have heard about it. His head has already healed—that fast! I'd left that broken lamp in their room. If Linda saw the mess, she didn't say anything. It probably cleaned itself up. She carried the lamp up to the lounge, all in one piece again, said she found it in her room. I pretended to know nothing about it. She probably blamed Hugh.

XXX. We shared a pizza today & began to talk about things we hadn't before. Linda asked Rhoda where she was from. Rhoda said California. Linda said, "I mean your nationality." Rhoda put her little nose up in the air & said, "I'm American." So Julio inquired where her *parents* were from. Same answer. Finally, Linda asked if she was Chinese & Rhoda said yes.

Then Linda asked Julio where he was from. Even tho he doesn't have an accent, we knew he was some kind of Latino. He said his family moved from Puerto Rico to NYC when he was too young to remember. His parents never talked about PR. They wanted to forget. He never understood why. They lived in a shitty neighborhood in NY & he got out of there as soon as he could. The whites looked down on them. Even at school. Only other PR kids would have anything to do with him.

"Like West Side Story," Doreen said. Julio shook his head. "I never got mixed up with gangs." An Italian girl next door got out by going to college. Julio knew he could do that, too, so he worked hard in school & got rid of his accent. He graduated with a scholarship but would've had to stay in NY to use it. Instead, he came here. Once he got away from the Spanish-speaking community, he discovered he was an exotic. The girls loved him. He qualified that—they loved to have sex with him. "I was just a dish to be tasted. Not something to take home to Mom & Dad."

Doreen asked if he finished college. No, he had to work, so he could only take a few courses at a time. He lost touch with his family. His dad was killed in a robbery. He had no phone, so nobody could reach him until after the funeral. "They never caught the guy who killed him." He gritted his teeth. "Then my mom married some joker who didn't like her kids." That's all he'd say about his past.

Rhoda's nose was still in the air & the longer Julio talked the more elevated it got. Finally, she snipped, "You're not the only one who had it hard. At least you could go to college." Did she imagine she was a victim of prejudice? Doreen said, "When I was in school, the Oriental kids were the smart ones." Rhoda huffed & said she had better things to do than study 24 hrs a day. She wouldn't admit she wasn't one of the smart ones. She didn't get a scholarship & her parents refused to pay for college. Why didn't Doreen already know this stuff? She & Rhoda were roommates before they came here.

Linda said people aren't prejudiced against Chinese like they are Puerto Ricans & Negroes. Rhoda looked at Linda like she was out of her mind. "Have you ever been to the West Coast?" No, she hadn't. Rhoda huffed again. "Well, then. You just don't know. They hate us there. Even the Mexicans do." She glared at Julio as if she expected him to hate her like the Mexicans did. "I couldn't get a decent job unless I worked in a laundry or bakery." Doreen reminded her that she had a good job here, in a bank. "Well, I had to go 3000 miles from home to get that." Julio asked if she stayed in touch with her family. "No. I don't live up to their expectations." While Rhoda was talking, I noticed Wendel kept looking down, not saying a word.

* * *

Enough for now. Rick set the notebook aside, rubbed his eyes, and went to his study. He took out his lists, reviewed and expanded them. Thumbing through the phone book and his personal directory of subcontractors, he added errands and phone calls. Barry, his electrician. Derek of Crawford Heating and Air. Molly Maid. Dampier's for a porta potty. Waste Management for a construction dumpster. A house mover to lift the building. Yellow Pages listed two, but one was in Jacksonville. He'd try Crosby and Sons. By now he was tired enough to sleep.

The following day, Rick called Jerome, a college student who did occasional odd jobs. Jerome said he could meet him at the Wilson House that afternoon. Rick loaded his ladder and tools and stopped by a hardware store for a roll of clear plastic, furring strips, and a box of staples. When Jerome arrived, they removed the boards from the ground floor windows and replaced them with plastic sheeting.

While he was there, Dampier's delivered a portable toilet and washing station. Afterward, Rick strolled through the building. Big improvement—the windows now admitted enough light they could see to work.

That evening, after completing paperwork, he returned to the journal:

XXXI. Awhile ago, Rhoda spotted Linda & Hugh's keys under the piano bench in the parlour. How could we have missed them that night? I don't think we did. It's part of the cruelty of this place, to hide the keys when we still had an opportunity to escape, then give them back after all hope was lost.

Linda jingled her keys in our faces. "Somebody's doing this. Nothing happens unless we're asleep or out of the room. Maybe if we catch them in the act, we can get out of here." That made sense. Her strategy was to have someone in the kitchen, the messiest room, at all times. She volunteered to take the first watch. Hugh was to relieve her when she got tired. She made a list of shifts.

How long should a shift be? We have no way to time ourselves. Linda said she'd let us know when it was our turn. She told us not to pick up after ourselves. "I want this place to get really messy." That was unnecessary. We're the laziest slobs imaginable.

At first, it creeped me out the way things just cleaned themselves. Was someone in the house with us? How did they manage to do it without being seen? How did they get in & out? By now we're so used to it, we take it for granted. I hope Linda's idea works.

XXXII. Linda woke me when it was my turn. The refrigerator & cupboard doors were open. She said she can't see in them when they're shut & didn't want anything to get in there to restock them. That open refrigerator bugged me. All my childhood I was yelled at to shut the refrigerator. So I sat with my back to it. If something could sneak in behind my back, let it. I took a book with me but had to clear an area of the table b/c it was piled with dirty dishes & leftovers. I drank coffee until I was wired, but when I wanted a doughnut, they were all gone.

When caffeine couldn't prop my eyes open much longer, Doreen took over. After I slept & went down for something to eat, Wendel was in the kitchen reading with his book on his lap b/c there was even less room on the table. I managed to find some cereal & used the last of the milk. When Julio came in to relieve him, Wendel drew a mug of beer. He said he was glad we weren't running out of beer. He should be worried about the ice melting. If it stops renewing itself, he'll have to drink his beer warm.

XXXIII. As I wrote this numeral, the number of letters struck me—a lot just to write 33. No wonder the Roman Empire fell. Back in my former life, I dated my entries, but here I don't know what date it is. Besides, I don't write on a regular basis, just when I feel like it. I know I've been here way more than a month. It seems like forever. Forever? I hope I won't be here that long.

XXXIV. Earlier, I wanted something to drink but couldn't find a clean glass & had to wash one. The kitchen was impossible. I had to restrain myself from cleaning—imagine that! Running out of clean dishes is bad enough, but I started to worry we'd run out of food & starve to death.

Louie had cleared himself a spot on the kitchen table & was snorting a line of cocaine. He said it helps him stay awake. But before his shift was over, I heard Linda scream at Louie, "Why'd you fall asleep?" Louie shouted back, "I didn't!" I rushed to the kitchen. It was clean! Linda got in Louis's face, "Don't lie to me!" Julio & Doreen pulled them apart. Julio suggested they sit down & talk about it. He led Louie into the dining room. Linda shut her mouth & followed.

Louie insisted he only nodded off for a split second. "I swear to God! I woke up before my head hit the table." If he was telling the truth, the kitchen was cleaned & restocked in that instant. I asked who came in. Louie only shook his head. "Well, what did you see?" Louie threw up his hands. "Nothing! The minute I opened my eyes, the place was clean." Wendel said he'd been in the kitchen just a few minutes earlier & Louie was awake. It's not humanly possible to clean up that mess inside an hour. Linda started to wail, "Now we'll have to start all over!" Louie slammed his fist on the table & said, "Fine! But don't ask me to help."

So we're back where we started. Honestly, I'm glad more food appeared & I don't have to wash dishes. Linda is grieving over her derailed idea. She was crying so hard you could hear her all over the house, but she's quiet now. Has she given up hope? How can we go on without it? We need hope.

* * *

So do I, Rick thought, closing the notebook. Hope had deserted him when Amy got sick. At first, he was careful not to burden her with his worries. As her illness progressed, he had to bolster the children. After she died, people insisted on asking how he was coping. He always lied. Even now he refused to acknowledge he was skirting the edge of a pit of despair. December. Almost Christmas. How could he make it without her?

Maybe he should thank Bob for giving him a project to keep him busy.

THE DRIVER'S LICENSE

On Wednesday, work on the yard was underway by the time Rick arrived. To his dismay, the shady back yard now lay open to the sun.

Carlos shook his head. "We had to take down that live oak after all. My man dropped this cherry tree where it wouldn't hit the house and it fell on one of them oak limbs. Ripped off the limb and split the tree. There wasn't no way to save it."

As though to ease his disappointment, Rick rescued the little houseplant he'd found under the tree. It had miraculously survived being trampled.

Inside the house, Rick salvaged the most intact pieces of the plaster ceiling medallions. He enlisted Carlos's man, Lester, him to help clean out the trash. Once cleared of debris, Rick was pleased with the condition of the flooring. Although badly stained, it could be refinished.

Lester beckoned to Rick. Tangled among shreds of an old jacket was a cigarette lighter and a dented soda can. "Lookee." He pointed to a small wad of stainless steel wool in the crease of the can. "Crack," he said. "They ware smokin' crack in here."

Rick took the can from him and wrinkled his brow. He'd never seen crack paraphernalia before.

When Lester cleaned out the fireplace, he set aside some pieces of metal. "Boss," he addressed Rick, "if you don't mind, I'll take these."

"What do you want them for?"

"Scrap metal. It'll fetch me a couple bucks."

"Sure." Rick couldn't figure out what some of the fragments were, but he understood what happened to the missing doorknobs and light fixtures. Someone had "salvaged" them.

Lester carried his treasures outside, then returned to work. When he lifted a shovelful of rubbish, a small card fluttered to the floor. "Hey, lookit this." He held up an old driver's license. "I ain't seen one like this in years." He handed it to Rick. A black and white photo of a woman wearing glasses peered through water stains. The print was unreadable. Almost absent-mindedly, Rick tucked it among the papers on his clipboard.

Shortly afterward, Lester doubled over and clutched his belly. "I don't feel so good. D'ya mind if I go outside?"

Rick sniffed the air. It couldn't be the crack pipe, but who knew what was in the dust they were breathing?

After lunch, Carlos said he'd like to tour the house. Most of his men went with him, but Lester, who had eaten a hearty lunch despite his bellyache, grimaced and said, "I ain't going back in there. Place gib me the heebie-jeebies." His friends laughed.

When they returned, Carlos said, "Well, I didn't see no ghosts." He leaned toward Rick and lowered his voice. "I kept feeling somebody was hidin' in there, but we didn't find anyone."

Rick secured the boards that covered the doors. Then he announced, "There's no way anybody can get in now without cutting the plastic, unless they climb up to the second floor."

Lester crouched down and peeked under the building. "I bettcha they crawl under here and go up through that old cellar door."

Rick bent down and looked at the steps dangling from beneath the floor joists. He began to feel queasy. Why? When he stood up, the sensation went away. Rick went inside and nailed the cellar door shut. When he tried the door to assure himself it wouldn't open, the queasiness returned. He hoped he wasn't coming down with something.

For the rest of the afternoon, he measured rooms and sketched the floor plan. By evening, Carlos' crew had transformed the yard from a jungle to the promise of a landscape. Before locking up, Rick searched the house to ascertain no one remained inside.

The following morning, Rick decided to bring Amy's hanging plants indoors. All summer, they'd dangled happily from the eaves of the carport, but they were tropicals that wouldn't survive an upcoming frost. Temperature the past few nights had dipped into the thirties, but thankfully no frost had crept under the carport. He cleaned the pots and trimmed spent leaves. He took the vine he'd saved at the Wilson House and studied Amy's plant with the heart-shaped leaves until he understood how to pot the new one. He had plenty of empty containers from plants that had succumbed to neglect.

By then, it was time to go to the Wilson House. Waste Management delivered a construction dumpster. Jerome arrived after his last class. Together they hauled several pieces of rotting furniture out to the dumpster, including a couple of mattresses that reeked of urine. That was enough for the day.

Back in his study, Rick reviewed his lists, made a few phone calls, and left messages. While waiting for replies, he found his place in the notebook.

XXXV. Escape remains our foremost desire. Since we've found no way out of the house, we've taken to our private escapes. For most of us it's booze: Julio's wine, Wendel's beer, Doreen's vodka, my Scotch. Louie's is cocaine. Linda likes valium. The day after the party, she found a bottle of valium in a medicine cabinet & gave some to Hugh & the other girls.

Later, I caught Doreen in the parlour with the valium & a bottle of vodka. I tried to stop her, but she'd already taken most of the pills. I yelled for help. Julio stuck his finger down her throat to make her vomit. She bit him. Despite that, he stayed with her while she slept it off. When she woke, she carried on like she was in pain, but she was only upset to still be alive.

She's not the only one who's tried suicide. One day when I felt especially hopeless, I took as many pills as I could & washed them down with Scotch. When I woke up, nothing had changed. No hangover. Not even a headache. Only more misery. Why can I suffer depression but not a hangover? It makes no sense.

Music helps. That's one reason we set up the lounge. We can listen to music & mellow out. Doreen started smoking pot, then Julio & Wendel, & occasionally the others. I used to take pride in the fact that I didn't use illegal drugs. I looked down on people who did. Even tho I drank a lot, my justification was, at least it's legal, & I never drove under the influence. If someone lit up a joint, I'd give them a dirty look.

Today, I crossed that barrier. The lack of consequences was part of it. If Scotch & valium didn't kill me, neither would pot. I'd welcome getting arrested & hauled off to jail. At least I'd be out of here! Today, Doreen passed me a joint. Instead of waving it by, I took a drag. Then another. It helped a little. Wendel brought up some chips & dip & that helped, too. I'm ashamed of myself, but at the same time, I feel a little better. I think.

XXXVI. I'm starting to worry about myself. I spend too much time in my room, drinking myself senseless, reading trashy books. I don't brush my hair or teeth or bathe or change my underwear. Of course, I don't have any clean underwear or hairbrush or toothbrush. I haven't even thought about asking for them. When did I last bathe? With 5 people sharing one bathroom, it's hard to get in.

No, that's bullshit. I just don't care. Does it make sense for the house to clean itself & everything in it, but not us or what we wear? Give us cigarettes & booze & drugs, but not clothes? Back in the real world, I bathed every day b/c I had to work. Here, it doesn't matter.

Nothing matters. I can drink myself to oblivion, but when I wake up I'm fine. If I stopped eating, I doubt I'd starve. It wasn't so bad when we were busy trying to find a way out or catch whoever's responsible for keeping us here. But we've tried everything. There's nothing left to do but eat & drink & smoke & listen to music. I'm tired of reading those mindless novels. The plots are so predictable, the characters the same, just different names, contrived circumstances. I started one I'd already read & didn't realize it till I was halfway thru. I used to read good literature. The library here has better books, but whenever I finish a trashy romance, I go back to the same shelf & get another.

Linda asked why I still had pizza sauce on my blouse. I said I don't have any way to clean it. She said take it off & go to sleep & it'll be clean when I wake up. She leaves her clothes in her room when she takes a bath & they get clean. That's easy for her. She has a private bathroom. I don't intend to parade naked thru the house just to clean my clothes. Besides, who does she think she is? My mother?

My mother. I haven't thought about her lately. How long ago in real world time did I last call her? Does she miss me? Does she know I'm missing? Did anyone from work call her? Did my landlady? Did I leave her phone number or address where anyone could find it?

XXXVII. An embarrassing thing happened to me the other day. I'm almost too ashamed to write about it. I had to use the bathroom real bad but Rhoda was in there, w/ the door locked. I didn't think I could make it downstairs. Louie's door was also locked & he wouldn't let me in. You can't hurry Rhoda, so I tried to wait. I couldn't. The minute she opened the door, I peed all over myself. Rhoda wrinkled her nose & said, "No wonder you stink all the time." That made me so mad! I pulled off my panties & threw them at her. The bathroom was free now, but I didn't need it anymore. I was too upset to do anything but go to my room & cry. My skirt dried but didn't clean itself. Later, my underwear showed up on my dresser, clean & folded. It's still there. I've been going around with none on. I guess I've sunk about as low as a human being can & I don't even care.

XXXVIII. I finally put my panties back on. They feel nice, I guess. I'd take a bath if I had clean clothes. I'm tired of wearing a skirt. I'd like some jeans. All of us have been wearing what we came in, mostly Halloween costumes. Wendel had regular clothes under his monk's habit & Doreen wore her everyday clothes—bell bottoms & a psychedelic shirt.

Louie doesn't have his wig anymore, but he's been strutting around in those high heels like he's at Versailles. I keep waiting for him to break an ankle.

Today Louie showed up in a suit & tie—still wearing those heels! We all had a good laugh. Then we asked where he found the clothes. In his closet, he said. He had no idea how they got there, but he was tired of his costume & wanted a suit. Julio said, "No new shoes?" Louie looked down his nose and said, "I prefer these." We convinced him that costume heels with a suit was a faux pas. Finally, he exchanged them for dress shoes. I can see why he prefers the heels. He's shorter w/out them. He can't look as far down his nose.

When he complained he was too warm, we suggested he take off his coat. He still looked out of place in a tie. Julio kept poking fun at him until he took it off. At least he no longer dresses like a French king. Shortly after we came here, I looked in my closet but there were no clothes. I wish I had something different to wear.

XXXIX. Today, Doreen had on new clothes & gushed about everything she found in her closet. I came back to my room, opened my closet, & guess what? I found jeans & shirts! All my size. Seems all I had to do was ask. Then I looked in the dresser & found underwear. All brand new. I don't know why we didn't think to ask for clothes before. We get most everything else we want. Except our freedom. Now I can change clothes, but I should bathe first.

XL. I haven't bathed yet. I picked out a pair of jeans and a T shirt & headed to the bathroom, but Rhoda was in there. Neither Louie nor Linda let me use theirs & by the time Rhoda was done I was no longer in the mood. Those clothes are just like the ones I had at home, but they're not them. Identical, but not mine. It's so wrong. I know I should be happy to have new clothes, but I don't want NEW clothes. I want MY clothes.

XLI. I'm so ashamed of myself, but I need to get it out. I avoid looking at my closet b/c I know what's in there. Clothes that aren't mine. Every time I think about them, I drink until I can't remember what I wanted to forget. I don't know when I last bathed. I don't know how long I've been here. Non-time is so nebulous. Some of my companions have been wearing new clothes. They may be bathing, too. I notice them wrinkling their noses at me, but I don't care.

I got tired of my room & went out to the lounge. The others were mellowed out on pot & I joined them. Rhoda passed out & Julio & Doreen disappeared together. An album of love songs was playing. I couldn't help thinking about what was happening in Doreen's room. It's been so long since I've been with a man.

My body began to come alive. Hugh sat beside me, but I considered him useless. Besides, that would make Linda mad. Wendel is nice, but I've never been with a black guy & wasn't ready to cross that line. Besides, I wasn't sure I could entice him away from his chocolate brownies.

Louie sat across the room, lost in reverie. I couldn't take my eyes off him. Despite his loathsome personality, he's a feast for the eyes. I hadn't noticed him being involved with any of the other girls & I was just high enough to lose my inhibitions. So I moved over beside him & tried to cuddle.

Louie turned his head, looked down at me, & sniffed. "You stink."

I slapped him. I tried to tear his nose off. He grabbed my wrists & pushed me across the room. I tumbled to Julio's feet just as he emerged from Doreen's room. I couldn't help crying. Hell, I was bawling uncontrollably.

Julio picked me up, carried me into the bathroom, filled the tub with water & bubble bath, & undressed me like a baby. It felt nice to have someone take care of me. He left me soaking in the tub, still crying, & returned with a slinky robe & a bottle of wine. After I was clean, he handed me a tooth brush, emptied the tub, & cleaned my glasses. They were so crusted with salty tears, no wonder I couldn't see. Then to my surprise, he undressed himself, turned on the shower, & poured two glasses of wine. We climbed into the tub together. This time I didn't resist.

When I was a teenager, one of my boyfriends insisted on having sex wherever we could find a place, no matter how awkward. We didn't dare use our bedrooms & neither of us had a car, so we did it in sheds, behind bushes, etc. My comfort didn't matter to him. I was so young & desperate for love, I didn't stand up for myself.

With Julio it was different. I never had it so good. Even in the bathtub, he made it as pleasurable as a featherbed with silk sheets. Now I'm sorry I spurned him. And now he knows I'm not a frigid bitch, after all. We had more wine, he gently toweled me dry & put the robe on me. He led me back to the lounge, to Louie, who was drifting in his own little world. Louie came out of his trance to find my sparkling clean self before him. We went into his room together.

What a disappointment! He had no interest in satisfying me. When he was done, he got up without a word & went to his bathroom. I heard water running. So, he had to wash me off him! He didn't even invite me to join him. I went back to my room for another cry. I'm so ashamed of myself. I'm no Vestal Virgin, but I never dreamed I'd go w/ 2 guys the same day. Now I don't think I want to be with a man ever again. Not even Julio.

* * *

Rick wondered how these people could indulge in drugs, alcohol, and sex with no worry about side effects or disease. He reminded himself they were fictional characters. Their troubles were created for entertainment.

He'd spent his youth on the sidelines of the sex and drug culture. Playing baseball in high school kept him straight. Then he met Amy, who was an angel. Together, they were mere spectators to the 70's, as the wild innocence of the 60's spiraled down to the sobering 80's, with its AIDS and crack cocaine. Sometimes he toyed with the idea he missed out on the fun, but no. He and Amy had been busy building their future, rearing their children. Looking back on that time, he had only one regret— it had been too short.

XLII. I've tried some of the new clothes but they're so stiff, especially the jeans. Maybe if I can get them worn in a little I'll like them better. I left my old clothes in the bathroom & they showed up in my bedroom, clean and folded. So I wear them. I found some pajamas & sometimes I stay in them all day.

Neither Julio nor Louie have mentioned our little tête-à-têtes. Were our "romantic" encounters so insignificant? I expected both of them to ask for more. I don't want sex with either of them, but I want them to ask. Am I so undesirable? They couldn't have been disappointed with my love-making, could they? Does Julio think I'm going with Louie? That wouldn't stop him. Maybe he wants me to go after him, but I'm not about to.

XLIII. Wendel came into the lounge all excited about a science fiction story by Robert Heinlein. "Maybe this is what happened to us." He started to tell us the plot: a guy builds a house shaped like a tesseract. Rhoda interrupted, "What's a tesseract?" I'm glad she asked so I didn't have to. Julio tried to explain that it's some kind of 4-D geometrical shape. Louie said you can't build something in 4-D. Doreen wanted to know what 4-D means. Louie looked down at her & said, "The 4th dimension is time."

When they finally let Wendel speak, he said the guy unfolded a tesseract to what it would look like in 3-D & built the house in that shape. Then they had an earthquake & the house collapsed inside itself. Here, Wendel got real excited. "What happened in the story was like what's happening to us. Instead of letting you outside, all the doors led to other rooms." He flipped the book open as if he was going to read it to us.

Julio stopped him. "Just tell us how it ends. Were they able to get out?"

"Yeah, they climbed through a window."

Nobody said a word. Wendel deflated.

Finally, I said I don't know what a tesseract looks like, but this house looked ordinary enough when I saw it from the outside. Rhoda said she didn't recall any earthquake, do we even have them in Florida? Nobody thought so, but if there was one, we'd have felt it in the cellar, wouldn't we? Poor Wendel. I guess he expected us to take him seriously. But, you know, if that story had told us how to get out, we'd have done it.

* * *

Rick pondered. A house built in the shape of a tesseract? He'd never read anything by Heinlein and had only a vague idea what a tesseract was. How could you build a house like a four-dimensional shape? He turned on his internet and googled "tesseract house." Heinlein's story "And He Built a Crooked House" was published in 1941. Several sites showed tesseracts and some purported to unfold them. He found photos of "tesseract" houses, all very modern and unconventional. He was skeptical as to how livable they would be.

XLIV. A strange thing just happened. I finished writing & lay back on my bed, not even reading, just enjoying my room. Maybe I fell asleep. When I rolled over, I saw something on my bedside stand—my driver's license & car keys! Where did they come from? I had them in my pocket when I went to the party, but thought I'd lost them.

That's not a good photo of me. Somebody told me they train those clerks to take bad pictures. If they take a good one, they're fired. Actually, I think they're just in too much of a hurry to do a good job. I heard they're going to put color pictures on licenses soon.

* * *

The driver's license Lester found! Rick rushed to his office and flipped through his clipboard. It wasn't there. He searched his desk and the floor, even rifled through his trash can. After hunting unsuccessfully in his truck, he leafed through the file folder for the house. Not there, either. What had he done with it? Had he accidentally dropped it in the house? Had it been scooped up with the trash? The thought of rummaging through the dumpster crossed his mind. What a spectacle that would make! Now he wished he'd examined it more closely.

Hold on—this was only a coincidence. He had no reason to assume the discarded license had any connection to the story.

The phone rang. His electrician. "Hey, Rick."

"Thanks for calling back, Barry. I have a job for you, an old house I'm fixing up. It'll need complete rewiring." Rick gave him the address. "First, I need temporary service."

"Sure thing, Rick. I can get over tomorrow."

No sooner had he hung up than Elsie from Molly Maid returned his call. "I'm pretty booked up but we can come out Monday," she said.

"There's no electricity yet."

"What about water?"

"Oh, it'll be some time before that's hooked up. I just need it clean enough to work in." He explained the circumstances. "I'll truck in some water for you."

"Good."

Now things were rolling. This promised to be an expensive project. Bob wanted him to check on the historical value of the house and the possibility of financial assistance. Rick turned to the Internet, googled "National Register of Historic Places," and clicked on the link for grant money. No, they didn't provide grant money, but tax credits were possible. He was referred to the Florida Division of Historical Resources, but their grants were available only to non-profits. For tax credits, he was referred back to the National Register. He felt like he was watching ping-pong! The bottom line was—he needed more information on the history of the Wilson House. Where should he look for that? Amy always used to steer him in the right direction. What would she suggest? The public library. Neighbors. County records. He started another list.

Run-down Houses

On Friday, when Rick drove to the Wilson House to meet with the electrician, he spotted an old man touching up paint on the sign of the law firm next door.

The frosty morning had yielded to warm sunshine. Soon, Barry arrived. "Looks like it's gonna be a nice day," he said and slipped off his jacket.

Rick provided him with the floor plan and they walked through the house together. Barry noted what wiring the electrical code required and Rick discussed additional features he wanted. Barry put his coat back on. "It sure is cold in here. You'll want good insulation or this place'll cost a fortune to heat. And cool."

Rick agreed. "Send me an estimate and I'll let you know when we're ready to start wiring."

After Barry left, Rick glanced at the parlor floor where Lester had found the old driver's license. Aware of the absurdity of his obsession, Rick searched the room, then the rest of the house, but little trash remained. No driver's license.

As he locked the door to go home, the old man from next door walked over. "Good afternoon," he said. His eyes swept the yard and he nodded with approval. "I'm sure glad to see someone's cleanin' up this place. I've complained to the city for years but nothing ever got done."

Rick looked at the fellow's paint-stained clothing and introduced himself, tentatively extending his hand.

The man reached toward Rick, frowned at the paint on his palm, and wiped his hands on his jeans. "I'm Ben Whitehead. I own the law firm next door."

Yes! This was someone Rick wanted to talk to.

"I'm retired now, or supposed to be," Ben said. "I still have to ride herd on that bunch in there. Are you the one who bought this place?"

"No, I'm the contractor. Tell me, how long have you been in your building?"

"I bought it shortly after it was moved here—forty, fifty years ago? I thought the neighborhood was on the way up at the time. As you can see, it didn't work out quite the way I figured." He gestured at the Wilson House. "I've offered to buy this place a time or two. I'd have torn it down, but the Historical Society would put up a fuss. Publicity from crossing them would hurt my business more than leaving it standing. So I paid to have that fence put up. At least I don't have to look at it all the time." He indicated the dilapidated house next door. "I've threatened to sue that nutcase, but I know it wouldn't do any good."

"Who lives there?"

"Harvey Balrush. That's who I bought my building from. He had his all fixed up before he moved in. Painted it green and it looked real nice. Hard to tell now."

Rick nodded.

Ben went on. "Balrush showed a lot of promise as a young man. He was in real estate and owned all these lots. But after he moved into his house, he went downhill. I think he lives on disability now. You never see him outside."

"What do you know about the history of the Wilson House?"

"Is that what you call it?"

They sat on the edge of the porch and Ben answered Rick's questions. No, no one had ever "fixed up" the Wilson House or connected utilities. Yes, all kinds of drunks and druggies tried to live there. "The police run them off, but before long, they're back. It's a wonder it never caught fire."

"I've heard rumors the house is haunted."

The old man laughed. "You always hear that about old buildings, especially empty ones."

"I understand you had a paralegal who suffered a nervous breakdown and blamed it on ghosts?"

"How'd you know about that?"

"My son's friend is related to her."

"Yeah, she even filed a Workman's Comp claim. I'm not sure if she was in fact mentally unstable or just trying to scam me. She came up with the idea of ghosts after one of those Halloween parties The Inn throws every year. Their employees want people to think their place is haunted, but their spooks are undoubtedly contrived."

"What did the lady say she saw?"

"She never claimed to see anything. She alleged she heard someone screaming." Ben thumbed the Wilson House. "In here. And the usual. Loud noises. Music."

"Music?"

"Yeah, she said she heard someone playing the piano. Or songs of the 60's and 70's. She'd pull one of us over to the window and say, 'Don't you hear that?' Well, of course, we didn't. I tried to reason with her. The bums who stayed in there made the noises. And the music, well, that coulda come from anywhere. To top it off, she'd claim to hear a clock chiming. I told her to keep her window shut."

Rick grimaced. Piano music? Clock chiming? "You know, I heard the police talked to a couple of crack heads who got scared when they heard a clock chime in there."

"Coulda been where she got that idea. When she started to imagine our place was haunted, she had to go."

"What did she say happened in your place?"

"She never claimed to see or hear anything, only that she felt something cold."

"Cold?"

"Something cold crept up behind her and squeezed her. Nobody else complained about anything like that." He looked at his hands again. "I need to get back to my job before the paint dries. If there's anything I can help you with, let me know."

"Maybe there is something. I have a cleaning crew coming Monday. Would you let me connect a hose to your water?"

"Why, sure. Let me show you where the outside faucet is."

After Rick took leave of Mr. Whitehead, he peeked around the fence to look at the Balrush house. Mold and lichen provided more color than the faded paint, which flaked and curled, exposing rotting siding. Most of its gingerbread trim was missing. The front porch sagged nearly to the ground and the turret appeared ready to follow. Parked at an angle near the back, almost hidden by weeds, was a rusty sports car. One wheel, missing a tire, was propped on a crumbling cement block. The other tires were flat and the hood gaped slightly open. Rick moved around for a better look—an Aston Martin! What a shame.

That house looked worse than the Wilson House. It dawned on him —usually an inhabited house will deteriorate less rapidly than an empty one.

That evening, he thought about Mr. Whitehead's paralegal. Was she actually crazy? She wasn't the only one who had felt something cold squeeze her. If anyone but Kyle had related such an experience, Rick would have passed it off. His own imagination crept up behind him and laid a cold hand on his shoulder. He shrugged.

Later, he continued reading:

XLV. Linda's trying to catch someone again. Louie won't help & the rest of us are less than enthusiastic. Today when Julio was watching the kitchen, he came up with an idea. He wrote a note, "Help! We're trapped in here—Big white house w/ green trim on E Univ Ave, W in gable window—Get us out!" He put it in a Coke bottle, & when Rhoda relieved him, he tried to flush it down Linda's toilet. Of course it was too big. He tried to remove the trap under the kitchen sink to drop it thru there, but even when he found a pipe wrench, he couldn't get the pipes to come apart.

Rhoda said she had a makeup bottle small enough to go down the toilet. Julio cleaned & dried it out & stuffed in the note. By now, all of us were aware of this latest shot at freedom. Linda had Hugh keep kitchen watch while we went into her bathroom. That must have been a sight—7 people crowded around the toilet, watching it flush. We all cheered when the bottle didn't come back up & the toilet didn't clog.

Nobody said anything about where it might go. Was this impossible house connected to sewer pipes? If it was, where would an object go? Would anyone find it? If they did, would they open it, retrieve the note, actually read it? Act on the message? We didn't talk about that. We need to hold on to some hope.

XLVI. Today I mentioned our message in the bottle. What a mistake! Julio mentally traced where something in a real house goes when it's flushed down a toilet. If, by some incredible stretch of imagination, someone found a bottle floating in a sewage treatment plant, fished it out, cleaned it up, & read the note, then what? If they didn't think it was a prank, & took it seriously, if they located the house & went in looking for us, what would they find? If we can't get out, could they get in? If they did, would they be trapped in here with us? The more he talked, the more depressed he got. Then he fell silent. When Linda called him for his next shift, he said, "I'm not doing this anymore. It's pointless."

XLVII. I wandered into the parlour to get a bottle of Scotch. Instead, I sat down at the piano & opened it. No one has paid any attention to it. We only use it to set drinks on. For a few minutes I sat there trying to remember when I last played. When I was 10 or 11, I took piano lessons. I had a stepfather who liked me. He was the only person I ever let call me "Red." Not only did he pay for piano lessons, he encouraged me. He found a teacher who loved music more than perfection—Mrs. Annenberg?

At first, I played only with my right hand. Mrs. A. was patient. Eventually, I learned to use my left hand, too. One thing she taught me was to reverse the melody & chords, playing the chords with my right hand & picking out the melody an octave lower with my left. That made the music interesting. By experimenting, I learned some rudiments of arranging & could even adapt music to suit my ability. Unfortunately, my formal instruction was as short-lived as my mother's marriage. I hadn't touched a piano since. In a way, I wanted to now, but didn't know where to begin. I closed it & came up to my room.

* * *

Rick paused. He thought he'd heard piano music at the Wilson House. It probably came from a neighbor's piano. Something nudged his memory—the fireplace. The homeless had used it for heat. When Lester cleaned it out, among the scraps of metal were twisted steel strings which had puzzled Rick. Now he knew what they were from—a piano! But how did it get in the house? And why? It made no sense to leave a piano inside when they moved the house, and he doubted squatters dragged it in. Ben Whitehead's account of what his paralegal heard came to mind. So there was a piano. Who played it? The homeless? The writer of the journal?

He crossed the room to his spinet. A film of dust covered it. He'd lied to Bob about keeping house to Amy's standards. Before he went to get a dust rag, he opened the piano and fingered a few keys. The notes rang clear and inviting, but he had no idea how to put them together into a song. He lifted the front and observed its construction. More solid than a tank. How did the homeless manage to reduce one to firewood?

He and Amy had bought this one so their children could take lessons. To Amy, every child should learn music, and Rick agreed. Kyle balked at lessons and Amy didn't push him, but Kristin gave it a try. Rick remembered her tortured practicing. Although neither mastered piano, both later played in their school band. Kristin tackled the baritone and Kyle was almost proficient on the trumpet.

Rick had been surprised to learn that Amy took lessons when she was a child. That must have been a challenge because she was born with a deformed right hand, only a tiny thumb and one vestigial finger. She refused to let that handicap her but by the time he met her, she no longer played. She said she'd lost interest. That wasn't true. A few times when she believed herself to be alone, he'd caught her practicing. He told her it sounded good, that she should play more, but she laughed it off, saying she wasn't good enough for an audience. Even him.

As he dusted, he realized his piano, like the one in the journal, was used only as an end table. It held a lamp and a display of family pictures. He'd kept the piano in hopes his grandchildren would someday want it. He put the dust cloth away and went back to the journal.

XLVIII. When Wendel was watching the kitchen today, Louie came down the main staircase & through the hallway to the kitchen. I asked him why he didn't take the back stairs. Louie just ignored me & opened the refrigerator. Wendel said Louie never uses the back stairs. When I asked why, Louie's nostrils flared & he said, "Those are the servant's stairs." Then he took a Pepsi out of the fridge & left.

What a silly hang-up! That got me thinking about hang-ups. The night of the party, when he was stoned out of his mind, Louie went through the kitchen door & ended up in the foyer. That's the only time anyone's gone thru one of those "outside" doors. We're afraid to. I wanted to ask Wendel why, but he was buried in a book. Another Heinlein novel.

I went to the back door & told myself, don't be silly. I reached for the doorknob but my fingers froze. I took a deep breath, grabbed the knob & turned it. It was as if I stood on the front porch w/ the front door open. I was looking into the foyer. But I was in the kitchen & should have seen the back porch.

Logically, I knew nothing would happen if I stepped across that threshold, but I couldn't. Something swished—I jumped. It was Wendel turning a page. The only other sound was my heart pounding. I held onto the doorknob with my right hand & extended my left hand, the expendable one, into the foyer. No physical barrier stopped me but I jerked my hand back & slammed the door. Wendel just kept reading.

XLIX. I don't know how much longer we can keep watching the kitchen. I take a shift, grab some sleep, then I'm on again. We are down to 5 on rotation & we're running out of food. Today when Doreen was in the kitchen, Linda said she'd go get Rhoda to take her place. Then she raised her voice, "Don't fall asleep before I come back!" Doreen made a weird growling noise & shouted, "I am not a child! You can't talk to me like that!" Doreen stomped up the stairs & Linda sat down & boo-hooed. I fetched Rhoda for her.

L. We didn't get very far this time with kitchen watch. Hugh fell asleep & we had to restrain Linda from killing him. Now she wants 2 people on each shift. It seems like I just took a shift but she said Wendel & I are up next.

I don't dare drink b/c I have to stay awake, but I need solitude. Times like this I really appreciate my little turret room. I light a candle and turn off the lights. Candlelight enhances the colors of the room, making the cream-colored wainscoting & the blue walls almost glow. I lie on my bed, look at the ceiling, & pretend I'm looking at the sky. That row of flowers & vines at the top of the walls helps me imagine I'm in a garden. I wonder, was it stenciled? It has brush strokes. Painting that entire border would've been a big job. It would be a cheery little room if only sunlight came through the windows. Still, this is my favorite part of the house. This room suits me, so comfortable, roundish like a womb, with the little round bed.

* * *

Rick imagined the turret room as it would have been in its prime, blue and white, wainscoting and stenciled borders, just as she described. "Roundish" room with its "little round bed"—wait! They'd removed a ragged round mattress from that room. Another coincidence? No, the author of the journal had intimate knowledge of the Wilson House. Had she stayed there? Why? For atmosphere, inspiration? Did she sleep on that dirty mattress? He shuddered.

LI. We're done with kitchen watch. Rhoda dropped out & we were down to 4 people. The rest of us started to hide from Linda. We'd pretend to be fast asleep behind locked doors, so she had to pull shifts by herself. Finally, she had to go to the bathroom. She hollered for help but nobody responded. She made a dash to her bathroom & when she came back, the kitchen was clean & restocked. Thank goodness! She didn't throw a fit. She only whimpered, "I wasn't gone 2 minutes. Two minutes! I didn't even fall asleep."

LII. Despite the unavoidable acceptance of our situation, we've never entirely given up on finding a way out. Today, Wendel came to the lounge while we were listening to music and held up the Heinlein book he was reading. He said maybe this is what happened to us. These people were in a bomb shelter & there was a nuclear war. They took a direct hit & were blown into the future.

We exchanged dumb looks. Finally, Louie said the cellar is not a bomb shelter. Linda contended they could have had World War III when we were in the cellar. Rhoda said if they did, what we were blown into is nothing she'd call a future. Wendel pouted. He said he wasn't saying this is actually what happened, but maybe it was something similar, some kind of space-time anomaly.

I've been at parties where people spent all night talking about such things & coming up with all kinds of weird angles. But we just sat there until Julio asked how they got back home. Wendel hung his head & said they didn't. They learned to live in that future world.

Does that mean we have to learn to live in this impossible world? Julio took a drag on his joint & said, "What's the use? Even if we find an explanation, if it doesn't help us get out of here, what good is it?"

* * *

Rick wasn't certain when this was written, but he remembered living under the threat of nuclear war. His older sister told of having "duck and cover" drills in school. When a horn sounded, teachers herded the children away from windows and told them to crouch against the wall with their arms sheltering their heads. The powers-that-be eventually decided that what might protect you from a conventional air raid was of little use against a nuclear bomb. By the time Rick was in school, the same method was called "tornado" drill.

To stretch his legs, Rick wandered into Amy's library. She'd spent over thirty years collecting books. After Kristie moved out, Amy made a home for them in Kristie's room. He scanned the shelves. To his surprise, there were a handful of paperbacks by Robert Heinlein. He never knew Amy read science fiction. What were the names of the books the journal referred to? He found nothing with "Crooked House" in the title. Wendel hadn't named the one about the atomic bomb. Rick read the blurbs on the covers but nothing sounded familiar. The public library should have those books, but a glance at his watch told him they'd be closed now. It was time for bed anyway.

WEEKEND VISIT

Saturday, Kyle brought the kids over to spend the weekend. Balmy weather was in the forecast, temperatures in the seventies. Rick was glad they could play outdoors. The boys had brought their basketball and little Judy played on the swing set. For lunch, they grilled hamburgers.

While they ate, Judy asked, "Where are all of Grandma's flowers?"

"They're just not blooming this time of year." Rick pointed to the azalea bushes. "Those'll come out in about three months." Then he looked at the empty beds where Amy used to plant annuals. Last fall, when she was too weak to do anything, he set out flowers under her supervision—pansies, snap dragons, and petunias, cool weather plants that later succumbed to summer's swelter. He excused himself and went to his bathroom to wipe away tears.

He returned in time to prevent a food fight. "Hey, if you kids behave, and help me clean up, I'll take you to a movie." The table was cleared and dishes washed in record time.

That evening, once the kids were tucked in bed, Rick thought about Amy's books. Perhaps he could read one, but Judy was already asleep in that room. He went back to the notebook:

LIII. With no TV, we have to make our own entertainment. Julio & Rhoda & Doreen provide us w/ soap opera. We watch Julio slip into Doreen's room while Rhoda's asleep, or Doreen slip into his when Rhoda takes a bath. Whenever Rhoda's not asleep or bathing, she hangs onto Julio so tightly I don't know how he can breathe.

One day, Julio tiptoed out of Doreen's room & opened his door quietly. I thought I'd have a little fun & shouted, "Julio, why are you sneaking around like that?" He gave me this mock-sheepish grin & whispered, "Shhh, I don't want to wake Rhoda." Then Doreen came out of her room, yawning & stretching like she'd been asleep. She "innocently" asked, "What's going on out here?"

Today was better—a little slap-stick. Rhoda cut her bath short while Doreen was in Julio's room. Linda tried to warn her, "I wouldn't go in there now if I were you." So of course Rhoda barged right in. It sounded like a fox got loose in the chicken coop. Doreen, half naked, flew out of there & into her room. Then Rhoda ran back to the bathroom for a good cry. A minute later, Julio emerged from his room, suave as ever, smoking a cigarette. Even Linda rolled on the floor laughing.

* * *

Rick chuckled. It was good to find something light in the journal.

LIV. Utopia. The perfect existence. We don't have to work, pay bills, or pick up behind ourselves. Everything is provided. All my adult years, I've dreamed of such a life, where I could do as I please, day & night, & not worry about anything. Why then am I not content? I used to wish I could inherit a million bucks & be set for life. Of course I'd have to pick up after myself, unless I had servants. Then I'd have to manage them, so this is better, right? I don't have to deal with servants & everything is done for me. Hell, I don't even have to deal with my housemates. I can stay in my room & avoid them. So why am I not happy?

When I think about not having to go to work or deal with my landlady or bills, life here doesn't seem so bad. But I miss watching TV & listening to the radio & going to movies. I never cared about the news but I wonder what's going on in the world. I've never been an outdoor person but I enjoyed going to the beach. I long for sunshine & fresh air. I'd settle for a thunderstorm, or even a hurricane. Even for a miserable humid night full of mosquitoes. As long as it was real.

LV. Running into dead ends hasn't entirely stopped us from looking for answers. Occasionally, I pick up the phone to listen for a dial tone. I saw Wendel try it today. As far as we know, no one has received our message in the bottle. Even tho Julio scoffed at Wendel's latest theory, yesterday I found him in the library reading a book on physics.

Today, he dropped acid &, out of the blue, started quoting some weird stuff from Einstein. Then he went into this long spiel about space-time & how some quirk could account for what happened to us. Even sober, I couldn't have followed him. If he figured out what caused this, he still has no clue how to get us out.

Sometimes I brood about what my disappearance meant to the world. The day after the party, I didn't show up for work. They probably assumed I had a hangover. Gus put me in the VW with Virgil. Did he realize Virgil & I weren't at whatever party he went to? Did my coworkers wonder what became of me?

After a few days, my boss would have terminated my employment & filled the position with another warm body. Did anybody try to call me? Mail my last paycheck? Report me missing? Does anyone remember the redhead who drove a Mustang convertible?

My landlady would come looking for her money. Would she call the police? They couldn't find me, but I'd feel better knowing someone was looking for me. After a time, I'd be officially evicted & she'd throw out my stuff. I had nothing of real value, but it was mine.

Rhoda came up with the notion that there might be duplicates of us out there in the real world, living our lives. In that case, no one would miss us. Julio said, which of us are the real ones? The duplicates out there or us in here? Now, that was just too weird. Doreen said sometimes she thinks she's in a coma. Linda feels the same way, but would all of us be in a coma? Even if we were, would we all have the same dreams? I put in my 2 cents, maybe we aren't having the same dreams. Maybe they are just illusions in a dream I'm having. That got sour looks. Then Rhoda had the nerve to say that maybe I was a figment of her imagination.

What was going through my mind is, if it's just my dream & they're only illusions, why couldn't I dream about better people? More interesting people. People I could get along w/. But who I would choose to inhabit my dreams? There was no one I knew in "real" life I'd wish to share this timeless coma state with. Not even any movie stars or celebrities. Nor a dog or cat. Or a goldfish. A half bottle of Scotch waited for me in my room. That was my companion. Johnny Walker himself.

LVI. Did I set the tone for the group? Today we sat in the lounge talking about the lives we left behind. We've indulged in this discussion a dozen times. With each telling, past lives become rosier. Bullshit. We all worked dead end jobs, alienated from relatives, few friends. Some, like me, started college & dropped out.

So, if no one misses us for days or weeks or months, would anyone report it to the police? If each disappearance was reported, would they see a pattern? Eight people in one city vanishing w/out a trace? Would they connect our absences? Would they trace us to the party? To this house? If they did, what would they find?

Out in that other world, someone may be living in this house. What would they say if the police knocked on their door looking for us? Gus knew Virgil drove me to the party. Would the police question Virgil? I'd love to be there when they did. Another thing we all have in common —Virgil brought all of us to the party. Each of us had been invited by someone who had been invited by Virgil. None of us had been invited by him directly & none of us knew Virgil before that night.

LVII. Today, Louie was savoring a bottle of Crown Royale while the rest of us commiserated. After we finished our tales of woe, he bragged about his mama & how she has connections. "She won't let this rest. She'll make them keep looking for me." Julio asked just how did he think they'd find us? That didn't faze Louie. "She has connections in Washington. She'll get the FBI on the case."

Doreen laughed at him (if you could call it a laugh). "And where will they look?" She got louder. "Will they look here? How would they do that? Where is HERE?" She got right in his face. "We are NO-where!"

By now she was screaming. "WE don't know where we are or how we got here! No one can find us HERE!" Then she sat back & covered her face with her hands. "We are nowhere."

Louie took a swig of whiskey straight from the bottle. It dribbled down his chin onto his dress shirt. Then he took another swig, brooded for a minute, then took another, and another, until he passed out. The rest of that expensive whiskey ran down his white cuffs onto the floor.

If a policeman, or anyone else, has come looking for us at this house, they didn't get inside wherever we are. If they could get in, would they be trapped like us? That's a silly thought. We may not even be in the same universe anymore. Sounds like something Wendel would say.

* * *

This was the last page of the first notebook. Rick laid it on the arm of his chair. He was disappointed that the comic relief had been cut short and the story reverted to melancholy weirdness. It was getting late and the kids would be up early.

The next morning, while Rick cooked breakfast, David came into the kitchen with the notebook. "What's this?"

"Give me that." He snatched it from David's hand. "It's something about the house I'm working on."

"The haunted house?"

"It's not haunted."

"Can we go over there? I want to see it."

"Your parents said no."

"We don't have to tell them."

"I won't go against their wishes."

After Allison picked the children up, Rick came across the notebook he'd taken from David and recalled his reaction. Why did he snap at the child? Somehow, he'd felt like his privacy had been invaded. Why? The journal was nothing personal to him. True, the subject matter was inappropriate for children, but David likely hadn't read much, if any, of it. He put it on his desk, on the bottom of the stack. That evening, he picked up the next one.

SECOND NOTEBOOK

LVIII. When I went down for something to eat, Wendel was in the kitchen frying a steak. I told him how good it smelled. He offered me some & said, "I've got a big potato in the oven. I'll split it w/ you." I found salad ingredients in the refrigerator, so we had a well-rounded meal.

While we ate, Wendel started reading. "Mysterious Island" by Jules Verne. So he's off Heinlein now. I told him I was tired of the trashy novels I'd been reading. He jumped up, left the room, & came back with a book. "Here. I just finished this. It's good." Another Verne book, "Around the World in 80 Days." That was nice of him. I'd heard about that book but hadn't read it.

LIX. I was looking forward to reading something different, eager to go around the world in 80 days. However, I didn't get very far before I realized it wasn't science fiction. It dealt with the real world, albeit some 100 years ago. I didn't want to be reminded of the real world. That's why I'd been reading romance novels. So I returned the book to Wendel & told him why I didn't want to read it.

Not to be daunted, he came up w/ another Verne book, "From Earth to Moon." That's more like it. Only problem, it's more difficult than what I've been reading. I have a hard time following it when I drink. So I've been alternating between the Verne book & a romance depending on how straight my head is.

LX. Earlier today, I put away nearly a 5th of Scotch. As I staggered to the bathroom, an aroma rose from downstairs—fried chicken! I tripped

& fell down the stairs. I should have been injured, but I wasn't. My glasses fell off & I had to hunt for them, but they were ok.

Wendel was in the dining room chowing down on a plate of fried chicken. He said there was more on the stove. I stumbled over to a chair, but that's as far as I got. He must have felt sorry for me. He got up & fetched me some chicken. It tasted as good as it smelled. I told Wendel he was a good cook, but he said he didn't cook it. He just wanted some & found it on the stove. I told him I was almost finished with the Jules Verne book. He asked if I'd read "Twenty Thousand Leagues under the Sea." Yes, & I liked it. He said "Mysterious Island" is a sequel & he's done with it, so I can have it.

LXI. I found Hugh in the library reading a comic book. What surprised me was, when he left the library, he went through the front door! I peeked down the hall & saw him come in the back door & go to his room. That was the 1st time I'd seen anyone use an outside door. Wendel said Hugh's done it before. "You know he's not going to exert more effort than he has to."

Wendel found some pork chops in the refrigerator & asked if I wanted one. Oh, yes! We also made mashed potatoes. I wanted another vegetable & thought of something I hadn't eaten in awhile—acorn squash. I found a nice one in the refrigerator, cut it in 1/2, scooped out the seeds, & baked it w/ a big dab of butter. It was fun working in the kitchen with Wendel. I set the dining room table w/ the fancy china & silverware. Everything was delicious. While we ate, Doreen kept coming in & looking at the food. Finally, she asked if she could have some. Wendel said sure. There were still some vegetables, but we'd eaten all the pork chops.

LXII. Hugh startled me when he came in the kitchen door. I asked him how he does that. He said it's no different than going thru any other door. So I opened the door & looked into the foyer, but that's as far as I got.

I tried a new outfit today. Jeans & a red sweater, identical to my old red sweater. People say redheads shouldn't wear red but it looks good on me.

Sometimes I wish for other things I once had. Wishing doesn't bring the actual item from my former life, only something like it. I was nostalgic for a candleholder I'd bought at a yard sale. It was glass, with loops & curves of different colors which captured the light from the flame. An identical one appeared in my room. Nearly identical—my old one was chipped. Even so, I like the new one. Almost as much. I turn off the lights and watch the colors swirl.

Wishing for my old journals brought me a notebook to write in, then a 2nd one when I needed it. I think about my old journals. Even though I never re-read them, that's where I poured out my soul (if I have one). What if the police read them to look for clues to my disappearance! Strange men reading my secret thoughts? How embarrassing!

* * *

Rick dropped the notebook. He never intended to invade anyone's privacy. Should he stop reading it? Wait a minute! Rick laughed at himself —so caught up in the narrative, he was thinking of this as a true story. Fiction is written with readers in mind. That made him wonder if the author had finished & published this novel. Would the library have a copy? What else might she have written? As if she'd gone forward in time and heard his thoughts, entry LXII continued with:

The therapist who suggested I write a journal told me I should write professionally. I thought about it, but I could never think of anything interesting to write about. Now I'm in the middle of stuff I know some people would get off on, but who's going to read it?

LXIII. You know, even with a houseful of people, I get lonely. Eating helps, but I get tired of the usual comfort foods like cookies & chips. Today I hankered for a pot roast with vegetables, nothing extravagant, just satisfying. It's impractical to cook just one serving of pot roast, so I went all out. Louie came in while I was cooking, wrinkled his nose & left. Then Rhoda poked her head in & said, "What's that smell?" I ignored them.

Wendel drifted in on the aroma & asked what I was making, so I invited him to join me. He said it was the best thing he'd ever eaten. He forked a chunk of rutabaga & asked what it was. When I told him, he said hadn't eaten one before. I use turnips or rutabagas b/c they seem to bring out the flavor of beef. We talked some more about books. It was nice to sit down to a good meal & just chit chat.

Although I'd cooked enough for 6 people, Wendel & I took our time & polished off nearly the whole pot. I dumped the few leftovers down the garbage disposal. Wendel grimaced when I did that, but I wasn't about to leave them for people who don't appreciate my cooking.

LXIV. I'm still shaking from what happened today. Julio & Louie were arguing. I don't know who threw the first punch. I dashed out of my room when I heard a lamp break. Everybody else watched from their doorways, trying to stay out of the way. I don't think we could have stopped them. Altho Louie's bigger, Julio's more street smart. He twisted Louie's arm behind him, took him to the floor, & was beating his face to a pulp. Louie squirmed out of the hold & punched Julio in the gut. When Julio doubled over, Louie came down full force with both fists on the back of Julio's neck. I heard a crack. Julio sprawled face down on the floor & went limp. Doreen rushed over. Wendel yelled, "Don't move him!"

* * *

"No! Don't move him!" Rick echoed. Then he looked around as if to assure himself he was alone. How foolish to allow himself to get sucked into a story like this!

I knew Louie broke Julio's neck. Bruises heal, but a broken spine? Louie retreated to his room. He must have looked in the mirror, b/c he charged back out yelling, "My face!" It took the combined strength of Wendel, Hugh, & Linda to stop him from finishing Julio off. They steered Louie into his bathroom & Linda ordered Hugh to get some ice. Rhoda & I struggled to keep Doreen from rolling Julio over. After what seemed like forever, he began to moan & move his limbs. Finally he sat up & Rhoda was able to coax him into his room & lock the door. I could breathe again.

After things settled down, Linda said, "We can't have any more of that. What if somebody gets seriously hurt? We can't get to a doctor." So we decided to sleep it off & hold a meeting in the "morning" after everyone calms down.

LXV. Linda summoned everyone to the dining room. Overnight, the damaged lamp had been repaired, & both boys' injuries were healed. I can't say the same about their feelings. They sat at opposite ends of the table glowering at each other. Wendel took the role of peacemaker. After we went round & round, everyone promised not to fight physically again.

After Louie left, Julio stayed at the table, holding his face in his hands. "He broke my neck, you know. I heard it snap. I couldn't feel anything below my neck. I couldn't move anything." He looked up at us. I've seen Julio in disbelief, anger, despair, but never have I seen him look so scared. "I could have been paralyzed for life."

* * *

Rick tossed the notebook down in relief. Maybe this is why he didn't read fiction. Too emotionally involving.

On Monday, the Molly Maid crew brought buckets, brooms, mops, and cleaning supplies. Elsie wrinkled her nose at the nasty sinks and toilets.

"Don't bother with those," Rick said. "We'll replace them. The only fixtures that need to be cleaned are the ones in the antique bathroom upstairs."

Before they started, Rick assembled the workers and asked them to be on the lookout for an old driver's license. "We found it when we cleaned out the trash. I was going to keep it for research, but seem to have lost it." A few times one of them brought Rick a scrap of paper or cardboard, but none were the missing license.

Rick took pictures and samples of wallpaper and paint chips, recording each source. He'd brought a couple of two-by-fours to better secure the cellar door. At one point, awkwardly trying to hold a board while nailing, he hit his finger. He stifled a curse, cognizant of the women present. Nora heard his reaction and came over.

"Are you okay?"

"Yeah," He shook his hand to dissipate the pain. "Just need more hands than I have."

"Let me help you."

She held the board for him, standing on the top step to be out of his way. When they were done, she doubled over and grabbed her belly. With a quick, "Excuse me," she rushed by and Rick heard her retching in the back yard. Unable to resume work, she sat in Elsie's car until someone took her home.

Was it coincidence or was something making people sick? Rick wished he could open enough windows to air the place out. At least no one complained about phantoms or ghosts.

He expected the clean-up to take a week but they finished that day. The place began to show promise. He took more pictures.

With so many people all through the house, Rick was certain no unauthorized person had come in. Yet when he locked the door, he had the eerie feeling that someone remained inside.

That evening, Bob came to his house. Rick updated him and showed him the photos.

"Wow! Big improvement. You'd hardly know it was the same place. I'm beginning to think I made a good investment."

Rick nodded. "I've already talked to my electrician and a few other folks, but we need to start with the foundation. I'll call a house mover to see about jacking it up. Once the building is stable, we'll work on the roof."

"I always pictured a metal roof," Bob said. "Most houses of this era had them. I can't see going to the expense of a slate roof, just because that's what it originally had."

Rick agreed. "Metal will be less expensive and not so heavy. Strong as this baby is, she's over a hundred years old."

They spent an hour going over details. The notebooks lay on Rick's desk in plain sight, but he forgot to show them to Bob until after his friend left. Then he picked up the one he'd been reading.

LXVI. We were listening to music in the lounge today when a strange thing happened. Wendel went down for a beer. He came back w/out one, looked around at everybody, then went back downstairs. He returned looking baffled. I asked what's up. He said, "Was anyone banging on a door?" We all looked at each other & shook our heads. None of us heard anything, but, then, it's a big house. "Did anyone go downstairs when I did?" Nobody had moved. Julio asked if there was a problem. Wendel said, "It sounded like somebody was banging on the other side of the cellar door, like they couldn't get out, so I opened the door." He shook his head. "Nobody there. Hugh's the only one downstairs & he said he wasn't banging." We chalked it up to just one more weird thing.

LXVII. Linda's a great one to lecture about fighting. She threw the first punch. Yesterday I was going down the back stairs & she was coming up. Her hands were full of chips & dip and the stairs are narrow. We bumped elbows. Instead of saying excuse me, Linda barked, "Why don't you watch where you're going, Red?" Oooh! I retorted with, "Why are you so clumsy, Bitch?" She dropped the potato chips and punched the side of my head. My glasses flew off & clattered down the steps. I got her in the belly and she dropped the bowl of dip. Before I could get out of her way, she slipped on the spilled dip & fell on me. We both slid downstairs and rolled around on the floor, punching & grunting. She grabbed my hair & I pulled hers.

If Hugh & Wendel hadn't pried us apart, we'd still be fighting. Hugh took Linda to their room & Wendel held me while I cried. I had potato chips in my hair & my mouth bled all over his shirt. He picked up the pieces of my glasses, took me into the kitchen, & got some ice for my face. He said I wasn't injured too badly & suggested I go up & take a hot bath, then I'd feel better.

Instead, I went to the parlour for another bottle of Scotch & drank myself to sleep. When I woke up, my glasses were on the bedside stand, good as new. I looked in the mirror—no swelling. I checked the rest of my body. No bruises, as tho' nothing had happened. Sometimes I'm glad when things fix themselves, but it's just not natural.

LXVIII. One thing came out of that fight w/ Linda—I'm using outside doors. Today I was in the dining room & she came out of her room, headed in my direction. My only exit was the outside door. I opened it & slipped thru to the parlour. It felt weird, but like Hugh said, it didn't hurt. Later I tried the front door. I had to brace myself, but it was no different than going from one room to another. And it does save steps.

LXIX. Wendel asked if I like soul food. What did he mean? He rattled off a list of things, some I'd never heard of. Barbecue ribs was on the list, so he cooked up a mess. For dessert we had sweet potato pie. I seldom notice the color of Wendel's skin anymore, but I told him no white person can make sweet potato pie this good. He said he didn't fix it. He wanted one like his grandmother used to make & found it in the refrigerator. We talked about what ingredients she used, & the recipe sounded the same as mine. Did she have some secret she didn't let out? Wendel didn't know. Maybe it's just a talent only black people have. Anyway, we polished off the ribs & put a dent in the pie. Wendel wouldn't let me put the leftovers down the garbage disposal. He set them out for whoever wanted some.

* * *

Ribs and pie. Rick felt hungry. He remembered he had ice cream in the freezer and ate a bowl before he went to bed.

93

Ghosts in the Neighborhood

Tuesday morning, Rick decided to talk with a few more neighbors. The optometrist's office across the street from the Wilson House was busy and no one had time to chat. Next door at the graphic design shop, the young people who ran it knew nothing of the history of the neighborhood. The Wilson House had been in place before they were born. All they knew was that it was haunted.

"How do you know it's haunted?" Rick asked. "Have you ever been inside?"

A young man spoke up "No, but that's what I've always heard. That's what everybody says." His coworkers nodded sagely, but none could tell Rick who or what haunted it, or why.

A girl volunteered, "I heard it was built over an Indian burial ground."

"Across the street?"

"I guess."

"Have you noticed anything unusual over there?"

Several heads shook. "Sometimes homeless people stay there. But that's not unusual."

Afterward, as Rick crossed the street, a shadow flitted across his peripheral vision. On the sidewalk in front of the Balrush house, a drab figure stood at the mailbox with a stack of envelopes. Harvey Balrush! Rick shouted, "Hello!" The man glanced up, turned abruptly, and scampered to his front porch, Rick in pursuit. "Hey! I'd like to talk to you." Mr. Balrush tripped on a warped board but managed to vanish through his front door before Rick could stop him.

Rick picked his way carefully over the damaged decking and knocked, politely at first. "Mr. Balrush, I'd like to talk to you." Silence was the only answer. He knocked again and shouted. While waiting for a reply, Rick studied the correspondence the man had dropped. Mostly junk mail, but one envelope caught his eye. The return address read, "Jeffrey A. Smart, Attorney at Law." Bob had to go through an attorney to buy the house. Maybe he'd have to go through the attorney to talk with Mr. Balrush.

He left the Balrush house and walked down the street to the bed and breakfast. The Inn displayed a plaque from the National Register of Historic Places. A young woman answered the door.

Rick introduced himself. "I'm renovating the Wilson House. You've done such a nice job on your building, I'd like to get some ideas."

The girl ushered him to a small office near the back of the house where Mrs. Richardson, a white-haired matron, sat at an ornate desk. When Rick extended his hand, she clasped it in both of hers. "I'm so glad you're restoring that old house. Let me take you on a little tour, and then we can sit down over coffee."

Rick tried to pay attention to the décor while he followed Mrs. Richardson's narrative.

"I've worked here since I was a girl," she said. "When the owner, Mrs. Prevatt, retired, I took over management."

In the parlor, he asked about the old-fashioned radiators.

"Yes, Mr. Hoover, who built this house, had steam heat installed."

"Do these still work?"

"Oh, yes, but they've been modified. Hot water runs through them now."

Rick looked at the high ceiling. "How do you cool the place?"

"With a heat pump. That's one modern feature the Prevatts installed. No one would rent a room if there was no air conditioning."

Upstairs, he nearly lost count of the number of bedrooms.

"The Hoovers needed a big house. They had fourteen children."

"Fourteen?"

"Yes. People had large families in those days, but he had two wives. Not at the same time, of course. He wore the first one out after ten babies, then he married a young girl who gave him four more, before she wore him out. He died of a heart attack." In a stage whisper, she added, "In bed, so I'm told."

The bathrooms looked authentic, with claw-foot tubs and pedestal sinks, just like the master bathroom in the Wilson House. One even had an old-time water closet toilet. "It didn't originally have so many bathrooms, did it?"

"No. After Mr. Hoover died, his widow sold the house to a Bascomb family who ran it as a hotel. They added bathrooms and closets. After the Prevatts bought it, they had period fixtures installed and had to redo some of the walls." She shook her head. "The Bascombs divided it up so badly."

The restoration appeared seamless.

After the tour, Mrs. Richardson led him to a breakfast nook. The young woman brought coffee and a plate of scones, serving one to Rick. "Thank you, Tanya," Mrs. Richardson said. "We're famous for our blueberry scones. We get our berries from an organic farm in Earleton. Now, what else would you like to know?" Before Rick could respond, she went on, "The Hoover House was built in 1893."

As Rick sipped coffee and nibbled on his scone, she related the history of the residence through good days and bad. Because of its size, upkeep was an issue. "That's why the second Mrs. Hoover sold it to the Bascombs, the ones who made it into a hotel. After Mr. Bascomb died, his widow married a rich man who restored the house, just before the 1929 crash. Then he put his gun to his head."

Mrs. Richardson shook her head. "Twice widowed, the dear lady lived out her days in the house. After she passed in 1958, it sat empty until Mr. Balrush rescued it and moved it here." She smiled. "Then the Prevatts bought it and renovated it, and established our bed and breakfast." She went on about the care they'd taken to restore the building to its original appearance while they modernized the plumbing and wiring and installed air conditioning. "You must come to me with any questions you have about renovating old houses."

Rick helped himself to another scone. "I definitely will. What can you tell me about the Wilson House?"

"I never studied that one. It's a shame no one took care of it. Mrs. Prevatt used to complain to the code enforcement people, but they never did anything. One year, I don't remember which year exactly, when we had a hurricane, I can't recall its name. That was back when they named them all after girls. Anyway, it wasn't really a bad hurricane, but it spawned twisters, and they blew the roof off that old house. Those slate shingles flew all over the neighborhood. Some of the pieces hit our Inn and did an awful lot of damage. One of those shingles flew through a window and made a hole in a bedroom wall!

"And…oh, you don't need to know all that. And that Mr. Balrush—he still owned the Wilson House—he didn't do a thing to help us. He didn't even say he was sorry. Nor did he fix the Wilson House. If the Historical Society hadn't repaired the roof, I guess that whole building would be rotted to the ground by now. But you know, they didn't do one thing to help us. Good thing we had insurance."

"Do any of these houses have cellars?"

"Cellars? We don't have cellars in Florida."

"Did you know the Wilson House originally had a cellar?"

"No, I didn't know that. Well, it used to sit on that hill where they built the courthouse."

"How long have you been hosting Halloween parties?"

"Well, we've had them off and on for years. Why do you ask?"

"Did anyone ever throw a party at the Wilson House?"

"No. No one has ever done anything with that house. Except the homeless, that is. They try to live there, until the police throw them out."

Tanya brought fresh coffee.

Rick said, "I've been told these houses are haunted."

Mrs. Richardson gave him a naughty smile. "Well, you always hear that about old houses." She added cream to her coffee. "Are you interested in ghosts?"

Rick paused, his cup halfway to his mouth. "Do you have any?"

Tanya sat down with them. Mrs. Richardson beckoned Rick to bend closer and whispered, "We have one. She's a young lady who used to live in this house. We don't know her name but she may have been a Hoover or a Bascomb. They say she died of a broken heart. Her lover went off to war and never came back. Instead of mourning in black, she wears white. She looks so lovely in white. Sometimes she sits on the staircase and you can hear her crying for him, her lost love."

Rick's eyes darted in the direction of the staircase. "Is she there now?"

"Maybe, but she only manifests herself when she wants to. I don't hear her now."

Tanya interrupted, "She was there yesterday. I couldn't see her, but I heard her."

Rick looked at Tanya. Her expression was serious. His back tingled. "What about the other houses? The Wilson House. Is it haunted?"

"I don't know anything about that. You know, I've never been inside that one."

Tanya spoke up, "Remember Jessica that used to work next door? She told us it was. She had to quit her job because the ghosts started coming into the lawyer's office."

"Yes, so she said."

Mrs. Richardson's change of tone surprised Rick. "You sound like you didn't believe Jessica."

"I don't know what to believe. You see, our young lady is a friendly ghost. I've never met an unfriendly one, and what Jessica told us about that one, well, it was pretty unfriendly."

Rick finished his coffee, set the cup down, and leaned back. "If someone doesn't know your young lady's there, and walks down the stairs, what happens?"

Mrs. Richardson and Tanya looked at each other. Mrs. Richardson replied, "Why, nothing. Why should anything happen?"

"If a living person walked through her, would they feel anything?"

"Maybe. Once in a while a guest will say something about a cold draft at the foot of the stairs."

Rick remembered what Kyle had told him, and what he'd heard about Jessica's experience. He tried to recall the location of air conditioning vents, a likely explanation. "What about your ghost, would she feel anything?"

Mrs. Richardson smiled. "I don't think so. She's dead, you know."

Did Mrs. Richardson really believe in the ghost or was she enhancing the atmosphere of her establishment? Her charm detained Rick longer than he'd intended. A mantle clock in the parlor chimed. "I'm sorry, I need to go. I have a dentist appointment."

After he got home that evening, he decided to read more from the journal:

LXX. In the real world, I always watched my weight & refused to nurture my psyche with food. I tried to fill my emptiness with Scotch. Here, it doesn't matter. At 1st, I was too shocked, too numb to eat. Then I started eating whatever I felt like, the hell with everything! But I don't think I gained an ounce.

Wendel was chubby when he came here & he eats like there's no tomorrow. Also, he uses a lot of bacon & salt pork when he cooks, but he doesn't look one pound heavier. Since we started cooking & sharing meals together, he seems to eat less compulsively, but I've been packing it away. No change. One good thing about Wendel is that he likes anything I fix. I experimented with some new flavoring for spaghetti sauce today. The taste was off, but he ate it anyway & said he liked it.

I left what we didn't eat on the stove & listened for reactions. Doreen snuck in & tasted it. She said, "Eeew!" & spit it out.

LXXI. Hugh fell downstairs today. I don't know why—he's not much of a drinker & I don't think he'd done any drugs. He just walked to the back staircase, & over he went. Head first. I heard him bump, bump, bump down. I rushed over to the stairs. Hugh lay there, head on the floor, the rest of him still on the steps. I couldn't get past him so I ran down the main stairs. Julio was right behind me. Hugh made no sound & didn't move. I was afraid he was dead.

Linda stood at the top of the staircase going, "Oh no! Oh no!" By the time she came down, he'd started to grunt & turn over, then he slid the rest of the way to the floor. I got him some ice & Julio helped Linda take him to their room. I couldn't help noticing his smell. Hasn't he been bathing? Oh well, I'm no one to talk.

LXXII. Hugh seems to be ok. In the real world, we'd have taken him to a hospital. If I could say I pitied anyone, it would be Hugh. While the rest of us indulge in our dysfunctions, Hugh sleeps. When he's awake, he does little but sit around. He listens to music, but when the record's over, if no one puts on another, he still sits there. His depression must be fathomless.

Linda doesn't help. She criticizes him for doing nothing, but if he does something, she criticizes that, too. Once I asked him why he puts up with her. "B/c I love her," he said. She's not the type you'd expect a man to fall in love with—heavy set, uncouth, all mouth, loud & vulgar, & she seldom smiles. I wasn't raised to be a lady, but even I picked up a few social graces. Linda could be almost pretty if she took care of herself & had better manners. She was all full of sympathy for Hugh yesterday, but today she's back to belittling him. I wish she'd make him take a bath.

LXXIII. Doreen and Rhoda woke me arguing about records. I'd fallen asleep to the beat of "A Hard Day's Night" & I guess Doreen wanted to play more Beatles, but Rhoda didn't. I have to agree with Rhoda. As much as I like the Beatles, I can't listen to them 24 hrs a day. But Rhoda wanted to play "The Sound of Music" again. I used to love that, but now whenever I hear about hills being alive, I want to strangle her. They compromised on "The Fantasticks." That was fine, until "Try to Remember" came on. I try NOT to remember. I gave up & went down for something to eat.

Wendel was cooking bacon & eggs & offered me some. I'd finished "Mysterious Island," so after we ate, we went to the library. "Try this," he handed me "Dune" by Frank Herbert. It takes place on a planet that's all desert. We just sat together in the library, reading, for the longest time.

LXXIV. Eating is one thing you have to do to stay alive. When I was a kid, if I wanted to eat, I often had to fix it myself. So I learned to cook. I started using box cakes & canned soups, until I got my hands on a cookbook. I learned to follow a recipe & eventually made everything from scratch.

My maternal parent didn't like many of the dishes I made, even when they turned out right, but some of her live-ins did. Mostly, I cooked for myself. I became adept at one-serving meals, like a sausage, potato, carrot, and maybe a few Brussels sprouts boiled together in one pan. (Hold that thought! I haven't had that in awhile.)

Out on my own, I became Betty Crocker. I collected recipes & tried new foods. Not all the time. I went through cycles. My creativity would wane & I'd cook just to live until my mood changed. Sometimes I'd eat out, but restaurant food gets boring, & I hate those waitresses who try to get chummy: "Did he stand you up?" You can eat only so many hamburgers, & besides, they make you fat.

At work, I'd show off at covered-dish luncheons. My best was a baked medley of vegetables, eggs, cheese, & bread crumbs tossed with fresh herbs. (Yes, another one I must make!) Since I changed jobs frequently, no one ate the same dish twice. Once I took a fancy cake, which impressed everyone. The boss suggested I make a career of baking. Was he planning to get rid of me? But just b/c you enjoy a hobby doesn't mean you want to do it for a living. That takes the fun out of it.

Right now my belly is full of fried chicken & mashed potatoes. I cooked for Wendel again. It feels nice to share a good meal with someone who appreciates it. Best of all, after many attempts to fry chicken just right, I finally succeeded. Wendel says mine rivals his grandmother's.

* * *

All this talk of food made Rick hungry. He seldom made one-serving meals. He'd cook a batch that would feed him for several days. Unfortunately, he was out of leftovers. He rummaged through his refrigerator and freezer for inspiration. He settled on a fried egg sandwich and was glad he hadn't run out of bread.

Rick spent Wednesday pulling permits and contacting subcontractors. He called Crosby and Sons House Moving to get an estimate on lifting the building. The secretary told him Tracy could meet him the following morning.

By now it was his habit to read a little of the journal every night. That evening was no exception.

LXXV. I guess it was inevitable. Two physically healthy people spending a lot of time together, one thing will lead to another. Wendel & I'd been reading together for hours every day, silently, at the dinner table or any quiet spot we could find. That can be difficult, w/ 6 other people making a ruckus. We went to my room to read until Julio put on some heavy metal music at full volume. Then we went up to Wendel's attic. It's quieter there, & private. That's where it started.

His being black makes him no better or worse a lover than anyone else. Men are all the same when you turn out the lights. Wendel made no complaints about my love-making, either. He's a good man & he's kind to me. I haven't experienced much of that in my life. I wouldn't say we love each other. Our common love is food, with books for dessert. But we're both lonely & want someone to love us, or at least give us affection.

LXXVI. I told Wendel that since I've been reading his books, he should read one of mine. Back in the real world, I enjoyed classics like Dickens, Jane Austin, & Thomas Hardy. After Wendel started loaning me books, my appetite for good literature returned. I found "Bleak House" in the library. Today Wendel was ready for another book, so I recommended "Great Expectations." We sat together in his room with chips & dip & Charles Dickens. When we got tired of reading, we made love. That's a pleasant way to spend an afternoon. (Since I don't know what time of day or night it is, I call it what it feels like.)

Later, we joined the others in the lounge to listen to music. Wendel likes black artists, like Aretha Franklin and Marvin Gaye, but he doesn't get to listen to them as often as he'd like b/c we have to take turns & he's not very confrontational. Linda & Hugh get a double dose of country music, b/c there are 2 of them. But with me on Wendel's side, there were 2 votes for Louis Armstrong. Surprisingly, altho Louie listens mostly to classical music, he likes jazz too, so today there were 3 votes for Louis Armstrong & no argument.

Then Doreen interrupted "What a Wonderful World" w/ "Where's Hugh?" I hadn't seen him upstairs since he fell. All eyes turned to Linda. "He's sleeping," she said. Julio asked if he was ok. Linda said of course, why wouldn't he be?

LXXVII. Today, I hankered for lasagna. I didn't want to just find some. I wanted it fresh from the oven & I wanted to make it myself. I found pasta in the cupboard & everything else I needed in the fridge, even fresh oregano. Preparation took hours. Wendel helped. We peeled & cut real tomatoes, not canned, for the sauce. The worse thing about making lasagna from scratch is handling those hot noodles, even with the right utensils. Wendel noticed me struggle with them & said, "Here, let me." He took over so gently, I didn't mind. He burned his fingers, but said it was ok, they'd heal overnight. Some of our housemates came into the kitchen when they smelled it baking. Julio asked when it would be ready but Doreen wrinkled her nose & remarked, "I wondered what that smell was." By the time it was done, everyone else must have fallen asleep b/c nobody asked for any. Fine by me. Wendel & I couldn't finish it off, so I hid the leftovers in the back of the refrigerator where I hope no one will notice. It's better the 2nd day, even cold.

I KNOW THIS HOUSE

Thursday, Rick arrived at the Wilson House to find a Ford Ranger in the yard and a small fellow with a ponytail peering under the building. When the person stood up, he realized it was a girl, quite attractive, wearing denim and jewelry. She couldn't have been over thirty. "Is Tracy here?" he asked.

She smiled and held out her hand. "I'm Tracy." Hers was the voice on the phone. "I know. You were expecting a man. A lot of people won't do business with me if they know up front I'm a woman."

Rick mumbled a greeting.

"I know this house. My dad is one of the 'sons' in Crosby and Sons. Our company moved all these houses back when he was a kid."

"Really?"

"Yeah. My grandfather took him to work that day, so he saw the whole operation."

"That must have been a sight to see."

"I guess so. These Victorian houses are more trouble than most because they're so tall and wide. You have to take down power lines, street signs, and sometimes trees. And the fireplaces and chimneys require special handling."

Rick looked up University Avenue and tried to imagine the Wilson House squeezing down the street.

"The permits were so expensive they moved them all in one day. That's what amazes me. *One* house a day is a job."

"Gee. They must have started at dawn and worked past dark."

"I guess so. They hired another company to help, but good thing it was summer. Long days, and with the students gone, almost no traffic."

"So, your dad still has the equipment to lift it?"

"He's retired. And yes, *I* have the equipment. We're tied up this week with another job but we can do it next week."

"That's fine."

"Do you want us to build the foundation?"

"You do that?"

"Sure do."

They circled the house together. As they inspected the back porch, Tracy said, "I don't understand why they left this one dangling, but we can fix it." When she saw how the east porch was caved in, she shook her head. "This one's too far gone. We'll have to remove the whole thing. If you want it replaced, your carpenters can do that."

"Right. By the way, do you know anything about this house having a cellar?"

"Yeah. My dad told me it did. It was the only house in town that had one, as far as he knows. Of course, they couldn't move the cellar with the house."

"Yeah."

"If you don't mind," Tracy said, "I want to look around inside, just to see if there are any potential snafus. A house this old can surprise you."

Tracy stomped on floors and kicked baseboards.

"You're wise to do the foundation before any other work. Even with the most careful lifting, some things will shift." Tracy's gaze drifted around the room. "You know, it's curious. I've been in lots of old houses, some of them empty for a long time, and there's usually more deterioration. I don't know why, but when someone lives in a building, even if they neglect the maintenance, it holds up better than an empty one. This one looks pretty beat up on the outside, but inside it doesn't look like it's been empty that long. It almost looks like people have lived here."

"Only homeless people."

"Uh huh."

"Speaking of curious," Rick said, "we found some things I suspect were in the house when it was moved."

"Really? Like what?"

"Some furniture, but I guess the homeless could've brought that in. I'm thinking of an antique radio cabinet."

"Where did you find that?"

"In the attic."

Tracy nodded.

"But even more curious, I think there was a piano here." Rick described what Lester had found in the fireplace. "I can't see the homeless bringing in a piano."

"No. And we wouldn't move a house with a piano inside."

That evening, Tracy called. "I told my dad about the house. He was glad someone was finally doing something with it. You know, it bugged me, what you said about the stuff you found in there. Especially the piano. He said the house was totally empty when they moved it. They cleared out everything that wasn't nailed down. He remembers, because he found a jar of old coins in one of the other houses. He searched all four houses for more treasure, even in the attics, but he didn't find anything else. Nothing was left inside."

After they hung up, Rick leaned back in his chair. So, everything he'd found in the house, including the remains of furniture, had appeared after the move. Why would anyone move a radio into a place with no electricity? Why something as bulky as a piano? He wondered if Harvey Balrush used the house as storage. Did the diarist have any connection to him? Rick felt his pulse quicken. Here was a puzzle to solve. He reached over his desk for the notebook. Maybe it would contain some answers.

LXXVIII. I don't know whether to be mad at Wendel or what. My mouth was watering for leftover lasagna but it was almost gone. I thought one of the others had found it, until Wendel came out of Hugh's room with a dirty dish with a smear of tomato sauce. When he saw me scowl, he said, "I noticed Hugh hadn't been out of his room for awhile, so I took him something to eat." What could I say?

Later, I noticed his bookmark was about ½ way through "Great Expectations," so I asked how he liked it. He said it was pretty good. "What do you think about Pip's sister?" Now, Dickens has all kinds of screwball characters, but that bitch takes the cake. Even my sorry mother treated me better than she treated Pip. Guess what Wendel had the nerve to say? "She's pretty nice."

He was faking it! He wasn't reading the book & he hadn't seen the movie. The withering stare I gave him would have made Pip's sister look kindly by comparison. Poor Wendel looked like he was ready to panic & run.

"What have you been doing?" I screamed. "Why did you deceive me?"

"I'm sorry." He shut the book w/out the bookmark. "I just couldn't get into it."

After we disrupted the whole household, yelling & screaming & stomping off, I downed ½ a bottle of Scotch, then sobered up enough to think. He probably had trouble with the language. It takes me a chapter or 2 to get into Dickens each time I tackle one of his books. Thomas Hardy is easier to read, so I found "Tess of the D'Urbervilles." Maybe he'll read that.

LXXIX. Everyone who's been complaining about my cooking takes an interest when they see Wendel eating with me. Doreen's the worst. She hovers around until we're finished. I'd throw out the leftovers but Wendel doesn't like to waste. (I put them down the garbage disposal when he's not looking.) I don't mind him taking food to Hugh.

I've never seen Doreen with a book, but now she's so interested in what Wendel's reading, she hangs over him & quizzes him about it. Over & over. It's gotten so bad, if she's around, Wendel goes to my room where he can read in peace. I know he's really reading "Tess of the D'Urbervilles" b/c he said he doesn't understand Tess' husband, why he had such an attitude about her past when he was guilty of the same thing.

LXXX. Hugh hasn't been upstairs since he fell. Today, Wendel asked when I last saw him. I couldn't say. We drift through our unmeasurable existence, broken up by sleep & meals. Hugh seldom comes to the kitchen & lately he hardly leaves his room. Good thing—he stinks so bad. Linda doesn't do much for him, so Wendel has assigned himself as Hugh's caretaker. He enlisted Julio and Louie to manhandle him into the tub for a bath.

LXXXI. Sometimes we sleep in the attic but I'm more comfortable in my room. Wendel moved a few of his things in. Normally, I don't let a guy move in with me b/c of the mess they make. Here any mess gets cleaned up, but I'm used to sleeping, reading, & drinking whenever I want to.

He finished reading "Tess." We talked about the book, but he didn't give it back to me. Then I found out he gave it to Doreen! Why? She wanted to read it & he thought I'd already read it. I did, a long time ago, & didn't plan to now, but it's my book & I expected it back. Wendel shook his head. "But you got it from the library. It's everybody's book." Technically that's true, but I feel like I own it. Why couldn't Doreen ask ME for the book?

I finished "Bleak House" & started another romance. Maybe Wendel thought that put me in the mood for love. Last night he tried to wake me when he felt amorous. I didn't, & he didn't know how to arouse me. We ended up arguing & I kicked him out of my room. Later, he apologized but I didn't accept it. Until he brought me a sinfully tasty rice pilaf. Then I had to forgive him.

* * *

Rick set the notebook aside. All those books—he was sure Amy had read them. Maybe some were in her library. He glanced at the clock. Was it too late to make a phone call?

Kyle answered on the fifth ring.

"I was beginning to think you weren't home," Rick said.

"Just got in."

In the background, Rick heard raised voices. "What's going on?"

"Allison's playing referee. We went Christmas shopping and left the kids home. You'd think they were old enough, but the boys decided to torment their sister. Of course, they claim she started it."

Rick smiled. It had been the same with Kyle and Kristie.

"What's up?" Kyle asked.

"I have a question. Remember when you went inside the Wilson House? What did you find inside?"

"Just a lot of garbage."

"No clock, right? What about a piano?"

"No. Nothing like that. Some broken chairs, maybe. I remember a mattress."

"In a bedroom?"

"Downstairs, I think. There wasn't much upstairs. Why'd you ask?"

"Just curious."

"You're going ahead with that house, aren't you."

Rick squirmed. "Any time I'm there, it's full of workers. And, no, nobody has seen—or felt—any ghosts." He was lying about going there alone and not telling the whole truth about his workers' odd experiences. But who was the parent here anyway?

Kyle sighed. "Please be careful."

"I will."

"Allison needs to talk to you." He handed off the phone.

"Dad, do you want the kids' Christmas wish lists?"

"Let me get something to write on." Rick wrote down her suggestions. Afterward, he stared at the list. Christmas. Without Amy, how was he going to cope? Despite the list, he had little clue as to what kids these days wanted, or what was good for them. Amy always handled Christmas. Last year, she couldn't go to stores, but she told him where to go and what to buy and reviewed his purchases before he wrapped them. Now he was lost.

As if in answer, his daughter Kristie called. "Dad, would it inconvenience you if we came for Christmas?"

"Why, of course not!"

"I mean, for two weeks. While school's out."

Two whole weeks? "I'd love to have you. When are you coming?"

"We get out next Friday, so expect us that weekend."

"Great! You can help me with Christmas shopping. I haven't even started."

"Be glad to. Have you put up a tree yet?"

"Uh, no."

"Good. Wait for us. The kids will enjoy it."

Where to put the tree? They didn't have one last year. When Rick looked around for a likely spot, he noticed accumulated dust on almost every surface, and dust bunnies in corners and under furniture. He'd better get busy. And groceries. He should ask Kristie what her kids eat. And bedrooms. He needed to change the sheets. Kristie and Steve could sleep in her old room, but were the kids too big to share bunk beds in Kyle's old room? Sandy was in high school now. That would make her fourteen or fifteen, Michael two years younger. If they couldn't share a room, Michael could sleep on the couch.

It was too late to start house cleaning, so he read a little more.

LXXXII. It was a mistake to let Wendel move in with me. His mere presence disrupts my life. Now I have to do things around another person with his own habits. When I want to write in my journal, I have to get him to leave, b/c I don't want him, or anyone, to know about it. Earlier, I told him I just wanted some time for myself. He left & went up to his attic. I actually felt relieved.

Later, when I went to the attic, Doreen was there, "discussing" "Dune Messiah" with Wendel! That pissed me off. Has she finished "Tess"? She hasn't read the first "Dune" book, so why's she starting w/ the 2nd one? When I showed up, she left. I jumped all over Wendel. "What's your problem?" he asked. "She has a right to read, too."

I stomped down to get a bottle of Scotch. And I hadn't been drinking so much lately.

* * *

Rick paused and stretched his legs. *Dune* was one science fiction book he was familiar with. He hadn't read it, but Amy had, and they went to see the movie. They hired a sitter and made it a date night, only to be disappointed. Amy said the movie wasn't near as good as the book. He heard they were now remaking the movie. Maybe the new one would be better.

LXXXIII. Doreen can't let matters rest. She played "I Want to Hold Your Hand" full blast. Somebody made her turn it down, but when she flipped the record over she cranked up the sound again for "I'll Cry Instead." I ran out to the lounge w/ a bottle, smashed it down on the turntable, & shattered the record. Now, both of us know all we have to do is leave the room & everything will get fixed, but she began to sing at the top of her lungs, "Look what they've done to my song, Ma." Only the first line & she just kept repeating it, over & over & over. When I screamed at her to stop, she screamed back, "I have every right to sing," & went on & on! Was she itching for a fight? I didn't take the bait. I went all the way down to the cellar to get away from her & her noise.

That's where Wendel found me, crying. He held me until I stopped. "Let's get out of here," he said & we went up to the kitchen. He asked me to help him with Hugh, so I did. I have no idea where Linda was. Wendel took Hugh some warmed-over soup. He was lying on his pallet on the floor. It takes more than one person to get him to a sitting position. While Wendel propped Hugh up, I fed him soup. Like feeding a baby, I guess. I've never fed a baby.

LXXXIV. I asked Wendel to recommend another book. He suggested "Foundation" but when he told me about it, I declined. It's a planet that's all city, no open countryside. I've been cooped up here too long. I don't want to be confined, even if only in my imagination. So he brought me "Stranger in a Strange Land" by Heinlein.

LXXXV. Doreen keeps borrowing books from Wendel. Then she hovers around, waiting for me to leave the room so she can talk to him. No way can she read those books that fast! I've been letting him stay in my room just to keep him away from her, but he gets on my nerves & then either I kick him out or leave the room myself. He always tries to make up afterward. I never do. I don't need a man that badly. But Wendel has a sweet romantic side to him & he needs a woman. Maybe he needs one to mother him, but I'm not the mothering type.

National Register of Historical Places

Friday the 13th dawned cool, with rain in the forecast. Rick wondered when the mild weather would break and they'd get a freeze. He had an appointment with Derek Crawford, his heating and air man, just after lunch. After he drank his coffee and read the paper, he tackled house cleaning. He barely heard the phone over the vacuum cleaner. It was Tracy Crosby.

"Rick, we're about finished with this week's job. We can start on your house Monday."

"Okay. Anything I need to do first?"

"I just need a copy of the permits. Oh, to get the equipment in, we may have to take down a few more sections of fence. We'll put them back up when we're done."

"Sure. No problem."

After he finished all the housework he cared to do, he settled down to paperwork and decided to see about listing the house on the National Register of Historic Places. Where to start? He turned on his computer and pulled up their website. Qualifications included the "age and integrity" of the property, and its "significance." Is it at least fifty years old and does it retain some degree of its original appearance? Yep. Does it have historical or architectural significance? That, he couldn't answer. He located the application form at the Florida Division of Historical Resources website and printed it. The amount of information required overwhelmed him. He called Mrs. Richardson at The Inn.

"I wasn't involved with applying for historic status," she said. "Mrs. Prevatt did all that, but she's no longer with us. What I do know is, you'll want a good history of the place. Mrs. Prevatt spent a lot of time at the courthouse and library. You should talk to Mrs. Johnson at the Historical Society. She knows a lot."

"How do I find her?"

"She's in the phone book, Ellen Johnson. I think the library has a file on these houses."

He reached Ellen Johnson's voicemail. After leaving a message, he made himself a ham and cheese sandwich, grabbed the journal, and read while he ate:

LXXXVI. I can't believe the nerve of Doreen. She showed no interest in Wendel before I got w/ him. Now, she not only tries to monopolize him, she wants to eat with us! We cooked a pot roast & I set the dining room table for 2. When it was ready, I saw a 3rd place setting. Wendel said he'd invited Doreen to join us. Not NO but HELL NO! I picked up the pot & dumped the whole meal down the garbage disposal, roast beef & all. Poor Wendel. He said, "All you had to do was say you didn't want her to eat with us."

LXXXVII. I HATE DOREEN! I HATE DOREEN! I HATE DOREEN! & I HATE WENDEL! I thought we had something good going. Sure, we argued & sort of split up a few times, but all couples do. How could he do this to me?

After a day of seething, I began to feel sorry for blowing up over the pot roast. Remorse is not one of my traits, but I made a chocolate cake, Wendel's favorite. While it was baking, I expected him to catch a whiff & come downstairs. When I iced the cake, I listened for him, but the only one who came in was Julio. He said he hadn't seen Wendel. He tried to get a finger full of icing. I slapped his hand with the flat side of the knife, threatened him not to touch the cake, & went in search of Wendel.

I knew he wasn't downstairs. Louie & Rhoda were upstairs in the lounge. Rhoda tittered. When I looked at her, she shut up. I checked my room in case he'd returned, but it was empty. I went up to the attic. No one there. The bathroom was vacant. Finally, I asked Louie if he'd seen Wendel. Rhoda burst out laughing & said, "Look in Doreen's room."

I didn't even knock. They hadn't locked the door. There he was, his shiny black ass sticking up, his face in her crotch. Both jerked around, but before they could say anything, I slammed the door, stamped downstairs, & threw that cake on the floor. I stomped on it & ground it into the linoleum. I didn't leave one edible crumb. Then I took off my shoes & ran up to Doreen's room. They still hadn't locked the door. Doreen was almost dressed but Wendel was struggling to get his pants on. I threw my shoes at them. Doreen ducked. Both shoes, cake mess & all, hit Wendel. Then I got a fresh bottle of Scotch & retreated to my room.

Later on, I stumbled thru' the lounge to the bathroom. Everyone but Wendel & Hugh were listening to music. Doreen stood up & said, "I'm not going to say I'm sorry." She was careful to stay out of my reach. "But Wendel is the only one who's really nice to me. And you're not nice to him at all."

"Then why don't you go after Hugh?" I retorted. "He needs someone to be nice to him."

Apparently she was too stoned to think straight. "I tried to, but he can't get it up."

Linda heard this and went after Doreen, who ducked into her room & locked the door. Linda pounded on the door, shrieking. When she couldn't get to Doreen she went downstairs & pounded on Hugh.

LXXXVIII. I'm not letting go of Wendel that easily. I don't want him back, but nothing's going to stop me from getting my revenge. He left a book lying around & I ripped it up & threw it in the fire. I broke one of his records in half & put it back in its sleeve. Did he suspect I was the culprit? He said something about it being squashed in the stack, then he took his favorite records to his attic. The records eventually fix themselves, & the books reappear whole, but at least I have the temporary satisfaction of destroying something & witnessing his consternation.

* * *

Rick closed the notebook. All those petty conflicts! He finished his sandwich and tidied the kitchen. By then it was time to go to the Wilson House.

Derek Crawford arrived. Rick said, "There's already some ductwork that was put in when the house was renovated, if it's still serviceable."

After examining the ducts, Derek's advice was to replace the old ones. "I assume you want to keep these antique registers. You'll need additional ducts and vents, too. This house was designed for heating, not for air conditioning. I'll work up an estimate and send it to you."

From there Rick went to the public library. A dozen library employees milled around. He addressed the first one who made eye contact. "Where would I find historical records?"

"They're at the Matheson History Museum," she said.

"Oh." Although the Matheson wasn't far, Rick decided to drive over rather than tie up a space in the crowded library parking lot. Besides, it was raining.

At the museum, he was told that the archives were in their building across the street. "But there's nowhere to park. You might better leave your vehicle here and walk over." He was glad he'd brought his umbrella.

The handsome brick building had once been a restaurant. Rick didn't realize it had gone out of business. *I guess I don't get out enough.*

A woman rose from her seat. "Hello. I'm Rita. Can I help you?"

Rick explained his mission. Rita ducked behind a large bookcase that stretched nearly the whole width of the room. He scanned the shelves. All the books seemed related to history in some way. Several shelves were devoted to books on historical houses, both in Florida and elsewhere.

Rita returned with an armful of file folders. "I think these are what you're looking for, but if you need anything else, let me know."

"Thank you." Rick set his clipboard on the table beside the folders and sorted through them. None were labeled "Wilson House" so he opened the "Whitehead Law Office" file. Maybe it would yield some clues. It did. Information dealt with all four houses being condemned and sub-sequently rescued. The file was full of old newspaper clippings and doc-uments. Some were handwritten and others had been typed on an old typewriter whose letters were either worn or needed cleaning. Such a typewriter had seen him through college. He plodded through the file, expecting the information to be in chronological order, but it wasn't. Worse, a newspaper column on page two continued on page eight, but the pieces weren't attached. It was like putting a puzzle together.

After an hour or so, he needed a break. He walked over to the library and found the science fiction section. As he scanned the shelves under "H," a sallow young man who was shelving books asked, "Can I help you find something?"

"Yes, I'm looking for a book by Robert Heinlein. 'A Crooked House?' It's about a tesseract house."

"That's a short story." The youth pulled a paperback from a shelf, opened it to the table of contents, and handed it to Rick.

"Another book I'm looking for—I'm sorry I don't know the title—is about some people in a bomb shelter who are blown into the future."

The young man nodded. *Farnham's Freehold.* He handed Rick an-other book.

"You seem to know a lot about science fiction."

"I live and breathe it."

"If you can help me with one other thing, there's a story about some people trapped in an old house—a Twilight Zone type situation. They're given everything they need, but they can't get out."

The boy looked puzzled. He shook his head and said, "No, I'm not familiar with that one. If you find out the title or author, let me know, okay? I'd like to read it."

"Sure." He checked out the two Heinlein books. Exiting the library, a damp wind assaulted him. At least the rain had stopped.

Rick spent another hour at the archives. He found information on the Wilson House in an unrelated file and brought it to Rita's attention.

While she prepared a folder for it, he Xeroxed several newspaper articles and other documents.

At home, he shuffled through the material and spent the rest of the day trying to put it in chronological order. Once he'd accomplished this, he found gaps in the information and knew he'd have to return to the archives, but not today.

What should he read tonight? He started with the notebook:

LXXXIX. I'm so lonely. I really wish I could get out of here & go home. Do I still have a home to go to? But anywhere would be better than here. Nobody cares about me & I don't care about them. The longer we're together, the worse it gets.

I've been thinking about my mother. Even though we never got along, at least she'd care about what happened to me, wouldn't she? I hope she misses me. I wonder if anyone tried to contact her. Did anyone know her name or how to reach her? It'd be 6 months or more before she'd try to call me. Maybe not even then. She'd be mad b/c I hadn't been in touch. Of course, when she tries, she won't find me. How hard would she look? When I'm drunk enough, I cry for her. Or am I crying for myself? Someone no one loves or misses? I'm sure it's been more than 6 months by now. It may have been eternity.

XC. A new development. Rhoda can't be content to let Doreen have a man w/out moving in on him herself. Her eyes follow Wendel, & when Doreen isn't around she snuggles up to him. And Wendel lets her! Yes, he cheated on me with Doreen, but I thought he had higher standards than that.

Doreen didn't forsake Julio when she took up w/ Wendel. Julio doesn't object, but I wonder how Wendel feels about it. Wendel & Rhoda have little opportunity to be together unless Doreen's asleep or w/ Julio. Rhoda actually eased her grip on Julio just to be w/ Wendel. Rhoda doesn't have her own room & doesn't dare use Doreen's for their little trysts. Wendel has no lock on the door to his attic & Doreen's not above storming up there if she suspects they're together. When I know one or the other is w/ Wendel, I make it a point to tattle. That causes no end of chaos. Poor Wendel hates to be caught with his pants down, but he doesn't seem to be capable of keeping them up.

XCI. As if our little soap opera wasn't entertainment enough, it just got better. Julio loves having a harem & doesn't mind sharing. Once I overheard him trying to talk the girls into a 3-some. Today, he wanted to include Wendel in a 4-some. I heard him follow Wendel up to the attic, telling him how much fun it would be, Wendel protesting the whole way. Poor Wendel. He just wants a woman, not to be part of some sex club. I pity the way Doreen & Rhoda play him as a pawn. He may have imagined himself a Casanova, but he's beginning to look like a lost puppy.

* * *

Rick set the notebook aside and thought about going to bed. It had been a long day, Friday the thirteenth. Unlucky for Red, maybe, but it had been a good day for him. The house movers were coming Monday, an estimate for heating and air conditioning was in the works, and he'd made progress applying for historical status. In addition, although he'd never been interested in science fiction, he was now on that path. Whether that was good or bad remained to be seen.

Parade of Homes

Saturday morning saw more rain, a good day to be cooped up indoors. Rick organized his Wilson House file and studied the documents. A handwritten page seemed to have the oldest information:

> Hiram Wilson built the house in 1888. He moved here from Philadelphia after inheriting a comfortable fortune. Although the design of the Wilson house is similar to its neighbors, Hiram included some features more typical of houses in Pennsylvania, such as a cellar with a furnace. He was careful to build on the highest elevation in the city so his cellar wouldn't flood.
>
> He moved to Florida for investment opportunities and his wife's health. Though an invalid most of her days, she outlived her husband. Hiram invested in the orange business and lost heavily in the freezes of the 1890s. After that, he became involved with a variety of ventures, including railroads, land speculation, and the turpentine industry, all of which further drained his fortune. At some point after his wife's death in 1932, the house was sold at a tax auction.
>
> Harold Griffis, the next owner, renovated the house, installing a more modern kitchen and bathrooms. His family occupied the place long after other houses in the neighborhood had been reduced to rental property and eventually abandoned. His children sold the property to the city in 1968.
>
> Ellen Conner, 10/18/71

Rick wondered if this was the same person as Ellen Johnson.

A newspaper article from November 14, 1968 announced plans for a new courthouse to be built downtown. Several old buildings, mostly empty and falling to ruin, were to be razed. Construction was slated to begin in January.

On November 26th, a photo was published, showing some old brick stores being demolished. Rick vaguely remembered those buildings. One had been a hardware store where his parents did business when he was a child, but to his recollection, the others were empty and boarded up at the time.

The next piece was a lengthy letter to the editor by Ellen Conner in which she deplored the destruction of the city's historical buildings. She had been unable to save the old stores, but in her opinion, the Victorian houses merited preservation. She singled out the four that stood on Second Street and detailed their history.

Rick thumbed through more articles. Ellen Conner rallied a group of like-minded citizens, including an attorney who filed an injunction to prevent destruction of the houses. An editorial branded Miss Conner as a "naïve troublemaker" who was "impeding progress." Rick had to chuckle. In another letter to the editor, Harvey Balrush proclaimed that he owned four lots on the east side of town. He promised to purchase the buildings from the city and pay to move them.

A photo dated January 11th showed a young Mr. Balrush at the city commission meeting. The caption stated that he bought the houses for one dollar each.

In June, a Sunday supplement, titled "Parade of Homes" showed pictures of the four houses as they rolled down University Avenue. Onlookers lined the sidewalks. In one photo, a man with a camera stood precariously in front of the Wilson House. The pictures showed power lines tied back, and trees with street-side limbs sheared off, making them appear to lean away from the onslaught.

In the photos, the Wilson House looked much as it did now. Curiously, it was the only one with an intact chimney. From what he could see, those in the other houses had been partially dismantled.

An hour later, he decided that was enough for the day. He still had much to do before Kristie's family arrived. That afternoon, when he took a break from house cleaning, he read more of the journal.

XCII. Wendel actually had the audacity to apologize. He said he thought it was ok for him to go w/ more than one woman, like Julio does. He thought the rules of the real world didn't apply here. Does he want to be romantically involved w/ me again? No chance! I didn't even accept his apology. But he started me thinking.

The rules of the "real" world? He's right, they don't apply here. At least not the laws of science. But social rules? Between people? Do they apply? Should they? We behave no differently than people in the "real" world. Maybe we take it more to the extreme, or maybe it's b/c we're too confined to hide misbehavior. I've broken rules here I never would have out there. I never drank as much. Or used drugs at all. And we seem to have no consequences. I never get a hangover & my liver hasn't failed. Even if it did, it'd probably heal itself. I was with two guys in a single day. We don't work but we get fed. Everything's done for us. Truly, the rules of the outside world don't apply to us, except that we still have feelings. And those feelings can be hurt.

XCIII. I've resumed cooking only for myself & I eat alone. I wait until the others are asleep or high. I miss Wendel's company, but I don't really miss sex w/ him. He's so predictable, so unimaginative.

Today I fixed filet mignon. I didn't know Louie was up. He wandered in & said, "I know a wine that's perfect with this." I told him I don't really care for wine but he left the room & returned with a bottle of a red something that I can't pronounce. Of course, Louie announced the name of it in perfect (to my ear) French. He said it complements the taste of the meat. He was right. I felt obligated to share my dinner w/ him. He took only a few bites of food w/ his wine, but I really enjoyed the taste, if not the company.

XCIV. I feel like a prisoner in solitary confinement. No one to talk to, not even a prison guard to bring me food. Even in my solitary life in that other world I had some social contact, but I don't want anything to do with these people. Out there I had freedom. I want it back. I'd even be happy to go back to work. At least I'd have free time to do what I wanted, maybe go to a movie, but that's indoors, I want to be outside. I want to drive around in my Mustang, go to the beach. Maybe watch a movie at the drive-in.

I miss my car. I still have the keys. I tried to throw them away, but they came back. I loved my car. It was the one bright spot in my pathetic life, the only thing that was truly mine. It was a used car, but I owned it free and clear. It was so cool to have a convertible, even if I seldom put the top down. Seems whenever I did, I'd get sunburned, or it would rain.

XCV. Louie must be pretty lonely. He doesn't have any friends here, not that he's made much effort to be friendly. I don't have any friends either, but I'm used to it. I suspect he was once popular in his own social circle, but no one here is up to his standards. So what happened today surprised me.

I stay holed up in my room until the house is quiet & everyone else is asleep. "Tonight" I made my usual "midnight" raid on the kitchen & discovered someone had beat me to it. The oven was on. Louie came in with a bottle of white wine. "Do you like quiche?" he asked. It smelled good, & since he invited me, I joined him. He'd already put a formal place setting in the dining room, and now he put out another. It almost felt good to have conversation over a meal, not that we discussed anything momentous. I told him I'd never made quiche. I didn't admit I'd only tried it once before. Louie said he doesn't make his own pie crust. I told him pie crust isn't hard to make & offered to show him how. (The wine must have gone to my head.)

After we ate, he picked up a rather thick book that had been lying on the buffet. "What are you reading?" I asked.

"Ulysses." His bookmark was about 2/3 of the way thru. "If you like, I'll give it to you when I'm finished."

I never read it, although a lit professor once told me I should. I like long books when I'm in the right mood, b/c if it's a good story, I don't want it to end. Right now I'm reading "Pride & Prejudice." I can't believe I never read it before. My education is so incomplete.

* * *

That reminded Rick of the books he'd checked out at the library. He put the notebook away and picked up the collection of Heinlein stories. First, he read the one about the tesseract house. Interesting. Now he understood why Wendel was so excited about the parallel between his circumstances and the story. What else was in this collection? The table of contents listed a story with the title, "—All You Zombies—." Intriguing, but he still had a house to clean.

While dusting the bookshelf in Kristie's old room, Rick noticed a copy of *Dune*. Another surprise. Amy never mentioned she had that book. Later, he sat down to supper with the zombie story. It turned out not to be about zombies after all. It was about a person who was her/his own mother and father. Were all of Heinlein's stories this weird?

* * *

Kyle and Allison invited Rick over for Sunday dinner. The children were excited about Christmas and the anticipated visit by their cousins. Rick asked Kyle what he knew about his mother's interest in science fiction.

"Mama read all kinds of things."

"True. I thought she liked classical literature most, but her bookcase has quite a collection of Heinlein, and other writers."

"Some of those books may have been mine or Kristie's."

"I hadn't thought of that. Look them over next time you come. If you want them back, you can have them."

That evening, rather than reading more Heinlein, he continued with Red's journal.

XCVI. Louie took me up on the pie crust offer. I was in my room reading when I heard a knock on the door. It's been so long since anyone came to my room, I almost didn't hear it. "I'm going to make quiche," he said. "Will you make the crust?"

I showed him how so he can do it on his own. Then I watched him put the filling together. Quiche isn't that hard to make. Apparently, there are many kinds. The last time, he made Quiche Lorraine, the only kind I was familiar with. This time he put spinach in it. After he put it in the oven, he went to the dining room to set the table, for 2! I was still wearing my pajamas & had flour on them, so I decided to go change. On the way up, I thought an elegant dinner called for dressing up. I found a nice pants suit in the closet & even did my hair and put on makeup. When I returned to the dining room, Louie smiled in a way I'd never seen him smile before. We had a pleasant dinner.

Louie just picks at his food. I think he still watches his weight even tho there's no need to. Nobody gets fat here. For some reason, I didn't gobble my food like usual. I slowed down & discovered I could taste it better. Maybe that's what Louie does, taste it more. I ate less, but was just as satisfied.

He's done with "Ulysses" & gave it to me. I'll finish "Pride & Prejudice" first. Louie had a poetry book, by someone I'd never heard of, Adonis Castleberry. He read a few poems to me. Maybe it was the wine, but I thought they were weird, impossible to follow.

XCVII. Since I started haunting the midnight hours, I've noticed Louie up & about at the same time. Like me, he's avoiding the others. Tonight I was reading by the fire when he came in & asked how I like "Ulysses." I said I hadn't started it yet. He just hmmmed. I asked what he was reading. Dante's "Inferno". I hmmmed. That was our conversation.

I read the "Inferno" a few years back. Good reading, but seeing Louie w/ it made me think about Virgil. Not Dante's Virgil, ours. Dante's Virgil led him into Hell, but delivered him out again. Our Virgil just led us into this hell & abandoned us. At times I wonder about him, what kind of person he actually was, what power he had over our fate. Did he do this on purpose? Why? He collected the 8 of us & brought us here. The other people at the party left, & so did he.

I lied about "Ulysses". I didn't want to admit that I'm having a hard time reading it. Why does it have that title? As best I can tell it's about some Irish guys, & none of them are named Ulysses. I read the "Odyssey" in school & liked it, but I'm not sure about this. The professor who recommended it was also into Faulkner & required us to read some of his novels. I read them, but I had a hard time. Too foggy. Maybe I already have too much fog in my brain. I couldn't see my way through Faulkner & this book's even worse. I really tried, but I can't make heads or tails of it. Not even sober. Call me uneducated, but I like books that just tell a good story.

* * *

Rick leaned back and smiled. All those books. He was surprised that these characters—boozers and druggies—would read such literature. He thought back to his college days. Faulkner's novels were hard to understand and he never tackled *Ulysses*. He missed the *Inferno*, but he had a general idea what it was about. After he graduated, he seldom read fiction. There was too much else, and he liked to stay anchored in the real world. Amy, of course, read just about everything, but she never pressed him to read what he had no interest in.

XCVIII. Louie isn't so bad once you get to know him. We have similar tastes in music & literature. We both like the classics. Today he wanted to talk about Dante's "Inferno" but I didn't & I told him why. So he asked me what I thought about "Ulysses". Now I've made honest attempts to read it, but it puts me to sleep. I turned the question around and asked him what he thought. Louie went off on some literary criticism spiel that confused me more than the book itself.

Since no one else was listening, Louie played a Vivaldi album. When that was finished, he put on opera. Instead of telling him I don't like the way those women screech, I just listened. The music woke Doreen. When she complained, I told her she just wasn't cultured enough.

Somehow we got on the subject of baths. Maybe b/c Rhoda was hogging the bathroom again & I wanted to take one. Louie invited me to use his tub & mentioned he has a collection of gourmet bath salts. I took him up on his offer & enjoyed the luxury. However, I locked the door so he couldn't get in. I don't want him to get any ideas of us becoming lovers. I remember our one and only encounter and don't want to repeat it.

Message in a Bottle

On Monday, Rick arrived at the Wilson House to find a yard full of equipment and a semi backing in with the largest "I" beams he'd ever seen. He squeezed his truck into a corner where he hoped it would be out of the way. Several men surrounded the house, their eyes following Tracy as she gestured and called out orders. He didn't interrupt, only watched from a safe distance. Some of the workers went around with pry bars to separate the back and east porches. Finally, with the beams in place, they rolled huge hydraulic jacks under them. Tracy approached Rick and explained what they were doing.

An hour later, with a few creaks and groans, the house rose several feet in the air. Then came a splintering crash as the east porch fell. "We'll level the house temporarily," Tracy said. "Then we'll work on the foundation. Once we put the house back in place, I think you'll be pleased."

He nodded.

A cry came from under the house. Tracy bolted. Ducking under the building, she emerged with a middle aged man whose hand dripped blood. She took him to the washing station to clean it off.

"How bad?" Rick asked.

"Oh, I'm okay," the man said. "I just got cut on some glass."

"Glass?"

"Yeah. That old rusty sewer pipe come apart and a bunch a' gunk fell out. I tried to shove the pipe outta the way and a piece of glass fell on my hand."

Rick looked at the cut. He might not need stitches, but what about infection? "Do you want me to take you to a doctor?"

"Naw. Tracy's got a first aid kit."

As Tracy led the man to her truck, she called out, "Clean up that glass before anyone else gets hurt."

A young man came from under the house with a shovelful of rubbish. Rick looked at it closely and picked out two pieces of glass which seemed to fit together, into, yes—a small makeup bottle!

This can't be! Rick examined the shards. A rusted metal cap remained tightly screwed to the neck but the bottle had split in half. He found himself looking for a scrap of paper inside. The debris was unrecognizable but seemed to fall in layers. If anyone were to ask about his interest in this piece of trash, he didn't know what he'd say. He wrapped the fragments in newspaper and put them in his truck.

After watching Tracy and her crew work all day, leveling the house and digging the trench for the footer, Rick was as worn out as if he'd done the labor himself. He bought Chinese take-out on the way home and read while he ate:

XCIX. Was it a dream? It seemed so real. I ventured into the lounge to listen to music. Louie put on an album of soft classical music that put me to sleep. I dreamed the cushion beneath me was hovering in the air. Then I heard a huge crash. You know how in dreams you fall and wake up? When I fell, I grabbed the person next to me—Wendel. He said, "What was that?" We held onto each other, hardly daring to breathe. Finally I whispered, "Did you hear something?" He said, "I dreamed I was in a boat & we crashed into rocks."

Rhoda ran into the lounge screaming, "No! I gotta get out!" She ran downstairs. Julio followed her to the bannister and looked down. I asked what was going on. He said, "Nothing, just a bad dream. Rhoda thought we were having an earthquake." Then he snorted & said, "She's trying to get out of the house." She opened the front door, then slammed it hard.

C. Today, the aroma of cooked steaks wafted thru my closed door. It was so tempting, I went down to see about it. They'd left one uncooked steak in the fridge so I claimed it for my own. Louie came down and said "bernaze" sauce was just the thing to go with steak. I had no idea what he was talking about, but I didn't let on. He said he'd make some, also a salad, if I'd share the steak with him. What could I say? I watched him make the sauce. I was familiar with most of the ingredients, except tarragon. I like the taste, so I'll add it to my repertoire.

While we were eating, somebody played the "2001" soundtrack. When it came to "Blue Danube," my imagination started waltzing with the music. I recalled my idea the night of the Halloween party, of a formal event in this elegant house.

One positive result of my involvement with Louie is that I've come to appreciate the house again. The interior, that is. Louie fits the setting. Both are beautiful to look at & show good taste, on the surface, anyway. The dining room was made for formal dinners and the parlour for classical music. Move the furniture, roll up the carpet, and there's room to dance.

I told Louie my idea & he liked it. So that's what we did. We didn't need to move much furniture for just the 2 of us. I found a formal gown in my closet—a blue brocade in a rose pattern. The neckline is just low enough to make my throat look graceful. I fixed myself up & found a string of pink-tinged pearls & a pair of matching earrings, even a pearl bracelet. Colorful enough with my red hair. A crinoline came with the dress. My room is too small for the skirt to flare out when I twirl, so I went out to the lounge to try it. I felt like I was in a fairy tale.

I missed out on my Sr. Prom. I went to the Jr. Prom with a pimply-faced boy & wore a dress my mother found in a thrift shop. In the middle of my Sr. year we moved, & I didn't know anyone at the new school. I thought about asking a guy to take me to the prom, but that would be too mortifying. I didn't have anything to wear, anyway. The old dress hadn't survived the move. I missed out on a lot that year. I spent prom night alone, in tears. Some memory.

To my surprise, Louie put on his Sun King costume, the one he wore Halloween. Everything was clean & pressed. Even a new wig! Good thing I wore high heels, b/c so did Louie. Those women in movies who dance in heels always amaze me, but it's not so hard if you stay on your toes. When he saw me, he smiled & said, "You look lovely." I felt lovely, too. He took my right hand & kissed it with flare.

By then no one was in the lounge, so we moved the record player downstairs. We dimmed the lights in the parlour & lit candles. He chilled a bottle of champagne & we waltzed until our legs gave out. We didn't talk much. I was lost in my private fantasies & Louie probably was, too.

In the past I had a hard time w/ this type of dancing b/c I try to lead rather than let the guy do it. But this time I had no trouble letting Louie lead. He didn't hold me close, just one hand on my waist and the other holding mine. That was fine with me. Usually when you dance with a guy, you feel warm where he touches you. Louie's hands were cool. He didn't want me to put my left hand on his shoulder but had me hold up a corner of my skirt. I have to admit it's an elegant way to dance. When he spun me around, my skirt would swirl, just like in the movies.

* * *

Rick thought back to his senior prom. He couldn't remember what color dress Amy wore, but she had been lovely, too.

The phone interrupted him. "Dad?" It was his daughter, Kristie. "You had me worried when you didn't return my call."

"When did you call?"

"This afternoon. I left a message. I also tried your cell phone, but you didn't answer."

Rick had forgotten to check messages, and the noise at the Wilson House likely muffled the cell's ring. "Is anything wrong?"

"No, I just wanted to confirm we're heading out Friday afternoon. If I'm not tired, I may drive all night and get there Saturday."

"Don't do that. Why not stop halfway at a motel?"

"I may. I'll call you when we get to Lake City."

"I needed to talk to you anyway. What do the kids like to eat?"

"Don't worry about that. Just have some milk and cereal on hand. I'll go grocery shopping when I get there."

"That can wait 'til you're rested. I'll order pizza."

After they hung up, he realized Kristie sounded like she was driving by herself. What about Steve? Maybe he had to work. As a teacher, Kristie had a full two weeks' Christmas break. It was too bad they had to take separate cars.

He checked his messages. Someone named Ellen Johnson had returned his call. Who? Oh. The Historical Society. He called her back. "Mrs. Richardson at The Inn suggested I talk with you. I'm working on the Wilson House...."

"Oh, yes. I noticed some activity over there. I was worried someone was tearing it down, but Mr. Balrush assured me you were fixing it up."

"You talked with Mr. Balrush? I tried to, but he won't answer the door."

"I know. He's very reclusive, but he talks to me."

"Well, I want to list the house on the Historical Register and need some history."

"You've come to the right person. Why don't you come over tomorrow afternoon, say one o'clock? I'll have time to talk then." She gave him her address.

Rick recalled the makeup bottle and retrieved it from his truck. He wanted to wash off the dirt, but that would ruin any evidence. Evidence of what? He was past feeling foolish. He pulled the first notebook from the stack and thumbed through to the account of the message in the bottle. A small makeup bottle, small enough to go down a toilet drain, with a note inside. He examined it under the bright kitchen light but couldn't tell whether the contents had been paper, or what.

In his years building and repairing houses, Rick had encountered many things flushed down toilets—tooth brushes, toys, you name it—often resulting in clogs. It was conceivable someone could accidentally drop a makeup bottle in a commode. But why, of all places, the Wilson House!

He rewrapped the glass and wondered if there was any way to determine what had been inside. Documentaries he'd watched on TV came to mind. Archaeologists had been able to read fragments of writings a thousand or more years old. Could they give him answers about this note in a bottle? Would they think he was nuts?

Curiosity grappled with self-respect. There was no question of calling anyone tonight, but if he decided to, who could he call? He looked in the phone book for the archaeology department at the University, but could find no listing. Surely they had one. He googled it. It was located at the Museum of Natural History. He could find no reference to old documents, but stumbled across "What to do if you find a dugout canoe in a lake." Close enough, he hoped, to a bottle stuck in a drainpipe for half a century. At least these researchers could steer him in the right direction. If they didn't think he was crazy. He jotted down a couple of phone numbers before he let himself get lost reading about prehistoric canoes buried for centuries in the mud of Florida lake beds.

At the Wilson House the next morning, Rick asked Tracy about the injured man. "Oh, Jimmy'll be okay. He had to go home sick."

"Is his cut infected?"

"No, the cut's fine. He started throwing up shortly after he got here."

That was the third worker who'd taken sick.

"By the way, Rick, what do you want to do about those old cellar steps? I'd like to run floor joists through that gap."

"They can be removed. I want to make that space into a closet."

"Sounds good."

Fortunately, the morning brought no mishaps. After lunch, he drove to Mrs. Johnson's.

Not unexpectedly, Ellen Johnson, the founder of the local Historical Society, lived in the historical section of town, in a modest limestone bungalow. And she looked the part—probably in her eighties, petite, silver hair twisted into a bun. Her gentle Southern manners, Rick suspected, were merely a veneer beneath which the "troublemaker," no longer naïve, lingered.

She ushered him into a room lined with book shelves and filing cabinets. "Would you like some sweet tea? And oatmeal cookies?"

"Yes, thank you." Rick settled into a comfortable chair. "Mind if I take notes?"

"I expect you to."

"I read the file on the Wilson House at the Matheson. Are you the same person as Ellen Conner?"

"Yes. That was my maiden name."

"I'm hoping you can give me more details and," he smiled sheepishly, "some tips on listing it on the National Register."

"Oh, that's not as difficult as it looks. You only have to fill out the forms, answer the questions." She set the tea and cookies on a little table between them. "The house was built by Hiram Wilson. He was from Philadelphia and moved to Florida in 1885 after he inherited a tidy sum of money. He was interested in the orange business. Also, his wife, Edith, suffered from some unspecified illness and needed a warm climate. They went to Miami first, but it was too humid, so they settled here. They built the house in 1888. Edith's health never improved, and neither did Hiram's fortunes." She lowered her voice. "I came across rumors that she was a closet alcoholic, or addicted to laudanum. Probably true."

Mrs. Johnson sipped her tea before continuing. "Anyway, the freezes of the 1890's nearly wiped Hiram out financially. After that, he tried investing in railroads and several other things, never successfully. Finally, in 1916, he put his gun to his head."

"Oh!" Had he heard this story before? Yes. "Mrs. Richardson said one of the owners of her house committed suicide, too."

Mrs. Johnson nodded. "Not every Yankee who came to Florida in those days got rich. And some of them took it hard when they didn't. The Wilson children didn't fare very well, either. After their mother passed, they piddled away what was left of the family fortune. In 1938, the house was sold for taxes."

Rick wondered if the inhabitants of the other houses had better luck.

"More tea?" Mrs. Johnson asked.

"No, thanks."

"Harold Griffis, the new owner, renovated the house, then he had a stroke and died. He'd added two bathrooms, though, so they could take in boarders. His wife, Alma, ran the boarding house for years. She was the last owner to live in the neighborhood. The other houses on the street had become rentals. By the time Alma Griffis passed away, her children were only too happy to sell the property for what they could get."

"It sounds like the people who lived there had bad luck. Mrs. Richardson said the same thing about her house."

"I know. Some say it's because they were built over an Indian burial ground."

"Were they?"

"Who knows? That little hill has been dug up and bulldozed so many times, any evidence was destroyed long ago."

"But what would that have to do with it?"

Mrs. Johnson shrugged her shoulders.

"After the renovations by Mr. Griffis, did anyone else fix up the house?"

"No. His wife lacked the money."

"What was your experience with the house? I mean, you've been inside, right?"

"Oh, yes. Not before the city condemned it, but I went in a few times before they moved it, and after." She stood up and took an old photo album from a shelf. "Here are the houses before they were moved."

The pictures showed a street of empty Victorians surrounded by azalea bushes so large they nearly obscured the porches. Huge live oaks trailed ghost-like wisps of Spanish moss. In front of the Wilson House stood a pair of sabal palms that reached the second floor. A few broken windows made the façades look wretched. Sunbeams slanting through the trees failed to dispel the gloom. No wonder people thought those houses were haunted. "May I have a copy of these?"

"Certainly. My printer is out of color ink, but I can scan them and send them to you."

Rick gave her his email address. "Tell me about the cellar."

"Mr. Wilson was a Yankee, so he thought a house should have a cellar. It wasn't like a northern cellar, extending all the way under the house. It was small, about the size of a single room. It had a furnace and storage for canned goods."

Rick shuddered. That was about the size of the one described in the journal. Who could have guessed the size of the cellar after the house was moved? "What do you know about the squatters who stayed there?"

"Not much. They didn't do very much damage, which is surprising."

Rick took a deep breath and asked, "Did you ever notice a red haired woman there? Or a Mustang convertible?"

"No, no cars, and I don't recall any redheads."

"Are you aware of any disappearances connected with the house?"

"Well, no. Why do you ask?"

"Just some things that have come up. Did anyone in the Historical Society have a son who disappeared? Named Louie or Louis? Tall, good looking, blonde hair, blue eyes."

"That sounds like Louise Badger's son, only his name was Calvin, not Louis."

"Did he disappear?"

"For a while. He and his mother had an argument and he ran away."

"How old was he?"

"He had to be in his twenties. He was pretty shiftless, wouldn't work, wasn't married, just lived off his mother. I heard he had a cocaine habit. That may be what they argued about."

"Do you know what became of him?"

"He showed up again several years later. By then he'd settled down. Never finished college, but at least he was off drugs. When his mother could no longer care for herself, he worked and took care of her."

Rick swallowed. "Did they have a house in the historical area?"

"Oh, yes. A beautiful house. But they don't live there anymore. They had to sell it when she went into a nursing home."

"Are they still in town?"

"Louise died a few years ago. I have no idea what became of Calvin."

Rick changed the subject. "I've heard rumors the Wilson House is haunted."

Mrs. Johnson smiled. "Well, isn't that part of the charm of these old houses? What good would they be if they weren't haunted?"

"Did you ever experience anything unusual when you were in there?"

"No. Have you?"

Rick forced a laugh.

Mrs. Johnson straightened her back. "Aren't all things a little haunted? If not by ghosts, or the past, by something?"

On his way home, Rick pondered what Mrs. Johnson said about Calvin Badger. It was uncanny. Did Red know the real person and use him in her story? That night he couldn't resist reading further:

CI. Today, we listened to a Mozart opera sung in English. Of course, who doesn't like Mozart? I enjoy the singing better when I can understand the words. Doreen came in and said, "Eeeyoo. Opera." She couldn't wait for it to end so she could put her record on. Beatles, of course. Always Beatles.

I find it unbelievable how uneducated most of my housemates are, even the ones who claim they went to college. None of them finished. Neither did I, but at least some of it sunk in. The other day, Louie & I were reading in the parlour. I was trying to read "Ulysses". I had paged ahead to a different section of the book to see if it got any better. It did for a while, then the fog rolled back in. Anyway, I was trying to decipher it when Julio came in, pulled the book up to look at the title, and said, "Why are you reading that garbage?"

Louie didn't give me time to answer. He said every cultured person should read it.

Instead of backing down, Julio asked what it was about. Louie's explanation was just as unintelligible the 2nd time around. Julio tried to pin him down on the plot. Louie went on & on but Julio only shook his head & said, "You're not making any sense." I told him not to knock it till he tried it. Julio walked off, saying, "I wonder if he's actually read that book."

CII. Today Louie shared more poetry with me. It was a different poet this time, again someone I'd never heard of. The others drifted through the lounge while he read. Linda and Doreen kept going but Wendel paused a moment to cock his head & listen before he went up to his attic. Julio listened with a sardonic smile, shook his head, & went downstairs. I told Louie I used to write poetry when I was younger. He asked if he could read some. I didn't bring my poems to the party! Besides, I think my mother threw them away. I told Louie if I could remember any I'd write them down.

Later we fixed Boeuf Bourguignon. I looked up the spelling in my cookbook, as well as the recipe. It's very good, but it's really just beef stew w/ more steps & fewer vegetables. If I'd seen the recipe before, I'm not sure I'd have gone to all the trouble. I'd just make beef stew.

CIII. What I could remember of my old poetry seemed childish, so I wrote a new poem. When I get a chance, I'll copy it here. I wrote it on another piece of paper b/c I don't want Louie to know about my journal. When I showed it to him, he said he couldn't read my handwriting & asked me to read it aloud. I started to, but he interrupted me. "Like this." He straightened his back, held the paper out at arm's length, & in a theatrical voice, quoted the first line. I was more than a little embarrassed b/c we were attracting an audience, but I read it anyway, imitating his style. He nodded sagely & said, "Yes. Fascinating. Very deep." I heard a chorus of groans. What do any of them know about poetry?

CIV. Louie and I decided to have another dance. This time I wished for a shimmery green gown that's close fitting & shows my figure. Louie wore his royal attire again. He looked me up & down, handed me a silk handkerchief & had me hold it with my left hand when we danced. Like

I held my skirt the last time. At 1ˢᵗ, we waltzed, then he put on a foxtrot. I told him I didn't know that one. He demonstrated the steps & told me to follow. When I was a kid I wanted to take dance lessons but never got the chance. I'd watch dancers in movies & imitate them. It must have been just enough to give me an edge. I didn't do too badly, I think. Louie didn't say anything either way.

Halfway thru our dance, Doreen came down pulling Wendel by his nose, so to speak, & Rhoda had Julio (figuratively) by the penis. Both guys wore tuxedoes, Rhoda was in an elaborate Chinese outfit, & Doreen had a formal gown. "Now, wait a minute," I said. "This is a private party."

Louie looked at them & sniffed. "Well, at least they're properly attired." He let them dance, but he didn't share our champagne. Of course, all they had to do was get their own bottle. None of them knew the proper way to waltz, they just "slow" danced, hanging on to each other. They didn't even try the foxtrot or cha-cha, just bounced around like they would to rock music. Louie rolled his eyes and whispered, "They act like they're at a sock hop."

Sock hop! That's a word I hadn't heard in awhile. I was glad Louie didn't try to educate them.

* * *

Rick chuckled. He hadn't heard that word in some time, either. After the children were grown, before Amy got sick, she had talked him into taking a ballroom dance class. Neither became very proficient, but they had fun. Rick was surprised that most of the men were as enthusiastic about dancing as the women. When he let himself get beyond his macho persona, he had to admit he enjoyed it as much as Amy did.

GROK

Rick didn't feel like reading more of the journal that night. Maybe he'd read one of Amy's books. Among her Heinlein books was *Stranger in a Strange Land*. Hadn't this come up in the journal? When he was in college, his friends were all abuzz over this novel. He wasn't interested in it at the time, and he didn't know Amy had read it. Rick took the book from the shelf and opened the front cover.

An inscription jumped out at him, "Dear Amy, will you grok me? Love, Henry." Who was Henry? What did he mean—"grok?" The thought that flew into Rick's mind was not pleasant. He saw no date on the inscription. The book was printed in 1961, long before he met Amy. Did she have a previous boyfriend he knew nothing about? It was unthinkable she might have….No. That was unthinkable.

Rick looked for inscriptions in other books. Some had former owners' names, or Amy's, written inside the covers. One name was Henry Fletcher. Rick fished out a phone book. His fingers trembled so badly he could barely turn the pages. A few Fletchers were listed, but the only Henry was co-listed with a Mary. It wouldn't do to intrude on what might be a happy marriage. He needed more information.

Amy had saved her high school yearbooks. No Henry Fletcher in any of them. She also had a collection of yearbooks from her teaching days. He opened one. In the faculty section, on the same page as Amy, a handsome man smiled from a photo. Henry Fletcher.

Rick resisted jumping to conclusions. Who could he talk to? The kids might know this Henry Fletcher, but he didn't want to burden them with suspicion. Bob's wife had been Amy's friend. He dialed their number.

By chance, Melody answered. "Let me get Bob," she said.

"Wait, let me ask you something first. Did you know one of Amy's co-workers named Henry Fletcher?"

"No. The name doesn't ring a bell."

Bob came to the phone with, "How's the house coming?"

"Great. Tell me, have you ever heard the word 'grok?'"

"What does it mean?"

"That's what I'm trying to find out."

"Why don't you google it?"

Of course. Rick slowed down enough to give Bob an update on the Wilson House. "I'm going over tomorrow to see how the foundation's coming. Why don't you come by?" Rick waited for Bob's excuse.

"I'm busy tomorrow. When are you going over next?"

Surprised, Rick said, "I can go any time."

"How about Thursday? Maybe around lunch?"

"Great!" After hanging up, he turned on his computer and googled "grok." It wasn't as bad as it sounded. Heinlein had coined the term, which meant "drink" but encompassed much more, closer to "understand completely." So why did Henry want Amy to "drink" him? He needed to know more about this fellow.

The following morning, Rick called the high school. "Does Mr. Fletcher still teach there?"

"Who? No, we don't have a teacher by that name."

"Well, he used to teach there. Do you know where he is now?" Rick heard some muffled conversation, then a familiar voice, the secretary who had been there for years.

"Why are you looking for Mr. Fletcher?"

"I've been going through Amy's things and found some books that might be his."

"Oh, I don't think Mr. Fletcher will be needing his books. You see, he passed away a few years ago."

"Oh. I'm sorry." Had Amy ever mentioned a fellow teacher dying? "I didn't know that. He and Amy were friends, weren't they?"

"Oh, yes. Everyone liked Mr. Fletcher. Well, almost everyone."

"I don't recall her going to his funeral."

"Well, she did. I was there, too. His family took him back to Alabama for burial."

Rick had taken this investigation as far as he could for the moment, but he didn't plan to let it rest.

Meanwhile, he went to check on progress at the Wilson House. A cement truck stood in the yard and Tracy's crew was pouring the footer. "We'll give the concrete time to set," she told Rick, "Then we'll lay the foundation."

When Rick got home, he went through more of Amy's books. In *The Time Machine*, he found, "Henry, I'm surprised you never read this. It's a classic." Below this was written, "Thank you, Amy, for turning me on to H.G. Wells. My education was sadly incomplete." Inscriptions in some books were dated, indicating they had exchanged reading material for years. Although Rick found nothing inappropriate, uneasiness continued to torment him. Apparently, Amy had lived a double life, one part which hadn't included him.

When he grew tired of sifting through Amy's books, he returned to the journal:

CV. Today, Doreen started a fire in the upstairs lounge—on purpose! Why? Nobody can figure it out & she won't say. We always leave trash lying around. The room eventually cleans itself, but it didn't have a chance to yet. She must have piled everything flammable together & set a match to it. I heard Linda scream, "Oh my God! Oh my God! We can't get out! We'll burn to death!" I rushed out of my room. Wendel was throwing a trash can full of water on the fire. I helped put it out. Then I ducked back into my room while they chewed Doreen out. Later, I thought about how the house takes care of itself. It probably would extinguish a fire on its own, but we can't take that chance.

* * *

Rick turned the page. A few shreds of paper hung in the spiral as though pages had been torn out. An entry was missing.

CVII. I can't believe it. I thought Louie & I had something good going. I'm glad I didn't have sex with him again. But Doreen must have thought we were sleeping together, b/c when I woke up this morning, she was in his bed! Even tho that's the last place I want to be, it stings.

All along, he was playing me for a fool. How could I fall for it? All his "high literature!" Translation: poetry that really makes no sense. He'd read those poems to me in a lofty voice, never in private of course b/c he had to irritate the others. Then we'd discuss the "meaning". And I was writing such "poetry" & reading it aloud for him (within the others' hearing of course) so he could impress everyone w/ his "deep" under-standing.

I'd even copied them in my journal. When I looked at them today, they were so bad I was ashamed. I hated to, but I ripped out the pages. I didn't want to lose my other stuff but I couldn't leave them here. I tore the pages to shreds. When I went to the bathroom, they put themselves back together. I tried to destroy them by burning them in the fireplace, but when I got back to my room, they were back in the notebook! I wish I'd never written them in my journal. This is my private place, for my thoughts. Those damned poems were Louie's, not mine. Finally I shredded them again & put them down the garbage disposal. This time they didn't come back.

I'm glad I didn't read that awful "Ulysses." I did what Wendel did to me when he pretended to read "Great Expectations," except I was more clever. Whenever Louie asked how I liked it I gave him some pompous adjective & that seemed to satisfy him. I bet Julio was right. Louie hasn't read that book, either.

And his music—Louie found records he hadn't played before. Some pieces were really weird & I didn't like them, but I pretended to. When the others complained, I'd look down my nose & tell them they just weren't cultured. In other words, I was becoming, like Louie, a snob. I guess in my own way I've always been a snob. Now I became an insufferable one. Despite my attempts to fit into his "high class" world, he betrayed me. With Doreen.

Her transformation caught me by surprise. She was probably getting tired of Wendel. When she saw I was successful gaining Louie's attentions, she decided she wanted him, too. She must have observed how I dressed. She changed her appearance to appeal to him. She shaved her legs & armpits. She wasn't willing to cut her hair but Rhoda helped her put it up in a French twist. She put on makeup & sleek clothing. Louie noticed.

I'm still in shock. Too upset to cry. I'm not going to let on how much they hurt me.

* * *

Rick closed the notebook. Poor Red. Just when it looked like things might work out for her, it goes downhill again. The boy Calvin that Ellen Johnson told him about—could he have been Louie? Calvin was a loser. Well, Louie sounded like a loser, too.

It was getting late. Time for bed.

The following day, the Wilson House still hovered above the ground on its jacks. Stacks of concrete blocks sat in the yard and Tracy's crew was putting finishing touches on the footer.

"We'll start laying the foundation tomorrow," she said. "And some of the men don't mind working Saturday, so depending on the weather, we may finish up. If we do, I'll call the building inspector Monday."

"Sounds great. I'll call my roofer so they can get ready."

Bob arrived and surveyed the work. "Impressive."

A few more concrete blocks had been stacked on the makeshift steps so they could reach the front door. "Let's go in," Rick said. "I'll show you around."

Bob frowned. "Maybe we shouldn't go inside until they're done."

Tracy laughed. "Our few hundred pounds isn't going to make any difference."

On the front porch, Bob stamped his feet as though trying to shake the house. "Feels solid enough."

"It should," Rick said. "Did you see the size of those jacks and I beams?"

Bob hesitated at the front door and took a deep breath before going in. "Floor feels level."

Tracy smiled. "It is."

They walked through the rooms. Tracy pointed out a few stress cracks from lifting the building.

Bob said, "They don't look too bad. Will they be easy to repair?"

"Should be," she said. "We'll mend what we need to and your carpenters can do the rest. Fortunately, the fireplace and chimney held together nicely. Good workmanship."

Rick and Bob discussed how close to its original appearance they wanted to restore the house. Upstairs, Rick pointed out the partition between what he called the lounge and the turret room. "Originally, this was all one room. Do you want to keep it like this or remove the wall?"

"Might look better if we remove it. That'd bring in more light."

Rick felt his heart sink. He didn't know why. "On the other hand, if the house is a residence, it could be an extra bedroom."

"If it's a business, storage?"

"Oh, no." Rick swept an arm around the windows. "Not with this view. Maybe a small office or waiting area."

"Just do what you think is best."

Okay, Rick thought. I will.

As they walked back toward the stairs, Bob paused to scuff his shoe across a dark area on the floor. "I wonder what this is."

Rick bent down to swipe his finger across it—soot! "I never noticed this before. It looks freshly charred." He looked at Tracy.

She squatted down to examine the burn. "I don't know. I don't let my workers smoke inside a building, and we haven't done anything that would cause this."

"The homeless?" Bob asked.

Tracy shrugged. "I haven't seen anyone here, or any indication of a break-in. I don't know what happens after we leave, but I know I lock up every day."

Something nudged Rick's mind. The journal. Doreen had set a fire in the lounge. In a manuscript written many years ago. He stared at the spot and frowned. Doreen's fire could have no connection to this.

When he got home, Rick called Roger Alvarez. "We should be ready for the new roof next week."

"Good timing. Let me come over Tuesday for a second look and we'll get started right after Christmas."

Rick was pleased. Several companies had balked at the steep pitch of the roof but Roger had waved it off. "We've done houses like this in Micanopy and Melrose. No problem."

Rick busied himself preparing for Christmas and Kristie's visit. There was more to do than time permitted. Tidying the kitchen, he came across the broken makeup bottle from the Wilson House and the phone numbers for the Museum of Natural History. What story could he tell them that might make sense?

He reached a graduate student named Troy, who seemed willing to listen. Briefly, he explained his role with the Wilson House and its historical significance. "I found an old diary in the house. One entry tells about putting a note in a little bottle and flushing it down the toilet. They wanted to see if anyone would find the bottle and respond to the note. Well, we found a makeup bottle in a drain pipe and think it may be the one. I wondered if anyone in your department could help me find an answer."

To his relief, Troy said, "Wow, that's interesting! I'm sure somebody here could look at it. Most everyone's on break right now. Can you bring it over after Christmas?"

"Sure. Who should I ask for?"

"Call ahead of time and ask for me."

That evening, he continued to read from the journal:

CVIII. I refuse to let them know I'm upset. I just put my nose in the air & go on. To get back at Doreen, I fixed chicken cordon bleu, just 2 servings, & invited Louie to dine with me. He chose a nice white wine. Doreen snuffled around, but Louie paid her no attention. I can't figure him out.

Louie let Doreen into his bed, but he didn't let her move her stuff into his room. When he wasn't around, I told Doreen she'll never live up to his standards. Before she could sass me back, Wendel came in, & I said she's scraping the bottom of the barrel. Louie's not as good a lover as Wendel. Poor Wendel looked more miserable than usual, but he deserves it. I wonder if he's still sleeping with her, or w/ Rhonda, or both?

CIX. I got hungry & warmed up some chili I'd hidden in the back of the refrigerator. Louie came into the kitchen, looked in the pot, & left w/out a word. He has no interest in "down home" cooking.

There was only a little chili left & I thought about Hugh. Was Wendel still feeding him? Linda lacks the patience. When did he last eat? I took the pan into his room. Hugh rolled over & looked at me. "Are you hungry?" I asked. His mouth half-curved into a sort-of smile & he said, "Yes, thank you." I helped him eat. He needs another bath. I don't know what's wrong w/ him. I don't know if he has some kind of medical condition or if he's just that depressed or lazy. Miserable as my life is, I wouldn't want to be him.

CX. Louie's playing some of that weird music he calls classical. I wish I had earplugs. Doreen's out there fawning on him, pretending to like it. Wasn't she making fun of that music not so long ago? She went a step beyond me & found some art books. They were discussing painting & sculpture. Neither of them know what they're talking about. I do. I studied Humanities in college & thought about majoring in it. I should have, b/c I liked it. But my advisor discouraged me, said there was no future in it, so I went into Business & found it so boring I dropped out & ended up with no future, after all. Then I ended up here.

Louie must have been exposed to some esoteric art criticism at one time. There were people like that in my class. All Doreen knows is what she reads in the books & doesn't understand. Their discussions are almost comical. I try to set them straight, but there's no changing Louie's mind & Doreen goes along with him no matter what she really thinks. Just like I did with his music & "poetry."

CXI. Louie & Doreen held a formal dance today & Rhoda edged her way in. I decided to crash their party. I wished for a red dress with a low neckline & a slit up the leg. Louie's eyes lit up when I entered the parlour. He was trying to teach them to waltz. Rhoda started to get the hang of it but Doreen's pretty clumsy. Both were a disaster when he tried to show them other ballroom dances. He got frustrated with them & danced with me. They were reduced to dancing with each other, bouncing around like they were at a sock hop again. I bet they don't try another formal dance unless they want me to show them up.

WHO WAS HENRY?

Just after noon on Saturday, Kristie's minivan pulled into the driveway. Rick was surprised to see Sandy at the wheel. He asked Kristie, "You're letting her drive?"

Sandy threw her shoulders back and said, "I'm fifteen now. I got my driving permit."

"I don't let her drive on the interstate, or at night."

"You look pretty tired. I didn't expect you 'til later. You were supposed to call from Lake City."

"Sorry. After school let out, we finished packing and left home last night. I drove straight through. Almost. I stopped at rest areas for naps. Would you mind if I lie down for a little while?"

"Please. When's Steve coming?"

"He's not."

The pride in Sandy's face crumbled to sullenness. Michael kicked a tire.

Kristie turned toward them. "Kids, help me unload the van." They carried the luggage inside. "Sandy and I will take the bunk beds. Michael can stay in my old room." Kristie took Rick's arm and pulled him toward his study. "Let's talk." Then she took a deep breath and dissolved into tears. "Daddy, I'm leaving Steve."

Rick put his arms around her.

"He's been seeing another woman. Maybe more than one, I don't know. Anyway, it's over."

Rick held her while she sobbed. He blinked away his own tears. "Marriages can be saved," he said quietly. "Even with things like this. Have you tried marriage counseling?"

"It takes two, and he won't go. There's more to it. I don't want to talk about it. Let me take a shower before I lie down. I need to wash off the road dirt."

She left Rick to handle the children. No, they weren't hungry, and no they didn't need to bathe or nap. They'd slept in the car. Rick avoided discussing their parents' situation. He had no clue how to handle children's grief over loss of a parent. He hadn't handled things very well when Amy died. He diverted their attention to boxes of Christmas decorations in a corner of the living room. "We need to get a Christmas tree. Would you like to do that now?"

Sandy nodded. Michael said, "First, I want to see your haunted house."

"Who told you it was haunted?"

"David. He said his dad won't let him go over there."

"Well, if it's okay with your mother..."

Kristie, emerging from the bathroom, said, "Yeah, it's okay. Go on. I'll probably sleep better if no one's here."

In the truck on the way to the Wilson House, Rick ventured, "How are you kids doing?"

"I hate Daddy," Sandy said. "And I hate Mama."

"Why?"

Michael spoke up. "Because she's moving us here. She already checked us out of school. I was supposed to play basketball. Now I can't."

Rick glanced at Michael, whose shoulders were nearly level to his. "They have basketball here, too."

"Yeah, but I bet they already picked their teams."

On the other side of Michael, Sandy wept. "I had to leave my friends. I don't want to be here!" She unbuckled her seat belt.

Rick hit the door lock and pulled over.

"It's okay," Sandy sobbed. "I'm not going to do anything stupid." She jerked her seat belt and re-fastened it. Rick wanted to hug her, but couldn't reach around Michael. "I'm okay," she insisted. "Let's go."

By the time they reached the Wilson House, both children were calm. Stacks of cement blocks in the yard had been replaced by I beams and equipment. A cold front had blown through Thursday night, but the weather hadn't impeded Tracy's crew. The house sat proudly on its new foundation.

Michael nearly climbed over his sister to get out of the truck. He stood in front of the house with his mouth open. "It sure does look spooky."

"No it doesn't," Sandy retorted. "It's ugly."

Rick forced a smile. "Maybe now, but wait till she's fixed up and painted. Go ahead, look around. There's nothing here that can hurt you. Just stay away from the equipment." The children followed Rick as he walked around the perimeter, appraising the foundation work. When they came to the gap that allowed access to the crawl space, Michael peeked under the house.

Sandy shouted, "Don't go in there!"

Rick motioned to him. "I'm sure it's safe, but let me check first." He stuck his head through the opening and felt a wave of nausea. He hoped he wasn't coming down with something. "We shouldn't go under here without a flashlight. Let's go inside."

Both children were fascinated by the back stairs. "I thought only rich people had back stairs," Sandy said. "Like plantation owners."

"Well, the man who built this house had a lot of money." Rick was poised to say more but they didn't seem interested in the building's history.

Sandy opened the former cellar door. "What's this?"

"This house once had a cellar. The steps were in there."

"Where are they now?"

"We removed them. It doesn't have a cellar anymore. That was before they moved it."

Michael stood on the new plywood floor and gazed at the underside of the staircase above him. "Awesome. Like Harry Potter's room under the stairs."

"You can have it," Sandy said. "Can we go now?"

The church he and Amy used to attend sold Christmas trees every year. While the children were choosing a tree, Kristie called. "Dad, will you stop by Satchel's? I ordered a couple pizzas. If you'll pay for them, I'll pay you back. I tried to put it on my card, but they only take cash. Kyle and them are coming over for supper. That's okay, isn't it?"

"Of course."

They had time to set up the tree before Kyle's family arrived. The cousins were delighted to see one another. Sandy, Rusty, and Judy decorated the tree under Allison's supervision. Michael and David went their own way, and Kristie took over the kitchen. Rick and Kyle settled in the study with pizza and beer. When they made a trip to the kitchen for a second helping, Michael approached Rick with *Stranger in a Strange Land*.

"Grandpa, are you reading this?"

"I thought about it. But if you want to, go ahead. It was your grandmother's book."

"I know." Michael opened the book to the inscription. "Who was Henry?"

Rick grimaced. "Another teacher."

Kyle said, "Henry Fletcher? Yeah, Kristie and I had him for Senior English. Mom wouldn't let us take her class."

"Apparently, he and your mother had a lot in common. Her bookcase is full of books he gave her."

"Yeah, they were buddies."

Kristie had been watching Rick's face. "You act like you're jealous of him."

"Of course not. It's just that your mother never talked about him. I was surprised to find these books." Rick paused. "Did you know he died? If she went to his funeral, she never told me."

"You just forgot," Kyle said. "I went to his memorial service with her."

Kristie began to laugh. "Hey, Kyle, I think Dad's jealous of Mr. Fletcher!"

"Jealous of Twinkletoes? Dad, do you know what he died of?"

Rick suspected he was the butt of a joke.

Kristie sobered. "Dad, Mr. Fletcher was just a good friend. If she didn't talk about him, it's because she was afraid you wouldn't understand."

"Understand what?"

"Henry Fletcher was gay. He died of AIDS. Everyone liked him. Just about everyone, that is."

Kyle nodded. "They held the service in the high school auditorium. It was packed."

"Oh." Why had he doubted Amy? Still, it stung that she hid this friendship from him. Did she consider him a homophobe? On reflection, he admitted he used to join his construction workers' banter about homosexuals. And maybe he brought those jokes home and told them to Amy. Couldn't she see through that?

On further reflection, he never told her about Jody, thinking *she* wouldn't understand.

Rick didn't personally hire Jody. One day he noticed a husky young fellow working with his head carpenter. "Who's this?" Rick asked.

Cecil beckoned the guy over. "Rick, this is Jody. He's the best trim carpenter I've come across. I didn't think you'd mind. I already gave Sylvia his information for the payroll."

Rick always trusted Cecil's judgment. "Welcome aboard." He extended his hand.

Jody's handshake was firm, but he had little to say and quickly returned to his task.

One day in the office, Sylvia whispered to Rick. "Do you know about Jody?"

"What about him?" Rick's thoughts flew to the many problems his employees had posed through the years—drugs, alcoholism, criminal backgrounds—but Sylvia's answer floored him.

"*He* is a *she*."

"What?"

Sylvia laid a photocopied paper in front of him. "Look at the driver's license."

Nothing looked unremarkable, until Rick put on his reading glasses and saw "Sex: F." His head tried to wrap around this. "Has anyone complained?"

"No. Jody gets along well with everybody. I don't think anyone else knows."

Rick was not above hiring a woman for what was traditionally men's work, but this? He drew a deep breath and shook his head. "Well, if he, or she, can do the job, I guess it doesn't matter."

Rick never brought the issue up with Jody, but at first he caught himself treating the carpenter with the deference he would a woman. He never told Jody's secret to anyone else, including Amy. Eventually, it slipped to the back of his mind, and he let Jody be himself.

Later, when the house was quiet, Rick asked Kristie, "Why didn't you tell me you were leaving Knoxville, and moving here?"

"I didn't want to tell you over the phone."

"What about your job? Where are you going to stay?"

"I've been looking for an apartment over the internet. I have a job lined up, at Hawthorne High, to take over for a teacher who's on maternity leave. I've applied for a temporary Florida teaching certificate. All I have to do in Knoxville is get my stuff. Steve can have the house."

"What?"

She waved him off. "Oh, he'll pay me for it. And child support. I didn't want to live there anymore. I wanted to come home."

"This is so unexpected. I don't know what to say."

"You don't have to say anything. Can we stay here until I find a place?"

"Of course."

Once he was alone, Rick beat the palm of his hand with his fist. He wanted to beat Steve's face for what he'd done to Kristie.

To get his mind off the problem, he picked up the journal.

CXII. Doreen can't have something w/out Rhoda wanting it, too. I don't know how those 2 ever existed as roommates. One "day" they're tight friends, then turn around & they hate each other. Too much drama for my taste. In the "real world" I'd have avoided them like the plague. Rhoda started fixing herself up to get Louie's attention & it worked. He's delighted to have classy-looking women around, so he gave Rhoda what he thought she wanted—sex. I'm not sure if that's what she really wanted or if she just wanted what Doreen has. Doreen doesn't seem to mind too much. It gives her more access to Julio. Poor Wendel has retreated to his attic.

CXIII. Louie now has 2 peacocks to parade around, one on each arm. It's comical. Even this house isn't big enough for such pageantry. Today I found the 2 of them hovering over him—can you imagine?—one giving him a manicure, the other a pedicure! Seeing Doreen and Rhoda with Louie seems to eat at Wendel, but I don't feel sorry for him. He had his chance. Our relationship wasn't perfect, but I didn't dump him for somebody else.

CXIV. I'm more miserable than ever. Twice I've come out of my shell only to be slapped in the face. Better to stay in. Less ventured, less pain. Sometimes when I feel lonely I sit w/ Hugh. He makes no demands on me. Maybe Wendel didn't either, but it felt like he did. I just can't get past seeing him with Doreen. Rhoda's involvement with him was an anticlimax. As for Louie, it eats at me the way he lavishes attention on Rhoda & Doreen like he used to on me.

I worry about Hugh. I don't think he gets up off his pallet except to go to the bathroom. And he's starting to stink again. I asked what was wrong but he said, "Nothing. Just tired." Yeah, I get tired, too. Tired of this place, these people.

CXV. Why do people find me so unlovable? It's not just b/c I'm not like them. Oh, I know that puts people off at 1ˢᵗ, but when they get to know me they either like me or don't. Even as a child, I never felt loved. Even by my mother. I was a burden, not a joy, just some baggage to drag around. There'd been a "father" once, but he abandoned me when I was a baby. Growing up, I saw him maybe 4 or 5 times. When I was 16, I tracked him down, thought I wanted a relationship w/ him. What a mistake. Grandparents? I've always envied people who love their grandparents. And are loved by them. None of my relatives wanted any more to do w/ me than my paternal parent did. Maybe b/c I was a product of my mother, but couldn't they see I wasn't her? That I was different? I was different, wasn't I?

And why do other people not like me? At school, I tried to be like the "good" kids, make good grades, draw nice pictures, but teachers always acted impatient, if not disgusted, w/ me. Sure, my clothes weren't as nice as other kids', but at least I didn't smell bad.

Even worse were people who pitied me w/out bothering to know me. Then they didn't have to decide whether to like me or not. They could put me in a category of something other than human. I had trouble learning to write. I was sloppy at coloring, couldn't stay in the lines. One principal wanted to put me in special education. At a different school, of course. Thank goodness I had a good teacher at the time who stood up for me. Then we moved, & I went to a different school, different teacher. Well, I learned good handwriting, but I never did color inside the lines. That was a form of rebellion they couldn't punish me for. I think I should have been left handed, but they wouldn't let me try.

* * *

Rick couldn't help feeling sorry for her. He wondered what made her think she was different. Did she have a facial deformity? Actually, it appeared she brought much of her misery upon herself. Still, he didn't understand the teachers' attitudes. Amy always stood up for her students, and so did Kristie.

He closed the notebook with a sigh. *I don't need any more of this tonight.* Poor Kristie. As a father, he wanted a better life for his children. And he'd always liked Steve. Was he such a poor judge of character? If only Amy were here to help steer him through this.

The next morning, Rick had coffee fixed before Kristie and the children stirred. As he finished the first section of the newspaper, Kristie came in and hugged him. "Good morning, Dad." She and the children were already dressed. She eyed his pajamas and asked, "Aren't you going to church?"

Rick shook his head. "They won't miss me. I haven't been in almost a year."

"Well, that's part of your problem. You never get out. You have no social life."

"What kind of social life is that? Serving on this committee and that committee? And I do get out."

Michael whined. "Can I stay home, too?"

Sandy followed with, "Yeah, me too. I don't know anybody there."

"No, we're all going." Kristie looked at her father. "Will you come with us?"

Rick nodded and took his coffee to his room to sip while he dressed.

At church, the older parishioners remembered Kristie and made a fuss over her children. Rick was greeted warmly by the pillars of the church, including several widows, one who was not content to merely shake his hand but clasped it between both of hers while inquiring about his health. Now he remembered why he stopped going to church.

Piano music drifted from the sanctuary. Rick and the children followed Kristie to a pew near the front. Rick would have preferred to sit in back. He glanced at the piano player, a slender young man he hadn't seen before. "What happened to Margie?" he whispered to a man behind him.

"Oh, she graduated and moved on to better things."

When the collection plate was passed, Kristie took a few dollars out of her purse, but Rick waved it by. He sent a check every month. During the service, he let his mind wander to his agenda for Monday and what to do about today's dinner. His plan to cook a roast had been derailed. He heard rain drum on the roof and wished he were home.

In the social hall after the service, Sandy and Michael were introduced to a few teenagers but opted not to join the youth group.

They ate at Applebee's. While waiting for their food, Kristie took a small tablet out of her purse and said, "We need to do some Christmas shopping. What have you done so far?"

"Nothing, really. Allison gave me her family's wish list, but it's at home."

Kristie took out her phone and called Allison. While they ate, Kristie worked on her list. Afterwards, they visited so many stores, Michael began to squirm and whine like a two year old. Sandy was happy only because her mother promised she could drive home if the rain stopped. Between shopping and Sandy's driving, Rick's blood pressure soared.

Once they got home, he called Bob, who invited him to come over and watch a football game. That was what he needed. "Shall I bring a six pack?" he asked.

"I have plenty. You could pick up some wings," Bob said.

By the time he returned home that night, everyone was in bed and the house was quiet.

CHRISTMAS

Monday, the foundation of the house passed inspection with flying colors. It was raining again. Rick examined the attic and was relieved to find no new leaks. Anxious to move forward, he noticed the date. "Oh my God! Tomorrow's Christmas Eve!" Kristie was taking care of his Christmas shopping and nearly everything else, but he hadn't bought her a gift yet.

Years of shopping for Amy had taught him how to choose a good gift for a teacher, but the stores were more crowded than ever and a few items he looked for were out of stock. He finally found a sweater and scarf ensemble in blue, Kristie's favorite color. He chose Amy's size, hoping his memory was correct, that they were about the same.

When he returned home that afternoon, the house was empty except for a note from Kristie saying she and the kids had gone Christmas shopping. After he wrapped Kristie's gift, he sat down with the journal:

CXVI. I'm like a ghost in this house. I don't leave my room if I hear anyone out & about. Today, I hankered for meatloaf & went to the kitchen when I thought everyone was asleep. While I was putting it together, it sounded like a herd of elephants coming downstairs. I got ready to flee if they came into the kitchen, but they went into Linda's room, her & the 3 guys. Hugh's bath time. Since they didn't bother me, I finished my meat loaf & put it in the oven.

The crowd in the bathroom wrestled Hugh into the tub & left. He gets so dirty doing nothing, he has to soak clean. While the meatloaf baked, I worked on mashed potatoes. I heard Linda crying in her room

& a male voice soothing her. I paid no attention until I sat down to eat. Then I heard a bump, then another, then a rhythmic bumping—from Linda's room! About the time I finished my meal, Linda's door opened. I peeked into the hall. Julio came out, went upstairs, & called for Louie & Wendel to help get Hugh out of the tub.

I couldn't believe it! Hugh right there in the next room taking his bath while Julio screws his girlfriend!

CXVII. Louie's not capable of keeping 2 girls sexually satisfied, so Julio has 3 on his string, including Linda, but at least he doesn't parade them. If the truth were known, I suspect the only person Louie cares to satisfy is himself.

I'm surprised at Linda. Hugh's no longer able to do anything for her, & I don't just mean sex. Still, she has something I never had, a long-term relationship w/ someone devoted to her. It's obvious he was, at least at first, before he sank into nothingness. Linda's mean to Hugh, but I think she just wants better things for him & doesn't know how to motivate him. Hugh always takes her abuse as if he deserves it. He never seems to resent the way she treats him. No man had ever been that good to me.

CXVIII. Wendel & I have become friends again. Not *that* friendly. I still can't look at him without thinking about Doreen. He's made no overt sexual advances but I can tell he's lonely. When I was in the library, he handed me Asimov's "Foundation" & said "I think you'll like it." I told him I'd think about it. That's the book about a planet that's all city, no open space. I wasn't interested in it before.

I hate Doreen. She took Wendel away from me, & then she had to take Louie. More than that, she took away the little (though imperfect) pieces of life I'd found here. What does she have that I don't, other than lack of shame? She's not as pretty as me. Is she good in bed? I could ask Wendel, but what if I don't like the answer?

Linda goes into Julio's room when Doreen & Rhoda are occupied with Louie. I suppose she needs something from a man even if it's only phys-ical love. Julio also gives her comfort & companionship. I envy her.

CXIX. Trying to drink less, I joined one of their pot parties, but I didn't expect to drop acid. Julio tried to get me to try LSD before, saying how wonderful it is. I always resisted, but w/ no cops & no consequences, I thought, what the heck. I'd always heard it was supposed to expand your consciousness, give you a "religious" experience. Well, the religion I grew up with was "do unto others before they do it unto you." I didn't want any help with religion. Still, I was disappointed. Oh, it gave me quite a high, a little different from pot or Scotch, but nothing really spectacular. Consciousness raising? Maybe my brain cells are already so burned out they can't raise anything. Religion, consciousness-expanding —malarkey!

* * *

Religion. Amy rose unbidden in Rick's thoughts. He seldom thought about religious matters, but at times he wondered where Amy was now. Could she see him? Know what he was going through? As her last few days had stretched out to eternity, Amy told him she looked forward to being out of pain. Yet she held on, saying she didn't want to leave him. But leave him she did. Afterward, everyone consoled him that she was in a better place. He found no solace in going to church. But he was glad Kristie did.

Amy had been a devout church-goer, yet they seldom discussed spiritual matters. Beyond the teachings of the church, what were her beliefs? It was too late to ask now. They had been so close, he thought, but here was another aspect of their lives they hadn't shared.

He set the notebook aside. It was nice to have the house to himself for a few hours, especially when he found himself thinking about Amy. Much of the time, he tried to keep her out of his mind. Not to forget her, only to not dwell on her absence. Especially now. He leaned back in his chair. This time last year, she was unable to leave her bed and he seldom left the house, unless a hospice worker or family member gave him a few hours' break. He'd gladly trade his freedom to have her back. He knew he was being selfish—she was no longer in pain. But he was.

The phone rang.

"Dad, have you taken out anything for supper?"

"No." He'd lived alone for so long he'd forgotten how to plan for a family.

"Don't worry, I have it covered. We'll be home in an hour or so."

"Okay." He chided himself again on his selfishness. The whole family was suffering. And Kristie's children—on top of everything else, they'd lost their home and their father.

He must have dozed off. Car doors and children's voices intruded. For a moment he forgot where he was. As he struggled to wake up, the kitchen door slammed. "Grandpa, we're home!" He staggered to his feet and stuffed the notebook in a drawer.

"Dad, are you okay?"

Rick shook his head to clear it. "Yeah. I guess I fell asleep."

"I'll have supper ready in a jiffy."

Tuesday morning, Rick half-woke and watched the sky outside his window slowly grow lighter. His bedside phone jarred him fully awake. As he grabbed for the handset, he glanced at his clock. Not quite eight. He nearly dropped the phone before he got the receiver to his ear. He gulped, "Hello?"

Someone laughed, then Roger Alvarez said, "Hey, Rick, what—did I wake you?"

"No, I'm awake. My daughter and her kids are here on Christmas break. I didn't want to wake them. They're used to Central Time."

"I'm about to head over to the house if you want to meet me."

"Sure. I'll be there in half an hour." Rick drove through MacDonald's for coffee and an egg sandwich.

Roger was waiting. "I just want to be sure there's nothing unexpected before we begin the roof."

Rick showed him things Tracy had pointed out and took him into the attic. "I checked for leaks yesterday—nothing I'm worried about. The worst place is the valley by the turret."

"Good. I'll give you a call Thursday."

Rick's cell phone rang.

"Dad? Where are you?"

"Hey, Kristie. I'm over at the Wilson House."

"I woke up and couldn't find you. Why didn't you tell me you were leaving?"

"I didn't want to wake you. How are you and the kids this morning?"

"We're fine. They're still asleep. I have some last minute Christmas shopping to do. I plan leave the kids here."

"They're big enough. I'll be home soon."

The rest of the day was spent in last minute details. With the children's help, Kristie wrapped gifts and piled them under the tree. Between phone calls with Allison, she directed the children in the kitchen. Rick tried to stay out of her way and retreated to his study.

Before long, he heard a tentative knock on his door. Kristie said, "Dad?"

"Come in."

Kristie threw herself onto the couch. "The kids are getting ready for church. You're going with us, aren't you?"

He nodded. "Have you finished wrapping presents?"

"Yes. Usually Christmas Eve finds me rushing to get things done but I had to be better organized this year."

Rick stifled a smile. Kristie, the epitome of organization.

The Christmas Eve service was filled with Amy's absence, but the presence of Kristie and her children was a comfort. After they returned home, Kristie said, "You kids get your baths. When you're ready for bed, you can hang your stockings on the chair by the wood stove."

Rick waited until the children left the room. "Aren't they a little old for stockings?"

"They need some babying right now. Besides, you were filling our stockings until we left home."

Rick laughed. "You're right. I remember, when Kyle moved back in, he expected a visit from Santa. Your mother told him he was grown now, and he was quite put out over that."

Kristie laughed with him.

It was still dark when Rick heard the children. Whispering, they crept into the living room for their stockings. He listened to their quiet expressions of delight before they retreated to Michael's room.

It had been the same when Kristie and Kyle were children. And he and his siblings had done the same a generation before. Last year, very early on Christmas morning when he gave Amy her medication, they reminisced, imagining the scenario in their children's homes, miles away.

Amy was so strong. She'd always criticized people who died at Christmas. "Their families will always grieve on a day they should be joyful." Despite her suffering, Amy hung on until a few days after, rallying to enjoy a visit from Kyle's family on Christmas day. After that, days and nights ran together. He took a deep breath to smother a sob, thankful that he had hours before breakfast, enough time to compose himself.

Christmas Day was more pleasant than Rick anticipated. Surrounded by children and grandchildren, he was able to bask in Amy's memory, if not her presence. Only one thing marred the day. Steve called to talk with his children, then he wanted to talk to Kristie. She hung up on him. When he called back, she turned off her cell phone. Later he called on Rick's home phone. After he wouldn't take no for an answer, Rick turned off the ringer.

Kyle arrived with his family. "What's wrong with your phones? I've been trying to call you."

Kristie broke down in tears. "Steve won't leave me alone."

"I'll handle this," Kyle went into Rick's office and closed the door. Rick couldn't hear the conversation, but Kyle emerged with a satisfied expression and gave his sister a thumbs up.

That evening, after Kyle's family left, they settled down to watch *It's a Wonderful Life*. During one tender domestic scene, Kristie rushed from the room and could be heard sobbing in her bedroom. Michael acted oblivious, but Sandy rose from her seat, hesitated, headed toward Kristie's room, then took refuge in the bathroom to cry. Rick went to Kristie's door and knocked.

A broken, "What?" came through the door.

Rick answered softly, "Kristie, it's me."

"Oh."

Without a word, he sat on the bed beside her and patted her back.

Kristie curled up into a ball under the shelter of his arms like she had when she was a little girl. "Daddy, how did life get to be so much of a mess?"

NEW ROOF

The day after Christmas was always an anti-climax. Rick sat at his desk doing paperwork when Roger Alvarez called.

"Rick, I'm bringing my crew over today."

"Already?"

"Just for prep work."

"I'll meet you there."

Kristie sat at the kitchen table with her laptop. He asked, "What are you doing?"

"Checking for places to rent. You?"

"I'm going over to the Wilson House."

"Do you want to eat something first?"

"I had leftovers earlier."

At the Wilson House, Roger's crew was unloading ladders and tools. One of the workers looked like a child. It was a woman! As she scurried up a ladder, Rick asked, "Who's that?"

"Oh, that's Erin. Don't worry, she took dance lessons all her life. She's safer on that roof than those rednecks are."

Rick watched the workers peel off the old roofing, sending the sheets cascading to the ground. He carried his wallpaper catalog into the house. At home, he'd tried to match designs to the samples he'd taken and decided he could do better on site. While so occupied, he heard a shout outside, followed by Kristie's voice. "You kids STAY BACK!"

He rushed to the front porch.

A voice from above shouted, "It's okay now. You can go to the front door."

Kristie bustled across the yard carrying a small cooler, her children in tow.

"What are you doing here?" Rick asked.

"I brought your lunch." Once under the shelter of the porch roof, Kristie said, "The kids wanted to come over and see what you're doing. Is it okay? Can they stay with you while I go look at a place?"

Rick hesitated. He'd taken his children to work with him many times, but those were new houses, mostly single story, with predictable hazards. "I guess, but they have to stay close to me. I probably won't be here long."

"Thanks, Dad." She kissed him and started to leave, but hesitated. "Oh, tell me if the coast is clear."

Rick waved to Roger, who stood on the ground by the corner of the house. When Roger nodded, Rick said, "Go ahead." Then he turned to his grandchildren. "Well, what would you kids like to do?"

Sandy shrugged her shoulders. "Michael wanted to come. Mama said he couldn't unless I did, too. I wanted to go with her, but she made me come here."

Michael piped up, "I just wanna check out this spooky house some more."

"Go ahead," Rick said. "Just don't go outside without me. Sandy, maybe you can help me with something."

"What?"

In the dining room, Rick opened the wallpaper catalog. "I've been trying to find a match for this, but they don't make this design anymore. What do you think?"

Sandy paged through the catalog, glancing occasionally at the walls. Finally, "This isn't exact, in fact it's not really close, but it's a good design for a dining room."

Rick examined the sample, then looked at the room. "You're right. Thank you." He earmarked the page and scribbled a note on his clipboard before they moved to the next room. At the foot of the stairs, they encountered Michael coming down. "Boy, it sure is noisy up in that attic! When's lunch?"

"You have to wash first," Sandy said.

Michael disappeared and came back holding his hands up. "There's no water."

When it was safe to cross the yard, Rick took the children to the washing station.

Michael watched the workers on the roof. "Grandpa, aren't those guys afraid they'll fall?"

"They don't act scared," Sandy said.

"Oh, I'm sure they have a healthy fear of falling," Rick said. "Just enough to make them cautious."

"It looks like mountain climbing." Michael said. "Do ya think they'd let me go up there?"

"*I* won't let you go up there. Do you see how steep that roof is?"

"I'll be careful."

"Mama'd have a fit!" Sandy said. Her eyes widened. "One of them is a woman! I wouldn't want her job. I don't know how they can work up there."

Rick smiled. "They're professionals. They do this all the time. If they couldn't handle it, they'd get a different job."

The children followed Rick to his truck for a roll of paper towels. Sandy pointed at Harvey Balrush's house. "Now, that place looks spooky to me."

Michael peeked around the fence. "Yeah. Look—there's something moving around in there! Is it a ghost?"

Rick chuckled. "No, somebody lives there."

Sandy wrinkled her face. "You're kidding, right?"

"No, it's an old fellow. He used to own this house."

"What's he like?" Michael asked.

"I don't know. I never met him."

After they ate, Rick and Roger discussed the condition of the roof. Roger said, "The slate shingles over the turret are sound and don't need replacing. Of course, the slate won't match the metal, so it's your call."

Rick looked at the roof. His imagination compared shiny new tin with the vintage slate. No, they wouldn't match, but the slate was part of the history of the house. "If they're good, let's leave them be."

Sandy shouted, "Michael, come back here!" Rick's head whipped around to the ladders. The roofers had taken them down. Sandy stood at the end of the fence looking toward the Balrush house. Rick rushed to her. Michael was climbing the porch steps. Before Rick could stop him, Michael knocked on the door and peered through a window. Then he spun around and ran back.

"Boy, that guy sure is weird," Michael said. "And that house smells bad."

"Michael, don't bother that old man. He doesn't hurt anyone. Go sit in the truck. I'm almost ready to go."

Over supper, Rick asked Kristie about the place she'd checked out.

"I didn't like the neighborhood. I'll keep looking."

Later, she settled at the kitchen table with her laptop, and the children watched TV. Rick joined them, but what they wanted to watch didn't interest him. Rather than ask them to switch channels, he went into his study to read:

CXX. I was in the library today, minding my own business. Linda stomped in & said, "Were you in my bathroom?" I said no & tried to get by her, but she blocked my way.

Julio came in & asked what the problem was. She said somebody scared Hugh. "I went in our room & he asked who was in the bathroom. There wasn't nobody there." Julio cocked his head & said, "Why should it scare Hugh for someone to be in your bathroom?" Linda threw up her hands. "'Cause he didn't know who it was. He was ½ asleep & thought somebody came in. He heard them say, 'Darn,' but nobody came out. We were all upstairs. Except her." She jabbed her finger at me. Julio said, "Oh, Hugh probably fell back to sleep. What's the big deal?"

I left Julio trying to reason with Linda & returned to my room. I don't know why something like that should scare Hugh. Come to think of it, "Darn" is a rather mild expletive for this bunch.

* * *

Rick had left his door ajar. Michael came in.

"Goodnight, Grandpa."

Hastily, he closed the notebook.

Kristie was on her son's heels. "Don't bother your grandfather when he's busy."

"I'm sorry."

Rick smiled. "He came in to tell me goodnight." Michael hugged him and left.

Kristie looked at Rick. "Whatcha reading?"

"Just something about the Wilson House. I'm doing research so I can get it listed on the National Register of Historic Places."

"Really? Would you like my help?"

"I'd love your help." Rick opened his file cabinet. "I've been to the Matheson archives. They have a lot of material." He put the notebook in the drawer and pulled out his historical file. "When you have time, look at this and give me some direction."

"Sure. I'll do that before school starts."

Friday morning, Sandy accompanied Rick to the Wilson House.

Roger said, "It's surprising, but the roof's in pretty good shape, even after all those years of neglect. We didn't have to replace very many boards. We're getting started on the underlayment now. I want to have it dried in before it rains this weekend."

"That's great."

Rick wanted to measure windows one more time before ordering new ones. "Measure twice, cut once." He'd discovered a discrepancy in the window sizes, so "Measure three times" seemed prudent.

He explained to Sandy what he was doing and why. She held the end of the measuring tape for him. Sure enough, window openings that appeared identical were not. The windows must have been custom made when the house was built. He charted their dimensions. New windows would come in standard sizes. He'd have to modify the openings and cover the faults with trim.

Sandy looked out at the Balrush house and said, "Grandpa, did Michael tell you what he saw over there yesterday?"

"No."

"He said he thought he saw a skeleton. Then it moved, and he realized it was a man. I don't think he'll bother that old guy again." She giggled. "He also told me he peed in the downstairs toilet. He didn't think about the water not being hooked up."

He and Sandy went home for lunch. "I want to go look at a place," Kristie said. "I'll take the kids with me."

Rick paged through catalogs for windows, narrowing down his choice. Then he savored his solitude. With the house to himself, he could read more of the journal.

CXXI. Earlier today I couldn't think of anything I wanted to do. I wandered down to the parlour for a bottle of Scotch, but didn't even feel like drinking. I sat down at the piano, opened the lid, & started to toy with the keyboard. A few chords started to come back, then some of the notes of "Fur Elise." How long has it been since I touched a piano? How many centuries have I been here? I hit many wrong notes, then it began to flow. I played the piece over & over, got lost in the music, carried away to a place where I felt free, complete, unburdened.

Then Louie broke the spell. "Cut that out! I can't hear the record." I played to the end of the melody, closed the piano, & went in search of a book. I feel better now.

CXXII. After Linda had been with Julio today, she & I were alone in the lounge. I don't know where the other girls were, maybe in Julio's room, having an orgy. I asked Linda. "How can you stand to have sex with him? He screws everyone & everything." She said, "I know. But Julio is very loving. He's just oversexed. And I'm human & I have needs. And Hugh can't do anything anymore." I asked if Hugh knows about Julio. She started crying. "Yes, but he doesn't care. At least Julio acts like he cares." She cried harder. Although it was distasteful to me, I put my arm around her. She buried her face in my shoulder & cried for a long time. "I really love Hugh," she said. "When I'm making love to Julio, I pretend he's Hugh." I started to feel a little sorry for her. I also envy her. She has someone to love even if he can't return her love. I've never really loved anyone.

CXXIII. When did I start being everyone's mother confessor? Julio & Rhoda had an argument. Afterward, Julio went into Doreen's room. Rhoda huffed & started talking to me. She said she gets tired of sex all the time. I said if she's tired of Julio, why doesn't she dump him? She gave me this convoluted excuse—basically b/c Doreen wants him. Rhoda didn't ask me not to tell anyone, & I don't have the sympathy for her I have for Linda, so the next time I caught Julio alone I told him what she said. I thought he'd get mad. Instead, he raised one eyebrow & said, "Is this an invitation?" I turned my back on him, went to my room, & slammed the door. Julio didn't dumped Rhoda. Instead he keeps her stoned so she doesn't mind screwing him. Or she passes out so he can have Doreen. I don't know where Linda fits into the mix. She doesn't make demands on Julio the way the others do. They don't seem to mind Linda's trysts with him. Maybe they need a break.

CXXIV. I haven't been drinking as much & I feel better. So much better, I played the piano again. I opened the bench & found some basic instruction books. I played around with those simple exercises until I got tired. Nobody bothered me.

About the time I finished, Wendel came down & asked how I like the Asimov book. I'm ½ way thru, so we started talking about it. Just like old times. He said there's a series of them. He's reading the next one now & he'll save it for me. Then he went into the kitchen & fried some bacon. I couldn't resist. I offered to cook eggs. It felt good to share a simple meal with someone who's not putting on airs.

* * *

This softer entry relaxed Rick. He dozed off. He woke when he heard Kristie yelling at the children. "Just go to your rooms and stay there until I tell you to come out!"

Rick put the notebook away and headed to the kitchen. Michael passed Rick, bumping into him. "Say excuse me!" Kristie shouted.

Michael grumbled something. Sandy stomped by without a word.

"How was house hunting?" Rick ventured.

"A waste of time. I don't like the neighborhoods where I was looking. Besides, everybody seems to think it's still Christmas and don't want to do business."

"What's wrong with the kids?"

"They've been fighting all morning. I'm sorry I took them." She sobbed. "I was hoping to find a place during Christmas break and get my furniture and stuff before school starts."

"Let me call Bob. Maybe he can help." Bob answered on the first ring. "Kristie's looking for a place to rent. East of town. Do you know of anything?"

"I'll check with my property manager and get back with you."

"Thanks." He turned to Kristie. "Bob'll see what they have and call me back. By the way, I'm going back over to the Wilson House to check on something."

"Will you take Michael with you? Get him out of my hair?"

"Sure."

A few minutes later, Michael came in. "I'm sorry I bumped into you, Grandpa."

Rick smiled. "Did your mother tell you to apologize?"

"Yeah, but I really am sorry."

"You're forgiven."

"Sandy wants to go, too."

"Sorry," Kristie said. "Your grandpa doesn't need to referee when he's working. Besides, I need her to help me clean and cook."

"You're going to spoil me," Rick said.

He took his window catalog with him. The roof underlayment was nearly done. He stood in the yard comparing his window choices with the appearance of the house.

Roger said, "Rick, if you want those porches roofed, you need to have them repaired pretty quick."

"Yeah, I'll get my framing crew out here."

Michael stayed at Rick's side and behaved, but several times Rick caught him staring at the Balrush house. "You're quite fascinated with that place, aren't you?"

Michael nodded. "Grandpa, it smells like something died in there. Maybe that's the haunted house Uncle Kyle went into, not this one."

Rick laughed. "No, Mr. Balrush lived there at the time. But I guess if there's such a thing as a living ghost, he'd be the one."

After Rick got home, Kristie said, "Bob called. He has a house that'll be available in February, but I don't want to wait that long. He also has a two-bedroom duplex that some college students just moved out of. It needs to be cleaned. I told him I can do that."

"You need more than two bedrooms."

"I can make do. I'm going over to Bob's for the key."

That evening, Kristie approached her father with the Wilson House file. "Do you want to talk about your historical research?"

"Sure." He took the file from her and opened it. "I printed this application for historical status and the guide for completing it. Some of the information I know already or can easily get, but all in all, I feel somewhat overwhelmed. I don't like paperwork."

Kristie smiled. "I know. I've glanced through the file. What is all this stuff?"

"Some notes and things I copied at the Matheson."

Kristie looked over the application. "Well, the house is old enough. I think it should qualify. What's the story behind it?"

Rick gave her a brief history.

"Wow. That's interesting. It should be fun putting all this together. What about that spiral notebook I saw you with the other day?"

"Oh, that's something I found in the house, so I was looking it over. I don't think it's relevant, just something one of the vagrants left."

The next day brought a balmy south wind. In the morning, Kristie went to check out Bob's duplex, and both children accompanied Rick to the Wilson House.

When they stepped inside, Sandy said, "It's warmer outdoors than it is in here."

"Let's open some windows," Rick said. "This is a good time to air the place out."

"But they're covered with plastic."

"Not the ones upstairs." Some were too hard for the children to open so Rick went behind them. Wrestling with a particularly stubborn sash, he disturbed a piece of molding, which fell off.

Michael peered into the hole. "There's something in there."

"It's a window weight. That's what they used in the old days to hold the window open or shut." He closed, then opened the window again. "Do you hear the rope on the pulley? The weight counter-balances the weight of the window. Must have been good quality to still work after all these years."

Sandy said, "I just love these old houses. I want one someday."

In the turret room with all the windows open, Rick basked in the breeze. *Someday this will be a pleasant room again.* After he finished what he'd intended to do that day, they closed the windows and went home for lunch.

Kristie returned from the duplex apartment. "It's a mess. There's a bad leak in the kitchen, water all over the place. The carpets and some of the drywall need replacing. I turned off the water and told Bob. It'll be a month before that place is ready."

"You're welcome to stay here as long as you need to."

"Thanks, Dad." She hugged him. "I need to get my things from Knoxville before school starts. I guess I'll have to rent a storage unit until I find a place." She turned toward the kitchen. "Let me fix some sandwiches for lunch."

Rick went into his office. He felt a headache coming on.

THE CEMETERY

"Dad, lunch is ready. Ham sandwiches." Leftovers from Christmas.

When Kristie offered Rick pecan pie for dessert, he declined. "I think I have a headache."

"You aren't getting sick, are you?"

"No, of course not. I never get sick."

"You never get headaches, either." She made him take vitamin C with his aspirin. "On my way home, I picked up some flowers."

"Flowers?"

"For Mom's grave. You're going today, aren't you?"

Rick shrugged his shoulders. "Why?"

Blinking away tears, Kristie put her fists on her hips. "It's been a year. Today. Surely you haven't forgotten."

"Of course not." That's why he had a headache.

"I think it's only fitting we take flowers."

Amy loved flowers, but she always said, "Bring them to me when I'm alive. Don't wait till I'm dead." Rick said, "All right."

At the cemetery, Kristie righted the bronze vase attached to the grave and asked, "When's the last time you were here?"

Rick turned away. "I never come here." Amy's body had failed her, but her spirit never failed. Wherever her spirit might be now, it had nothing to do with this body. While Kristie arranged the flowers, Rick gazed around the grounds. Perhaps someday he'd explain to her that he felt no connection to Amy here.

On the way home, the children squabbled in the back seat. Kristie frowned into the rear-view mirror. "Stop that at once!" They turned away from each other and stared out the windows.

After they got home, Rick mumbled to Kristie that he had something to do and left. He drove to the Wilson House and sat in his truck. The roofers had gone home. He was grateful for the solitude.

A raindrop hit the windshield. He glanced at the house. Roger had the roof dried in, but there was an open window in the turret room. Hadn't he checked them all before they left that morning? He dashed to the front porch and noticed the lock was open. Did Roger fail to lock up? He closed the window and walked through the house. Everything was secure. When he closed the padlock, he second-guessed himself and pulled on the lock. It held. He ran across the yard, dodging raindrops, and drove home.

Kristie left supper and a note that she'd taken the children to Kyle's to spend the night. After he ate, Rick pulled the notebook he'd been reading out of the drawer.

CXXV. Am I imaging things? I was taking a nap & thought I felt air blowing, pleasantly cool. Was I dreaming? There's no reason for air to blow b/c we don't have a/c here. Don't need it. It didn't smell like a/c anyway. It smelled fresh, sweet. I'd forgotten how much I miss fresh air.

CXXVI. Poor Hugh. He keeps sinking lower & lower. Today, he wet & soiled himself & just lay there on the floor in all that mess. I don't know why most messes clean up on their own but this one didn't. Probably b/c Hugh's in the middle of it. Linda didn't want to leave him like that. When she couldn't get him to move, she got the other guys to help. I overheard Wendel ask, "Is he dead?" Linda shrieked at him, "No, he's not dead. Are you going to help me or not?" The 4 of them weren't enough. They asked me to help, too. I didn't want to get near that stinking mess but I couldn't get out of it. He was like a bag of jelly & it was all we could do to get him into the tub.

We left Linda to clean up. Shortly afterwards, I heard her screaming. Not her usual angry yelling—this had panic in it. She had Hugh by the hair & was struggling with him. At first I thought she was trying to drown him, but no, she was trying to pull him up. Hugh was coughing & choking & she was all wet. She said she left him in the tub to soak while she made him a fresh pallet. When she returned to the bathroom he'd slid down in the tub & his face was underwater. His eyes were open & he was staring up at her. She didn't know how long he'd been like that.

Linda cleaned him up & the guys hauled him out of the tub & called for recruits. He was so limp it took all 7 of us to get him into PJs. Finally, after he was comfortable, Linda went upstairs with Julio. By now, Hugh was sitting up, but he wouldn't talk or eat or anything. Was he brain damaged from almost drowning?

CXXVII. Rhoda noticed me & Wendel discussing books & began to move in on him. She continues to share Julio's room & Louie's peacock parade, & previously she showed little interest in Wendel other than to take him away from Doreen, but now she's begun elbowing her way into our conversations. I don't go into Wendel's attic & I won't invite him into my room b/c I don't want to become romantically involved with him again, so she has plenty of opportunity. She's worse than Doreen. At least Doreen takes pleasure in things. Rhoda just takes them.

CXXVIII. I was nearly finished with "Foundation" & looking forward to the sequel, when I saw Rhoda descending the attic stairs with a smug look on her face & a book in her hand—the book Wendel had promised to give me when he finished! It's not about the book. We have a whole room full of books. Nothing stops me from getting that book after Rhoda's done w/ it. Hell, what stops me from asking for a 2nd copy? It's not about the book. It's about reading the same book as someone else & talking about it. There's so little else to talk about here. It's about human contact, having something in common with someone. I've been yearning for that all my life.

***

Rick sighed. He and Amy had much in common, but they never discussed books because they didn't read the same things. Wouldn't it have been nice to read her books and talk about them? He wished he could talk with her about the journal. What would she make of it?

Shortly after breakfast Sunday morning, Sandy called her mother and said she wanted to come home.

"Anything wrong?" Rick asked.

"No. Kyle's kids are younger than her. The boys are closer in age to Michael, they have more in common. I'll pick her up on the way to church. Are you coming with me?"

"I went to church twice last week. I need to go over to the Wilson House. I found it unlocked yesterday and need to check on it."

All was well at the Wilson House. Rick went home to fix dinner. *It doesn't hurt me to cook for Kristie once in a while.* Once he had dinner in the oven, he had time to read before she got home.

CXXIX. Today when Julio was between women & I was feeling snarky, I asked why he didn't have VD. His answer: "I don't think there are any germs here. Haven't you noticed nobody catches colds or anything?" I asked what was wrong with Hugh. He didn't know, but later I found him in the library reading a medical book. He said he was trying to find something that would help Hugh. I hope he can.

CXXX. I finished the book I was reading & went to the library for another. Julio asked what I was looking for. When I said a romance, he lifted his eyebrows & said, "Oh?" I ignored him. He pulled down a book & handed it to me—"Everything You Ever Wanted to Know about Sex but Were Afraid to Ask." I asked if that's where he learned everything he knows. He ignored me, grabbed his medical book, & went upstairs.

I flipped thru a few books & took one into the parlour. My eyes fell on the piano & I decided to play awhile. What I learned as a kid is coming back to me. I can now play "Love Me Tender" almost flawlessly.

* * *

Rick paused. Amy used to play that song when she didn't know he was listening. Even with an incomplete right hand, she also played it flawlessly.

CXXXI. While I was listening to Billy Joel today, my housemates trickled in. After my record, Linda put on Elvis, then Julio chose Clearwater Revival & passed a joint around. I noticed Linda smoking, too. She used to turn her nose up at it worse than I did. Julio offered everyone some acid, but I wasn't interested. Doreen put on a Beatles record she hadn't played in awhile, "Sgt. Pepper's," & Louie brought out his cocaine. I thought I'd see how it compared to LSD. The problem was, it made me more alert & that's the last thing I want. Well, I guess I've tried everything now. Even with no consequences, that stuff doesn't appeal to me.

* * *

Rick shook his head. Drugs and sex. He'd wondered how long before Red would succumb to her companions' vices. All in all, that was a naive era. To his knowledge, only pot, LSD, and powder cocaine were available then. Today, he couldn't keep up with the designer drugs that hit the news every week. And sex—these people knew nothing about AIDS.

CXXXII. Someone tried to burn my piano book! I bet it was Rhoda or Doreen. I found a corner of it in the fire. It's funny how the fireplace doesn't use up the logs but it will burn paper. I was livid. But before I could find either of them to exact my revenge, I found the book back in the piano bench, fully restored. At least they can't take my music from me.

* * *

The timer in the kitchen went off. Dinner was ready. Kristie would be home soon. He put the notebook away.

That afternoon Kyle brought Michael home, and David and Rusty accompanied him.

"Grandpa," Michael asked. "Are you going to the Wilson House today?"

"Already went. Why?"

Michael's face fell. "Rusty and David want to go over there. I thought we could take them."

"Their father doesn't want them there."

"How come?"

"Why don't you ask them?"

David said, "He says it's haunted."

"So?"

David shrugged his shoulders.

Rick said, "He's afraid they'll get hurt."

Michael accosted Kyle. "Why can't they go see the haunted house? Nothing will hurt them."

"I just prefer they not go."

Kristie asked, "Kyle, what's the problem? Don't tell me you actually believe in ghosts."

Kyle grimaced. "I don't, really. But I had an experience in that house years ago and I don't want my family there."

"Oh, really? Tell me about it."

Kyle shook his head. "There was an unnatural coldness about the place, almost a sense of doom. I felt like something hostile was squeezing the life out of me." He shivered. "I wasn't alone. A couple a friends were with me, and they had a similar experience. And it was broad daylight."

Kristie laughed. "I was in there the other day and didn't notice anything."

Kyle set his jaw. "That's my final answer."

That evening, Kristie approached Rick with the historical file. "I've looked at applications on line and they all seem to have a detailed history of the houses. I've looked at your notes, but I need more. What all have you done?"

Rick recounted his interviews with the neighbors and Ellen Johnson.

Kristie took notes. "What about that old guy next door? Have you talked to him?"

"I've tried, but he's very reclusive."

"Bob must have talked to him."

"No, he wouldn't talk to Bob, either."

"How did Bob buy the house?"

"Through the man's lawyer. Jeffrey A. Smart."

"Well, I'll talk to *him*. Maybe he can get me an interview."

Rick agreed. If anyone could crack Harvey Balrush's isolation, it would be Kristie.

Rick woke Monday morning to Kristie's arguing with the children again. "I don't care. You're going with me." They quieted when Rick entered the room. "Good morning, Dad."

"Mornin'. Have you made coffee?"

"Yeah." She filled a mug for him and returned to the stove. "How about some eggs?"

"No, thanks. Just coffee. Where are you going?"

"Over to the school. Someone's there today and I need to see about my classroom." She cooked herself an egg and sat down with him. "This afternoon, I'll see about renting a U-Haul. Hopefully I can head to Knoxville tomorrow for my stuff. What are your plans?"

"Well, this afternoon, I'm supposed to meet my carpenter at the house." He thought a minute. "I was planning to go to Bob's New Year's Eve party tomorrow night, but that's not important. I can go to Tennessee with you."

"Thanks, Dad. That would be a big help." Kristie lifted her fork, then set it down. "You know, New Year's Eve isn't a good time to be on the road. I can wait another day. You should go to Bob's party. You need to get out socially. Have you thought about dating? You're still young enough."

Rick gave her a crooked smile. "Kristie, I'm quite capable of running my own life."

"Of course." She took a bite of egg. "Don't fix anything for supper. I have leftovers ready to warm up."

After Kristie and the children left, Rick called Troy at the museum. Yes, this was a good time to bring his "message in the bottle" over.

Rick was glad the university was between semesters. Plenty of parking spaces were available. As he entered the building, he thought about how he and Amy used to bring Kyle's children to the museum. He must bring Sandy and Michael.

Troy seemed delighted to be given a mystery to solve. He carefully removed the newspaper wrapping and gently probed the bottle's contents. "So, somebody flushed a bottle with a note down the toilet, hoping someone would find it and respond. I never would have thought to do that. Unfortunately, it didn't get very far."

"So, you don't think I'm crazy?"

"Well, it's not exactly the Dead Sea scrolls, but it's interesting. I can't say whether this is paper or not, but I can find out."

"Even if it is, I'm sure there's no way to read it."

"You might be surprised. We don't have that capability here, but there are imaging techniques that have worked miracles with unreadable old manuscripts, even some that have been erased and written over. But I don't think yours is valuable enough to ask them to look at."

"I have to agree."

Troy turned to his computer, brought up a form, and began typing. He asked for Rick's contact information. "Do you know when the bottle was flushed?"

"No. The diary didn't have any dates. The person just wrote things down."

"That's unusual. When was the house moved?"

"In 1969."

"So, it's been in the drain over fifty years." When he finished, Troy said, "I'll be in touch when I know more."

Rick had some time before meeting with Cecil. He went home and resumed reading the journal:

CXXXIII. The romance book I was reading aroused desires I've been trying to ignore. I believe Julio put something in the joint we smoked today. I also suspect he orchestrated the whereabouts of our housemates. I drifted off into an erotic dream & when I came back, Julio & I were alone in the lounge. Rhoda was asleep in his room & Doreen & Louie had paraded down to the dining room for an elegant dinner. I had no idea where Wendel & Linda were. So we were alone. Julio approached me, took off my glasses, put his arm around me & kissed me. Before I knew it, I was returning his kisses & it went from there. We made love right there in the lounge! I didn't care if anybody saw us. One thing about Julio, as much as he enjoys sex, he also knows how to make a woman enjoy it. Afterwards, I felt so content.

But we weren't done. We only came up for air. We dressed & went downstairs for something to eat & a glass of Julio's favorite wine. One glass only, to heighten the mood, not drown it. Then we went to my room. I don't remember how long we were there. It may have been minutes, hours, days. Julio likes things I don't but he didn't push me to try them. I didn't have to fantasize about anyone else. But then, who else is there to fantasize about?

Eventually Rhoda woke up &, not being able to find Julio, she pounded on my door. I'd locked it, so she couldn't get in. Julio just turned over, cuddled me, & said, "She'll go away eventually." She did.

Then he kissed me, got up, dressed, kissed my hand & left me in a state of euphoric confusion. He was probably going to Rhoda, then he'd go to Doreen, then to Linda. And I am all alone. I know I can't keep Julio for myself. Nobody can. The other girls don't even try. But somehow, I feel some power over my circumstances that I didn't have before.

Once I was able to move, I got dressed, went downstairs, & played the piano. Simple songs, but sweet.

* * *

Rick paused to catch his breath. He was glad his family wasn't home right now. This was a good reason to hide the journal from them.

CXXXIV. They're trying to keep Julio away from me. I can never seem to be alone w/ him. I hoped he'd come to my room but he hasn't. They must be working day & night to keep him occupied. Great! Rouse my desires then leave me dangling. I knew this would happen if I got involved w/ Julio.

Today, I probably did the wrong thing, but I don't care.

It was time for Hugh's bath. Linda pays no attention to him until he gets so ripe she can't stand it. She never spends time with him, even when he's clean. I bet she never feeds him, either. He'd die of starvation if it was up to her. If anyone can die here.

He must have been easier to manage today, b/c nobody asked me to help. I happened to be in the kitchen when they all went back upstairs. I took Hugh some leftover pizza. He thanked me, ate a few bites, then set it down & smiled at me. He seldom smiles. It made me feel all warm inside. So I seduced him. At first he was worried about Linda coming in, then he said, "No, she won't be back till bedtime." He seemed a little sad, but after I kissed him, he smiled again. With much coaxing & extra stimulation he was actually able to perform. "Thank you," he said afterward. "I haven't been able to do that for a long time."

I'm not sure how I feel now. Not like I did after Julio. I don't feel dirty or anything, but I don't feel good about myself either. I know Hugh won't tell Linda. She'd kill him.

NEW YEAR'S

The phone rang. It was Steve. "Can I speak to Kristie?"

"She's not here."

"She's not? Where is she? She's not answering her phone. Are the kids there?"

"No, they're with Kristie. I'll tell them you called." The man was crying! "Is something wrong?"

"Yes, something's wrong. She left me. And now she won't even talk to me."

Rick didn't want to talk to him, either. "Did you try marriage counseling before she left?"

"Yes, but she wouldn't go."

Rick rolled his eyes. "I'll tell her you called. That's all I can do. I can't make her talk to you. Maybe she'll let you talk to the kids. By the way, we're heading your way Wednesday to get their things. That won't be a problem, will it?"

A sob came over the phone. "No. I'll be sure not to be home when you come."

Rick looked at the clock. It was time to meet his carpenter.

When he arrived at the Wilson House, the roofers were at work and Cecil Brewer was inspecting the front porch. "This one just needs a little TLC. It won't take long to fix," he said. They walked around to the back porch. "This will take some work, but we can have it ready before they finish the main roof." When they reached the east side, Cecil laughed. "What—did you say there was a porch here? Is your dumpster big enough for all this rubble?"

Rick laughed with him. "I know this one's a total loss. You'll have to build it from scratch."

"We'll start on Thursday."

"By the way, this house was likely covered with lead-based paint. Is your RRP certification up to date?"

"Yes. I keep it for whenever I work on an older home."

"Good. Mine is, too, so we're covered." Lead paint had performed well for years, until they'd become aware of its dangers. Undisturbed, it was no problem, but they'd be disturbing a house-load of it. By law, he was obliged to protect the health of his workers, and of the environment. Rick made a mental note to check his supplies.

After he, Cecil, and Roger discussed porch roofs, Rick went home. Kristie and the children hadn't returned. He had a little time to read:

CXXXV. I'm sinking again. I don't feel like cooking, & at times I don't want to eat. I haven't been joining their pot or whatever parties b/c I hate just about everyone. It seems there's nothing & no one I can have w/out someone taking it away from me. I hate Louie b/c he's a phony & he doesn't care about me anymore. Actually, he never did care about me. I hate Doreen b/c she took Wendel, then Louie, away from me. I hate Rhoda b/c she took Wendel away from me again & won't let go of Julio even tho she doesn't want him. I hate Julio b/c he's such a whore. I hate Linda b/c she's such a bitch. Did I leave anyone out? Oh, I hate Hugh b/c he's nothing. Most of all I hate Wendel b/c there'd been a grain of hope for us & he turned away from me. Twice. Needless to say, I hate myself, too.

CXXXVI. A few days ago Julio was in the parlour reading. When he set the book down, I looked at the title. "I Will Fear No Evil." That sounded intriguing, so I asked him about it. "It's good," he said, "You can have it now. I'm finished." I didn't realize until I looked closer that it was written by Heinlein. He must have borrowed it from Wendel. I almost didn't read it for that reason, but I rationalized that Wendel didn't give it to me, Julio did. It's about an old rich guy who has his brain transplanted into the body of a young woman. Since Julio recommended it, I shouldn't have been so surprised by all the sex. I couldn't believe this was the same guy who wrote "Space Cadet" & other adolescent tales. I enjoyed it anyway.

I believe Julio set me up by giving me that Heinlein novel. He came to my door & asked if I like it. I said yes. "Better than those romance novels?" Then he grinned. It gets me, he's so confident that girls want to jump into bed w/ him, but next thing I knew, that's what I did. Or rather, I let him jump into mine. I've discovered why Julio craves so much sex. Not only desire—it's an opiate, like eating, only better. It lifts me out of myself, helps me set my troubles aside. At least for awhile.

CXXXVII. When the other girls realized Julio & I were back on good terms, Doreen, & especially Rhoda, started to monopolize him again. If they can't find him, they pound on my door. If I so much as speak to him in public, they snatch him away.

Yesterday, he & I were in the kitchen. Rhoda shouted down the back stairs for him. I asked, "Why do you put up with that?" He said, "I really have no idea." But he must have put some thought into it b/c he kicked her out of his room & she had to move back in with Doreen. She wanted to move in with Louie but he wouldn't have it. And she no more wants to be in Wendel's attic than he wants her up there.

CXXXVIII. Doreen wanted to move in w/ Julio, but he must have learned his lesson b/c he wouldn't let her. She doesn't like sharing her room w/ Rhoda so she picks arguments with her. Their catfights are dreadful. Even Wendel in his attic and Linda downstairs complain about the commotion.

They tried to argue me out of my room. "You've had your own room all this time & we've had to share." I'm not sure which one wanted the room & who was willing to share with me, but I only laughed in their faces. They had no support from the men, so they tried to enlist Linda. She dressed them down & told them to just grow up.

* * *

When Kristie returned, Rick told her Steve had called. "He said he won't bother you when we go for your stuff."

"Good. I don't think he'll try anything, anyway, if you're with me."

"He said you wouldn't go to marriage counseling with him."

"Oh, he did, did he? Did he tell you about all the times I tried to get him to go and he wouldn't? He only wanted to when I got serious about leaving him."

On Tuesday, after checking on the Wilson House, Rick picked up the U Haul and brought it home. Kristie and the children were dismantling the Christmas tree.

"It's bad luck to leave it up past New Year's Day," she said. "And I don't need any more bad luck."

Rick helped them. Then he hauled the naked tree to the back of his lot where he piled brush for wildlife. "I need to get ready for Bob's party. Would you like to go? He won't mind."

Kristie shook her head. "No. You need to get out with your friends. The kids and I'll watch the ball drop, then we'll go to bed. We need to get used to going to bed on time before school starts, because I have to be at work by 7:30. By the way, I made an appointment with that lawyer Jeffrey Smart for next Monday. I tried to arrange for Mr. Balrush to meet with us, but the secretary said I had to talk to Mr. Smart first."

"Don't you have school Monday?"

"No. It's a student/teacher holiday. Don't ask me why. I didn't plan the calendar."

Rick was one of the first to arrive at Bob's. The weather for the past week had been balmy, but a cold front had arrived, putting a chill on festivities. Bob asked Rick to help set tiki torches around the deck and start a fire in the brazier. Tasks accomplished, Rick fixed himself a rum and coke and settled in a lawn chair. Throughout the evening, he chatted with mutual friends. Most were interested in his work on the Wilson House.

"What are Bob's plans?" a woman asked. "He's not going to move there, is he?"

"No, he plans to sell it. It's a good location for the right business."

Her husband said, "Yes, good for a business. I wouldn't want to live there."

"Why?"

"I've always heard those houses were haunted."

Bob's wife Melody said, "Really, now. You don't believe such nonsense, do you?"

"No, but our daughter and her husband spent their honeymoon at The Inn. They saw a lady in white walk down the stairs one night. Then she disappeared."

Rick felt a chill. He stood up to go inside.

Melody shook her head. "She must have been dreaming. What about you, Rick? Have you seen any ghosts?"

Rick laughed. "Of course not."

Bob's house was comfortably warm. Across the room he spotted a flash of red hair. Inexplicably, his heart leaped. The woman was talking to Bob. He approached cautiously.

"Rick," Bob said. "Let me introduce you to my new associate."

When she turned to greet him, he met her eyes. Brown, like most redheads. Not blue. He couldn't account for his disappointment.

When Rick got home, a nostalgic aroma greeted him. Kristie had baked cornbread and cooked a pot of hog jowls and black-eyed peas. "I missed those last year," he said.

"Well, maybe your luck will be better this year. Mine, too. Have a bowl, then we need to get some sleep. It a good twelve-hour drive." She sat with him while he ate. "Allison's coming for the kids in the morning. I appreciate all the help I'm getting. I don't know how I could do it alone."

"You shouldn't have to."

* * *

The trip to Knoxville and back was grueling but uneventful. Kristie's friends helped load her furniture and belongings, and Steve stayed away.

When they returned, Kristie sent Rick to bed while Kyle's family helped her unload at her storage unit. Where did Kristie get her energy?

That night, Kristie went to bed early. Rick watched TV with the children until he got bored. Then he went to his room to read:

CXXXIX. What am I going to do about Rhoda? Doreen stopped bugging me about my room but Rhoda kept on. Finally I had enough of her jabs & shouted at her, "Why don't you just move down to the cellar?" She got silent & gave me a stare that chilled my spine. She must be part snake. Then she struck. Before I could find the presence of mind to defend myself, she snatched my necklace! Then she gave this mirthless grin, ducked into her room & locked the door.

CXL. Rhoda uses my necklace to get back at me. If I'm too drunk or stoned to move she'll sport it right in my face. Once when she and Doreen weren't in the room, I snuck in but couldn't find it. She offers to give it back if I give her my room.

I fight back using Julio. That's not fair to him, but he doesn't complain. I try to outmaneuver Rhoda to keep Julio from her, just like she & Doreen did to me. I let him sleep in my room when I honestly want to be alone. Why is it, when you try to hurt someone else, you only end up hurting yourself? I don't try to keep Julio from Doreen b/c I need a break once in awhile. My appetite for sex in no way matches his.

Doreen got tired of fighting w/ Rhoda, so she started on me. She threw it in my face that she took Wendel away from me. I should be over that by now, but I guess I'm not. To get back at Doreen, I went up to Wendel's attic under the pretense of borrowing a book & tried to seduce him. "I'm sorry," he said. He held both my hands to keep me at arm's distance. "That's over between us. Really. We can't go back there.

Let's just be friends." His rejection was so gentle, somehow I didn't feel spurned. He apologized again for cheating on me. I asked if he was still going with Doreen. He refused to discuss it.

* * *

What a start for the New Year, Rick thought. He set the notebook aside and took a deep breath. Sometimes he wondered why he bothered to read it. He thought about the redhead he'd seen at Bob's party. What was he thinking when he spotted her across the room? Why was he disappointed when she wasn't Red? If there were an antithesis to Amy, that would be Red.

WICKER FURNITURE

Sandy accompanied Rick to the Wilson House the next morning. It was another unseasonably warm day, with a stiff breeze from the south. As they drove down the street, the sun reflected off the new metal of the partially-completed roof.

"Wow!" Sandy said. "That looks nice. They sure got a lot done in a hurry."

Roger walked over to Rick's truck. "How'd your trip to Tennessee go?"

"We accomplished what we'd set out to do. Boy, that new roofing sure brightens up the neighborhood."

"Don't it though?"

Rick watched the workers hoist a sheet of metal up to the roof. It settled into place with a clang. He glanced at the dumpster and saw a chair leg poking up. Was someone using his dumpster for personal trash? He peeked inside and found a half-rotted wicker chair. Cecil's helper approached with another. "Where'd that come from?" Rick asked.

"That porch on the other side of the house," the man replied. "There was a whole set of furniture under that collapsed roof. And some flower pots."

Rick found Cecil by the ruins of the east porch. "Dangest thing I ever come upon," Cecil said. "I thought this house was moved here?"

"It was. And supposedly all the furniture was removed first."

"Well, somebody set up housekeeping on this porch. It was quality stuff, too, when it was new."

Yet another conundrum. Rick watched Cecil and his helper drag a wicker love seat from the rubble. A few broken patio pots half full of dirt lay scattered on the ground nearby.

Rick took Sandy inside and gave her the wallpaper catalog. "See what you can figure out for the parlor. I'm going next door to ask some questions."

By luck, Ben Whitehead was at the law office. "Hey, Rick. Good job you're doing over there. Is there something I can help you with?"

"I just had a question. We're replacing the porch on this side of the house..."

"Oh yeah, the one that caved in."

"Yes. What's puzzling is, we found some wicker furniture in there. How do you suppose it got there?"

Ben wrinkled his forehead. "I have no idea. I never saw any furniture on that porch. Of course, I couldn't see the porch after we put up the fence. You suppose the squatters put it there? No, wait—the porch roof collapsed *before* we put the fence up. No, I have no idea how it got there."

A young man at a nearby desk mumbled. "Maybe the ghosts did it. Like they moved my Hankerson file."

"Ghosts don't move furniture!" Ben hollered at him. "Or files." To Rick, he said, "Every time they misplace something, they blame it on the ghosts."

"I thought you didn't have any."

"I don't. By the way, you ever see anything of that ghoul on the other side of you?"

"I saw him go to his mailbox once. How does that man live? Does he ever go out?"

"Not anymore. I haven't seen him in maybe twenty years. I know he gets groceries delivered, and probably anything else he needs. They send the bill to Jeff Smart and he takes care of it. I suspect he was running out of money and that's why he sold your house."

When Rick returned, Sandy was upstairs paging through the catalog. "I think I found something close to what used to be in this room."

Rick looked at her choice. "Good. Let's open the windows again."

Sandy set the catalog on top of the bannister. A gust of wind blew it down. "Why is it so windy today?" she asked.

"A cold front's coming in tonight. We always get a south wind before one moves in." He pointed into the master bedroom. "The wallpaper in there used to have a peacock pattern." Why was he so sure of this? What little remained on the walls was so faded he could hardly tell. Was that mentioned in the journal?

His musings were interrupted by a shadow flying past the windows, shouts from workers on the roof, and a metallic crash. He looked out in time to see a sheet of metal slide across the ground. By the time he got downstairs, Roger was at the front door.

"Rick, this wind is too much. We're gonna stop before somebody gets hurt."

"Sure." He heard his own heart pounding. At least no one fell off the roof, or had been in the yard when the roofing fell.

Cecil said, "I'm glad they're quitting for the day. I was getting nervous."

Rick and Sandy went home for lunch. Kristie said, "I'm going to the school to prepare my classroom and work on lesson plans. Sandy can go with me, and I'll take Michael over to Kyle's."

Rick had the house to himself. He made phone calls and did paperwork. Then, after completing a few household chores, he decided to read from the journal:

CXLI. I woke up to the loudest racket! I thought it was a thunderstorm. Only we don't have weather here. Turned out to be cannons —the 1812 Overture. Louie probably put that on. Anyway, the first BOOM brought me out of my bed & into the lounge. The lights were low. Someone handed me a joint. I guess they forgot I wasn't speaking to them. I forgot, too. The pot calmed me down & I stayed & listened for awhile.

CXLII. Yesterday I saw Doreen in front of the fireplace, tearing up paper & burning it. Afterward, Rhoda accused Doreen of burning her sketches. I wasn't aware that Rhoda draws. Louie probably influenced her to think she can. Rhoda needs to relax—her drawings will come back, just like my piano book. But that's not the point, is it? Burning Rhoda's stuff is a mean thing to do.

The other day, I found my curtains open. Somebody must have been in my room. As I closed them, I noticed movement in one window & looked closer. Julio & Doreen were in his room performing acrobatics in bed. Gross! Out of curiosity I looked thru another window and saw Rhoda in her room. In another, I saw Louie's curtains, but they were closed & all I could see was his light.

Since then, I've been spying on my housemates to see what they're up to, who's in bed with whom. There's little to see, nothing very exciting. I never cared for X-rated movies—I spy only out of boredom. And meanness. Yesterday, Julio caught me peeking. He winked & gave me a big smile. Rhoda saw this & closed the curtains. Now she makes sure they stay closed. All I see Louie do is snort cocaine. Today I caught Doreen trying to spy on me!

CXLIII. I've been cooking again, usually just for myself. Once in awhile I'll cook for 2 & invite someone I'm on speaking terms w/. Sometimes Wendel. If the food is up to his standards, Louie will dine with me. Julio & I use food as foreplay. At times, Linda joins me & we have agreeable little chats. If no one else eats w/ me I try to get Hugh to eat. But I don't try anything else w/ him.

Today I found Linda & Wendel cooking together & they invited me to join them. We had a nice meal, but I noticed he was more attentive to Linda than to me. After dinner, Linda went to her room to try to feed Hugh. Wendel & I went upstairs, exchanged pleasantries, then he climbed up to his attic & I retired to my room. As I curled up with a book I heard someone else come upstairs, hesitate in the lounge, then ascend to the attic. How could I have been so blind? It's not Julio Linda's having sex with! I broke out a bottle of Cutty Sark.

CXLIV. I hate Linda. She has 2 men to herself & I have none. One thing consoles me in a twisted way—I was able to get Hugh to perform when Linda couldn't. I've stopped cooking & seldom eat. Only drink. I no longer try to feed Hugh or care if anyone else does. I avoid everyone & they avoid me. Even Julio.

Yesterday, he knocked at my door & I stumbled over to unlock it. After I managed to get it open, I passed out. Thru the haze in my brain I heard him say, "Shit on this." I was dimly aware of him picking me up off the floor & dumping me on the bed. He slammed the door behind himself. I've lost my last friend.

CXLV. I got tired of isolation & joined the group in the lounge. Louie put on some classical music, starting with the William Tell Overture. No one objected. Who can complain about the Lone Ranger? Julio passed around a joint. Then another. After that, we were too stoned to dispute Louie's choice of Mussorgsky. Pictures at an Exhibition. I closed my eyes & strolled along, looking at pictures. Then "Night on Bald Mt." came on.

One thought lead to another. It reminded me of Dante's Inferno. What circle of Hell had I descend to? Virgil—a recurring nightmare— I leave my Mustang in front of Gus' building & this VW bus comes up, the old kind with the V front. V—for Virgil? Vice? Victim? Voodoo? Vanish? I screamed at Louie to play something else. Rhoda put on one of her musicals, one I'd heard 100 times before, but at least it brought up no sinister memories.

* * *

Rick put the notebook away when he heard Kristie's car pull up.

"You know, Dad, I'm a little nervous about starting the new job." After the children left the room, she said, "Also, they're going to an unfamiliar school. I've always had time to introduce them to their new teachers before throwing them to the lions."

"You'll do just fine. So will the kids."

"I know."

Saturday at breakfast, Kristie said, "I'm going over to the school again, but the kids don't need to go with me. Do you want me to take them to Kyle's?"

"I thought I'd take them shopping."

"Shopping?"

Sandy smiled. Michael scowled.

Rick said, "I mean, yard sales, and the flea market."

Both were okay with that. Michael asked, "Can David and Rusty come, too?"

"Well, I can't fit that many in my truck..."

Kristie said, "You can take my van and I'll drive your truck. That is, if Kyle and Allison say they can go."

Despite the mild cold front and a spattering of rain, the day turned out pleasant. All five children had Christmas money to spend. They made the rounds of yard sales and second hand stores. Rick was shopping for items for the Wilson House and found a vintage vent cover, some old door knobs, and a chandelier with a few prisms missing. "We may find more prisms at the flea market," Rick said. "People buy them as curiosities, then get tired of them." They ate lunch at Sonny's Barbecue.

At the flea market, Sandy took Jessie under her wing, so Rick only had to keep up with the boys. The children bought a few trinkets but Rick's shopping was not as productive as he'd hoped. The adjacent Antique Village had mostly furniture and dishes.

Towards the back of the last shed, in a rather neglected booth, Rick spotted a vintage door set on a pair of sawhorses, a makeshift table. Under a pile of rusted tools, he found another antique floor vent. He settled on a price with the proprietor and said he'd return the next day with his truck.

"I got another old door like this at the house," the man said. "I'll bring it tomorrow."

Once again, Kyle's children begged to go to the Wilson House. Rick told them they had to get their parents' permission.

Kyle's family joined them for Sunday dinner. Rick asked his son to help him pick up the doors from the flea market. When they arrived at the Wilson House, Kyle carried one to the front porch. "I don't want to go inside."

"Oh, come on. I'll protect you."

Kyle hesitated, then followed. "Sure looks different. Not as dark." They leaned their doors against a wall.

"Let me show you around. Tell me if you feel a ghost."

Kyle followed Rick through the house. He seemed to relax when nothing spooky happened. Afterward, Rick asked, "Well?"

Kyle shook his head. "I don't sense anything."

"Your kids have begged to come here. What do you say?"

Kyle took a deep breath. "I'll think about it. If I let them, I'll come with them."

THE MISSING SLEDGEHAMMER

Monday morning, as Rick prepared to go to the Wilson House, Kristie said, "Dad, I'm going to see Mr. Smart today and arrange a meeting with Mr. Balrush."

"I'm surprised you have time for this."

"I'm in good shape for school, and I'd like to get this done. Sandy and Michael can stay here. I have chores for them."

At the Wilson House, Rick found Cecil sifting through the remains of the east porch.

"What are you looking for?"

Cecil scratched his head. "We left some tools in the house Friday. Didn't see any sense in carryin' them home. This morning, nothing looked disturbed, but we can't find the sledgehammer. Thought maybe we'd left it out here by mistake."

"I have one at my house you can use. Let me know if anything else comes up missing."

Now that the east door was no longer barricaded by the collapsed porch, Rick was able to assess its condition. Most of the glass panes were broken and the wood sadly rotted. "Cecil, why don't I get a new door today so you can replace this one while you're rebuilding the porch?"

"I was thinking about that myself."

After Rick measured the door, he drove to Lowes, then Home Depot. He couldn't find anything that came close to matching the original, so he bought a simple solid door that would serve until he could find something more authentic. By the time he returned, Cecil and his crew had started building the new porch.

Unexpectedly, Kristie drove up. "I went to see that nutty lawyer, but he won't talk to me. Can you go over there with me?"

"What lawyer?" Rick scratched his head. *Her divorce attorney?* "What does he want with me?"

Kristie gestured at the Balrush house. "*His* lawyer. He wasn't busy, but he said he'd only talk to Bob or you. Confidentiality, he claimed."

Jeffrey A. Smart's receptionist was a heavy, pasty-faced woman who didn't stir from her chair. After Rick told her his business, she yelled, "Mr. Smart, someone to see you."

A pale, scrawny man crept out to the waiting room, rubbing his hands. "Come in, come in." Hunched over, he shuffled into a dusty office piled with books and files. Kristie took the vacant chair in front of the desk. Mr. Smart cleared a pile of papers from a second chair for Rick.

Kristie glanced at her father and took the lead. "As I said before, the owner of the Wilson House wants to apply for historical status. I'm acting as his agent, doing the paperwork. I need as complete a history of the house as possible. That's why I want to talk to Mr. Balrush."

"Oh, Mr. Balrush won't talk to you. He doesn't talk to anybody but me."

Kristie sat back in frustration.

Mr. Smart continued, "I've been Mr. Balrush's attorney since before he bought those houses. I know as much about your Wilson House as anybody, as much as Mr. Balrush does, maybe even more."

Kristie took a steno pad from her purse. "Okay, what can you tell me?"

Still rubbing his hands, Mr. Smart brought them up to his chin. "Well, you see, my time is valuable...."

Rick took a deep breath. "My time is valuable, too. How much do you charge for a consultation?"

Mr. Smart lowered his hands to his chest. "I charge $175 for a consultation, as long as it doesn't go over an hour."

"Fine." Rick stood up. "Tell my daughter all you know, and send Bob your bill." He handed the lawyer Bob's card.

Without being asked, the woman rolled her chair to the open doorway and thrust a document through it. Mr. Smart tiptoed around his desk, took the paper from her, and adjusted his glasses. He laid the agreement in front of Rick and said, "If you will sign here…"

When Rick emerged into the fresh air outdoors, he took several deep breaths to clear the dust out of his lungs. Then he laughed. *Amy would have gotten a kick out of that. I feel like I've just escaped from a Charles Dickens' story.*

When he returned to the Wilson House, the furniture in the dumpster reminded him of questions he'd forgotten to ask. He called Kristie. "Are you still at Mr. Smart's?"

"Yes. We're nearly done."

"Ask him a few questions for me. Did Mr. Balrush store things in the house, specifically, a piano, an antique radio, and wicker furniture? Oh, yes, also a grandfather clock."

He listened as Kristie related the message to the attorney and heard him reply, "Not that I'm aware of. I would have to ask him."

"Kristie, have him ask Mr. Balrush and let us know."

Before Kristie could speak, Rick overheard, "Now, beyond consultations, I charge…"

"Just tell him to find out and send Bob the bill."

That afternoon, the savory aroma of spaghetti sauce greeted Rick upon his arrival home. *How did Kristie manage to do so much in one afternoon?*

"I made it, Grandpa," said Sandy.

"And I made the garlic bread," Michael boasted.

"All you did was put it in the oven."

Michael's face fell, but he recovered when Rick tasted a piece and told him it was the best garlic bread he'd ever eaten. "Toasted to perfection."

That night Bob called. "How's my house coming?"

Rick updated him and told him to expect a bill from Jeffrey Smart.

Bob groaned audibly.

"I'm sure you'll recoup the loss with benefit of historical status. Besides, Kristie's not charging for her work."

"Oh."

"Remember, you told me to do what I thought necessary and send you the bills."

"So I did."

"I may have saved you money on the roof. Roger said the slate shingles over the turret are sound and don't need replacing. Of course, they don't match the tin. I don't think that's a problem, but you can come by and see what you think."

"Okay. I'll swing by tomorrow."

The next morning dawned cold. Kristie and the children left early for school. Before Rick finished his first cup of coffee, the phone rang.

Kristie was sobbing. "Dad, can you come get us?"

"What's wrong? Where are you?"

"Out on Hawthorne Road. My van broke down. My first day and I'm going to be late!"

"Settle down. I'll be right there." He found Kristie with her head under the hood, the children shivering in the van.

"I think the fan belt broke. Steve was supposed to have everything checked out before I left. Typical!"

"Hop in my truck. I'll take you to school, then I'll tend to it."

When he returned to Kristie's car, Rick ascertained that the serpentine belt had indeed broken. At one time, he would have fixed it himself. Mid-career, he'd calculated that, dollar for dollar based on his time, it was cheaper to pay a mechanic. Besides, he had a towing rider on his insurance. He called Hoggetowne Auto and asked Rose, the shop manager, to send a tow truck.

Despite the frosty morning, he arrived at the Wilson House to find the roofers and Cecil hard at work. Since his help wasn't required, he went home and lit a fire in his wood stove. Then he poured his second cup of coffee and settled down to read.

CXLVI. I haven't written in awhile. I've been too preoccupied. And too ashamed. I've found something worse than drinking. Worse than drugs. I'm ashamed to put this on paper but if I don't, it will haunt me. Maybe alcohol affected my brain. Or is that just an excuse? I started doing something I've never done before. Ever. Stealing.

At first I picked up things the others left lying around. Little things. Unimportant things. I'd take them into my room & stash them out of sight. Especially things belonging to the other girls—jewelry, makeup, books. It gave me a wicked sense of self-satisfaction.

Then I began slipping thru unlocked doors. One day when Linda was in the attic w/ Wendel, I went into her room. Hugh rolled over & looked at me, so I went to him. He hadn't been cleaned up in awhile but I unzipped his pants anyway. "It's no use," he whispered & turned away. Spurned me! I spit on him. He didn't even respond. I went into his bathroom & washed my hands. Then I went through Linda's stuff & found a negligee I liked. Hugh didn't say anything.

When Linda missed her nightgown, she accused Rhoda of taking it. Rhoda denied it, but everyone knew it was her. As other things came up missing, more suspicion was heaped on Rhoda, even by Doreen. She'd go through Rhoda's stuff looking for her belongings & they'd get into terrible fights. They could just wish for a duplicate of whatever's missing, but they wanted their own things, not a replacement.

Once when Rhoda was with Julio, Doreen asked me & Linda to help search her room. We didn't find what Doreen was looking for, but we did find my necklace. No one had the presence of mind to realize it was not Rhoda's modus operandi to conceal her thefts—she always flaunted what she took.

To keep the suspicion focused on Rhoda, I tried not to steal from her, but once I made a mistake & took some cologne I thought was Doreen's. Rhoda proclaimed that she too was now a victim. "You must have left it somewhere," Doreen told her, but a search of the house failed to produce it.

Alone behind my locked door, I'd wear the clothes and jewelry I took. I was careful not to use the cologne b/c they might smell it. (Later I squirreled it away in Linda's room. Linda never admitted finding it.) I'd arrange items around my room & gloat over them. Everyone's so used to my isolation, they didn't bother me. I was careful to put everything away before I opened my door again. I found a loose board in my closet & hid things behind it.

* * *

Yes! Rick thought. *The hiding place where I found the notebooks.* He still wondered why she felt the need to hide them. Who was she hiding them from? Furthermore, why had she abandoned them in the house? He continued reading CXLVI:

Eventually, things I'd stolen began to lose their appeal. Even throwing the household into consternation ceased to amuse me. Just to be mean, I started putting things back. In other people's rooms. Somebody would accuse someone else of taking their stuff. Of course, the accused would deny it. I heard them speculate whether the house was shuffling things around. If anyone suspected me, they didn't say.

Then one day when I was ½ drunk, I went out to the bathroom wearing Linda's negligee. She happened to come down from the attic & caught me. "There's my nightgown! What are you doing with it? Give it back!" I stuck my nose in the air & said, "It's not yours. It's mine." She would have ripped it off me had Wendel not restrained her.

The nightgown was soft & silky & caressed my skin, but one time when I put it on, it seemed to burn w/ cold fire. I couldn't get it off fast enough. I was too drunk to think straight. Totally naked, I stormed out to the lounge & threw the garment in Wendel's face. "Here, you asshole, take this. And take her, too, you two-timing slime."

Now, Linda never took care of herself & is quite pudgy, but I have a good figure that even alcohol hasn't ruined. I threw myself into Linda's face, not thinking about how my slender body has been less successful w/ men than her fat one. I stuck my finger in Wendel's face. "I had him first! Before you or Doreen did." Then I lowered my voice & said, "And I had Hugh last. I could get him up when you couldn't."

Instead of coming at me w/ claws, Linda buried her face in Wendel's chest & sobbed. "Please," Wendel said quietly, "there's no need for this." He stood up, picking Linda up w/ him. W/ his arms around her, he guided her up the attic stairs. There's no lock on the attic door, so I followed them, hurtling insults laced with obscenities. Wendel put Linda on the bed & tried to bar my way. I may not have been too drunk to walk but climbing stairs was another matter. I fell over backwards and tumbled down.

"You pushed me!" I screamed. Wendel hurried down to make sure I was ok. Julio rushed from his room. Wendel asked, "Will you take care of her?" Julio said, "Of course."

Julio took me into the bathroom & drew a tub of warm water. After I stopped crying, he brought me some fresh clothes. I was surprised. I expected him to take me to his room for sex. Instead, after I was dressed, he said, "Come downstairs, I have some hot tea for you." So we sat in the parlour, drinking tea & eating little sandwiches like civilized people until I felt better. Julio asked me to play the piano for him. I looked at him apologetically & said, "I don't really feel like it now, if you don't mind." He smiled. "I don't mind at all."

Later, after I slept & sobered up, I went down & played the piano for Julio. Louie, Doreen, and Rhoda came downstairs & sniffed on their way to the dining room. I didn't see Wendel or Linda, but no one interrupted my music with the record player.

Later, I apologized to Linda & Wendel. I didn't admit to anyone that I'd been stealing, but I found a way to put everyone's stuff back. One good thing came out of all this nonsense—I got my necklace back from Rhoda.

VIRGIL'S VW

The phone rang. Kristie's van was ready.

This was a good opportunity for an overdue oil change, so Rick decided to swap vehicles. He paid for Kristie's minivan and handed Rose his truck keys. As he left the office, a tow truck pulled in with a vintage VW bus. The kind with the V front. Stunned, Rick walked over to get a closer look. A young black man drove up in a Toyota.

Rose went out to greet him. "That sure is a beauty, Virgil. Or will be once it's restored."

Virgil? Rick nearly dropped his keys. This Virgil was a slender fellow, about five-nine, not much over thirty. Rick followed him and Rose into the office to eavesdrop on their conversation. Virgil was soft spoken and sounded well educated. When he and Rose were finished, Rick approached him. "What year is your bus?"

Virgil smiled proudly. "1967. The last year they made that model."

"Impressive. You're planning to restore it?"

"Yeah. She's not in bad shape but I want her roadworthy."

"Where did you get it?"

"Belonged to my daddy. I had to fight with my brothers for her after he passed. I finally bought them off, and she's in my name now."

"Who was your dad?"

"Virgil Jenkins, Sr. Did you know him?"

Rick swallowed. "I'm not sure. He was from around here?"

"All his life."

"I think I used to see this bus all over town. Quite some time ago."

"Probably. He got around. When he wasn't hauling us children, he was hauling somebody else."

"Do you know if, a number of years ago—did he go to a party at one of those Victorian houses on East University Avenue?"

"Wouldn't surprise me. He loved to party." Virgil laughed. "That's one reason I have so many brothers."

"Was he a big, jovial man?"

"I guess you could call him jovial, but he wasn't much taller than I am."

Rick studied the man, so different from the Virgil portrayed in the journal.

Virgil stepped away. "You'll have to excuse me. My students will be waiting."

"What do you teach?"

"Violin."

"It's nice to meet you."

"Same here. Have a blessed day."

Coincidence? Could the Virgil of the notebooks have been an actual person? Who was the writer? Did she draw on people she knew in real life? Once again he wondered if she had gone on to rewrite the story and publish it. Did she write anything else? How could he find out?

Bob was surveying the roof when Rick returned to the Wilson House. "I think it looks all right, tin on the main part and slate on the turret."

Rick nodded. "After all, she's over a hundred years old. She's earned the right not to be perfect. Come on in. There are some things I want to show you."

As they walked around inside, Bob remarked, "It'd be faster to build a house from the ground up."

"Yeah, but it wouldn't have this much character." He told Bob about the missing sledgehammer. "Even though I don't know how anyone could get in, I'm worried about more thefts. This is mostly a business neighborhood. Nobody around at night." By now they were in the turret room. Rick wondered how comfortable he could make it. Maybe a cot and an extension cord for a lamp, and a heater....

Bob interrupted. "I need to get back to the office."

Kristie was in a better mood when he picked them up. "I like the principal and staff. Nice people. The students, too, even though they gave me a run for my money. Testing the new teacher, you know. They've had a substitute since Thanksgiving, so I've got my work cut out for me."

The children were less enthusiastic. Michael said, "I asked my gym teacher about playing basketball and he said I'll have to wait till next year."

"I'll talk to him," Kristie said.

"Won't help."

"The girls here are so stuck up," Sandy complained. "I miss my friends."

Kristie said, "You'll make new friends."

"That's not the same."

"Well, I left friends, too. I don't want to hear any more about it."

Rick said, "I'm thinking of camping out in the Wilson House for a time. That'll give you and the kids more room. You can sleep in my bedroom and give Sandy her own space."

"No, Dad, I can't put you out of your house."

"It's okay. Cecil left some tools over the weekend and one came up missing. We'll be storing more expensive stuff there as we go along."

Kristie dropped Rick off at the auto shop for his truck. The old VW was on a rack being worked on.

When he got home, Rick dragged a camping cot out of his shed and a sleeping bag from the attic and carried them, a space heater, a lamp, and an extension cord to the Wilson House.

Roger's crew was getting ready to go home. "What're you doin', movin' in?"

"I thought if someone was here at night, nothing else would go missing."

"Yeah. A few times when we got here in the morning—you know how you can sense when somebody's home? Well, I had the feeling someone was here, even though the house was locked up and I don't know how they coulda got in. Or out. Without us catchin' 'em."

Cecil had run an extension cord into the house. Rick plugged his into it, and set up housekeeping in the turret room. What else would make it comfortable? A coffee pot would be nice. He could go home for meals and showers.

At home, before supper, he cleaned the coffee pot that had been in the shed since he retired. He also put a TV tray and a small radio in his truck, along with the box containing his plans, permits, and other paraphernalia on the Wilson House, including the notebooks.

When Rick returned to the Wilson House after supper, he noticed a car pull into Harvey Balrush's driveway. A young man hopped out with several grocery bags, set them on the porch, and left. When he finished unloading his truck, Rick noticed the bags were no longer there.

The cot was comfortable and the sleeping bag cozy. The floor lamp threw a gentle light. Better than a tent, he thought. Having met Virgil, Jr., Rick's interest in the journal was renewed. He took out the notebook and began to read:

CXLVII. Rhoda & Doreen continue to make my life miserable. To get back at them, I seduced Louie. Only hate could drive me to disregard my distaste for him. He's so mechanical—does he get any pleasure from sex? My experiences with Julio boosted my confidence. I'm learning how to play Louie. He'll never be the lover Julio is, but he's catching on.

CXLVIII. Louie must have bragged about our encounter to Rhoda and Doreen. They're trying harder than ever to keep the men from me. But I have a ploy they can't equal. I'll cook for either Louie or Julio & invite him to eat with me. Only me. Those girls can't drag a guy away from a good dinner, & they're lousy cooks.

CXLIX. With 8 people in this house, evenly divided bet. male & female, you'd think we'd end up in couples. Linda & Hugh were a couple, but she wasn't content w/ Hugh. Wendel & I were a couple, but he wasn't content w/ me. That leaves 2 men, neither of whom I can have for myself. I get tired of sex for its own sake. I want love. Or affection. At least companionship. I've never felt loved, truly wanted, cherished, by another human being. Not even out there. Not even by the woman who gave birth to me. Hugh is incapable of giving love & affection. Besides, he belongs to Linda. Louie is cold, giving only to himself. Julio is loving & giving, just so he can get sex. That leaves Wendel, a really nice guy. I shouldn't have been so hard on him. He didn't know how to say no to girls. Until he learned to say no to me, that is.

* * *

Poor Red. Rick laid aside the notebook. More tired than he realized, he turned off the light. The house was quiet.

In the middle of the night, the wind rose and rattled the ancient window panes, disturbing Rick's sleep. He nodded off again. A rhythmic squeaking woke him. What was that noise? It sounded metallic. Was part of the roofing loose? The rhythm reached a crescendo, then ceased altogether.

He slept, then woke from an erotic dream. He hadn't had one of those in a while. Amy wasn't in this one, only a shadowy figure, maybe one or two more. With guilty pleasure, he tried to recall the details before they escaped. A sensation of lying on a round bed, pleasured by, yes, three women! Lying in the center of an arbor, looking up at flowers and vines twining through a lattice. Where did this come from? All that sex in the journal?

His eyes opened. No round bed, but the light from the space heater shone on the stenciled border near the ceiling, flowers and vines twining through a lattice.

The bedroom door stood open. Hadn't he shut it when he came in? He got up to close it. The rest of the night, his dreams were pleasant.

Upon awakening, all he remembered were a few strains of piano music: "Love me Tender." It reminded him of Amy.

Another cold front had moved in. When the crews reported for work, Rick told the foremen about the noise he'd heard that night. "I thought the wind was blowing a piece of loose roofing, but the sound didn't seem to come from the roof. I couldn't pinpoint it. Then it went away."

"What did it sound like?" Roger asked.

"Like, squeaka-squeaka-squeaka-squeaka."

The men looked at each other. "We'll see what we can find."

Rick went home for breakfast. When he returned, Roger said, "We checked everywhere but we didn't find anything loose. Maybe it was a branch scraping against the roof. The wind must have blown it away."

Kristie and her family showed more equanimity that evening. Sandy admitted she'd met a cute boy in algebra class. The basketball coach made no promises but allowed Michael to practice with the team. Kristie was confident she could whip her charges into shape in no time. "And, Dad, I'll pay you back for my van when I get my first check."

Rick returned to the Wilson House and checked every room before settling into the turret room for the night.

CL. Yesterday—I shudder every time I think about it. I was acutely depressed. Not just melancholy. I mean the bottomless pit that would send me to a shrink in the outside world. I found some tranks in the bathroom but they didn't help. I smoked pot but that only intensified the feeling. So I did the usual. I got a bottle of Scotch even tho I knew I'd only sink deeper as the numbness wore off. I lit a candle & turned out the light.

Then I snapped. An immense wave of depression rolled up in me & broke out. I took the bottle by the neck, swung it, & knocked the candle over. Then I went to a window & smashed the bottle against it w/ all my might. The window didn't break but the bottle shattered & Scotch flew all over the room. My face began to sting. I brushed shards of glass &

blood & Scotch off my cheeks. The candle still burned, lying on my bed. The Scotch caught fire & burned w/ a blue flame. The curtains caught fire.

All this brought me a twisted sense of satisfaction & released the depression. Another wave struck & carried me, like a flood through a broken dam, out into the lounge where my housemates were listening to music. They scattered like bowling pins. I still gripped the neck of that bottle. I went to the record player & brought it down on the record as hard as I could. When I turned around, I was alone.

I headed to the stairs. When I went to hit the banister w/ the bottle, there was only a nub of glass in my bloody hand. I laughed, if you could call it a laugh. I threw that piece of bottle down. Then I smeared blood on the wall, all the way down the stairs.

I grabbed a lamp from the parlour & smashed everything in sight. When that lamp was reduced to almost nothing, I got another & went all around downstairs, swinging it, right & left. I took a sick delight in the noise & destruction. Linda opened her bedroom door & looked at me. I couldn't tell what was in her look. Not surprise, anger, disapproval, fear, or pity. Just—a look. She calmly stepped back into her room & closed the door.

By the time I got to the kitchen, I was exhausted & still gripped what was left of the lamp. I opened the cellar door to throw it down & the momentum took me w/ it. I stumbled & fell all the way down the steps & lay there on the floor, on that shag carpet, sobbing, until I passed out.

I had the most horrid dream. My room was all ablaze & the rest of the house caught fire. I was in the lounge with the others. The fire spread. We threw water on it, but it was too big. We retreated down the stairs. The fire followed us. We couldn't get out of the house. We stopped trying to fight the fire, only ran from the flames. Finally, we ended up in the cellar with that whole big wooden house burning above us.

A rumbling noise woke me. I panicked—was it the fire? I sat up & listened. It was only somebody moving chairs around in the kitchen & Black Sabbath blaring in the lounge.

I was shaking so hard, it took awhile before I could leave the cellar. I walked through the kitchen & downstairs rooms. No damage anywhere. I climbed the main staircase. No blood on the wall. I went into the bathroom & looked in the mirror—no cuts on my face. I looked at my hands—no blood, no cuts. I wanted to throw up. As I crossed the lounge to go back to my room, Julio, Rhoda, Wendel, and Linda were sprawled on the cushions, listening to music. They seemed to cringe when they saw me, but they didn't say anything.

My room was as pristine as ever. No ashes or smoke. No damage. My bed was made, & on the night stand was a fresh candle, an unopened bottle of Scotch, & a clean glass. This was worse than the depression, rage, even the nightmare. The only change was that my curtains were open, exposing those unseeing windows. I shut the curtains, took up the bottle of Scotch, & drank myself senseless.

* * *

Rick shuddered. The image of being trapped in a cellar while that large wooden house burned! He was tired but almost afraid to fall asleep. He set the notebook down and turned off the lamp anyway.

Sometime in the night, he turned over and his sleeping bag slid down. *Damn, it's cold in here!* By the light of the space heater, he noticed the bedroom door was open. Again? How did that happen? He didn't need to heat the entire second floor. He got up to close the door. Something he hadn't noticed before—it could be locked from the inside. He made sure it was firmly latched and locked. *Now it won't open by itself.*

As he slid into the sleeping bag, a siren screamed almost at his elbow. "Shit!" Flashing lights outside—a fire truck shot by on the street. He took a deep breath to steady his heartbeat. Yes—cold snap plus bad heaters equals fires. Every winter. He looked skeptically at his heater. It was in good condition but even with the door closed, it couldn't keep up with the draft from the old windows. *This is not working. I need a better plan.*

In the morning, Rick went home and soaked in a hot bath until the chill left his bones. Then he huddled by the wood stove, his brain searching for solutions. He called his son at work.

"Hello, Dad," Kyle said. "Is everything okay?"

"Sure. Why wouldn't it be?"

"Kristie told me you moved into the Wilson House."

"I'm only camping out there to keep things from being stolen. Speaking of camping, can I borrow your trailer?"

"You going camping?"

"No. I want to take it over to the Wilson House and stay in it."

"Why? Are the ghosts getting to you?"

"No. The cold is."

"Sure. We won't need it till summer. I emptied the holding tank the last time we used it, so it's ready to go."

"I'll come for it this afternoon."

When he returned to the Wilson House, Rick found several workers huddling over his space heater.

"Hope you don't mind," Cecil said. "We borrowed it. Just needed a break from the cold. Why don't you have the fireplace inspected? Then we can use it for heat."

"That's a good idea." Rick called a chimney inspector, who said he could come the next day. *It'll be warm by then. But not inside this house.*

That afternoon he went home to a peaceful household. While Kristie fixed supper, the children sat at the table doing homework. "How was school today?" he asked.

"Better," Kristie said.

Sandy got up and hugged him. "Thank you, Grandpa."

"You're welcome. For what?"

"Letting me have a bedroom."

He took his grandchildren with him to Kyle's, hooked up the camping trailer, and hauled it to the Wilson House. The children helped set it up and plug it in.

"Can we go inside the house?" Sandy asked.

"It's cold in there."

"We don't mind."

"Yeah. Help me get my stuff out of the turret room."

A Scream in the Night

The camper was much cozier than the old house. Instead of using its gas heat, he plugged in the space heater. Then he read from the journal. He was nearly through the second notebook.

CLI. Hugh has sunk even lower. He no longer eats or drinks or even gets up to use the bathroom. Linda's resorted to diapering him. Curiously, we seldom hear her yell & cuss at him like she used to. She's become almost gentle. Today, she was crying & said he's no longer wetting or soiling himself & seems to be losing consciousness.

Doreen & Rhoda still share a room. Rhoda makes occasional attempts to get my room but now she & Doreen are after Linda's. "You're not using it," they said. Linda sobbed, "But Hugh is." Doreen said, "Hugh isn't using anything." Rhoda added, "We can put him someplace else." But the guys wouldn't go along with that & they'd be the ones who'd have to move him, so Hugh's still in Linda's room.

CLII. Today, Linda went downstairs after spending a long "night" with Wendel. The neighbors (if they existed) could have heard her wailing a block away. We're all used to Linda's carryings on, but when we heard her scream, "He's dead!" we all rushed downstairs.

"He can't be." Julio felt for a pulse, then he put his ear to Hugh's chest, then his hand over Hugh's mouth. He looked into Hugh's eyes, lifted an arm, & let it drop. He slapped Hugh in the face & called for water. Nothing revived him.

I'd never seen a dead person except those already pickled & put on display in a funeral home. In the "real" world, people die discreetly in hospitals & are not seen again until the undertaker does his thing. The pupils in Hugh's eyes weren't dilated, like they describe in crime novels. But his eyes didn't move at all or even respond when Julio put a lamp in his face. His skin was cool but not cold. He wasn't stiff like I thought a corpse would be. Was he really dead? No one knew for sure. We didn't know death could happen here.

If he's dead, wouldn't his body begin to decay? We discussed what to do w/ it if it does. Will it get cleaned up like any other mess?

CLIII. Even Rhoda & Doreen kept a respectful watch, but now they've started in again about Hugh's room. Today we had a meeting. If Hugh isn't dead, then he's in a coma & none of us have a clue what to do about it. If he's dead, his body shows no signs of decomposition, but we have to do something. It's been eerie to go thru his room, past this corpse, to use the bathroom. Even Linda can't defend leaving him there. The only reasonable place seemed to be the cellar. "Not the cellar!" Linda pleaded, but Wendel agreed. "It's better than stuffing him in a closet. We can check on him, & if he shows signs of life, we can move him back up here." So Linda reluctantly carried his pallet down to the cellar. Hugh was so limp it took all of us to move him. He hadn't lost an ounce despite taking almost no nourishment.

The cellar stairs are too narrow to carry him down. We laid him on the floor, Julio & Louie got below him, Wendel stayed above, & we girls squeezed in wherever we could to ease him down, step by step. We tried to not bump his head, but we did. If he were alive, that should have produced some response, but we got nothing. Not a wince of pain. Like he really is dead. Once we got him down, Linda put a pillow under his head & a blanket over him. She didn't cover his face. She kissed him on the forehead & went back up to the attic with Wendel to mourn.

CLIV. Rhoda & Doreen let things rest "overnight" before they began to fight over Hugh's room. Wendel spoke up, "Maybe I'll move down here with Linda & one of you can have my attic." Of course neither wanted the attic. It wasn't until after their conflict reached a climax & settled down again that Linda said she didn't want that room anymore.

She moved her things into Wendel's attic, & in the end Rhoda got the room. Doreen's consolation is that she's closer to Julio & Louie than Rhoda is. Rhoda got what she wanted, her own private room & bath.

Every morning when Linda wakes up, the first thing she does is go down & check on Hugh. No change. His body hasn't been cleared away like an ordinary mess. We're able to hold onto a little hope, but we're all sobered by his non-death. We each harbor a silent fear that his fate could become ours as well.

* * *

The story was taking a different direction. Was the writer starting to kill off her characters? By this time, the space heater had done its job and could be turned off.

Sometime during the night, a scream jolted Rick awake. Was he dreaming? Another scream, then a third started at a high pitch and trailed away. He stuck his head out the camper door. Loud music and laughter a block or so away—a party? Probably students. When they get exuberant, they sound like they're being killed. He went back to bed.

On Friday, the fireplace inspector brought a chimney sweep with him. Rick had asked for a three level inspection, but after the sweep was finished, the inspector said, "You don't need a third level when a chimney's been in use, unless you've noticed problems. Have you?"

"We haven't used it. I was afraid to."

The man wrinkled his brow. "By the looks of it, I'd a thought you'd been using it a lot."

"Oh, vagrants that camped in here did. That's all. I was concerned because the house was moved about fifty years ago and has been vacant since."

"Well, it looks solid, no cracks, no bricks loose, or anything. Whoever built it did a bang-up job. Also, whoever moved it. They must have been gentle. I'll start a fire to check the draw."

Rick returned home for firewood. For the rest of the day, the workmen were able to warm themselves during breaks.

Before retiring that night, Rick checked doors and locks and the fireplace. Only a few coals remained burning. He settled into the camper and opened the notebook:

CLV. Things have settled down again. Linda checks on Hugh every day. Still no change. Julio & I have an occasional tryst. Sometimes I cook for myself & occasionally for anyone who wants some, except Doreen & Rhoda. At times, I eat only what's available. Wendel & Linda cook for each other & usually invite anyone who's about, including me. If I'm not in a Wendel-hating mood, I join them.

They're starting to act like an old married couple. Linda has become sweet-tempered, especially toward Wendel. She never turns her anger on him like she did Hugh. I'm jealous. I don't want Wendel, I want what they have together. Julio & I talked about that. He, too, desires what they seem to have found but admits he's not ready for monogamy. I admit I'm not ready for Julio! But it eats at me, & more & more often I blow off at little things. I seem to have replaced Linda as house bitch.

Today I was in the kitchen when Linda came up from the cellar. She said Hugh was the same. I grumbled, "It's his own fault. He never tried to help himself. He just let himself go." Instead of lighting into me, Linda gave me a sad smile. "Isn't that true of all of us? Haven't we wasted our lives? Isn't that why we're here? I can do nothing more for him. He has to find his way out himself."

I'd have been less surprised if she'd slapped me.

What Linda said keeps eating at me. Yes, I did waste my life. Is that why I'm here? Is this dead-end existence a consequence of my dead-end life? I don't want to think about it. I want to get drunk, even tho I know it'll only numb my brain but won't erase my thoughts. In the end, I can't avoid the truth & I know it. What good are escape mechanisms when you recognize them for what they are? I've had too much psychology for them to be fun.

CLVI. I'm recovering from an unnerving experience. I put on a good drunk. Maybe for days. I don't remember socializing, even eating. My bladder got full & I had to pee, but I couldn't move. I couldn't so much as lift my arm to take another drink. I tried to will my body to stir, to get up, to crawl if I couldn't walk, to the bathroom. Nothing. At 1st I attributed my lassitude to the depth of my despair. Then I tried to move my little finger— I was paralyzed! I couldn't scream or cry. I couldn't even blink my eyes. When my bladder could take no more, it emptied itself. I felt the warmth spread all over me & all over the bed. It wasn't unpleasant, physically, but even tho nobody was around, it was embarrassing.

After awhile it cooled & felt slimy. My mind began to clear but I still couldn't move. I thought about Hugh. Was he aware of his surroundings like this? Had I ended up like him? Would anyone make me comfortable & check on me every day like Linda does? Help me if I start to come out of it? How long must I lie here before anyone thinks to check on me? Before anyone misses me? Days? Could they even get in? Had I locked my door?

A cold dread settled over me. This was worse than being dead. I began to panic. How can you panic when you can't move? Finally, I resorted to something I hadn't done in a long time—I prayed. I hadn't prayed since I was a child, before I found out it never did any good. Then I began to worry. Does God, if he actually exists in the real world, exist "here" as well? Does his reach extend to this non-reality? There was nothing else I could do, so I prayed some more.

As the alcoholic pall slowly dissipated, I promised if I could get out of this, I would never drink so much again. I still couldn't move, but after awhile I fell asleep. It wasn't an alcoholic blackout. I know the difference. I began to dream. I dreamed that the windows in my room were open & sunlight filtered in thru the blossoms of a dogwood tree outside. Somewhere near the window, birds were singing. A spring breeze wafted in, stirring the curtains.

When I woke—miracle of miracles—I was able to move again! I rolled over, got out of bed, changed my clothes, & went to the bathroom. When I returned, my bed & everything else was clean again. The vision of that spring day was gone & the windows were as dark as usual, but that dream has stayed with me. I'm resolved to keep my promise not to drink quite so much again.

* * *

Finally, an entry that ended on a more positive note. Rick laid the notebook aside and turned out the light.

TRAGEDY

Rick slept soundly until he was awakened by a sense that something was wrong. Strange noises, a flickering light, the smell of resin. He bolted upright and looked out a window. *Oh, my God! The house is on fire!* Not bothering with shoes or coat, he grabbed his phone and rushed out the camper door. Wait. Was it only a dream? The Wilson House stood quietly unaffected, lit only by reflected light. He spun around. The Balrush house was engulfed in flames!

"Oh, no!" He raced around the fence, toward the fire, fumbling to dial 911. When the dispatcher came on, he shouted, "There's a house on fire on East University Avenue. There's a man inside!"

"What address?"

"Uh, I don't know. It's—I don't remember—one of the Victorians. You can't miss it!" As he ran, he cursed the makers of sweatpants with no pockets—nowhere to put his phone. The heat was too intense to approach the front door. He rushed to the back, only to be impeded by burning debris that cascaded from the roof. No side doors. A firetruck screamed down the street. He ran out to meet it.

"An old man lives in there," Rick shouted at the first fireman who jumped from the truck.

"Just stand back. We'll handle it."

Rick realized he was crying. And his feet were freezing. He returned to the camper for his coat and shoes, then went back outside. He leaned against the corner of the fence, watching the Balrush house collapse in burning fragments. The weeds around the old Aston Martin caught fire and the exploding gas tank drove the firemen back. They were unable to save anything, only spray water on the flames.

A man in a heavy jacket approached with a notepad. "Do you have some identification?"

Rick went into the camper to look for his wallet.

"What is your purpose here?"

Rick explained his role and the need for security. He wiped his eyes. "You didn't get him out, did you?"

"What do you know about the resident of that house?"

"His name's Harvey Balrush. I don't really know him, never talked to him. His attorney is Jeffrey Smart. He can tell you more."

"Were you and Mr. Balrush in conflict?"

Rick's jaw dropped. "What? No, of course not. He's—was—a neighbor. A very reclusive neighbor."

The man handed Rick his card. "Don't leave town without clearing it with me. I'll have more questions for you later." He left to talk with the firemen.

Rick found his glasses and read the card. Marvin Howell, Fire Investigator. "Does that jerk think I started the fire for some personal gain? Or revenge?" He crumbled the card in his fist, thought better of it, smoothed it out, and slipped it into his wallet.

No more sleep that night. Rick was sitting on the front steps of the Wilson House drinking coffee when Cecil arrived.

"Rick, what the hell is going on?"

He briefly related the night's events. "Why are you here, Cecil? Isn't it Saturday?"

"It's supposed to warm up today and I need to finish the porches so Roger can roof them. Why don't you go home and get some rest?"

At home, he told Kristie and the children about the previous night's tragedy. Kristie looked shocked. The kids had little to say. He crashed on the couch in his office, only half aware of the family going about their business.

Rick returned that afternoon to find yellow tape around the Balrush house and men picking their way among the cinders. "They had an ambulance over there this morning, when things were cool enough to handle," Cecil told him. "And that old guy's lawyer came over, asking questions. We told him we didn't know nothin'."

Rick dreaded nightfall. He was tempted to go home to his own bed. Then he had a talk with himself. He would have saved the old man if he could have. Even the firemen had failed. Did they feel as bad as he? Probably. Well, he had survived Amy's death. He could survive this, too.

He made his rounds of the Wilson House and yard before retiring. When he picked up the notebook that night, the first words echoed his mood:

CLVII. I dread sleep. Every time I try, the terror of that temporary paralysis returns. I resist the temptation to drink myself to sleep. Eventually, I succumb to total exhaustion. When I wake, I think about my old life & the seeming injustice of this non-existence. Over & over, I've mourned the loss of my car & my apartment & my belongings. Assuming time has not stood still "out there," all those things are gone.

I miss my mother, imperfect though she was. I've begun to understand why she was the way she was. She & I are not so different. We both coped with our miserable lives as best we knew. At least I didn't have children to impose my dysfunction on. That was a decision I made early in adulthood. I knew I wouldn't be any better a parent than she was. I sometimes wonder how she's coping with my disappearance. Does she miss me? I'm sure she does. I think she did love me even tho she didn't show it. She's probably distraught. I was the anchor in her life. Men were temporary moorings, but I'd always been there, despite our unpleasant & infrequent contact. I actually feel sorry for her.

* * *

Rick noticed the page was slightly puckered, as though it had been wet, and the ink was smeared. How did that happen? The pages around it showed no sign of water damage. Would a writer of fiction get so emotional about her creation?

CLVIII. I broke down crying during my last entry & had to stop. I wonder how long we've been here. Is my mother still alive? Will I ever know?

As dissatisfied as I was with my life in the outside world, it had some direction, if only to the next day, the next meal, the next paycheck. Here, even the next anything—meal, tryst, argument, is followed by an unending succession of "nexts" with no sense of accomplishment, no release.

Release—from what? I've given up on release from this "situation." Can I find release from this continual unhappiness? The constant quiet desperation? If I could come to terms with myself, perhaps I could find some peace, even in this interminable emptiness.

* * *

Like Red, Rick felt empty and longed for peace. This was not the first time in his life he'd faced trouble, but he'd never felt this before—a loss of innocence. His reputation had been assaulted.

Sleep brought no succor. In his dreams, Rick tried to run from an unseen menace but was unable to move or make a sound. When he tried to breathe, his lungs struggled to expand but there was no air.

He woke gasping. The space heater was still going and it was too warm in the camper. He turned it off and opened the door for a breath of fresh air. The notebook lay open on the table. One entry remained:

CLIX. I'm drinking less & getting along better with the others. I feel like something is spurring a change in me. Not a big change, & not always a good one, but I feel like I'm starting to move forward. Today, I went downstairs & cooked some macaroni & cheese. I fixed more than one serving & left the rest for anyone who wants some. Even Doreen or Rhoda.

Altho Linda seems happy with Wendel, she still checks on Hugh faithfully every day. Sometimes I hear her talking to him. I check on him sometimes, too. He doesn't even breathe. I recall that horrible drunken paralysis. I give thanks that I'm able to breathe, to speak, to move, that I have *some* control over my life.

* * *

That was the last entry in the notebook. Rick placed it at the bottom of the stack. Early Sunday morning, Kristie called. "Are you going to church with us?"

"Not today."

"Well, I made a breakfast casserole. I'll leave what we don't eat in the oven for you. Allison invited us over for dinner today."

"Okay. I'll meet you there this afternoon."

He went home and partook of Kristie's casserole, his favorite—sausage and cheese—Amy's recipe. It felt nice to have someone take care of him.

They spent a pleasant afternoon at Kyle's. After Kristie and her children left, Rick stayed to watch a football game with Kyle.

It was dark when Rick returned to the Wilson House, yet he made his usual rounds before retiring to the camper.

On Monday, Rick stayed at the Wilson House only out of a sense of duty. Roger's crew was nearly finished with the roof. "We have a little left to do on the porches and I've been waiting for a warm day to do the caulking."

Derek of Crawford Heating and Air arrived with his crew. They began removing old ductwork. Derek walked through the house with Rick to show him where he intended to run additional ducts to new vents. "I'll be knocking holes in the walls. I'm not RRP certified."

"That's okay. Cecil and I are." As much as possible, Rick avoided looking in the direction of the Balrush house. Although the fence hid the charred remains, it didn't hide the empty space above, or mask the smell of wet cinders. He ached to leave, to go anywhere, do anything, but deal with old houses.

Wayne, his plumber, came to give an estimate. After talking with him, Rick found himself in the turret room. Those windows looked out onto the street, thankfully not to the ruins next door. His eyes traced wavy lines in the antique glass. He hated to replace these old windows. They had such character, but they were impractical. Modern double-paned windows afforded better insulation. In a building this size, with high ceilings, energy costs had to be kept to a minimum. He extended a finger to trace one of those wavy lines and left a streak in the dust.

Out on the street, a car slowed to a stop. Rick wiped across the window to get a clearer look. Not a fire official's car, but a battered Nissan. It pulled into the Balrush driveway.

A few minutes later, a worker called, "Rick, somebody here to see you."

He found Jeffrey A. Smart on the front porch. "Can I help you?"

Mr. Smart rubbed his hands. "Yes. Tell me what occurred the other night."

Rick told him about waking up, discovering the fire, and calling 911.

"What efforts did you make to put out the fire or rescue Mr. Balrush?"

"There was nothing I could do. The house was engulfed in flames."

"How long before the fire department got here? Would you say, twenty minutes?"

"No, not that long. Almost immediately."

"Fifteen minutes?"

"More like five."

"And why were you here at that time of night?"

As though it's any of his business, Rick thought. He drew a deep breath and explained why he was staying in the camping trailer.

Mr. Smart looked at the camper. "Is that legally hooked up to water and sewer lines?"

Rick crossed his arms. "That's between me and the city."

"No reason to get upset. Just inquiring, you know."

"If you're done inquiring, I have work to do."

"Yes. Have a nice day."

Rick watched the old man cross the yard, hunched over. Bloodsucker, he thought. An image sprang into his mind. He laughed—Mr. Smart walked like the vampire in the movie *Nosferatu*! But why so many questions about an obvious accident? Did he need a lawyer? Maybe he shouldn't have talked to Jeffrey Smart without one, but the only one he'd ever dealt with was his real estate attorney. He used to bounce such questions off Amy. Even when she didn't have the answers, she'd help find them.

Later, Bob came by. He stepped around the fence to survey the Balrush place, then approached Rick. "I don't mean to sound callous, but with that eyesore gone, the property values in the neighborhood should improve. I wonder who his heirs are? That vacant lot might be a good investment."

Rick shook his head. "His lawyer should know."

After Bob left, Ben Whitehead came over. "That's too bad about old Harvey Balrush."

Rick nodded. Then he remembered Ben was an attorney. "Say, what type of law do you practice?"

"Mostly family law, some injuries and such. Why?" he grinned. "Not looking to sue anybody, are you?"

"No." Rick hesitated. "I was here the other night. I reported the fire. Now I seem to be under some suspicion."

Ben's face immediately sobered. "Suspicion for what?"

Rick told him about the fire investigator and Mr. Smart's questions.

Ben shook his finger at Rick. "Don't you talk to anyone about that night unless I'm with you. Yeah, I'll represent you. People always want to put the blame on somebody when things go wrong. And that Jeffrey Smart is nothin' but a bottom-feeder."

Now Rick was more concerned than ever. "Do you really think I could be in trouble?"

"Naw, you'll be fine if you listen to me. But anything you tell them, they'll twist your words and give you more grief than you bargained for. If anyone comes around asking questions, tell them to come talk to me."

Rick assured him he would.

That evening Rick picked up the next notebook.

THIRD NOTEBOOK

CLX. Today I went down to the cellar to check on Hugh. I talked to him about little things that wouldn't upset him. I can't forget my experience of being "dead" but aware of my surroundings. It was so horrible. I hope Hugh's not like that but that's why I feel the need to talk to him, just in case. He doesn't respond, of course, & he hasn't changed. At least he's not decomposing. Is the cellar preserving his body?

    CLXI. I feel like there's a great big hole in me & the more I try to fill it, the bigger it gets. Feeling this emptiness, I drifted downstairs & found myself in front of the grandfather clock. That hole in me is so big the clock won't fill it. Nor would this house & all that's in it. Am I doomed to feel this way forever? I looked at the clock. Both hands pointed to 12. Midnight. When we were in the cellar that last night of our lives, we heard the clock strike midnight. Then it stopped. And our lives stopped.

* * *

Rick laid the notebook aside to reflect. Why had he been so miserable the past few days? The Balrush fire had not directly affected him, but he felt guilty about the old man's death and his failure to save him. He argued with himself—it was not his fault, and he'd done what he could.

    Tuesday morning, Wayne began work on the plumbing and Cecil arrived to finish trim work on the porches. Rick oversaw containment of paint debris.

    Mid-morning, Cecil interrupted him. "Rick, I need to trim a few branches off that dogwood tree. I wanted to check with you first."

Dogwood tree? Rick had noticed a little tree by the turret windows but it was dormant and he hadn't taken note of its species. He followed Cecil to the front of the house.

"See those little branches? They brush against the eaves when the wind blows. I'm surprised Roger didn't take them off when he was doing the roof."

"Yes, sure, go ahead." Something nudged Rick's mind. The journal. Red's experience of being paralyzed. She'd dreamed of a dogwood tree blooming outside her windows. He studied the tree. Could the branches be seen by anyone lying on a bed in the turret room? They had raised the house a few feet when they built the foundation. Would that make a difference? So many little things. He wished he could talk to Red.

When Rick went out for lunch, he noticed a car parked in the Balrush driveway. Jeffrey A. Smart was snooping around inside the yellow tape. *Probably looking for any antiques that survived the fire.*

After school hours, a car pulled up and a gaggle of teenagers spilled out. Rick heard Cecil confront them.

"Wayne's my dad," a girl said. "I need to see him."

Rick called Wayne, who came down to meet them. He gave his daughter some money. "Hey, can we look around the house?" she asked.

"Yeah," a boy said. "I've never been in a haunted house before."

Wayne looked to Rick. "Is it okay? I'll stay with them."

"Sure." To the youngsters he said, "Just don't touch anything, and stay out of the rooms with the plastic sheets. There's lead-based paint dust in those rooms." He listened while Wayne led them, giggling, ooh-ing, and ah-ing through the house, up one staircase and down the other. He met them in the foyer. Wayne's daughter was twirling a party mask around one finger. Rick peered at it. It was so faded he could barely make out its color.

"Can I have this?" she asked.

"I guess so. Where'd you find it?"

"In that closet under the stairs."

How did it get there? The only trash in the house was construction debris. Didn't something like this come up before? Yes, on one of his first visits to the house, he'd found a remnant of such a mask on the cellar stairs. But this one was whole.

It was a busy day. Rick was relieved when all the workers left and the house was secure. That evening, he continued reading:

CLXII. The grandfather clock. Before this I'd never paid any attention to it. It's been in the foyer this whole non-time, silent, both hands pointing to 12. When I went down today, it stood there, daring me to do something. "Damn you!" I said. "You're useless. You should be counting time."

On a whim, I opened the glass door in the front & looked inside. I'd never seen inside a grandfather clock before. My landlady had an antique clock on a shelf & once she showed me how it worked, but this one's different. I was amazed at the wheels & the things that hang inside. How to wind it? It has no key. I reached in & pulled down on a chain. To my surprise, I heard a tick, then a tock, another tick-tock, then a series of tick-tocks. The clock was working! I pulled the chain down as far as it would go. A weight on the other end of the chain went up & the clock continued to tick. There was a 2nd chain. As I pulled it down, another weight went up. Then I closed the door & pulled up a chair.

I had nothing better to do. The house was quiet. I sat there & listened to the tick-tocks & watched the minute hand move. When the hand reached 3, "Ding-dong-ding-dong" echoed thru the house. Everybody rushed to the staircase & leaned over the railing to see what was going on. Doreen said, "What was that noise?" Julio came downstairs, looked at the clock & said, "What did you do?" I said nothing, just sat there, listening to the tick-tocks & watching the hands move. After a few minutes, everyone went back to whatever they were doing. At ½ past 12 the clock went, "Ding-dong-ding-dong, dong-ding-ding-dong". That prompted another flurry of interest. Every ¼ hour it added another phrase of the Westminster Chime. At 1:00 a loud bong sounded. I had started time!

1/1 **Noon.** The clock's still running. It just struck 12 again. Now I can keep track of time. Since I don't know what date it is in the outside world, I'll just start w/ Jan 1st. When I started the clock, it was midnight. Now it's noon. In all that non-time, I didn't write in my journal on any regular basis, only when I felt like it. Now, to keep track of days I'll write every 12 hours, noon & midnight. I think it's an 8 day clock, but just to be sure it keeps going, I'll wind it every 7 days. Then I can keep track of weeks, too.

Starting the clock may mean nothing, but I actually feel a little optimistic that maybe, just maybe, it'll make a difference. "Time" will tell.

1/1 **Midnight.** Whenever the clock chimes the hour, it attracts a small crowd. Everybody except Louie will stare at it like they're watching TV. Wendel opened the front, but he didn't touch anything.

A while ago, Rhoda banged on my door. She complained the clock wakes her up every time it strikes & it ticks so loud she can't sleep. She wants it stopped. I don't know how to stop it & thank goodness neither does she. I told her to just shut her door. She huffed & said she does but it wakes her anyway. (I can hear the clock upstairs, even with my door closed. When it wakes me, I just count the bongs to see what time it is.)

Of all people, Louie stuck up for me. He told her to give it another day or so & she'll begin to tune it out. He knows from experience. His mother had an antique clock in her historical register house. Doesn't he ever get tired of bragging?

1/2 **Noon.** I've never kept regular hours here, no reason to, no place to be at a particular time, & before I wound the clock, no way to keep track of it anyway. I eat & sleep whenever I feel like it. That's why it's interesting that I fell asleep after writing at midnight & had time to cook & eat a leisurely breakfast before noon. While waiting for the clock to strike, I practiced piano. Lately, the others haven't been complaining about my music so much.

1/2 Midnight. Linda has been busy fixing up the attic to make it more homey. She & Wendel found some dressers & rigged up curtain rods to hang clothes on. They arranged these around their bed to make a "room." I heard the noise & went to see what was going on. I asked Linda if she wanted to build some walls or at least hang curtains instead of clothes. She said no, she wants open space around her. "Don't you ever get claustrophobic?" she asked. "Cooped up in this house all the time?"

Instead of finding the furniture she wanted in the attic where it would have been convenient, Linda found it somewhere downstairs and kept Wendel busy carrying things up. I think she planned it this way, to keep him running up and down stairs for exercise.

* * *

Interesting development, Rick thought. He wondered what winding the clock and keeping track of time would mean.

Wednesday, shortly after Wayne arrived at work, he said, "My daughter's school just called. She got sick and I have to go pick her up. Her mother can't get off work."

Rick nodded. He had to leave work several times for a sick child when Amy couldn't leave school. "I hope it's nothing serious."

"She started throwing up. Probably just something going around, but I have to take her home."

Another intestinal illness. Wayne had watched the teenagers closely, so they couldn't have been exposed to paint debris. It must be something going around.

The roof was finally finished and Roger called the inspector. Derek's crew started installing ductwork. Barry, Rick's electrician, began work on the wiring. Rick tried to stay ahead of them whenever they made holes in the walls or otherwise disturbed old paint.

That evening when he settled in to read, he was relieved that the next journal entry was upbeat.

1/3 **Noon.** I've been busy. In my former life I made a bead curtain for my apt. & hung it in the doorway between the kitchen & living room. I liked it. There's no place in this room for a bead curtain & it doesn't go with the décor of the house, but I thought one would do nicely in Linda & Wendel's room. It would divide their area from the rest of the attic but still leave the space open. So I started working on one. You know, in my old life I never gave away anything I made. When I was a kid, I made things for my mother but she never appreciated them. She thought anything homemade was inferior to anything store-bought, so when I became an adult, I didn't even try. Even though my landlady would admire things I made, I never gave her anything, either. I should have. I never knew how good it could feel to make something for someone else.

1/3 **Midnight.** I'm almost finished w/ the bead curtain. It's more work than I remembered. At least I didn't have to run to the store for more supplies. All I had to do was wish for them. I guess I could have saved a lot of trouble by wishing for a bead curtain in the first place, but it wouldn't be the same.

1/4 **Noon.** The bead curtain is ready but I haven't caught Linda & Wendel awake to give it to them. Back in that other world, altho I had no real hobbies, I'd occasionally take a craft class. Then I'd have something to occupy myself w/ for awhile. Until I got tired of it. My apt. was nice b/c I made things like macramé wall hangings & ceramic knick-knacks. Anyone would think I was a busy little Suzy Homemaker, which I wasn't. I wonder what happened to all my things. Were they thrown out? Did my landlady have a yard sale? Did she give them to Good Will?

1/4 **Mid.** I finally found Linda & Wendel awake & presented them with the curtain. Linda cried—from happiness! Wendel said it was cool. Some of our housemates passed thru the lounge while Linda was gushing over the curtain. Louie wrinkled his nose. Rhoda said, "How tacky". Doreen took some interest in it, tho I couldn't tell what she was thinking. I helped them hang it. They put it across the side of their "room" facing the stairs. Linda said it gives her a sense of privacy.

1/5 Noon. I played piano this AM. It's so pleasant to lose myself in music. Playing is better than just listening. And I have to stay sober. It's a healthier escape from troubles than anything else I've tried, & I've been trying to escape for a long time. Even before I came here. What a wasted life! I don't want to waste any more. Who is this talking? The piano is giving me purpose. I don't remember having a purpose in life before.

Julio surprised me. He came down while I was practicing & sat by the piano. He watched my hands on the keyboard & said, "However do you manage that?" This made me self-conscious & I started making mistakes, but he didn't seem to notice. When I reached the end of my repertoire & turned the page, I told him I didn't know the next one yet & needed to learn. He smiled & left the room.

I'm surprised Julio likes the music I play, things they teach beginning students, easy pieces, good old American songs like "Beautiful Brown Eyes," "The Gift to be Simple," & Negro spirituals. My favorite is "When the Saints Go Marching In."

Jazz is Julio's passion. He can listen to it for hours. I like some jazz, but most of it has the wrong beat. Or no beat at all. Also, Julio likes to get stoned & listen to hard rock. Again, some of that is ok but a lot of it sounds like musical masturbation. Maybe that's why Julio likes it. I'm surprised he took pleasure in my music.

* * *

Rick smiled. A new side of Red was emerging. Previously, she'd given no hint that she did anything but read, drink, have sex, and fight with her housemates. Now she was playing piano and showing generosity.

Thursday, Rick received an email from Troy at the museum. He verified that the contents of the bottle were indeed paper, but that it was unreadable. He also asked if Rick wanted his "artifact" back.

Rick called Troy. "Thanks for looking into that for me. I don't need the bottle for anything."

"Then I'll keep it and use it as a teaching tool. What about the diary? Do you still need that?"

"Well, yes. I'm doing research on the house to apply for historical status."

"Can you scan that page and send it to me?"

Rick hesitated. "My scanner's broke. How about if I type up what the entry said and email it to you?"

"You don't need to go to all that trouble. It's not an important find, just curious, and I have the information you gave me."

Rick felt guilty for lying to Troy, but if he told the truth—a diary written in the seventies said a bottle with a note had been flushed down the drain of a house that wasn't even connected to water or sewer lines, and was recovered in 2019—who would believe him?

He fixed supper for Kristie and the kids. While he cooked, he watered Amy's plants. Apparently, Kristie'd had too much on her mind this week to tend to them.

When she got home, Kristie dragged her briefcase into the kitchen and dropped into a chair. After she inhaled the aroma from the stove, she smiled. "Dad, you're an angel. I'm so tired—I didn't know what we were going to do for supper. This has been the longest week of my life."

"But you've only worked three days!"

"I know. A stressful three days, but it'll get better. Thankfully, tomorrow is a planning day. I have to work, but no students. Monday's a holiday, Martin Luther King Day, so I'll have a long weekend."

"The Hoggetowne Medieval Faire is this weekend, you know. Your kids have never been to it. Why don't you take them?"

Kristie smiled. "I should. I hear it's three weekends now. I remember when it was just one. Maybe I can get with Kyle and Allison and we can all go. You, too, Dad."

"Maybe." Amy had loved the pageantry and entertainment. It wouldn't be the same without her. "I'd take the kids to work with me tomorrow, but the place is all torn up and the crews are trying to stay out of each other's way."

"It's okay. They can stay by themselves. Besides, they have homework to do."

Rick took some leftovers back to the camper to snack on. Good thing. There was so much food in the journal it made him hungry.

1/5 **Mid.** Today after I played piano, I went to my room to read but wasn't in the mood. I needed something else to occupy myself w/. I can't read & play piano all the time.

I lit a candle & watched the light dance thru the colors of my candle holder. Then I remembered—in my former life, one of my excursions into crafts was candle making. So I went down to the kitchen where I found wax, wick, etc. & spent the rest of the day trying to make candles. I realized that altho I remember the basics, I've forgotten the little tricks that make things turn out right. Maybe I can find a book on the subject.

1/6 **N.** When I woke up this AM & went down for coffee, I took it into the parlour & sat by the fireplace. It's curious how the fire keeps burning even tho no one adds wood. Winding the clock hasn't affected it. Fortunately, our food supply hasn't stopped, either, or anything else we depend on. While I sipped coffee, I watched the flames dance— relaxing, a comfort I've ignored too long.

1/6 **M.** Today, Julio followed me into the parlour & stayed while I practiced piano. He sat back, closed his eyes, & smiled, even when I hit wrong notes. I know "Love Me Tender" pretty well & don't need to keep my eyes glued to the page when I play it. Julio was moving a finger to the rhythm. He must have sensed me looking at him. He opened his eyes & the smile left his face. After I finished, he said, "You act as tho you really like me." I told him I do. "But why?" I could think of nothing better to say than, "Because you're nice." He was silent for a moment. Then he swallowed & said he thought girls only liked him for sex. "But there's so much more to you than that."

Julio continued to listen to my practicing, but he just stared at the curtains of the bay window. Before I finished, he left the room w/out a word. I shouldn't be so hard on Julio. My female companions & I are not exactly Vestal Virgins. He hasn't been so much of a sex maniac lately. I noticed this change even before I wound the clock.

I enjoy playing piano so much, I wonder why I didn't take it up before. Back in the real world, a piano was available several places where I lived, but I never laid a finger on one. Now I wish I had.

How did I get onto that? I was writing about Julio & my piano music and how I've been too hard on him. I think Julio genuinely likes music. Even imperfect music, like mine.

1/7 **N.** I found a candle-making book in the library & finally made some decent candles. While I was so occupied, I noticed Linda going down to check on Hugh. I hadn't visited him lately, so when I came to a stopping point, I went down. No change. I'm sorry I was so mean to Hugh. Sure, he made me mad a few times, but I shouldn't have treated him unkindly.

1/7 **Midnight.** It has been 7 days—1 week—since I started time. The clock has kept running & I just wound it. Over the past week, there've been changes. The men have started to grow whiskers. Julio was rubbing his chin the other day & asked Louie if he had a razor. Louie looked down his nose & said, "Of course I do. "When Julio asked to borrow it, Louie wrinkled his nose & said, "It's a personal item." I guess Julio found one. He's been clean-shaven since. Wendel hasn't shaved & looks a little chubbier. I may have to shave my legs & armpits unless I want to go "natural." I didn't foresee this. Starting time seems to have made our bodies come alive. What'll happen next? Wait long enough & find out! Meanwhile, whenever the clock strikes 12, AM & PM, I will pick up my pen & write.

1/8 **N.** All the non-time we've been here, our behavior bore no consequences. Now it does. To celebrate my 1st week, I drank nearly ½ a bottle of Johnny Walker Black & woke w/ a terrible headache. At 1st I didn't know why. I took aspirin & washed it down w/ more Scotch before I came to my senses. I'd forgotten what a hangover feels like!

1/8 **M.** Julio & I made love today. It was nice, of course, but different, enjoyable. My "lovemaking" used to have an edge of cheerless urgency, but today, I was more relaxed.

* * *

Rick pondered this turn of events. Red winds the clock, seems happier, and everyone starts to get along. He found this lack of drama a little boring. Or maybe he was just tired.

THE POTHOS

By Friday, Derek's crew had completed the ductwork for heating and air-conditioning. All that remained was to install the heat pump unit. "We'll do that after the wiring's done," he said.

Wayne said, "I'm 'bout finished with the rough plumbing. When the bathrooms and kitchen are finished, I'll install the fixtures."

Rick talked to Barry, his electrician, who said, "The downstairs bathroom is all wired. I'll finish those other rooms as soon as I can."

Rick called Cecil, his carpenter, and updated him.

"I'll be there next week to start on the trim work."

That afternoon, Kristie mentioned her mother's plants. "They're getting a little dusty. I'd like to put them outside for a good rainwater rinsing, but there's no rain in the forecast and it might get cold again next week. I need to collect rainwater for them. Some of them aren't doing well on this city water. It's the chlorine."

"I wonder if that's why some of her plants died."

"Could be. Mama used to collect rainwater for them. Those pothos are thriving, though. They can take almost anything."

"Pothos?"

"The vines with the heart-shaped leaves."

"I didn't know that's what they were called."

That evening, he was surprised to read:

1/9 N. I gave a candle to Linda & Wendel as a little "attic warming" gift. Linda was so pleased she almost cried again. I now have more candles than places to put them. No need to make more, I was thinking about what I could do next. Then this AM I found a potted plant by the front door. I called it a philodendron but Louie said it was a pothos & that he should know b/c his mother's in the garden club. Whatever.

So I decided to take up macramé & make a hanger for the plant. One that would go tastefully with the décor of the house. There was a book in the library & supplies showed up in my room.

* * *

Another coincidence? The plant he'd rescued from the backyard of the Wilson House was a pothos. Was that Red's plant? He tried to remember what kind of rope was attached to the tree above it. He should have paid more attention.

1/9 M. Since I started the clock, I've picked up the phone a few times to see if it works, but it doesn't. I asked Wendel & Linda about the radio. There's no plug in the attic. Wendel found an extension cord long enough to run up there, so we tried it. The radio turned on, but there was no signal, just static.

1/10 N. This AM most of us converged on the kitchen at the same time for breakfast. I fried myself an egg, then Wendel found a pound of bacon & baked it in the oven. That gave Linda the idea to make biscuits. I realized I was still hungry, so I stuck around for a biscuit & bacon. Doreen squeezed some oranges for juice & Julio fixed eggs for all of us. When was the last time we were so cooperative?

1/10 M. My fingers are sore from tying knots. Doreen watched me doing macramé & asked if she could try. I showed her a few knots, but she got flustered. "It's harder than it looks." I told her I've done it before, that it just takes practice. "Like sewing," she said. I asked if she knew how to sew. "Yes. My grandmother taught me, then I worked as a seamstress until I came here." I had no idea Doreen was anything more than a hippie. When I finished my macramé hanger, I put the plant in it & hung it in the foyer near where I found it. It's nice to see something alive in this house.

1/11 **N.** Today my hanging plant disappeared & no one seemed to know where it was. I snooped around & found it in Rhoda's room. At first I was mad. But I couldn't find her right then to have it out with her, & that gave me time to think. I decided to let her keep it. When I told her she was welcome to it, she didn't even thank me, but that's to be expected.

1/11 **M.** This afternoon, mellowing out in the lounge, Julio passed a joint around. When it got to Linda, she just handed it to the next person & said she was giving that up b/c she doesn't feel right about it. She never used drugs before she came here. Rhoda reminded her Valium is a drug. "But that's different. You get it from a doctor."

I let out my lungful of smoke & said that before I came here, I never used drugs, either. Just Scotch & cigarettes. At least they're legal. Listening to music with the rest of them started me on pot. Doreen said I used to act like I was too good for pot. "But you sure put away the booze."

That stung, but I didn't feel like arguing. Linda suggested taking the record player back downstairs. If we don't sit around here listening to music, maybe we won't use drugs. Doreen objected. She doesn't want to give up pot & didn't feel like moving furniture again. Neither do I.

1/12 **N.** The saga of the hanging plant. After I told Rhoda (nicely) that she could have it, this AM I found the plant, pot, hanger & all at the bottom of the back staircase. She must have thrown it down the stairs—the pot was smashed, dirt scattered all over. I don't know why she carried it up to the 2nd floor unless she was trying to get more height to cause more damage. I don't understand why it didn't get put back together the way things usually do. The plant had some broken stems, but it was still alive. I got a nice bowl from the kitchen & repotted it. This time I hung it in my room out of Rhoda's sight.

Hoggetowne Medieval Faire

Saturday, Kristie had it all arranged. They met Kyle's family in the crowded parking lot of the fairgrounds and tried to stay together. Many of the "Faire" goers were decked out in medievalesque garb. Kristie said, "That looks like fun. Maybe we can come in costume next year."

She and Allison strolled together, looking at crafts and clothes. Kyle tried to ride herd on the boys. Rick took little Judy's hand and Sandy accompanied them to watch a juggling act. The juggler's shapely assistant had red hair and blue eyes. Something about the color of her hair—Rick asked Sandy, "Does her hair look natural?"

Sandy laughed. "No. It's dyed."

Rick relaxed. Not Red. After the performance, he said, "Let's go find your mothers."

In front of a tent that sold ladies' costumes, Kristie and Allison were talking to a woman with straight brown hair. "You look familiar," Allison said.

"Yes, I'm a seamstress at Amber's Alterations."

Rick interrupted. "It's almost time for jousting. Let's get seats before the bleachers are full." They followed the crowd past venders with good-smelling foods: roast turkey legs, fresh bread bowls filled with soup, and other delectables. He told the children, "We'll eat after the jousting." They managed to get a few seats. The children sat on the ground in front of the bleachers.

While they waited, Rick thought about the seamstress. "Allison, did you get that woman's name?"

"No. She didn't say. Why?"

"She looked familiar to me, too."

"She's probably here every year."

That afternoon, as they made their weary way back to their cars, they passed the tent of a candle maker. Rick did a double take before he decided she wasn't Red, either.

David and Rusty resumed their plea to go to the Wilson House. After Kyle put the boys in the car, he said, "Dad, I'm caving in. Can I bring them over tomorrow?"

"Sure."

That evening, he recalled that Doreen had been a seamstress. There was a description of her in the first notebook. He found it—a hippie with "boring brown hair & eyes." Could it be? Virgil and Calvin/Louie were real people. Doreen, too? But this seamstress, whoever she was, was too young. By now, Doreen would be closer to his age.

1/12 M. Today we sat in the lounge, listening to records & musing about life & regrets. Julio admitted he'd like another chance at life. He thought he could do better, & perhaps w/ the right woman he could learn to love. I told him he'd learned that already. He said, "I still have a long way to go."

Linda & Wendel said they'd like to have a real home & family. They wouldn't mind having to work hard & they're willing to face the problems they'd encounter in the outside world as a mixed-race couple.

Doreen said, sadly, that she probably deserved to be here b/c of how selfish she's been. "I never did any good for anyone. I always saw others as being better off than me, so I never did anything for them unless it benefitted me."

Her words could have been my own. I'm ashamed that these people whom I'd spent such a long non-time putting down seem to have insight I still lack.

Rhoda put her little nose up in the air & said, "It ain't gonna happen, so there's no use even thinking about it." At least she went that far, but Louie tuned us out & wouldn't talk about the outside world.

1/13 N. Wendel, Linda, & I had breakfast together. He said he figured out why he used to eat all the time. "I feel better when my belly's full. Lately, I feel full in other ways." He smiled at Linda.

I don't usually get philosophical, but it slipped out, "When your soul is empty, it's hard to feel full, so you keep eating until you're stuffed. It doesn't cure the loneliness, but it takes your mind off it for awhile." Linda nodded but didn't say anything, just picked at her food.

1/13 M. Today, Louie was reading in the parlour. I asked what he was reading & he told me, but now I don't remember. If Louie enjoyed his book, he didn't show it. He looked bored. I'm bored, too. Starting the clock didn't remedy that. A few of the others were sitting by the fire. I asked, "Do any of you remember a time when you weren't bored?" Doreen said when we first came here she liked not having to work. She could do just what she pleased & didn't have to lift a finger. Rhoda said at 1st she thought this was Utopia. Linda frowned & said. "But that gets old."

Utopia. There's more to utopia than what we have here. I'm not sure what it is. I never found it in the "real" world & I sure as hell haven't found it here. Not even since I wound the clock. Oh yes, we are moving "forward" but to where? Old age and sickness and death? Still trapped in this non-existence? Sometimes I can't help being negative.

1/14 N. I still light my candles when I relax in my room. Occasionally, I put some in the upstairs lounge when we listen to music, or on the dining room table when we eat. But I'm careful about the flames. I still get flashbacks from that time I went into a rage & set my room on fire. I'm still haunted by that horrible nightmare about all of us being trapped in the cellar w/ this house burning above us.

Before I wound the clock, I was careless. In my drunken clumsiness, a candle would fall over or get too close to the bedclothes, but nothing bad happened. This AM, in my sober clumsiness, I set my book on the stand & accidentally knocked over the burning candle. I didn't wait to see what would happen, I almost caught it in mid-air. I don't know if starting time has changed this, & I can't take the chance. There are consequences now. That would be a horrible consequence.

1/14 Midnight—2 weeks! I just wound the clock. Changes continue to happen. Julio & Louie shave everyday & Louie asked if anyone knows how to cut hair. Doreen does & did a decent job. Julio is letting his grow. The girls have to shave their legs if they want to keep Louie's attention. Wendel is growing a beard. Only Hugh shows no signs of change.

I'll have a nightcap but haven't been drunk in the past week. I also try not to overeat. I play the piano & read. I found more craft books in the library & started looking through them for ideas. I feel almost alive!

I have no idea how much "time" passed between the Halloween party & the day I wound the clock—months, years, centuries? Maybe none at all. Or maybe time looped around, so if we get out of here we'll find ourselves somewhere in the past. Or another dimension. Or another universe. Who knows? I sound like Wendel.

All that non-time, we were suspended in a stasis. Nothing changed until I wound the clock. I stayed drunk or stoned as much as possible but even that doesn't account for the eternal fog I lived in. How long will "time" go on? Will we grow old here? Will we ever get out?

* * *

Sunday, when they arrived at the Wilson House, Kyle looked at the ruins next door, which still reeked of wet ashes. "That's a shame. That old guy was plenty weird, but he didn't deserve that."

Rick gave him a puzzled look. "What do you know about him?"

"Oh, when we scoped out this house, he came over yelling like a banshee and chased us off." Kyle laughed. "We were leaving anyway. Hank said the old guy held séances in his house, that he conjured up spirits."

"How'd Hank know?"

"His aunt told him."

"The crazy woman?"

"She wasn't crazy."

"What more do you know about Mr. Balrush? Or these houses?"

"Only that everyone says they're haunted. They say they were built over an Indian burial ground."

Rick shook his head and unlocked the door. "Stay close to me. Don't touch the plastic sheets, or even get close to them. There's lead in the dust, and it can cause brain damage." He grinned at Kyle. "You should have brought them here when the only hazards were imaginary ghosts."

David asked his father where he'd felt the ghost, but Kyle claimed not to remember. The boys kept trying to scare Judy, jumping out of doorways and around corners. Finally, Kyle separated them and put them in timeout.

Rick's cell phone rang. Rusty asked, "Who is it?"

"I'll have to look to find out," Rick said.

"You don't have a different ring for each person?"

"No."

After Rick finished the call, Rusty asked, "Can I use it to call Mama?"

"Sure." Rick handed him the phone.

That evening, Rick made his regular rounds before going to bed. The house was quiet. Suddenly–"Ding-dong-ding-dong. Dong-ding-ding-dong!" Something cold seized him. He spun around, looking for a grandfather clock. As the rest of the Westminster chime played out, he located it—in his pocket! He whipped the phone out and fumbled for the mute button. When he could breathe again, he checked missed calls. It was Kristie. He called back. "I'm gonna kill that nephew of yours."

"What?"

"Rusty. He was messing with my phone. He programmed in a different ringtone. I 'bout shit my pants."

Kristie laughed.

Rick returned to the camper. Bob called for an update.

"By the way," Bob said, "when you packed up that old radio, what did you do? Scoop it up with a shovel?"

"No, I picked the pieces up by hand. Why?"

"I found some trash in the box. Half a candle and some plastic beads."

A tingle crept up Rick's spine. "I have no idea how they got there." After Bob hung up, he stared at the notebook for a long time before he opened it to read on.

1/15 N. Louie tried to kill the clock. I don't know where he found the sledgehammer, but he smashed the glass in the face before Julio & Wendel stopped him. He shrieked something about it making him grow old. He seldom loses his cool like that. Afterward, we held a council. Louie & Rhoda want the clock stopped. Doreen doesn't care. To my surprise, it was Linda who said, "That clock is the only thing around here that's progressing. It's the only thing that shows a future. We need that right now." Wendel & Julio sided with her. Rhoda pouted & told Linda of course it doesn't disturb her up in the attic. Linda silenced her with a look. She took the hammer from Louie & threatened to hit him with it if he tried that again. Imagine—short, pudgy Linda brandishing a sledgehammer at 6 ft tall Louie! I guess she could have taken out his knees. Even funnier was the frightened look on his face. The clock healed itself while we were out of the room.

1/15 M. I played piano again today. I enjoy it so much I don't have to force myself to practice. Most of the others have stopped complaining.

1/16 N. I've been trying to take good care of my plant, but today I noticed it looks sick. I never had a plant before, but I water it every day. Was it permanently damaged when Rhoda threw it down the stairs? Does it need sunlight? I wish I had a real window. I looked in a plant book. It said it needs "low light," whatever that means. I swallowed my pride and asked Louie. He said the light in my room was bright enough. Then he picked up the bowl & said it has no drainage hole and the dirt was too wet. He said not to water it so much. I didn't know a plant could get too much water.

* * *

Rick set down the notebook. That plant had been bugging him. He tried to remember what the broken pot looked like. Was it a bowl with no drainage hole? He'd repotted the plant in one of Amy's containers and threw away the broken one. Would Carlos remember? He glanced at the clock. Too late to call Carlos. He'd call him in the morning.

Although Monday was a holiday, Barry and Cecil came to work. Another cold snap had moved in. Rick tended the fire so the workers could warm themselves. Despite feeling foolish, Rick called Carlos.

"What's up, boss?"

"I've got a question for you."

"Sure. What is it?"

"Remember that houseplant we found under the oak tree? There was a broken rope on the limb and the plant had fallen to the ground."

"Oh, yeah. I remember. You wondered why a homeless person would have a houseplant."

"Right. Do you remember anything about the rope or the pot? What kind of rope was it?"

"Oh, I don' know. It was old and rotten."

"Was the pot a regular flower pot or a kitchen bowl?"

Carlos paused. "I think it might a' been a bowl. I think there was some designs on it. Why'd you ask?"

"Just curious. I took the plant home and repotted it. It managed to stay alive."

"Oh, that's good. I was sorry about that nice tree."

That evening at supper, Kristie asked, "Dad, have you heard the news lately?"

"I try to pay no attention to the news. It's disgusting. That's why I get the paper. I can read what I want and ignore the politics."

She was silent for a moment. "I heard there's a new virus they discovered in China. It has people worried."

Rick smiled. "We get these new viruses from time to time. The media blows everything out of proportion, then it's never as bad as predicted.

Remember Zika? It was going to cause a generation of brain-dead babies, then it died down."

"I hope you're right."

"By the way, how's the application for historical status coming?"

"I'm sorry, Dad. I haven't had time to work on it since school started. I hoped to have some time this weekend, but we went to the Medieval Faire and I've been trying to get grades done. Report cards go out next week, if you can believe it."

Rick smiled. "Why don't you give it back to me? Work on the Wilson House is going smoothly and they don't require my constant supervision."

Back at the camper, he looked over the progress Kristie had made. He still didn't know where to begin. He put the file away and took out the notebook.

1/16 M. Now & then I get so involved in practicing piano, I neglect everything except keeping up w/ the clock. Nothing to report.

1/17 N. I had that dream again—my windows open & the dogwood tree outside. This time it wasn't blooming & the leaves were green. In my dream I stayed in bed, so all I could see was the tree & a little sky. Blue sky. How long since I've seen the sky? It must have been summer b/c I could feel the humidity. I could also hear a tree frog croaking, like they do when it's going to rain. I didn't tell the others about the dream, but when I went down to check on Hugh, I told him.

1/17 M. I didn't water my plant today. I sure hope it makes it. I cooked a big roast and vegetables & invited everyone to partake. Then I played piano until the clock struck.

1/18 N. Doreen asked me to teach her to play piano! I was too surprised to refuse. So I did what I could. I taught her the notes & the keys & how to position her hands & gave her the beginning instruction book. She asked if that's how I learned. I told her I'd had lessons as a child but after that I had to teach myself.

She got this look on her face. I couldn't tell if it was sadness or anger. She said she never had the chance to take lessons when she was a kid because her family was poor. Then she shook her head. "No, we weren't that poor." Her parents just didn't know how to handle money. The lights or phone would get cut off, even tho her dad had a good job & her mom worked, too. A few times they had to move b/c they couldn't pay the rent. They'd borrow money or hock things to pay bills. "We had some nice things but we couldn't seem to keep them." Her dad would get paid & they'd buy a new TV. Then they wouldn't have the money for the electric bill & they'd hock the TV. One time they made a bunch of long distance calls trying to borrow money, then they couldn't pay the phone bill & it got cut off. When Doreen was 12, her grandmother gave her a bike for her birthday. When they got behind on the rent, they wanted to pawn it.

"They wanted to pawn your bike?" Even my imperfect mother never did anything like that!

Doreen said, "Yeah. They did things like that all the time." Sometimes the kids even got their things back. But she'd waited all her life for that bike. Her brother had one but wouldn't let her ride it. "He was lucky, his bike was too rusty to pawn." She told her grandma. Her grandma chewed her parents out & afterward kept the bike at her house so they couldn't touch it. "Eventually, I figured out not everybody lived like that. I got out of there as soon as I could. It wasn't easy, but I learned to handle my own money." I was surprised, not only about her childhood, but that she'd tell me these things. I realize I no longer hate Doreen. I almost feel sorry for her.

1/18 M. We all seem to have fallen into a circadian rhythm. Quite often we spend our "evenings" mellowing out in the lounge. Last week's talk about giving up drugs didn't last. Today, even Linda broke her resolve & started sucking on a joint. Somehow the topic of Hugh came up. Linda said she'd always wanted to get married, have a house & children. When she met Hugh, she thought that was her chance. She began to cry. "I know y'all think Hugh was a lazy slob. But he was really a nice guy." Doreen said, "He must have been very different when you first met him."

Linda was almost sobbing by now. She said he was, but he had a hard life—an only child & his father was abusive. He died when Hugh was 13 & his mother worked 2 jobs but never let Hugh work. She tried to make up for his father's meanness & never made him stand on his own 2 feet. He was a fat kid & got picked on. She'd run down to the school to complain but never told Hugh to stick up for himself. He never applied himself in school & she'd make excuses for him. When Linda paused, Rhoda asked what she saw in him. Linda looked baffled. She said she didn't know. He was a nice guy, different from anyone in her family. "Even when I was mean to him, he was never mean back. Maybe I thought I could help him. Give him some ambition."

1/19 N. Today I was doing macramé. Doreen asked me to show her again how to do it. So I did. I even gave her cord & beads so she could make something. She said she'd never done any crafts before, but her grandmother had taught her to sew. If we can find a sewing machine, maybe I'll ask her to teach me. Sometimes I hear her struggling with the piano. I'm glad the others don't complain about her like they did me.

1/19 M. Altho the house still cleans for us, some of us have started cleaning up behind ourselves. I was going to cook this AM but Linda and Wendel were still in the kitchen. Linda said, "Give me a minute & I'll clear my stuff out of your way." I was able to start my breakfast w/out having to step out of the kitchen long enough for it to clean itself. So I tidied up when I was done & washed my dishes. It felt good.

Uncanny Manifestations

Tuesday afternoon, an SUV with the fire department logo arrived at the Wilson House. Marvin Howell, the fire investigator, approached Rick with a smile on his face. "I'm sorry I was so curt the other night. That was the third night in a row I'd been called out of bed, and there's so much paperwork to do afterwards, I can't catch up on my sleep."

"That's okay."

"Well, I want to apologize. I know you were under a lot of stress. I have some good news for you."

Did that mean he was no longer under suspicion?

"They performed an autopsy. It showed the victim didn't die in the fire."

"What?"

"He was already dead. Natural causes, most likely, but the lab results aren't back yet."

"How could they tell?"

"No smoke in the lungs. The body wasn't entirely burned. It appears he died in his bathtub and the firemen poured water on in time to keep him fresh." Marvin lowered his voice. "I shouldn't be telling you this. It's supposed to be confidential, but I knew you felt bad because you couldn't save the old fella. There was no one to save."

Rick was too astonished to think of anything except, "What caused the fire?"

"Preliminary results suggest it was one of those cheap electric space heaters. And that place was so cluttered, there was plenty of fuel. It's a wonder it didn't burn down before this." He shook his head. "Sad that anyone had to live like that."

Rick agreed. He felt a heaviness rise from his muscles and dissipate into the air.

That evening, Rick's cell phone rang. Thank goodness Michael had changed the ringtone for him. It was Bob.

"I called that Jeffrey Smart about the Balrush lot. He said the old guy has a sister who lives in California and she'll probably want to sell it. Maybe you can build something on it when you get finished with the Wilson House."

Rick groaned.

"Just think about it. We're not there yet."

1/20 N. Things definitely are changing. Hair & nails grow—I had to wish for a manicure kit. Overindulgence brings consequences. We'll grow fat if we aren't careful. I now cook more nutritious food. A bathroom scale appeared in the main bathroom & I allow myself dessert only when it gives me good news.

1/20 M. Linda put Wendel on a diet & started an exercise class. Even Louie joined, saying he needs to stay in shape. We use the parlour. We move the furniture to the sides of the room & set it back when we're done. I'm sure it would rearrange itself, but putting it back is good exercise.

Despite my inactivity for uncounted non-time, I'm no weaker than before. The guys seem to be as strong as ever. Doreen's strength surprises me. Those scrawny little arms of hers can do almost as many push-ups as the men. Rhoda joined only b/c Louie did, but she doesn't put out much effort. The only one who hasn't changed is Hugh. He doesn't show any signs of getting thinner.

1/21 N. Tonight it will be time to wind the clock again. Louie & Rhoda still resent me for starting time, so I'll make sure they're not around when I do it.

1/21 M. Three weeks. The deed is done, the clock's been wound.

1/22 **N.** I heard scraping noises in Rhoda's bathroom & went in to check. She wasn't there. I thought I smelled paint, but couldn't figure out where the smell came from. This isn't the 1st time I've experienced something like that. A few times I've imagined somebody besides us was in the house. There'd be sounds & smells, even shadows, but usually it's just a feeling. A creepy feeling. I attribute it to being drunk or high, but sometimes I'm sober.

I mentioned this to the group. Linda sometimes sees things out of the corner of her eye, like someone walking by, but when she looks, no one's there. Wendel said that happens to him, too, but never in the attic. Linda frowned. "I remember one day Hugh asked me who came into our room. He was half asleep & thought somebody used our bathroom, but we were all upstairs at the time." I remember that. Linda accused me of going into her bathroom when I hadn't.

Doreen said once when she & Julio were making love, it felt like someone was watching. Julio said he didn't notice that, but a few times he thought he heard sawing & hammering. "A record was playing, so that's probably where the sound came from. There are no ghosts here." Julio's not going to admit to any phantom noises or presence. He'll find a "scientific" explanation even if he has to make one up. I know it's not coming from the records. I don't know what it is, but it's weird.

* * *

Rick shuddered. He thought about the times he and the workers had imagined seeing and hearing things. The reasonable explanation was that some trick of sound and light peculiar to the structure caused the perception of a phantom presence. Kyle hadn't described it quite the same way, but Rick was willing to bet he sensed the same phenomenon. Had Red experienced it, too? He wished Amy were here so he could discuss it with her.

The next morning, Wayne approached Rick. "Do you know where I can find a temporary helper? Chris quit on me, and I'm trying to do things that need more than two hands."

Rick thought about Jerome. "I may get you someone this afternoon, but he goes to school and can only work part time."

"That would help. I have a man who can be here next week but I don't want to wait."

"Why'd Chris quit?"

"If I didn't know better, I'd say he was on drugs. He kept saying the house is haunted. He'd jump at every little thing, and he refused to work upstairs alone."

Curious, Rick thought. Chris probably heard rumors about the house and let his imagination get carried away.

Jerome came that afternoon. Rick found him at the foot of the stairs holding a sledgehammer. "Is this the one Cecil lost?" Jerome asked.

"I guess so. Where'd you find it?"

"Right here. Funny place to leave it."

He called Cecil. "You found your sledgehammer?"

"Not yet."

"Well, it's right here."

"Are you sure it's mine?"

"Your initials are on the handle."

"Well, I'll be damned. I looked everywhere. Thought it walked off."

Rick puzzled over it. Other objects that had mysteriously appeared flashed through his mind. The candle and beads Bob found with the radio parts. The party mask Wayne's daughter took from the closet under the stairs. The pothos plant in the yard. And no less, the notebooks themselves.

He allowed his eyes to wander about the foyer and hallway. Holes in the walls made by the electrician couldn't be ignored. He looked forward to their being patched and covered with new wainscoting and wallpaper. His gaze moved to the one undamaged wall, between the foyer and the parlor. What was he looking at? One area of wallpaper, about two feet wide and six feet tall, was less faded than the rest, as though something had sheltered it from the spoil of time. Something once stood there. A bookcase? Rick dropped the sledgehammer. The spot was the size and shape of a grandfather clock!

Later, he had no recollection of hurrying from the house to the camper. He vaguely recalled attempts to busy himself with paperwork. Mindlessly, he thumbed through Kristie's well-organized notes on the history of the Wilson House. He barely remembered driving home, hoping his grandchildren would offer a diversion.

Rick spent the night on the couch in his office. By the time Kristie and the kids left for school in the morning, whatever ailed him the day before had faded to a half-remembered delusion.

At the Wilson House, Rick asked who'd found the sledgehammer. No one knew anything about it. Once he was certain his presence wasn't required, he drove away without purpose, out to the countryside, cruising through new housing developments, avoiding the antique towns scattered throughout the region.

By the time he got home, Rick had convinced himself that, of course, the Wilsons had a grandfather clock. In those days, everyone who could afford one did. But the sledgehammer? He decided to spend the night at home again.

KRISTIE'S NEWS

That evening at supper, Kristie almost wriggled with excitement. "Dad, I've been asking around school if anyone knew of a place to rent and one of the math teachers has a brother-in-law who has a house. The kids and I went by after school today and looked at it. It's perfect—three bedrooms, close to Hawthorne, and the rent's affordable."

The smile on Michael's face and the relief on Sandy's confirmed their approval.

"That's great!" Rick said. "Is it ready to move into?"

Kristy nodded. "It's clean and ready to go. I just need to get the electricity turned on." She made eye contact with the children. "Maybe we can move some of the furniture in this weekend."

Rick was surprised at his relief. He'd soon have his house back. "I can handle the utilities for you. Which power company? Clay Electric?"

"Yes. Do you know where their office is?"

"Of course."

"Do you plan to stay in the camper?"

Rick shook his head. "No reason to. No one has bothered anything. The sledgehammer we thought was stolen turned up again."

"Do you want your room back?"

"Not tonight. The couch is comfortable enough."

Comfortable, yes, but he still felt out of joint. Why did he allow those innocuous happenings at the Wilson House to spook him? Amy entered his thoughts, a manifestation of reason. Would she think he was crazy? Overreacting? Could she find a reasonable explanation for things or would she be as stymied as he? He expected her memory to sooth him to sleep, but he tossed and turned for an hour before he could relax.

Friday morning, Rick drove to the Clay Electric office to get Kristie's utilities connected. The clerk recognized him as someone who'd done business with them for years. "She'd like to move in this weekend, if possible," Rick said.

The clerk typed into her computer and replied, "We might get you hooked up this afternoon."

Rick grinned. "That's great. Thanks."

When he returned to the Wilson House, Wayne presented Rick with a problem. "I know you want to use that antique tub and sink in the master bathroom, but the old faucets need to be replaced."

"Okay."

"Well, they don't make them anymore."

"What do you mean?"

"Modern sinks have holes six inches apart. Those are eight. I've looked everywhere and can't find that size."

"Let me find an answer." He walked down the street to The Inn.

Mrs. Richardson was happy to see him and insisted he sit down for a cup of coffee and blueberry scones. "I'm so proud of what you're doing for that house. But wasn't it so sad about Mr. Balrush?"

Rick nodded.

"I heard you were there that night?"

How did she know? "Yes. I was staying in the camper, for security."

She put a hand beside her mouth and whispered. "One of our guests said she heard someone screaming one night. It came from that direction. But I don't think it was the same night."

"I heard it, too. Different night. Just students. There was a party in the neighborhood."

"No, the party was behind us. It goes on over there all the time. Are you sure it wasn't Mr. Balrush?"

"It didn't come from his house."

She leaned back in her chair. "That's a relief."

Over coffee, Rick explained his quandary.

"Oh, that's not really any problem at all. When The Inn was first renovated, you could still get faucets to fit, but we ran into the same thing when we had to replace some later. You see, you don't use a one-piece faucet, you buy a set where the components are separate. Then it doesn't matter how far apart the holes are."

Rick scratched his head. "Now, why doesn't my plumber know that?"

Mrs. Richardson patted his hand. "He probably never put in antique fixtures before." She pushed the plate of scones toward him. "Have another?"

"They're delicious, but, no. I had breakfast earlier." He drained his coffee.

"Let me show you how we solved our problem."

Mrs. Richardson led Rick to the staircase. "It's in an upstairs bathroom. Walk on this side, if you will." She drifted to the right-hand railing. Rick followed her, looking to the left, wondering what was wrong with that side of the stairs.

The bathroom could have been a duplicate of the master bath in the Wilson House, and the faucet looked like it was made to fit. "You see how simple this is?" Mrs. Richardson did everything but take the fixture apart to explain how to install it. "We bought this at Baird's, but they've gone out of business. The big box stores should carry them."

"Thank you. If none of the stores have them, I'll check online."

She nodded. "And don't hesitate to come to me with any of your questions."

Rick smiled. "I didn't hesitate today."

Mrs. Richardson let Rick find his way out. Without thinking, he descended the stairs on the side Mrs. Richardson had asked him to avoid. Near the bottom, he thought he heard a sob. Looking around for its source, he felt the air thicken and grow cold. He realized he stood where the "young lady" was said to sit and grieve. He moved aside and restrained himself from leaping to the floor. Slowly, he turned, looking, listening for anything unusual. Nothing. He felt a draft and glanced up at the ceiling—an air conditioning vent! He laughed at himself.

Rick took his Wilson House file, including the journal, with him when he went home that afternoon. Kristie and the children were full of excitement. "My electricity's on already!" Kristie said. "How did it happen so soon?"

Rick grinned. "I have connections. I'll help you move in tomorrow."

"That would be wonderful."

Saturday morning, Kyle and his boys helped move furniture. After the first load, Kristie left Sandy at the house to arrange things.

"Sandy," Rick said when they returned, "When you finish school, I'm going to hire you as my interior decorator."

"Oh, Grandpa, I thought you were retired."

By the time they returned with the last load, Kristie had made beds, unpacked dishes, and had supper ready.

"Dad, if we could impose on you one more night—our clothes are still at your house."

"No problem."

Kristie and the children skipped church the next day to move the rest of their things. Rick cooked for them. By Sunday evening, he had his house back. He called Kyle. "Do you want me to tow the camper back to your house?"

"There's no hurry. Do you still need it?"

Rick thought a moment. "No, but maybe if I keep it there, people will think I'm still staying in it and leave the house alone. Besides, it's useful office space until they get done raising dust in the house."

1/22 M. I've been giving my plant only a little water every few days & it started to look healthy, but then it started to look sick again. My plant book isn't much help. Even tho I hated to, I asked Louie. He stuck a finger in the soil but washed his hands before he'd tell me anything. Now he says I don't give it enough water! I should water it when the soil gets dry & give it enough to make the soil moist but not soggy. I asked him about fertilizer. Of course he took this as an invitation to expound, but the more he talked the more he confused me. I did manage to glean from his nonsense that his mother gave hers fertilizer only once every so often. I'll try to get the watering right before I try fertilizer. I didn't know a plant could be so much responsibility. I thought they just grew. Another reason why I shouldn't have children.

1/23 N. I dreamed again about my windows being open. There was a thunderstorm. I could see lightning flash & trees shake in the wind. A few drops of rain blew in & sprinkled on me. When I told Linda & Wendel about this, Linda got this strange look on her face & said, "I dreamed it was raining, too." She could hear it on the roof. Wendel said he heard thunder, but he fell back to sleep & didn't hear it rain. It's funny that we'd dream about the same thing on the same night.

I wonder if there still is an outside world. I don't know where it would be. Look thru' a window & you see another room. Open a door & you're on the other side of the house, like it's inside out.

1/23 M. This evening, we were talking about our families. Someone asked Louie about his. For once he was too stoned to ignore us. He's an only child. His parents split up when he was 11 & it was just him & his mother. "My old man's a deadbeat," he said. "She's always having to go to court to get him to pay child support. When she does get a check, she gives it to me." Doreen said, "You're not a child anymore. Why does she still get child support?" "He's way behind. Just because I'm an adult doesn't mean he gets out of paying what he owes." Wendel asked, "She never remarried?" Louie straightened his back. "No. Not that she didn't have the opportunity. She's a very social person. But she has very high standards." I'm not sure if his cocaine hit him just then or if it was wearing off. He got this drifty look & went on, "She has this special friend. He's a congressman. Unfortunately, he's married. I've heard them talk about it. He said a divorce would ruin his political career." Louie got quiet again, went into a daze, & fell asleep.

I was surprised he'd open up like that. When he came back around, Julio asked, "Were you still living with your mother?" Louie frowned.

"What's wrong with that?" Julio stifled a laugh. "Shouldn't you have been out on your own? Why didn't you get married?" Louie straightened his back again. "I was waiting for the right woman. I have high standards, too."

"You?" Doreen quipped. "Or your mama?" If looks could freeze, Doreen would still be trying to thaw out.

* * *

Rick chuckled. He thought about Calvin. Yes, he and Louie could be the same person. He set the journal aside. *I shouldn't be wasting time like this when there's work to do.* He picked up the historical file. He'd managed to fill some of the gaps Kristie had indicated in her notes. He wished he could have talked to Harvey Balrush.

WILLIE'S DAD

The next morning, Rick called Bob. "Say, have you been able to contact Harvey Balrush's sister?"

"No, but Jeffrey Smart said she's coming next week to settle his affairs. He's supposed to arrange a meeting between us."

"Well, I'd like to talk to her, too. We're missing some information about the history of the house and she may know something."

"Sure. I'll let you know."

Rick reviewed Kristie's notes and returned to the Matheson archives for further research. At lunchtime, on his way to a coffee shop, he spotted a policeman he recognized as Willie's father, Tony. Rick hailed him. After exchanging pleasantries, Rick mentioned the Wilson House. "You know we're renovating it."

"Yeah," Tony said. "Coming along nicely, isn't it?"

"Yes, it is. What do you know about the house? I've been looking into its history so we can apply for historical status. Your son told mine it's haunted."

"Oh, boy! I could tell you lots, but I was on my way to lunch."

"Me, too. Let me treat you."

Over lunch, Tony recounted his observations through the years. Harvey Balrush had called the police department several times to have squatters evicted. Rick asked Tony to describe them.

"Oh, you've seen them around. They come in all colors, shabby, rotten teeth, poor health."

Rick described the people in the journal.

"Could a' been some of them. Hard to say."

"What about a red-haired woman with glasses."

Tony scratched his head. "The only redhead I recall was a black gal who dyed her hair."

"Did you ever see a Mustang convertible parked there? Or a Volkswagen van?"

"We had to tow a car outta the yard once, but it wasn't one of those. I think it was a Toyota."

"There was furniture in the house when we started working on it. Do you know how it got in there?"

"Oh, those street people would drag things in. And Harvey used it for storage."

Rick's heartbeat quickened. "What did he put in there? Do you know?"

"Boxes of stuff. Once there was an antique radio."

"What about a piano?"

"Never saw a piano."

"A grandfather clock?"

Tony laughed. "Nope. Funny you should mention it. One night we had to call an ambulance for a crack-head who was bleeding somethin' awful. We thought another guy stabbed him, but both of 'em told the same story. They said a big grandfather clock began to chime and it spooked them so bad they broke a window and jumped out. Cut him up pretty bad. They swore it was the truth. My partner and I searched the house. No clock of any kind." He sipped his drink. "But I tell you, that place is sure haunted."

Rick knit his brow. "What have *you* experienced there?"

"Nothing, personally, but I've heard lotta stories." Most of what Tony related was similar to what Rick had already heard. "They say the house —all four of them houses—were built over an Indian burial ground, but I don't know about that."

"Built?"

"Yeah. Their original location, where the brown courthouse is now."

Rick felt a chill. He looked up. There was an air conditioning vent above him. He sipped coffee before continuing. "Tell me, were there any reports of disappearances related to the place?"

"Disappearances?"

"Of people, maybe vagrants who stayed there?"

"None that I'm aware of."

"Do many people disappear unaccountably around here?"

"Well, this being a college town, sometimes kids drop out and go home and don't tell everybody, but I don't think the rate's any higher than any other city. Why'd you ask?"

"Just something that came up in my research."

Tony took a bite of his sandwich. After he finished chewing, he said, "Too bad about Harvey Balrush, isn't it?"

Rick nodded. "Did you know him well?"

"Only through my professional contacts. But he was one odd duck. They say he had lots o' money when he was young. That's how he could move all those houses, but he deteriorated real bad."

"What was wrong with him?"

Tony tapped the side of his head with his index finger. "They say he held séances in his house. Once he called us, said the spirits told him something, I don't remember exactly what."

"Did he hold séances in the Wilson House?"

"Wouldn't surprise me. Too bad the spirits didn't advise him on how to manage his money. If they did, they gave him damned poor advice."

That night, Rick resumed reading the journal.

1/24 N. We still struggle with boredom. Maybe that's why we clean up after ourselves. It's something to do & it brings a small sense of accomplishment. I cook & take Linda's exercise class, but I can do only so much cooking & exercise & crafts & reading & piano playing. How long will we be here? In some way, time seems harder to fill up than non-time did. Before, we could indulge in our escapes w/out consequence. Now the consequences are too unpleasant.

I don't often go back & read my old journal entries, but today I looked at a few of them. I can't believe how disagreeable I was. I was never that bad in the outside world. I couldn't have gotten away w/ it. I don't know how I got away with it here, unless it's b/c when people live together, the social barriers come down & they can be their true selves. Is my true self so mean? Well, I'm not the only one. But I always thought of myself as better than them.

As I look back, I'm not the same person who did all those mean things. Mean and self-destructive. I'm emerging from a fog, & not just the alcoholic one. It's funny, but before I came here, all those years of writing journals, I learned almost nothing about myself. All that time & paper & ink wasted. Now, I'm beginning to see myself & my actions in a new light. I see what a pitiful person I was. I think I'm getting better. It all began when I started the clock. By examining this non-life, I'm beginning to better understand my whole life.

1/24 M. I'm getting better at piano. Today, Julio sat in the parlour & listened. When I finished, he kissed my hand & we went up to my room to make love. That made my spirit sing. Afterward I went down & played some more. Since he enjoys my music, I'm practicing new pieces he'll like.

Doreen's been practicing, too. I hope I didn't used to sound as bad as she does. She spends less time w/ Louie lately. He & Rhoda still dress up & parade around the house, but Doreen seldom joins them anymore.

1/25 N. We all got together for breakfast this AM. Even Louie joined us, & Rhoda tagged along. Louie decided we should have Eggs Bene-dict. He found English muffins in the fridge but insisted on making the Hollandaise sauce himself. It was good, but by the time everything was ready, I was half-starved.

You know, I started out not liking any of these people, but now I get along ok w/ them. Except for Rhoda & Louie, but I don't hate them like I used to. I had good reasons for not liking everyone at 1st but they've changed. Or I've changed. Or both. Lately, life here isn't so bad. The worst thing is, we're confined w/ no way to get out. But we continue to get everything we need & most of what we want. I enjoy my music & crafts, & the books keep coming. I stay sober so I can concentrate. It's been so long since I watched TV, I don't miss it. And we have our little dinner parties & chit-chats.

1/25 M. I've been tidying up behind myself for some time but when I don't, it gets tidied anyway. Until today. I didn't make my bed & when I came back to my room, it was as rumpled as when I'd left it. I confided in Linda & she said the same thing was happening to her & Wendel. I wonder what this means. I hope it's not a sign that the house is going to stop taking care of us. If it stopped providing food, we'd starve.

1/26 N. I had another dream. The windows were open & a freezing wind came thru. It was night outside. Even with a blanket, I was cold. This time I dreamed I got up & shut the windows, but left the curtains open so I could watch the stars from my bed. How long since I saw stars? The curious thing is, when I woke up, the curtains were really open. I always keep them closed.

At breakfast, I shared my dream with Linda & Wendel. They've been having similar dreams, sometimes hearing rain & wind, squirrels scampering on the roof. Once they saw light coming thru the window with the big W. Occasionally they wake up cold & have to get another blanket. Then when they really wake up, the temperature's the same as usual.

Linda asked Doreen if she's had any dreams like this. She said no, but Julio has. He dreamed about his windows being open & a big magnolia tree outside was in full bloom. He could hear a mockingbird sing but couldn't see it. What does all this mean? Is there hope for us?

* * *

Magnolia tree? Yes, there was a magnolia tree on the east side of the house! The chill that shuddered down Rick's spine was becoming all too familiar. He drew a deep breath. Why was he surprised? The journal writer knew this. The tree was large enough to have sprouted after the building was moved. But she wrote it—when? The notebooks dated to a time when the magnolia would have been a sapling too small to blossom, let alone be seen from an upstairs bed.

He shut the notebook and read no more until the following evening.

1/26 M. Today something very extraordinary happened. Linda & Wendel cooked a big pot of chili & Wendel made cornbread. While he was setting the table, I heard Linda say she'd go ask the rest of us to join them. I was in the parlour playing piano for Julio & Doreen. After I finished my piece, we went to the dining room, even tho Linda hadn't come to invite us. Wendel asked, "Where's Linda?" We hadn't seen her. Julio suggested maybe she went upstairs to ask Louie & Rhoda. Like they would condescend to eating chili.

Wendel pointed to the side door & said, "She went thru there a few minutes ago." She didn't come into the parlour. Wendel's look was somewhere between puzzlement & concern. He went thru the dining room door into the parlour, looked in Rhoda's room, then the kitchen. He went down to the cellar, then up the back stairs. We heard him open & close doors, speak to Rhoda & Louie, then climb into the attic. He came down the main staircase, returned to the dining room, & said, "I can't find her."

When we jumped up to help him search, Linda came in thru the dining room door. Her eyes were glazed & she looked pale. "Where were you?" Wendel asked. "Nowhere." She collapsed into the nearest chair. "What's wrong? Are you sick?" She shook her head. "No, it's just that something..." She shrugged her shoulders. "Something... strange...happened." Wendel went down on his knees in front of her & held her hands. She finally cleared her throat and asked, "How long was I gone?" I calculated the time it would take for a quick walk thru the house. "Maybe 10 mins."

Linda nodded. "I was out on the porch."

We all echoed, "Porch?" She took a deep breath. "When I went out the dining room door, I was on a porch. The sun was shining." She smiled. "The porch is covered with vines, bougainvillea. There's a yard w/ more flowers & a tall board fence. There were bees & butterflies & a porch swing & some rocking chairs. I just stayed there, looking at the flowers." She sighed. "I wanted to go out into the yard, but I was afraid if I did I wouldn't get back in the house." She looked at Wendel. "I was afraid I wouldn't get back in anyway, but I did."

Wendel opened the door. He looked through the opening briefly, then stepped thru. We heard him in the parlour. Then he went out the front door. He came in thru the kitchen, shaking his head. "It's gone," he said.

I processed this the only way I knew how, by washing it down with Scotch. To hell with the hangover! But as I mused over my glass, I wondered why Linda came back inside. Why didn't she just keep going? Because she didn't want to leave Wendel? What if it had been me? Would I have stepped off the porch into the yard & from there out to the street? My first thought was, "Yes. In a heartbeat!" Then I wondered, what world would I be going out to? And when? If I knew, would I still have gone?

* * *

Rick closed the notebook. Yes, Linda's experience was extraordinary. He imagined himself in her situation. After being confined indoors for an interminable length of time, would he have gone back inside? Not hardly! He'd have kept going. Even if he didn't know what world he was returning to. He hated to be indoors more than a few hours. No wonder these people misbehaved so, being cooped up like that.

He shook his head. Again, he was being sucked into the story, forgetting it was fiction. Was this why Amy loved literature? So she could lose herself in a story? He regretted never having asked her.

This passage reminded him of something else. Once the house was finished, Bob might want him to oversee the landscaping. Flowers did sound nice, but probably not bougainvillea. In North Central Florida, it would have to be protected from frosts. Too much trouble. Besides, he didn't feel inclined to bring elements of the journal into his reality.

CONUNDRUMS

Rick's phone rang. Who'd call this late?

It was Kyle. "Dad, Allison wants to know if you've had your flu shot yet."

"I don't get flu shots. I never get sick."

"This might be a good year to get one. Have you heard about that new virus out of China?"

"Kristie mentioned it. Flu shots are just a stab in the dark. They never know what strain will be popular every year."

"Well, this isn't a flu, it's something else. I'm getting concerned. They put out a warning to the students today about travel to China. It's hitting pretty hard over there, and there've already been a handful of cases here in this country."

"Tell Allison I take my vitamin C every day."

1/27 N. I knew I shouldn't drink so much. Now I'm paying for it, but that's not the only reason I'm miserable. Linda's experience was disconcerting. Life settles into a pleasant, if dull, routine, then something like this happens. What do these things mean? Dreams of open windows & trees & birds & rain on the roof. Now a porch w/ bougainvillea & bees & butterflies? And our bodies coming alive, having to shave, putting on weight. Where is this leading?

1/27 M. Louie and Rhoda say Linda's lying about the porch, but the rest of us believe her. I've been going thru outside doors as usual, but so far, no porch for me. Today while I was learning a new song on the piano, Linda came in thru the parlour door! She looked so strange. She closed the door & leaned against it. I asked what was the matter? "Nothing." She smiled. Almost a saintly smile, if you can imagine Linda the (former) house bitch looking saintly. "I've been enjoying the porch. And the sunshine. It's morning on that side of the house." I rushed to the door & she stepped aside. Only the dining room. Linda shook her head. "No, it's not always there. Neither is the other side. And Wendel hasn't been able to find them, either. I don't know why I can. And nothing happens at the back door. I'm afraid to try the front."

She said the parlour porch is screened & has houseplants & wicker furniture, very pleasant. And a small yard w/ azalea bushes, but they're not blooming right now. "A high board fence goes all around the house. I can't see anything beyond it. I'm afraid to leave the porch. I don't know what will happen."

What could happen? Could this inside-out house put you on a different porch, another planet, or a totally different dimension? What would you find there? Something more bizarre than here? Other people? Nobody? Would you be alone & isolated for eternity? Not worth the risk.

* * *

Wicker furniture? The image of a chair leg sticking up in the dumpster flashed through Rick's mind. A set of wicker furniture crushed by the collapsed porch roof. A screened porch. Neither the neighbors nor the house mover had any knowledge of porch furniture. No one noticed the furniture before the porch roof collapsed. The roof collapsed before the fence was built. How could anyone hide furniture in plain sight?

For a moment he let himself doubt that the wicker existed outside the journal. But, no, it was real. He'd seen it. He'd watched Cecil and his helper drag the love seat out of the ruins of the porch.

Did the journal writer put the furniture there? How? Why go to all that trouble? To set the stage for this story? What kind of person would do that?

1/28 **N.** Rhoda is stalking Linda. If Linda gets up to leave a room, Rhoda follows. If Linda cuts through an "outside" door, Rhoda's so close behind I don't know how she can breathe. Linda tells her to stop, but Rhoda persists. Sometimes Linda goes back to her attic when she sees Rhoda. That's the only place Rhoda doesn't follow her. The attic and the bathroom. I wouldn't dream of crowding Linda like that. If the porches want to open for me, they will.

1/28 **M.** I don't know what's come over me. I've always had a healthy sex drive, but this is ridiculous. Julio & I have been going at it like we can't get enough. Just now, he helped me wind the clock. Four weeks. Almost a month. Then he went to the bathroom. That gave me a minute to jot this down.

1/29 **N.** Julio & I made love in my room until the bed was hopelessly messed up, then we went to his room. On the way, we saw Doreen. Julio asked her to join us. Thank heaven she refused! When the clock struck 12 noon, I came back to my room to write this. I think Doreen's with him now. I don't know how a guy can keep going like that. I need to rest once in awhile.

1/29 **M.** I'm sore now. This never happened before, but it's the 1st time I've done a marathon. I need to keep Julio at arm's length until I recover. It's strange how I'm willing to share a guy with another woman. I should want Julio for myself, like I did Wendel, but I know that's impossible. I actually feel guilty about my behavior. It's immoral.

1/30 **N.** I feel out of sorts, irritable. It's not the same as depression. I'm jumpy. If anyone crosses me, I snap at them. I tried playing piano but when I messed up & couldn't get it right, I started crying. I don't understand what's wrong w/ me. I don't think it has anything to do w/ Julio.

1/30 **M.** Now I know why I've been irritable. I took a nap & woke with a pain in my lower abdomen. I didn't recognize what it was until I used the bathroom—I've started my period! I haven't had one since I came here. It must be the clock. I found some tampons & Midol in the bathroom. Where is this taking us? We're certainly changing, coming alive again. Are we doomed to grow old here & die? Then what? What'll we do if someone does die? There's been no change in Hugh. I should be glad the cellar's big enough for all of us, but that's hardly a cheerful thought.

1/31 N. I've been using Scotch for medicinal purposes. You know, I enjoy it more when I don't overdo it. And it does help the cramps. I wonder if the other girls are having periods? Dare I ask? I'm not on such intimate terms with any of them. Come to think of it, I haven't had any close girlfriends since I was a kid. Maybe it was b/c of my mother —I couldn't relate to other women. But I couldn't relate to men, either. There's no point in blaming my mother. It's unproductive. I've always had the option of changing myself. Maybe that's why therapy never worked. I always expected the Dr. to fix me. Now I realize it was my responsibility to fix myself.

* * *

On Thursday, when Rick arrived at the Wilson House, Cecil met him. "When I got here this morning, both of the side doors were unlocked. I know Barry and I locked up last night. I don't know what happened."

"Anything missing?"

"No, and no sign of the doors being jimmied. It's almost like someone used keys."

Keys? There were no keys to the west door and Rick had the only keys to the east door. Someone must have picked the locks. "Maybe I'd better stay in the camper tonight."

Rick went home for his things. His house was quiet and peaceful. He missed Kristie's family but cherished the tranquility. He took the notebooks back to the camper with him.

That evening, before he made his last rounds, he heard a loud argument. It sounded like it came from the other side of the Wilson House, but when he stood in the front yard and tried to pinpoint the direction, he couldn't be sure. He recalled the screaming he'd heard before. Probably the same place.

He made sure all the doors were locked.

1/31 M. Just when I think things are getting better, they get bad again. It started w/ Doreen & Julio fighting & she kicked him out of her room. Somehow I missed that part, but Linda heard Doreen crying & went to comfort her. Doreen told her Julio wanted sex & she didn't. When he tried to talk her into it, she got mad & called him a whore. While Doreen & Linda were talking, Julio went downstairs to Rhoda's room & she obliged him.

Doreen found out & got into it w/ both of them. Then she went into another crying jag that made the ones Linda used to pull look like crocodile tears. Julio tried to apologize but she would have nothing to do w/ him. Rhoda gave Doreen a piece of her mind, & her attitude was so irksome, Julio called her a frigid bitch. Somehow Wendel & Linda got sucked in & they ended up arguing w/ each other. And there I was, trying to calm everyone down. Me, of all people, trying to be the peacemaker! I told them all to just go to their rooms & cool off, but of course that only made things worse. And Louie? On the sidelines, polishing his nails as tho everything was normal while World War III raged around him.

Finally, Linda went down to the cellar to cry to Hugh, Wendel went w/ Julio to his room to smoke pot, & I made Doreen some tea. Imagine me comforting someone! Doreen said she was on her period & didn't want to have sex. Julio didn't care about her period but she did. I made more tea & had a cup myself. Doreen said she's tired of sex all the time, but she's also fed up with Rhoda's shenanigans. Then she stopped talking, sipped her tea, & looked at me over her cup, like she was sizing me up, like she wondered if she could trust me. Now, I'd never given her any reason to trust me. In fact, I'd always given her every reason not to. She took another sip of tea, & said, "You know, what I really want is love, not just sex. I've had crushes on lots of guys but I've never really been in love. I'm not sure Julio's the one I want to be in love w/, but he's the only one here." Then she cried some more & said, "When I find the right man—I guess I should say 'if'—I don't want to share him w/ anyone. I want a man who'll be faithful to me." I nodded. That's what I want, too. I didn't ask where she thought she was going to find this "right man."

After awhile, I told her I just had a period, too. I also told her about my marathon w/ Julio before that, & I was glad I didn't get pregnant, even tho I didn't know if it could happen here. "It would be an awful thing to raise a baby here. Awful for the baby, I mean." She nodded & sipped her tea. Then she said, "I wonder if Julio would use a rubber."

2/1 N. I asked for birth control pills & found a packet on my bedside stand. Just in case! The last thing I need is a kid.

I had another dream. I got out of bed & opened the curtains & windows. It was dark outside, & cool, but I could see the stars! I stood at the window for a long time just looking at them. I'd forgotten how beautiful they are. Then I heard a whip-poor-will in the distance. It must be Spring. I don't remember going back to bed, but later dreamed it was morning & I could see the dogwood blossoms from my bed. When I actually woke up, my curtains were open, but the windows were as blank as always.

I keep thinking about these dreams & the sequence of time. I have no idea how our time here correlates with time "outside." I don't mean the hours of the day & night, which started at the arbitrary moment I wound the clock. I mean whether our 24 hrs here are the same as 24 hrs out there, whether a week here is the same as a week there, & so on. I wonder if they're at all synchronized or if they're so jumbled & out of whack it would give me a headache to think about it. My dreams have followed seasons changing: Spring, Summer, Fall, Winter, & now back to Spring. My first Spring dream came before I wound the clock but I don't know how long before. Now it's been over 4 weeks since I started the clock. A year of seasons in just over a month? Go away, headache!

* * *

Whip-poor-will. That's what Rick had always called those enigmatic birds that herald spring, calling at night from the woods, never seen during the day. Amy tried to set him straight. "It's Chuck Will's Widow," she insisted. "The Whip-poor-will is a different bird." He usually yielded to Amy's knowledge, but in this, he persisted in calling it the name he'd learned in childhood.

2/1 M. Doreen & I had tea again today. Imagine that! Like 2 little old ladies. For all I know, we could be old ladies depending on how time has passed in the outside world. I found a box of herb tea in the kitchen & used the china teapot from the dining room. While it was steeping, I got a cup & saucer that match the teapot. Then I heard Doreen in the parlour & invited her to join me. You know, I actually find myself enjoying her company. Sort of like I enjoyed Wendel's when we were cooking together and Julio's when I play piano for him.

2/2 N. This AM after I played piano for Julio & Doreen, Julio asked if we'd seen Linda & Wendel. Not since yesterday. Now this happens when sleep cycles are different, but at some point you see everyone. It's hard to avoid somebody even when you want to. Julio banged on the attic door & got no response. With a smug smile & raised eyebrow, he said, "Let's not disturb them." Leave it to Julio to assume they weren't just sleeping.

2/2 M. I found out where Linda & Wendel were. This afternoon, I was in the kitchen when the back door opened. In walked Linda, followed by Wendel carrying an armload of collard greens! I had to pick my jaw up off the floor. Linda's face was sunburned but she looked happy. Wendel was ecstatic. "There's a vegetable garden in the backyard," he said. I asked, "You weren't afraid to leave the porch?" Linda answered, "No, because we were together. But we couldn't leave the yard. There's a high board fence." She glanced at Wendel & the smile left his face. I asked what was wrong. They both said, "Nothing."

Doreen & Julio joined us. When Julio heard what happened, he went to the back door, but of course it only opened to the foyer. "What are these? Where did they come from?" A couple of coats were hanging on hooks near the door. Wendel said, "Oh, it was cold outside. I guess it's winter." Julio looked puzzled. "Then, where did the greens come from?" He's from up North. I told him collards grow in winter in Florida.

Wendel sure knows how to fix collards! We made a feast of it. Doreen mixed up a batch of cornbread, Julio & I fixed pork chops, & Linda made mashed potatoes. She must have been pretty hungry b/c she kept chewing on a raw collard leaf. We invited Louie & Rhoda, but all we got out of them was, "What's that awful smell?" I thought everything smelled delicious & I don't know when I've ever tasted anything so good.

Wendel said he was the 1st to find the back porch. He came back in for Linda & she was able to get out w/ him. That's why we didn't see them for a long time. They spent hours on the porch watching the sun set & the stars come out. When they got hungry, they came in. Then they found coats & blankets & spent the night outside. When the sun came up they had the courage to leave the porch & explore the back yard. They snacked on lettuce until Wendel noticed Linda was starting to sunburn. That's when they picked the collards and came in.

Wendel said he can get out to the side porches only when Linda's w/ him. That's weird, but why should it surprise me? This is the House of Weird. The entire time they were on the back porch, the rest of us were going thru those doors to the other end of the house, & Linda & Wendel were unaware of anyone using those doors. It's downright spooky. If they were sitting on the back porch & we were going thru that door, did we walk right thru them? Like they were ghosts? Or like we were ghosts?

* * *

Rick shivered. He recalled his experience a few days ago at The Inn, with the "young lady" on the staircase, and Mrs. Richardson's request to walk on the other side so as to not pass through her.

2/3 N. Linda & Wendel have been outside again. They must have been digging in the garden b/c their hands were dirty. Linda picked bouquets of flowers & put them in vases around the house. When she wasn't looking, Rhoda started to grind them down the garbage disposal! Doreen stopped her & told Linda. Rhoda pretended she was only putting more water in the vase. I suspect Rhoda was as much afraid of Linda's dirty hands as she was of her promised violence. Linda didn't know what kind of flowers they were. She was surprised to see anything blooming in winter. Louie looked down his nose & said the tall ones were snapdragons & the small ones, pansies. He criticized the way Linda put them in the vases & told her she needs to read a book on flower arranging. We told her to ignore him. The flowers look nice. They brighten up the rooms, almost like letting in sunshine. Louie sniffed & went up to his room.

2/3 M. We had mustard greens for supper. Wendel said he learned to cook greens from his grandmother. He uses fat back or bacon. Before they were cooked, Linda kept eating them raw. I tried one, but they're bitter & stringy, much better cooked.

At dinner, we asked them about the fence. They said it's weird. It goes around the back yard & the sides of the house are sealed off by the fence. The only way they can get to the side yards is thru the side doors. There are no gates. Now, who would build a fence like that? Dumb question. Julio asked if they've tried to climb the fence. "Yes," Wendel said. But he wouldn't elaborate.

* * *

That's odd, Rick thought. The privacy fence went all the way around the yard like a normal fence. He'd seen no evidence of interior fencing. He had to laugh himself back to reality. The doors of the house also opened to the outside, like normal doors, not to interior rooms like in the story.

NIGHT STALKER

Rick's sleep that night was disturbed by the sound of someone walking through the yard. He peeked through the camper windows but couldn't see anyone by the light of the street lamps. The first time, he got up and patrolled the yard with his flashlight. Nothing. All the doors to the house remained securely locked. He was relieved when dawn finally came. After his workers arrived, he went home to rest.

When Rick returned to the Wilson House that afternoon, he looked for footprints. Since the men were working mostly inside, it was unlikely any would have been trampled. Among the stubble of grass and weeds, he found nothing. In the southeast corner of the lot, however, was a patch of bare ground. There he found a print—a tennis shoe, a foot smaller than his. Someone *had* been prowling! A woman?

In the middle of the sandy patch, he spotted a light green plant about two feet tall. There was something about it…

Barry was crossing the yard toward his truck. Rick called him over.

"Barry, look at this."

"Yeah?"

"What is this?"

"Why, it's a mustard green."

Rick felt himself go numb. "How do you suppose it got here?"

Barry surveyed the corner of the yard. "Well, it's possible somebody had a garden here once, and a mustard plant went to seed and propagated itself."

Rick frowned. "Does that make any sense? Have you ever heard of the homeless growing a garden?"

"No. You're right. That don't make sense. Probably a bird dropped a seed. Or the wind blew it in."

"Yes, of course," Rick said. But he didn't buy it.

He stood in the yard for some time, idly staring at the stump of the live oak where he'd found the abandoned pothos plant. The mysterious journal writer whom he called "Red" had certainly lived in the Wilson House and possibly penned her story in the turret room. Hidden by the privacy fence, she might have tended a garden. Who was she? Why live in a house with no utilities? Even with the fence, how could she go undetected? For how long? Was she the nighttime intruder? Had she picked the locks? Taken the sledgehammer and brought it back?

That evening, Rick delved into the notebook as though he might find answers:

2/4 N. Rhoda no longer stalks Linda but she's taken to following Wendel unless Linda chases her off. She refuses to eat their vegetables b/c she "doesn't know where they came from." Like she knows where the food in the cupboards & fridge come from? When I go thru an outside door, I close my eyes, hoping I'll end up on a porch. Today, when I went thru the dining room door, before I opened my eyes, I smelled flowers! But it was only Linda's flowers in the parlour. I thought about bringing my hanging plant downstairs. Maybe it'd like some company, but I don't want anything to happen to it.

2/4 M. 5 weeks. Just wound the clock. Today, Louie & Julio had a heated discussion. Louie said, "How can you, of all people, believe in such fantasy?" Julio grabbed a vase of flowers & shook it in Louie's face. "Here's the evidence. And the fresh vegetables, where do you think they came from?" Louie brushed the flowers aside as tho they were an insect. "From the refrigerator, of course." Julio sputtered. "Turnips? With the leaves attached? Dirt still clinging to the roots? Since when did the refrigerator give us vegetables like that?" Louie turned away. "I wouldn't know. I don't touch dirty vegetables."

I asked what was going on. Julio said Louie denies the mere existence of the porches & the garden. I said to Louie, "Don't you believe what Linda & Wendel tell us?" He humphed. "Of course not." Then Rhoda butted in, "They're just lying." My turn to sputter. "What about Linda's sunburn? They're getting out of the house somehow, & if they can, maybe we can, too." Rhoda didn't say any more, but Louie did. "There is no outside." I couldn't believe he said that!

"But things have changed. It started when I wound the clock. Don't you remember?" Louie said, "The clock has always been running." Is he crazy or what? Julio said, "The clock stopped the night we came here." Louie left the parlour, walked past the clock, towards the staircase. "We've always been here." Then he went upstairs. Rhoda followed him like a puppy. I told Julio he scares me. Julio said, "I know."

We had turnips for supper, stewed with the greens. Linda ate a raw turnip like it was an apple. Wendel said they're sweet when they're young like these & gave me a slice. He was right, but I still prefer them cooked. We talked about Louie. Julio said, "He's in full denial. I'm sure there's a psychological diagnosis, but I can't recall what it is." I said, "I thought about reminding him about his life before he came here, but would he listen?" Julio shook his head. "Probably not. If he did, I don't know what it would do to him." Wendel said Louie's always been uptight, so has Rhoda. "But they'll get over it."

2/5 N. It appears we can get sick now. Linda was throwing up in the bathroom. When Wendel went in to help her, he threw up, too. I didn't want to get too close & catch it. I brewed some ginger tea for them. Linda said it helped, but Wendel said he wasn't really sick, just has a weak stomach. I mentioned to Julio about Linda eating raw greens & wondered if that made her sick. "Not unless they weren't washed well enough." After thinking a minute, he added, "I hope they're not bringing germs in from outdoors." I never thought about that. We don't have germs in the house & I thought it would be the same in the yard.

2/5 M. Is there something wrong between Linda & Wendel? Today she turned her nose up at his cooking! Then I caught her chewing on a raw collard leaf again. Louie, Rhoda, & now Linda acting weird—I hope we don't all go crazy. Linda also complains about our cigarette smoke. She said it makes her sick. Wendel quit smoking, but even that doesn't suit her. Rhoda told her it's probably b/c she's getting too much fresh air. I thought Rhoda didn't believe they can go outside.

2/6 N. Is Linda reverting back to being "house bitch"? She keeps complaining. We stopped smoking (even pot) in the public areas of the house & do it in our bedrooms, but she still says she can smell it. There's no way to air the house out. It's not like we can open windows. I wonder if Linda or Wendel could prop open a door? Would it work if none of the rest of us were around? Rhoda had been smoking in her own room until Linda complained. Now just to irritate her, Rhoda smokes out in the open, especially around Linda. I've toyed w/ the idea of quitting. I tried a few times in my former life but never could. Before I wound the clock, there was no point. Now I'm afraid if I quit I'll get fat. On the other hand, I worry about lung cancer.

2/6 M. Today Linda & Wendel came in soaking wet & said it was raining. I got onto Wendel about letting Linda get rained on when she's been sick. He tried to get her to come in, but she wouldn't listen. Linda said the azalea bushes are starting to show buds & a yellow jasmine vine on the fence is blossoming. How I wish I could go out & see them!

I managed to go all day w/out smoking. I asked Linda & Wendel about propping a door open for fresh air & they said they tried. They set a chair in the kitchen doorway, but when they let go of the knob, the door shut by itself and seemed to push the chair right thru the wall. They opened the door & looked in. The chair was back at the table.

When I was a kid, an old man lived next door. Whenever he'd shudder, he'd say a goose just crossed his grave. Well, wherever my grave might be, that goose just crossed it.

2/7 N. Awhile ago, Wendel was listening to music in the lounge w/out Linda. I asked where she was. "Upstairs sleeping." I asked if she was alright. He assured me she was. "Are you sure she's not still sick?" Wendel chuckled. "No, she's quite healthy." I had to ask, "Is there anything wrong between you & her?" From the look he gave me, I wondered if he thought I was coming on to him. "No, of course not. Why should there be?"

I don't see much of Louie lately. Maybe he & Rhoda are holing up in his room. I asked Doreen why she stopped hanging out w/ them. She said she got tired of putting on airs. Occasionally when Louie's not present, Rhoda will hover around like she wants to socialize with the rest of us but something holds her back.

2/7 M. I'm drunk & this is all I'm going to write.

2/8 N. This is what I was too drunk to write about. Yesterday AM Wendel joined me & Doreen for breakfast, again w/out Linda. When Doreen asked where she was, he said she was sleeping. "She sure does sleep a lot," I said. Doreen laughed. "What—do you think Wendel did away w/ her & hid the body in the attic?" An idea came to me: "No, maybe she hopped the fence & left him." Doreen laughed again. "I saw her when you were sleeping. She's still here."

Wendel had this stricken look on his face. Doreen prattled on. "By the way, I've been wondering why you 2 don't climb over the fence. Maybe you could get out of here." Julio had come in for a cup of coffee & said, "Yeah, I wondered about that myself. Maybe you could wish for a ladder." Wendel looked down & mumbled, "It wouldn't help." Julio asked if they'd tried. Wendel nodded. He gulped & said, "The fence looked like it was about 8' tall at 1st. I put Linda on my shoulders to look over it." He stopped. Julio prodded him, "What did she see?" Wendel shook his head. "Nothing. When she got up there, the fence stretched higher. It upset her so much she fell." Julio jumped up as tho to go check on Linda. "She's ok," Wendel said. "The ground's soft. A ladder wouldn't help. There's a live oak tree in the back yard. I climbed it as high as I could, but that fence just seemed to go up & up. I tried digging under it, & prying a board loose." He shook his head. "There's no way out. I try not to think about it. The fresh air & sunshine are enough."

Well, shut me up! I asked what they could see above the fence. "Only the sky." Julio asked, "What about other buildings, trees?" Wendel shrugged his shoulders. "We never hear sounds from outside—no cars, no voices, just the nature sounds inside the fence." I asked what they saw in the sky. "The usual. The sun comes up on one side & down the other. Clouds come & go. Sometimes it rains. At night there are stars, but I don't recognize any of them. We haven't seen the moon."

Julio stammered, "Airplanes?" Wendel shook his head. Doreen asked, "Birds?" Wendel's voice got so low I could barely hear him. "No birds in the sky. There are birds & bugs in the yard but we never see them fly over the fence. Maybe they're trapped here, too." Julio left & went up to his room. I lost my appetite. No wonder Linda sleeps so much. I got a bottle of Scotch.

Here I thought Wendel & Linda had found freedom, but it appears they are as trapped inside the yard as we are in the house. It gives me a headache to try to imagine the sky being turned inside out like this house is.

2/8 M. No change in Hugh. Linda goes down to see him every day & Wendel usually goes w/ her. I check on him from time to time & so does Doreen. Julio has a stethoscope & listens to Hugh's chest, but can't find a heartbeat. If by some miracle we can get out of here, what will we do w/ Hugh? Worry about that when (if) the time comes!

2/9 N. After breakfast, I went to the library & found Julio buried in a thick book. He must not have heard me, b/c when I pulled one off a shelf, he jumped & slapped his book shut. "What are you reading?" I asked. "More science?" He nodded and opened it, thumbing thru to find his place. "Sort of." I leaned over & saw pictures of brain sections. Eeeww! Julio lowered his voice almost to a whisper. "I've been reading medical books. At first I thought maybe I could find something to help Hugh. I haven't yet, but it's all so fascinating! It may never do any real good, but I'm getting pleasure from it." I never imagined Julio studying medicine. I'm proud of him.

2/9 M. Wendel made the best beef stew today. The vegetables all came from the garden—carrots, new potatoes, turnips, English peas, onions. I knew greens grew in Fla in winter, but I didn't know about the other vegs, so I asked him. "Oh, yes. The potatoes need more time to get bigger, but I found enough little ones for the stew. I think it's getting close to spring." Julio asked, "How do you know?" Linda answered him, "Because the peas are ready to eat." I hadn't thought about it before—we could be anywhere in the Universe, but what the dream windows reveal & what Linda & Wendel find in the yard sound like Fla. I tried to tell Louie and Rhoda how "gourmet" the stew tasted, but Louie wouldn't try it so Rhoda didn't either. Wendel's always been a good cook but now he excels. The garden vegetables are going to taste better than anything we find in the fridge.

2/10 N. Linda was chewing on raw turnip greens again. Doreen warned her it'll make her sick, but Linda ignored her. Then she rushed into Rhoda's bathroom to throw up. Doreen said, "I tried to tell her." I'll ask Julio if he can figure out what's wrong with her. Hopefully it's not catchy.

2/10 M. Today, Linda asked if I had any idea of how long we've been here. I only know how long since I started the clock—6 weeks tomorrow. For awhile she was quiet, then asked if she could tell me something & I wouldn't tell the others. I was surprised she'd confide in me, but also felt, well, kind of honored. I promised. She seemed to struggle w/ herself. I couldn't imagine what she was going to say, then when she did, I couldn't have been more surprised.

"When I was 15, I had a baby. My parents made me put it up for adoption. They didn't even tell me if it was a boy or a girl. After it was born, they told me it died, but I had to sign papers anyway. If it died, there was no burial I knew about." She straightened her back & clenched her fists. "They lied to me. Sometimes I think about that baby. I used to look at children the age it would be & wonder what it would look like. If I saw one that looked like me when I was little, I'd wonder if it was mine. I don't know how long we've been here. It might be all grown up by now."

I started to worry about my own mother again. Maybe time has stood still "out there," but maybe it hasn't. If & when we get out, we have no idea what we'll find. Or when.

2/11 N. Sometime during the "night," I went to the bathroom. The door was shut but no one responded when I knocked, so I went in. Linda was bent over the toilet, puking. I waited until she got done & flushed. After she washed her mouth out, she asked if I was sick. I shook my head. "Well," she said, "I hope you don't get what I've got." Then she left. What did she mean by that?

2/11 M. Six weeks! I just wound the clock.

2/12 N. Linda came into my room to talk w/ me again. At first, I thought she had something else confidential to tell me, but what she said could have been discussed in the lounge or kitchen, or wherever. She hopes one day she & Wendel will find a gate in the fence so they can get out. I asked what they'll do then. "Get married, of course." She's never known an interracial couple & knows such marriages are illegal some places. She supposed she'd have to live in the Negro community. Wendel said his family would welcome her, but her family, if they're still alive, would surely disown her. Linda sighed deeply. "Then, there's Hugh. If Wendel & I get out, I'll have to leave Hugh." I reminded her Hugh doesn't need any tending. "I know. But someday he might." I forgot to ask what's wrong with her.

* * *

Rick wondered why Red couldn't see what Linda's problem was. He'd suffered through morning sickness with Amy. She never ate anything as outlandish as raw turnip greens, but with Kyle, she couldn't get enough salads.

From there, his thoughts wandered to interracial marriage. When he was in high school, one of the white boys on his baseball team had a crush on the sister of their Black teammate. The resulting tension between the families, and threats by fellow students and the administration, had caused the Black students to transfer out. Now biracial couples had become so commonplace they barely turned heads. One of Rick's cousins married a Black man and, after the initial shock and anger, the family embraced him.

He glanced at the clock. How long had he been reading?

HARVEY BALRUSH'S SISTER

The night was quiet. The morning showed no footprints or evidence of a break-in.

Bob called. "Hey, I'm meeting with that Smart fellow and Harvey Balrush's sister at two o'clock."

"At Smart's office?"

"Yeah."

"I'll meet you there."

Cheryl Wedgewood looked like an aging hippie. When Rick was introduced, he mumbled, "Sorry about your loss," a phrase he always considered trite, but he couldn't think of anything better.

She and Bob discussed his purchase of the now empty lot. Rick only half listened to the transaction. He watched Jeffrey A. Smart, who had a stopwatch on the desk before him. Charging the bereaved sister by the minute!

Finally, it was his turn. Rick took out his list of questions. "I'm researching the history of the Wilson House. Anything you can tell me might help."

"Harvey had the history of all those houses written down, but I never saw it." She looked at Jeffrey Smart. "Do you have a copy?"

Rick expected the old lawyer to name a price for producing the document. Instead, he said, "No, ma'am. Mr. Balrush never mentioned it."

Mrs. Wedgewood dabbed her eyes with a handkerchief. "It probably got burnt up in the fire."

"Did he ever talk about the houses?"

"I don't remember much except that they were very old and had been empty a long time. Even condemned. I hadn't seen my brother in years and seldom got to talk to him. He wouldn't answer the phone. He'd become such a recluse." A tear escaped the handkerchief. "Harvey was doing well financially until he bought those houses and had them moved. He already owned the lots. I don't know why this one never sold. Harvey once told me it was because people thought it was haunted."

Bob spoke up. "Haunted?"

"Yes. There was a definite presence in there, but it wasn't malevolent, like his house."

"Malevolent?" Rick asked.

Mrs. Wedgewood shuddered. "Yes. I never set foot in his house a second time. After I moved to California, whenever I visited, I stayed in a motel."

"Someone told me Harvey used to have séances."

"That's true. He got into spirituality, but he didn't distinguish between good spirits and bad ones. Our parents tried to make him get help, but he refused. The deeper he went, the more reclusive he got. He sold his business and lived off the proceeds of the sale. My folks tried to Baker Act him, but..." She glared at Jeffrey A. Smart. "Someone put a stop to that. So he never got the help he needed. I was always afraid something bad would happen to Harvey." She tightened her fist around the handkerchief. "And it did."

"You mean the fire?" Rick asked.

"No. Before that. Those spirits sucked Harvey into that house and wouldn't let him leave." She almost sobbed. "I tried to get him to sell everything and come out to California. But he wouldn't."

Bob cleared his throat. "So, you weren't afraid of the spirits in the Wilson House?"

"No."

Rick put his list away. "Let me ask you a few things. Did Harvey ever put furniture in the Wilson House?"

"Well, he was into antiques, buying and selling, that is, when he still interacted with people. Sometimes he stored things in the Wilson House."

"Specifically, do you recall an antique radio, wicker furniture, a piano, or a grandfather clock?"

"I remember a radio, but none of the other stuff. Certainly not a piano. Harvey had a grandfather clock in his house, but it didn't work."

"Do you remember seeing people hanging around the Wilson House?"

"I didn't. Harvey complained about homeless people trying to stay there. And kids. They'd break in, out of curiosity."

"Did Harvey ever describe them?"

"No."

"Did he mention a woman with red hair?"

She shook her head.

Bob stared at him. Rick changed the subject. "Are you planning a memorial service?"

"No. I don't think anyone would come."

I would, Rick thought. He shook the woman's hand. "Thank you for talking with me."

"I'm sorry I couldn't help you more."

Hoping for an uneventful night, Rick stayed in the camper again.

2/12 M. Julio approached me for sex today & I made him wear a rubber. I'm taking B/C pills, but I think they require time to kick in and I'm not taking any chances. He said Doreen makes him wear a one now, too. He doesn't understand why. I told him we don't want to get pregnant. He said nobody's gotten pregnant. I reminded him that things have changed & now we don't know what to expect. Maybe he could look up in his medical books how long you have to take the pills before they start to work. He's been looking up Linda's symptoms & thinks she got a stomach bug that's hard to shake. He hopes it's not dysentery. He makes sure Wendel & Linda wash their vegs & cook them thoroughly.

We were in his room. After we made love, we fell asleep. When we woke, we'd had the same dream—windows open, sun shining, magnolia tree outside, only this time it wasn't blossoming. We could hear birds singing. It's weird. Our dreams were identical, detail for detail. Almost as tho they were real.

2/13 **N.** I had the strangest experience today. That's a curious thing to say. All our experiences here are strange. I was playing the piano, a piece I know by heart. I was lost in the melody & my eyes wandered to the windows behind the piano. All of a sudden I saw light behind the curtains—sunlight! And colors, green & pink! Flowers? I stopped playing & just looked. I was afraid to move. When I finally did, the spell was broken & the windows went dark. I now feel charged with energy & happier than I've ever felt before in my entire life.

I'm wondering—Wendel said it's winter in the back yard, but Linda said there are houseplants on the porches. My landlady always took her plants inside in winter so they wouldn't freeze. I'll ask Linda about this, although nothing about this place should surprise me.

2/13 **M.** I keep looking at windows hoping to see outside. Since Halloween, I'd been avoiding windows b/c what they don't show is so depressing. I'm still trying to cut back on smoking. Some days are better than others.

Linda brought in some yellow jessamine today. They smell so nice. I want to go outside & pick some myself. I asked her about the houseplants. As expected, it doesn't make sense. She said it stays warm on the side porches, almost as warm as inside the house, even tho they're open to the weather. I asked her to tell me more about the yard. She's able to walk around to the side porches from the backyard when she's alone, but Wendel can't go there. When she's alone, the fence abuts the front corners of the house, but when Wendel's with her, it meets the back corners. I told her this sounds like an illusion, but they've gone up to the fence & touched it & it feels solid. She doesn't mind being confined inside the fence. She was never an outdoors person, but now she loves the fresh air. Wendel always swore he wouldn't go into farming, but he really enjoys the garden.

2/14 N. Linda came into my room & laid the bombshell on me—she thinks she's pregnant! She had a period shortly after I started the clock, but hasn't had one since. She used to be as regular as clockwork. Also, she noticed changes in her body & recognized the signs. Having a baby doesn't frighten her, even tho we don't have a dr. here. She had no trouble before, but she worries about raising a child here. Since the baby would be Black, she's equally worried about & raising a mixed baby in the real world. I told her Julio's studying medicine & urged her to tell him about her pregnancy. She said she'd think about it. Afterwards, I tried to talk to Rhoda about the risk of getting pregnant, but she didn't want to hear it. I'll ask Linda to talk to her. I don't want to reveal Linda's secret, but it'll be out eventually. I don't know if Rhoda & Louie even have sex, but she still needs to be warned.

Speaking of Rhoda, I haven't seen Louie lately. Usually they manage to do something irksome every day.

2/14 M. Linda & Wendel spend most of their waking hours outdoors. They say the daytime out there doesn't coincide with the hours of our clock, but that doesn't faze them. Linda brought in some azalea blossoms —pink & white & those pink ones with the dark pink throat. Since the other flowers she brought in haven't faded yet, the place is beginning to look like a florist shop. Rhoda said it reminds her of a funeral parlour. Oh, go suck a lemon. Fortunately, Louie wasn't around to criticize.

Could the rest of us girls go outdoors if we got pregnant? Linda must have been knocked up before she got outside, but getting pregnant just to get out of here would be trading one prison for another. Wendel comes in all sweaty & covered with dirt. He must be working hard, despite the yard & garden taking care of themselves like the house does. He's having fun. He reads gardening books & has lost weight. Garden work benefits him even more than our exercise sessions do.

I asked Linda if there are any dogwood trees in the yard. She hasn't seen any, but she can't get to the front of the house where my windows would be. She said there's a magnolia tree outside Julio's window. Sometimes she sees Julio looking out the window but he doesn't seem to notice her, even if she calls to him. Julio said he dreams about looking out his window but doesn't remember what he sees.

2/15 N. Linda told everyone she's pregnant. Most of us are happy for her. We're also concerned. Rhoda of course is jealous, altho what she'd do with a child is anyone's guess. She'd be a worse mother than me. Julio said he'll study up on obstetrics, just in case. He confided in me that it's really too early for Linda to be sure. I didn't tell him about her other baby. If I were in her shoes I'd be scared to death, but she doesn't seem to be. Louie wasn't around for the big announcement. When did I last see him?

2/15 M. Louie is having a nervous breakdown. Rhoda complained that he wasn't bathing, which everyone thought was strange, but no one wanted to address it w/ him. Today Julio heard Louie crying & went into his room to check. Then Julio called for Wendel's help. Louie was sitting on the floor in his own excrement! The guys took him into the main bathroom to clean him up. Why didn't they use his bathroom? Linda, Doreen, & I went in & found out why. His bathroom was more than filthy. I'm not sure why it hadn't cleaned itself. We thought about cleaning it, but it was so nasty we didn't touch it. We hoped that if we gave it more time it would clean up on its own. One thing we're sure of —Louie can no longer pretend his shit don't stink!

This is the last thing I expected to happen to Louie. He's so persnickety. Nervous breakdown? Ok. But to lose control over his poop—to smear it like that—is the total antithesis of who he is.

Rhoda of course just stayed in her room & didn't lift a finger. After the guys were done w/ Louie they asked her to take him to her room & take care of him. She just stared at them & asked why. "Because he's your man & he needs you." She just sat there, like she didn't have a clue. That's when I realized she has no strength of her own. That's why she'd been clinging to Louie. She knows how to take, but not give. So Doreen & I looked at each other. Neither of us wanted the job.

Finally Julio spoke up, "Ok. I'll take care of him until he's better." He put Louie in his own bed & made himself a pallet on the floor. Louie cried off & on for hours. I made him tea & that helped a little. Wendel made him broccoli quiche but he barely touched it. Doreen gave him some Valium, but he threw up. Julio read his medical books & found a sedative in the bathroom cabinet that didn't make him sick. Julio also gave him a full body massage. Louie finally stopped crying & fell asleep.

2/16 N. Louie's still asleep but Julio assures me he's ok. As much as I don't like Louie, I'd hate to see him end up like Hugh. Fortunately, Louie's room is clean now, but Julio doesn't think he should be alone yet. If Julio needs to go to the bathroom or get something to eat, he'll get one of us to sit with Louie. Even Wendel & Linda take shifts, but Rhoda won't. She stays holed up in her room. We don't need another basket case, so Doreen & I made tea & sandwiches took them in to her. We had a regular little tea party. Afterwards, I swear she looked, well, softer.

2/16 M. Louie wakes up now & then & cries himself back to sleep. We do what we can. Julio keeps trying different treatments. Louie is unshaven, uncombed, unwashed, & wearing rumpled pajamas. What happened to our Sun King? Julio thinks it's better to let him rest than try to groom him. Nobody argued w/ that.

2/17 N. Louie woke up & this time he wasn't crying. Julio said he was getting better even tho he doesn't look it. He ate a little, then he started thrashing around. "I need some coke," he cried, & he didn't mean Coca Cola. He tried to go to his room. "No!" Julio told him. "That's your trouble. You're having withdrawal." But Louie wouldn't listen & actually fought Julio, who had to let him go. Louie turned his room upside down but couldn't find his cocaine. Then he started crying again. Julio brought out his pot & that seemed to help. Then Julio asked me to fix Louie some tea. After he drank it, Louie was calmer, but he kept complaining that he hurt all over. Julio gave him another sedative & put him back in bed.

I asked Julio if he knew what happened to Louie's cocaine, why the house didn't give him more. He was surprised when Louie couldn't find it. I asked, "If he took some, wouldn't that make him feel better?" "Probably, but the cocaine may have caused his breakdown in the 1st place. Or contributed to it. I don't think it's safe for him to keep using it."

Thru all this, Rhoda stayed in bed, so we girls decided to have another tea party. Linda asked Rhoda if she knew what started Louie's problems. "I think it was when he found a gray hair. He was real upset. He's afraid of growing old. Yes, I think that's when it started."

2/17 M. W/ all the excitement over Louie, I hadn't paid much attention to what else was going on. Linda & Wendel had stayed indoors, so I asked if anything was wrong. No, they just thought their help was needed. They did most of the cooking, only going out for more vegetables. I was impressed w/ how Julio took care of Louie. I thought the 2 of them hated each other. But then, I used to hate the others & now Linda & Doreen & I are on good terms. I think Linda & I might even be friends, but I'm not there yet w/ Doreen. I'm not sure I could ever warm up to Rhoda. Also, I don't know how the changes in Louie are going to affect her.

2/18 N. Linda came to my room again. She said sometimes she just needs a woman to talk to. I don't know when I became a soft shoulder, but I actually felt grateful to her for seeing me this way. Can you imagine that? Me grateful? We talked about her & Wendel & the baby & what it would be like to raise one here. "It doesn't seem fair to a child," she said. "I thought about asking Julio if he could do an abortion, but that doesn't feel right, either." I told her it might be better to raise a mixed baby here, where everyone will accept it, than out in the world where people are so prejudiced. She's thought about that. "But somehow, I think it'll all work out. That's what Wendel tells me. You know, he & I have found some real happiness together & maybe our baby will, too." She lowered her voice & said, "But if we ever find a way out, we'll go. That is, if Wendel & I can get out together. If we can, we'll know it's the right thing."

Then she teared up. "But I hate to leave Hugh. I feel so guilty about what I've done to him." I handed her a tissue & said, "As I see it, Hugh

did it to himself. He could have made other choices. The rest of us have."
Were these words coming out of my mouth? "If you & Wendel can get
out, you owe it to your baby to go."

I looked back at what I just wrote. It's so strange. I never really cared
about anyone else, but sometimes I find myself caring about my fellow
housemates. And what's more, I think some of them actually care about
me. That's a new twist. How long it will last? I suppose it could get
worse again, but I hope not. Most of the others have changed for the
better. They are kinder people than they used to be. They used to be so
selfish, no consideration for anyone else. What about me? Am I kinder,
too? Am I becoming considerate? I hope so.

2/18 M. Linda, Wendel, Julio, & Doreen helped me wind the clock. 7
weeks. Rhoda came out of her room & clicked her tongue. Linda glared
at her & she retreated. Louie made himself scarce.

* * *

Rick set the notebook down. Finally, these people were moving forward.
But to where? How would it end? Would they get out? He sat back and
thought about Linda and Wendel and their baby. Back when this story
took place, a white woman with a biracial child was ostracized. Now
days, no one gave them a second look.

He listened. No noise coming from the yard. Maybe that prowler
wouldn't come again. He missed the comfort of his own home. Did he
dare move back?

TOBACCO SMOKE

On Saturday, Bob came by to look at his new lot. Due to construction, the interior of the Wilson House looked worse than the last time he'd seen it, but he said little. At the top of the stairs, he wrinkled his nose. "You let them smoke in here?"

Rick sniffed. He detected a trace of tobacco smoke. "No. Especially when there's paint dust. I guess I need to lay down the law."

Bob shook his head. "I can't stand it."

Rick grinned. Bob was a reformed smoker, more bothered by tobacco smoke than non-smokers like Rick.

Cecil and his helper were the only ones working that day. "Rick, I don't let my men smoke inside, and I haven't noticed anyone else doing it, either. Maybe it drifted in from outdoors."

Rick wanted to spend the night at home, but he decided to stay in the camper again, just in case. Once settled in, he read more:

2/19 N. Doreen asked if Julio has asked me for sex lately. No, he hasn't. "Me, either, not since he started taking care of Louie. I hope he's ok." A thought struck me. "You don't think he & Louie...?" She shook her head. "No, his energies just have a new outlet." I'm not sure if she did anything about diverting his energies but I resolved not to approach him. I've lived w/out sex before & can do it again.

2/19 M. Louie's back in his room. He tells everybody to get out & leave him alone, but Julio ignores him & continues to monitor his health.

2/20 N. Linda & Wendel were all excited. They'd seen Julio at his window & he waved at them. When they came in, he was sleep. After he woke, he said he dreamed he was watching them but he didn't remember interacting w/ them. They asked if he could see beyond the fence. He looked puzzled & said in his dream he only looked down into the yard. When I go to my windows in my dreams, I look at the sky but not down into the yard or across the fence. My windows originally faced the street but I couldn't tell you what's out there now.

2/20 M. When Linda & Wendel were outside today, the rest of us sat in the lounge listening to music. We dragged Louie out of his room to join us. He didn't want to, but we decided he needed company. He still hasn't shaved & he's overdue for a haircut. We didn't intend to gang up on him, but Doreen told him Rhoda said he was afraid of getting old. He broke down & said, "I didn't used to be afraid of it. But I've done nothing with my life." So what? That's true of all of us. "Do you know how old I was going to be on my next birthday? 25!" I couldn't help laughing. I turned 25 on my last B-day, but I survived (I guess). And who knows how old any of us are now?

Julio said, "I know what we can do for Louie. Let's have a birthday party." We've celebrated no holidays the whole non-time we've been here, partly b/c we didn't know when it was but also b/c we didn't feel like celebrating. We party all the time but partying's not the same as celebrating. Julio went on, "If you're going to grow old anyway, you might as well enjoy it." So we made plans. I asked Louie what kind of birthday cake he wanted. Of course, he chose lemon chiffon, the most elegant & difficult to make, but he looked so sheepish, I agreed.

Doreen, w/ Rhoda's help, made a nice Quiche Lorraine. Julio iced some good champagne. Wendel brought in salad greens & Linda picked fresh flowers. We decorated the house & made funny B-day cards about growing old. Most of us came up w/ little gifts & we even found wrapping paper. I played "Happy Birthday" on the piano & we all sang. Louie was much cheered.

Only Rhoda was petulant. "When can I have a birthday party?" She was the last one to deserve a party, so we made no promises but decided to celebrate everyone's birthday in the order in which they come on the calendar, after Louie's. His was Aug 8th. As it turned out, Rhoda's did come next, Sept 10th. We decided not to wait a month to celebrate hers but to give it 24 hours for today's feast to digest.

2/21 N. I asked Rhoda what kind of cake she wanted. "Angel food," she said. Altho she's certainly no angel, I told her I'd make it. I had 2nd thoughts when the recipe called for 12 egg whites! Linda & Doreen promised to help me beat them. To everyone's surprise, when we asked what else she wanted for dinner, she broke down crying & asked Louie to choose for her. Louie requested standing rib roast.

2/21 M. For Rhoda's birthday, I baked, Wendel cooked, & Louie chose the wine. Wendel had never fixed standing rib roast before, but I found a recipe in one of my cook books & it turned out well. Even Louie liked it. Wendel added kale from his garden, cooked with bacon fat & served with cornbread. At dinner Rhoda astonished all of us by going for Wendel's soul food with gusto & barely touching the meat. She won't admit she's been starved for vegetables. When gifts were opened, she broke into tears over each one. You see, we each gave her little things of our own that she'd coveted. I gave her that necklace she'd taken from me a long non-time ago. We asked what was wrong, b/c we thought we'd failed to please her. She said she didn't know anyone cared about her. Actually, I don't really care about her, but I didn't say so. I was tired of the necklace. She seemed really touched, more by our gestures than by the things themselves. She seemed so genuinely grateful, I had tears in my eyes, too.

2/22 N. The next B-day is Julio's, Nov 30th, so he gets the next party. Wendel asked if we wanted to celebrate Halloween but everyone said, "No way!" Then we discussed other holidays. He said, "Why don't we celebrate B-days for now, then other holidays as they come according to the calendar." Everyone agreed. It's going to be a long time before Xmas.

While we were planning Julio's party, we heard Rhoda crying in her room & decided to put his off for another day, to let yesterday's ribs and cake settle.

2/22 **M.** How could I have been so obtuse? Linda & even Doreen said they'd seen it coming. Rhoda has been bawling every waking moment since her party. She's refused valium, tranks, even pot or booze. She said she needs to work thru this on her own. This is the 1st time I've seen any modicum of strength in her. She's like a little paper doll. Louie had been propping her up for so long, when he fell apart, she crumpled. I'd always seen her as a mean, conniving, avaricious little bitch. Now I know she's very needy. I may actually feel sorry for her. Doreen's been tending to her b/c Julio still has his hands full w/ Louie. When Doreen needs a break she calls me or Linda. On my shift I made Rhoda some tea. I didn't know what to do about the crying but Doreen & Julio both say to just keep giving her tissues. Poor thing, her eyes & nose are raw from wiping them so much. I remembered Louie has some nice handkerchiefs, so I asked for them. They're softer on her nose. He still has his crying jags, too, & sleeps after each one. He'll curl up in a fetal position & talk to himself. Julio has to make him bathe. What's happening to us? Are we all falling apart? All except Linda & Wendel. They spend most of their time outdoors. Maybe that's what we all need. Fresh Air.

* * *

Rick's phone rang early Sunday morning. It was Kristie. "Why don't you join us for church today, then come to our house for dinner?"

A home-cooked meal sounded good. "I'll meet you at the church."

Sitting in the pew with Sandy and Michael, Rick noticed a red mop of hair several rows in front of him. He couldn't explain the welter of emotions that stormed through him. When the congregation stood for a hymn, he tried to get a better look. Yes, it was a woman. Was she wearing glasses? His stomach quivered. He couldn't concentrate on the sermon.

When the service concluded, their exit from the pew was delayed by Michael's having to tie his shoe. Rick watched the congregants file by, the redhead among them. She was young, maybe eighteen, and no glasses. Rick relaxed. The journal writer claimed to be twenty five when she wrote it. Of course, that might not be true, but the innocent face passing in front of him could hardly have imagined, no less suffered, the tribulations that beset Red of the notebooks.

Rick followed Kristie's family home. Sandy opened the door for him. "Grandpa, I just love our new house."

"I'm glad. My house is a little lonely now with you all gone."

"You can come see us any time."

"Thanks."

At dinner, Kristie looked troubled. "What's wrong?" Rick asked.

"Oh, I'm probably just overreacting. The faculty lounge is abuzz about that new virus out of China. Two years ago, we had a really bad flu season. Half the staff and half the students were out sick. I didn't catch it, thank goodness, but Michael did. The school board was worried enough to supply everyone with masks. I just hate to see another flu season like that."

Kristie sent Rick home with a plate of leftovers. He warmed them and ate before he returned to the camper.

2/23 N. We're back on track w/ Julio's B-day. True to character, he requested the most sensual cake I know of, fudge w/ chocolate frosting. At least it's easy to make. He also wants a big steak w/ all the trimmings. Wendel, Linda, & I can handle it. Louie & Rhoda are better but Julio & Doreen are still tending to them.

2/23 M. Julio's party was a success. To everyone's relief, Louie & Rhoda perked up for it. Julio thought we should have a dance, so we brought the record player downstairs. It was so much fun. I don't know why we didn't think about this before. Louie taught the others some ballroom dancing & we got him to try disco, then we all regressed to rock 'n roll & those crazy dances from the 60's. Louie sure looked funny doing the Monkey. Sometimes I wonder what has changed in the outside world. If we ever get out, will we find that everything we thought was hip has become old fashioned? That we're just a bunch of old fuddy-duddies?

2/24 N. When I 1st started this journal, I hoped that writing things down would make me feel better. You know, it finally worked. I do feel better. The past doesn't bother me as much as it used to. I find myself feeling hopeful for the future, altho logic would tell me that there's no future here. Does logic apply here? This whole experience is totally illogical! We've decided a birthday party every day is too much. Having a day between Rhoda's & Julio's was better. The elevated spirits from Julio's party have lingered & we're looking forward to Linda's party tomorrow. Her birthday is January 12th. "Looking forward to." Now, that's a new experience for me.

Another new experience is sewing. Doreen is secretly working on a baby blanket for Linda, a little patchwork quilt. A sewing machine turned up in her room but it makes so much noise she doesn't use it unless Linda's outdoors, so she has to do a lot of it by hand. She let me watch & even let me do some of the quilting stitches. I don't have the skill she has.

2/24 M. Strange things happening. Linda & Wendel were absent for hours, then they came in through the front door! I thought they'd just cut thru from the kitchen, but Wendel had a basket of vegs & Linda had another bouquet of flowers, a variety I hadn't seen before. L & W were guardedly ecstatic. "We can both get all the way around the house," Wendel said. "Even the front yard," Linda added. "But there are no gates, so we still can't get out."

Can't get out? They can go outside & see sunshine & stars & rain. That would be enough for me. I asked them if there's a dogwood tree in the front yard. "Yes, right in front of your windows. And it's in full bloom."

So it's real, not just a dream. When I'm dreaming, are my windows really open? Am I seeing things that are really out there? "How tall is it?" I asked. "Could I see it from my room?" Linda smiled. "Yes, it reaches your windows."

* * *

The dogwood tree! It couldn't have been there when the house was moved. It must have sprouted from seed afterward. When was this journal written? The spiral notebooks were manufactured in the sixties or seventies, when the tree would have been a sapling. Did the author write this in recent years on old notebooks? Why? She seemed to capture the spirit of the 70's, as though living the era, without coloring it through the lens of nostalgia. What was at work here? He longed to ask her.

2/25 **N.** Today we celebrate Linda's birthday. When I asked what kind of cake she wanted, she said, "Just an ordinary cake." I suggested a basic 2 egg cake. "That would be fine. I like anything you make." So now it's cooling in the kitchen, waiting for icing & candles.

2/25 **M.** For Linda's party, Wendel prepared a delicious beef stew w/ lots of vegetables, served over rice, the way his grandmother always fixed it. We brought the record player down again & decided to leave it there for the time being instead of hauling it up & down. I also played Happy B-day & a few other songs. Doreen gave Linda the baby blanket & she was ecstatic.

After the party, everyone stayed up until midnight to help me wind the clock. 8 weeks. So much has happened. I can't believe the transformations I've witnessed in such a short period of time. We've all changed for the better, except Hugh. When I glance at my earlier notebooks I hardly recognize the person speaking from those pages.

2/26 **N.** This AM, Linda confided to me, "If we find a gate in the fence & can get thru, we're leaving. But I hope it's not before Wendel's birthday. We'd like you to make his cake." I asked what he'd like. She thought a minute & laughed, "Marble cake. Black & white together. That's the kind of baby we're going to have. He'll get a kick out of that."

Then Linda got quiet. "Will you promise me one thing? Will you take care of Hugh for me?" I said I would, even tho Hugh doesn't need much.

"Someday, if you get out, will you try to take him with you?" Did she realize what she was asking? How could I haul that lump of comatose flesh out of here? I couldn't get him up the cellar stairs! Yet my heart went out to her. "Yes, I'll do all I can for him." Of course, that's IF I can get out. And if I WANT to leave.

YOUNG WENDELL

Monday, Rick decided he needed a few more bits of information from the archives. From there, he went to the library to return his books. He ran into the young man from the science fiction section. The youth asked, "Did you ever find the title or author of that book you were looking for?"

Rick shook his head. "No. Have you come across anything like it?"

"Not yet. I'll keep reading. Maybe it'll turn up."

Rick crossed the plaza to the county administration building. As he passed the bus stop, a heavy set, dark-haired white woman sat on a bench with a little pecan-brown girl beside her. He didn't give them a second thought until a bus pulled up and the woman called, "Wendell, our bus is here." Rick spun in his tracks.

"Coming, Mama." A boy of the same complexion, a little older than the girl, ran to join them. Rick resisted the urge to shout to the woman, to say he wanted to talk to her. Before he could reach them, the family boarded the bus and it pulled away. What would he have said? If he told her why they caught his attention, she would think he was crazy. He sat on a bench to sort out his thoughts.

Were Wendel and Linda real people? But the story took place in the seventies. Linda and Wendel, if they were real, would be grandparents by now. It must be a coincidence. Yet Virgil had been a real person. So had Louie/Calvin. No, this little Wendell was only a coincidence. Had to be. Rick tried to dismiss the event from his mind.

2/26 M. Rhoda continues to cry off & on. She usually goes to her room for her crying jags, but today when I sat down at the piano, it sounded like she was on other side of the parlour door. Was she in the dining room? I went thru the doorway but she wasn't there. I could still hear her & now it sounded like she was in the parlour. I crossed the house. No Rhoda in the parlour, but I could hear her behind that door. I checked her room just to be sure my ears weren't playing tricks, but she wasn't there. Doreen came in & heard the same thing. It was eerie. Was Rhoda trapped between walls? That would be an ugly turn to the weirdness of this house.

We found Wendel in the kitchen & asked him to try the doors. He went out the dining room door & came back in. Then he went out the parlour door & returned, leading Rhoda! I was so relieved I hugged her. She was still crying, but also smiling. "I was on the porch," she said. "Do you mind if I go back out? I'm ok. Really. I am." Of course we let her go. I stood by her when she opened the door, but saw no porch, only dining room.

"I envy her," Doreen said. "I wish I could get outside. But I'm glad she can." I was surprised. I'd never known Doreen to be truly happy for Rhoda before.

2/27 N. Doreen's birthday. February 10th. She wants sponge cake. "You always were a sponge," Rhoda quipped. Doreen threw something at her, but it was all in fun. She wants fried fish & hush puppies. Wendel said he'd fix them. There's a cabbage in the garden, so Linda will fix coleslaw. I've been practicing dance music on the piano to give us a little more variety.

2/27 M. We had a good time at Doreen's party. Wendel's fish fry was a success & Doreen loved her cake. We danced to the piano. Rather, they danced to the piano. I had fun watching them. They were very forgiving of my mistakes.

2/28 N. Rhoda can get out to the parlour-side porch but not the others. She's afraid to step off into the yard. Why has she been given this privilege & not someone more worthy? I understand about Linda & Wendel. They've both made such personal progress. And then there's the baby.

We still have our daily exercise class & now that the record player is in the parlour we exercise to music. Doreen is trying to teach me to sew. You'd think someone who could play the piano could sew, but I fumble all over. Thank goodness she's patient.

2/28 M. I was in the kitchen getting something to drink when someone came down the back stairs—Louie! He used to be too stuck up to use those stairs. He must have noticed the look on my face b/c he grinned. He's starting to look like an aging hippie—hair shaggy & curly & he's growing a beard. But he stays clean & well-manicured, so I know he feels better. He seems calmer & smiles a lot, a real smile, not that old wrinkled-nose-just-turned-up-at-the-corners-of-his-mouth smile. He's given up drugs, except for a little pot or wine. Julio read up on drugs & convinced Louie that cocaine was addictive & hard on the heart. Julio said he didn't find any evidence that pot or LSD were addictive, but there wasn't enough information on the long term effects of acid, & with pot you're inhaling smoke, which can't be good. I see all kinds of positive changes in my friends (Friends!) but I seem to be lagging behind. I don't drink like I used to, but I can't seem to quit cigs.

3/1 N. I decided to let Feb have only 28 days. Wendel's B-day is March 18th. I asked Linda to keep him outside while I made his cake so it could be a surprise. He wants BBQ ribs w/ sweet potatoes for dinner. Julio said he'd cook. I asked Linda if there were any sweet potatoes in the garden. No. I forgot they grow in summer & it's late winter out there. Hopefully we'll find some in the fridge.

3/1 M. We've passed a milestone—sixty days. About 2 months. It seems like an eternity, but the eternity we spent before I 1st wound the clock now seems to have been no time at all. Maybe that's why I called it "non-time."

Wendel was pleased w/ my cake. He'd never seen a marble cake before. "It does look like a marble," he said after it was cut & he saw the chocolate & white swirled together. I'd even iced the cake w/ swirls of chocolate & vanilla frostings. Louie gave him a box of expensive chocolates. Wendel's eyes popped out when he tasted one. Then he shared them with everyone. "I'll get you another box," Louie offered. "No thanks." Wendel patted his now slimmer belly & said, "I shouldn't overindulge." All those vegetables must be going to his brain.

Rhoda's proposed gift was to give the study back to him & Linda. "It'll be a wedding present, too," she said. "Now that I can go outside, I wouldn't mind staying in the attic." Linda & Wendel thought it over & graciously declined. "We can go outside, too, & we're all settled in the attic." Linda didn't want to move back in there b/c she'd shared the room with Hugh. Rhoda settled for giving Wendel that painting in her room. Unfortunately they couldn't find a good way to hang it in the attic, so they hung it in the upstairs lounge where everyone can enjoy it.

3/2 N. Rhoda came in while I was playing piano. I told her I appreciated what she tried to do for Wendel & Linda. "It's the least I could do. I've been so mean to them. To everyone." Then she started crying. Here we go again, I thought. But she didn't go into it like I was afraid she would. She said, "I'm sorry, for being so mean to you. You didn't really deserve it." Actually I did deserve it. I apologized for being mean to her, too. We hugged like sisters. Then she stepped toward the door & said, "I wish I could take you w/ me but I don't think I can. It'll happen for you, too, in time."

3/2 M. Doreen's still giving me sewing lessons. I doubt I'll ever be as good as her. She used to make all her clothes, except jeans. She made a pair once, but it was so much trouble she went back to buying them.

3/3 N. We'll celebrate my B-day today. I wonder how old I really am. How much non-time passed before I wound the clock? When I look in the mirror it's the same face I've always seen. I'm not about to bake my own cake, so Doreen & Rhoda said they would. When they asked what I want for dinner, I told them to surprise me.

3/3 M. The girls apologized b/c the cake was from a box, not as good as my scratch cakes, but it's the thought that counts. Julio & Louie cooked hamburgers & French fries. Wendel & Linda made a delicious salad. I hadn't had a burger & fries since we came here. I was so touched by their kindness & attention, I cried. I should be cheerful, yet for some reason I feel depressed. But I'm not going to ask Julio for a pill. I put some rum in my coke at dinner & thought about getting drunk, but that no longer appeals to me.

3/4 **N.** I feel better than last night, but I still don't know where to go from here. We have one B-day left, Hugh's. How are we going to celebrate it?

3/4 **M.** Tonight I had help winding the clock, except for Linda & Wendel. They must have been outside. 9 weeks. I'm amazed every time I think about all that's happened since I started the clock, more than you'd expect in such a short period of time. Instead of things plodding on, developing one at a time in a linear pattern, it's like everything burst out in many directions at once.

3/5 **N.** Rhoda can get out to all 4 sides of the house. She's afraid to step off the porches, but she enjoys the fresh air & flowers. She doesn't see a gate anywhere. Lately, she's been cheerful, almost bubbly. I never imagined this side of her. She keeps telling the rest of us she wishes she could take us out with her. She did try to take Doreen. Doreen closed her eyes and Rhoda took her by the hand & led her thru the parlour door. But when she shut the door, Doreen was in the dining room & Rhoda wasn't! I heard Doreen crying & went to see what was wrong. Rhoda came in the parlour door & over to the dining room. Doreen wailed, "Why did you let go of me?" Rhoda shook her head. "I didn't. You were on the porch w/ me. Why'd you go back inside?" Just when I think I'm used to the weirdness of this place, it gets more bizarre. I'm not going to let anyone try to take me out to any porch.

3/5 **M.** I asked Rhoda if she's pregnant. Her eyes got wide & she said, "No way!" Then she whispered, "Louie & I haven't been sleeping together." So that's not how to get outside. But why her of all people? She was the most closed in, next to Louie. And she was the most mean & selfish. Even worse than me. It's true she's changed, but I would have expected Doreen, or at least Julio, to get out before her. I must stop being catty.

Julio says he still dreams about his window being open. Doreen said she spent the night with him recently & they had that same dream.

3/6 **N.** Hugh's birthday, June 8th. He's the last one on the list. Even tho he's not conscious, we thought we should celebrate. I'm all baked out so I made him a simple 1-bowl cake, not up to my usual standards. I hope he doesn't mind. I'm sure he won't even notice.

3/6 **M.** We put together some finger foods & went down to the cellar to sing Happy Birthday to Hugh, then we ate and went back upstairs. Linda cried the whole time we were down there. When we sang to Hugh, I imagined I saw a faint smile on his face. I didn't mention this to anyone. If he did smile, Linda didn't notice.

3/7 **N.** Linda & Wendel were acting strange this AM, almost furtive. They brought in several baskets of vegs, more than the 8 of us could possibly eat in a week. They cooked some, froze some, & prepared the rest for cooking. When the refrigerator was as full as it could get, they went up to their attic. With no explanation.

3/7 **M.** There's hope for us. When I took a nap today, I had a dream. Thru my open windows, I could hear the front door open & close. After I woke, I went downstairs & found an envelope lying on the floor under the mail slot. It was in Linda's handwriting, addressed to all of us. After I stopped crying, I called for the others.

* * *

Rick found a folded sheet of paper between the pages. The handwriting was different from that of the journal.

Dear Friends,

The morning after Hugh's party, we found a gate in the front yard. We haven't opened it yet. First, we wanted to tie up any loose ends here. We stocked up on vegetables for you all just in case it's awhile before you can get out to pick more. We're packing a few clothes and mementoes, just what we can carry. If you can't find us, it'll mean we've been able to get out. You all can have anything we left behind. We're sorry we didn't say a proper goodbye, but we worried about the gate disappearing. Please take care of Hugh. I hope he wakes up and all of you can get out. Be happy for us. All of you have been such good friends and we appreciate everything. Maybe we'll meet again on the outside. Until then, we wish you the best of luck.

   Love, Linda and Wendel

Rick leaned back with a grin. *They got out of the house!*

He thought again about the woman at the bus stop with the biracial boy named Wendell. This story was getting a little too weird. He looked at the handwriting on the note again. Definitely not the same as in the journal. Why did the writer go to the trouble of penning it in a different hand? He folded the note, replaced it in the journal, and started to put it away, but he wasn't sleepy, so he continued reading:

3/8 N. I'm a little miffed at Linda & Wendel for not telling us they were leaving, & we're all saddened by their departure. We hadn't realized how that budding little family had lifted our spirits. I hope they're faring well out there. We all talk about getting out, but most of us have reservations. Will we find the same world we left? But when? How much time, if any, has passed? Will we find ourselves in G'ville or somewhere else? Will I ever see my mother again? Despite misgivings, I'm happy for Linda & Wendel.

3/8 M. I dreamed about my windows again. They were open but the curtains were closed. It was dark outside & the wind was blowing. I could feel the breeze, it made the curtains billow. In my dream, when I got up to open the curtains, the windows went blank again. I don't know what that means. The dreams about my windows usually cheer me up, but this one was disconcerting. I miss our birthday parties. No one is up to holiday celebrations yet. We'll have to think of something else to do. Maybe farewell parties? I miss Linda & Wendel.

3/9 N. Yesterday when I checked on Hugh, he was as comatose as ever, but it seemed like he'd lost a little weight. This morning, I thought I saw his chest move. I put my hand by his nose—miracles of miracles—he was breathing! I ran up & got Julio. He brought down his stethoscope & heard a heartbeat! By now the others had descended to the cellar & we were whispering like we were afraid to wake him. We decided to take turns sitting with him.

3/9 M. This afternoon, Hugh wet himself. The guys helped me pull off his wet pants & change his bedding. When we moved him, he made grunting noises. Instead of dressing him, I covered his pallet w/ plastic wrap & towels. We thought about taking him upstairs, but if he's lost weight, it's not much.

3/10 N. This morning, Hugh opened his eyes. He tried to talk but his mouth was dry. I went up to the kitchen for a glass of water & yelled up the back stairs, "Hugh's awake!" Scrambling & door-slamming. Rhoda got there first. We helped Hugh sit up & sip water. After everyone saw for themselves that he really was awake, they began making Rip Van Winkle jokes. Julio brought a damp wash cloth & wiped his face. Once his eyes cleared & he had his glasses on, he glanced around & whispered, "Where's Linda?" We all looked at one another, thinking, "What should we tell him?" Doreen came to our rescue, "She's outside. She was able to get out of the house." Hugh smiled slightly & said, "Good." The guys helped him get dressed while Doreen & I changed his bedding.

3/10 M. We haven't left Hugh alone. We take turns sitting w/ him. After we changed his bed, he lay down for awhile, then said he was hungry. Louie sliced up fruit & I made chicken soup. While it was cooking, Rhoda went to her room & stayed there. I was a little peeved that she wasn't helping. When the soup was ready, Julio helped me prop Hugh up against the wall so he could eat. I could hear the others climbing up & down stairs but didn't think much about it. After he ate, Hugh had to use the bathroom. He couldn't stand up yet or walk, so we brought down a stock pot & the guys supported him so he could use it. I let them empty it.

3/11 N. I've never seen anyone recover strength so quickly. Julio spent the night w/ Hugh. He ate more soup & leftovers. Afterward, he was able to sit up w/out support, then he could stand, with support. Julio & Louie helped him climb the steps to the kitchen. Of course, that took all his strength & he got no further than the table, but that's ok. We ate breakfast together. Everyone cooked something: eggs, biscuits, sausage, fruit, hash browns. It was even better than a B-day party.

Hugh asked again about Linda. Right then, the clock struck & he about jumped out of his skin. I explained about winding it & starting time. He didn't mention Linda again. After breakfast, he was able to use the bathroom w/ only a little help from the guys. They took him to Rhoda's bathroom, of course, so he wouldn't have to climb upstairs. I followed them &, to my surprise, it wasn't Rhoda's room anymore—it was Hugh's again. That's what was going on all day yesterday. Rhoda moved out & the room had been given a more masculine touch. Rhoda grinned like she was the one who got a new room. She had moved to the attic. "It's ok," she said. "I can go outside now."

3/11 M. Clock winding time. 10 weeks. We told Hugh about Linda & Wendel. For some reason, he didn't seem surprised. He was sad about losing her, of course, but he showed no resentment. We told him we thought he was dead & that if he was only in a coma, we didn't know if he would ever recover. We said he'd been like that a long time before I wound the clock & over 2 months afterward. He didn't blame Linda. "She was right to move on. It wouldn't have done either of us any good for her to stay w/ me if I was like that." We told him Linda checked on him every day & made sure he was comfortable. He just nodded.

3/12 N. We decided to have a "Welcome Back" celebration for Hugh. I felt a little guilty about the sorry birthday cake, so I went to the trouble to bake a carrot cake. Doreen & Rhoda grated carrots for me. Louie & the other girls are fixing party food. When we were 1st here, we got tired of party food & eventually it went away. Now I'm looking forward to some. The record player's still in the parlour & Hugh's in there listening to music. Maybe we'll dance, if Hugh's up to it.

3/12 M. The party was a success. Hugh seemed stronger afterward & felt like talking. He told us about the dreams he had while lying in the cellar. This is what he told us:

"I dreamed I was lying on the ground under a house. I couldn't move. I couldn't even open my eyes, yet somehow I was aware of my surroundings. The house sat on concrete block pillars & there were floor joists above me. And a funny thing, there were a few steps, like the ones to our cellar, going up to a door. But I wasn't in a cellar. I was on the ground."

* * *

Rick's stomach seized into a knot.

"Sometimes I was cold, or wet, but it didn't bother me a whole lot. There was nothing I could do about it, anyway. I was aware of day & night. Sometimes I could hear it rain, or the wind would blow under the house. There were cockroaches & spiders, but I don't think they crawled on me. Also animals. Snakes & rats & frogs, sometimes squirrels. Once, a raccoon.

"Out beyond the foundation, there was grass & bushes & flowers & sometimes the leaves would fall & frost would kill the grass & flowers. I didn't really see these things, but I was aware of them. I don't know how many seasons went by. A lot of them. They just ran on & on. Sometimes I could hear people walking on the floor above me. I could hear music, people talking or arguing, sometimes singing.

"Then I started hearing Linda's voice out in the yard. She seemed to be talking to herself, or to the squirrels or the birds. Then she'd sing. I almost felt happy. Then Wendel was there w/ her. I heard them talking about a baby & getting married." He looked sad for a moment. "That's why I wasn't very surprised when you told me they were together. Sometimes they talked about me like I was dead, & they were sad for me. I wanted to call out to them, to tell them I wasn't dead, but I couldn't. Then one day I heard them go down the front steps & say goodbye to everybody. I heard a gate open & shut, & that's the last time I heard them."

That's what Hugh told us. I asked him if he dreamed about Linda talking to him in the cellar & the rest of us checking on him. He shook his head. He thought he heard us sing Happy Birthday, but it seemed to come from the floor above him. He wasn't aware of anyone coming down to where he was. I don't know why he dreamed about lying under the house & not in the cellar. It doesn't make much sense.

* * *

Rick closed the notebook without marking his place. It's only a story, he told himself. The writer knew there was no cellar after the house was moved. Her character Hugh wouldn't have known that. It's silly to get so deeply involved in a work of fiction.

He left the camper and drove to the safety of his own house. He didn't think he could spend another night at the Wilson House.

To his surprise, he'd brought the notebooks with him. Crossing the room to his file cabinet, he put them in the very back of the bottom drawer and caught himself locking the cabinet. He shook his head. *Do I think they're going to jump out and attack me while I sleep?*

DENIAL

In the morning, Rick called Kyle, "I think I'll bring your camper back. I'm not going to stay in it anymore."

"Sure. Do you need any help?"

"Naw. I can handle it."

Rick made a to-do list long enough to keep him too busy to think about the notebooks. After paying some bills, he drove over to the Wilson House.

So many crews were at work, Rick could barely find room to park. He had to ask Derek Crawford to move his equipment so he could hitch up Kyle's camper and tow it away. Once he'd parked it at Kyle's and transferred his belongings to his truck, he paused to consider, "Now what?"

The Wilson House was too full of activity and dust to use for office space, so he took his files home. He had to unlock the file cabinet to put his paperwork away. From the bottom drawer, he felt the lure of the notebooks, but he resisted. "I've wasted enough time with that nonsense," he said aloud. "I need to just give them to Bob." With that resolution, he was able to get on with his day.

The weather was fine enough to do yard work, mostly cleaning up debris from storms. As he dragged branches to the brush pile, he crossed the sunny open area between his patio and the tree line. Before Amy got sick, they'd thought about putting in a vegetable garden. This would be a good time to do it. She'd approve of his doing something healthy. He thought of the mustard plant at the Wilson House. No, on second thought, he wanted nothing to do with vegetable gardens.

That evening, the silence of his house weighed on his spirit. He locked his file cabinet before he went to bed.

On Tuesday, Rick drove to a salvage store in Lake City. There he found a vintage door for the east porch and some period light fixtures. He didn't return to the Wilson House until late afternoon. If the workers were gone by then, he was prepared to wait until the next day to take his purchases inside. To his relief, Cecil was still there. As he drove home, he chided himself. Cecil showed no fear of being alone in the house.

That night, when he filed his receipts, Rick thought about the notebooks. *I'll take them to Bob tomorrow.* He retrieved them from the bottom drawer and put them in his truck.

Bob's receptionist said he was out of town. Rick thought of leaving the notebooks with her, but he wanted to put them in Bob's hands.

They weighed on Rick's mind all day. He tried to remember what had frightened him—because Hugh had been lying on the ground under the house and not in the cellar? The writer had a good imagination. *Maybe I'm under too much stress.* But what was stressful in his life? Kristie's family had moved out, the Balrush issue had been settled, and things were moving smoothly.

When he got home, he absentmindedly carried the notebooks back into the house. He fixed a generous roast beef sandwich and opened a bottle of beer. Then he settled into his chair and reached for the remote. Channel surfing brought no satisfaction. The news obsessed about that new virus in China and he found no entertainment to suit his mood. When he got up to stretch his legs, he spotted the notebooks on the corner of his desk. "What the hell!" He shook his head. "I might as well find out what happens next."

3/13 N. Whatever happened to the Hugh I knew? The guy who just sat around doing nothing? This new fellow helps cook & tidy up & even makes his own bed! He has to rest frequently, but then he gets up & moves around again.

3/13 **M.** Rhoda came in w/ a bunch of carrots for supper. She finally got the courage to step off the porch & can walk around the house. All the way around. But she found no gate, only the high wood fence. I asked if she could see or hear beyond the fence. No. It's as tho the house is in a bubble. I think about Linda & Wendel & wonder how they're doing, what they found when they got out. I hope they're ok.

3/14 **N.** We decided to move the record player back upstairs. It bothered me when someone wanted to play records while I was practicing piano. Hugh continues to do well & gains strength & stamina by the hour. He doesn't sleep much, mostly cat naps. He said he's slept enough to last several lifetimes. Julio's been studying him as tho he's a medical phenomenon. I guess he is.

3/14 **M.** Rhoda was able to take Louie outside! He came in with dirt up to his elbows & the nicest red potatoes I've ever seen. Doreen refuses to let Rhoda try to take her out again. No one else has asked her to, either. Julio's too preoccupied, Hugh is basking in his new-found wakefulness, & frankly, the thought of it scares the hell out of me. This inside-out house took a lot of getting used to & I'm not ready for one that turns itself right-side-out at whim. And leaves the rest of the world inside out. Or something like that.

Rhoda convinced Louie to give it a try. She took his hand, he closed his eyes, & they got out the back door & down the porch steps. Rhoda said the moment Louie set foot on the ground, he started shaking. She was afraid he was having a convulsion. He couldn't talk. He went down on his hands & knees, put his face to the ground, & actually kissed it! Then he sat on the lawn, looked at the grass stains on his clothes, & laughed.

He said he'd never seen anything so beautiful. But he couldn't get around the house. He saw fences sealing off the backyard even tho Rhoda, standing right beside him, didn't. She wanted to lead him thru the fence, but he said he was satisfied w/ what he had. Then he saw the garden, went over, & started picking things & eating them raw. Rhoda didn't know what a potato plant looks like, but Louie does. He pulled one up & some nice potatoes came up w/ it. Then he dug w/ his hands to get the rest out of the ground. His nails were full of dirt and one of his nicely manicured nails was torn off. He actually laughed & said it'll grow back. I can't believe the change in him.

3/15 N. I dreamed my windows were open & it was a beautiful spring day. The dogwood was in full bloom. I got out of bed, went to the window, looked down into the yard, & saw azaleas blooming! In the middle of the lawn was a swing. In my dream, I went downstairs, out the front door, & sat on the swing for the longest time, w/ the sun on my face.

Now that I'm thinking about it, when I looked out my window, I didn't look past the fence to see what was there. I can't say exactly where the swing was or what it was suspended from, a tree or frame or the sky bubble, if anything. Linda said there was a swing on the dining room porch, but that would be in the shade. Anyway, it was a pleasant dream. Now that I think about it, in my dream it was early spring, but Rhoda & Louie have been bringing in vegetables that are ripe in late spring. So my dreams are not in sync with what they encounter out there. Bee-zarre.

3/15 M. Rhoda & Louie came in with today's harvest, all excited. "Where's Julio?" He was taking a nap. After he woke up, they asked, "Did you see us?" They said he came to his window & when they waved at him, he waved back, but he didn't speak. Just like he'd done w/ Linda & Wendel. He had no memory of this.

3/16 N. No dreams last night. I was looking forward to swinging in the sunny yard again, but it didn't happen.

3/16 M. Louie & Rhoda brought in fresh carrots & peas & Hugh helped them fix vegetable soup. The rest of us went upstairs to listen to music. As the Beatles' "Revolution" played, Julio blurted out, "As bad as we think it is in here, do any of you remember what we left out there? A mess. When I went to college, I thought I could make a difference, change things. But I couldn't. The ones who were yelling the loudest for change were really in it for what they could get. Do you think it's any different now? We have everything we want here. We're getting along well. Do you think it's as good as this out there?" Doreen whined, "But we're not getting anywhere here." Julio said, "Were you getting anywhere out there? I wasn't."

I worry about Linda & Wendel. Are they glad they left? But then, they were going to have a baby. If I were in Linda's shoes, I might take my chances out there rather than raise a child here.

3/17 N. Was it what Julio said? Or was I going there on my own? I dreamed about my window, & the swing, like before. While I was swinging I saw a gate in the fence, so I went thru it. Once I did, the sunny day was gone & it was night. The street looked familiar, a part of town I used to avoid. The air smelled like car exhaust. The street lights were so dingy they barely emitted light. The streets were dirty, too, garbage everywhere, walls covered w/ graffiti. There were people—scary people, black & white. They stared at me, then huddled together like they were conspiring. I didn't know what to do. Sleazy-dressed women —they had to be prostitutes—looked at me like I was competition. Then a scrawny little man came up & asked for money. I told him I didn't have any. He grabbed my arm & said, "Please, miss, I haven't eaten all day." His hand was dirty. I tried to shake it off. I tried to run away but couldn't move. I tried to scream but no sound came out of my mouth. The man was dragging me.

Then I woke up. Julio was holding my arm. I was shaking. "Are you ok?" He'd heard me screaming & came to see what was wrong. That was the first nightmare I've had in—I don't remember. I've been nervous & jumpy ever since.

3/17 M. Writing about my dream didn't help me feel better. I got a bottle of Scotch & proceeded to drink myself into oblivion. That's not what I intended—I just wanted to wipe that nightmare out of my mind. I thought getting drunk would help. I forgot about what overdosing can do. The more I drank, the less I could think. The less I could think, the more I drank. I got to where I knew I was in trouble. It was worse than the time I was paralyzed. Rhoda came in to check on me. All I remember was her, Julio & Doreen hauling me into the bathroom. Julio made me vomit. He put me in the tub & the girls bathed me. I was in & out of consciousness. I remember Julio gave me a pill. I threw it up, so they gave me a suppository. Yuk!

I woke up on Julio's bed. He was sitting on the chair beside me. The window was open. It was night & I could see stars. Then I went back to sleep. When I woke again, Julio was still there but the window was closed. I told him, "You always come to my rescue when I'm drunk." He just smiled. I told him about my vision of his window. He looked at it & said, "I'm sorry I missed it."

3/18 N. I still feel sick. I apologized to Julio & the girls & promised never to do that again. Julio grinned & said, "Good, because next time I might not be around to help you." Doreen asked what he meant. "Because if I can get out, & I find a gate, I'm going thru it."

"But the other day you were saying…" He interrupted, "I know, but I've put a lot of thought into it. If I get out of here, I'm going to medical school. Maybe I can make a difference after all." I didn't let him see me cry. Linda has her baby. Wendel has Linda. Julio wants to be a doctor. But what is there for me?

3/18 M. After I wound the clock (11 weeks) I thought, when it's time to wind it again, I may let it run down. What would happen? Would time keep on going anyway? I still can't get that dream out of my head.

3/19 N. Rhoda has been so thoughtful. She noticed I still didn't feel good & brought me some tea. We just sat & talked. I asked about outside. She described it in such detail I could picture it. She didn't mention my swing, so I asked about it. She looked puzzled & said there's not one in the yard, only on the porch. I asked if she'll leave if she finds a gate. "Maybe. I'm not sure. I'm in no hurry." She lowered her voice. "My life before this wasn't very pleasant. It's scary, thinking about going back. I don't know what I'll find." I couldn't believe she'd confide in me. I never, ever thought we could be friends.

* * *

Rick thought about the journal characters he'd found in the real world: Virgil who drove an antique Volkswagen; Linda and her biracial son, Wendell; Calvin, aka Louie, whose mother was a member of both the historical society and the garden club. Was there a Hispanic doctor? He thumbed through the yellow pages in the phone book. He didn't find one whose first name was Julio, but if he were a real person, he may have moved to a different city. Or he might not have gone to medical school after all. Perhaps his real name wasn't Julio. Or maybe he didn't exist.

Who was this writer? Why did she live in an abandoned house and leave hints of her existence for him to find? Why hadn't she published her story? The possibility that it had been an account of actual events briefly crossed Rick's mind again, but that was too preposterous. Nevertheless, he locked the notebooks in the file cabinet before he went to bed.

Things were shaping up at the Wilson House. Barry had finished wiring except for a few electrical fixtures. The plumbing was waiting inspection so Wayne could hook the house up to the city water and sewer systems. Derek's crew had finished installing ductwork, and a new heat pump was mounted by the back porch. With no more holes to be put in the walls, the interior was ready for plaster, paint, and wallpaper. Comparing fragments of ceiling medallions to pictures in a catalog, Rick ordered the closest match he could find.

The turret room was the first to be finished, with cream colored wainscoting and blue walls. Rick found a ceiling border similar to the original stenciled edging. Even without electricity, the generous windows admitted good light. He set up his office there but made sure to go home in the afternoon when the workers left.

The notebooks remained in the bottom of his filing cabinet. For days, he was too busy to think about them. One evening, while fishing something out of the drawer, he came across them. Why had he stopped reading? He finished his other business and delved into the unfolding story.

3/19 M. I still have no idea where I'm going or why. I take no pleasure in anything right now. I haven't played piano since my nightmare. Doreen noticed. She came in to cheer me up. She asked if I'd seen how attentive Julio has been to everyone lately. I hadn't. He was taking care of me & still studying Hugh, but I hadn't noticed him tending to anyone else. She said it's as if he's trying to make sure everyone will be ok w/out him if he's able to leave. I asked if she'd go w/ him. She shook her head & denied they're an item right now. It wouldn't be like Linda & Wendel. Besides, she's not sure she wants to leave. We talked about my nightmare. She knows there are such places in the outside world but it's not like that everywhere. I reminded her we don't know what's happened since we've been here. Maybe they had World War III. Maybe they bombed everything and there's no world to go back to. She shook her head & said, "I hope not."

3/20 N. I feel better today. Julio hasn't been able to get out of the house, but he's making preparations to leave if he can. Hugh is happy just to be awake & out of the cellar, or wherever he thought he was. Louie surprises me. He wears jeans now & even goes out to the garden in cut-offs & no shirt! He says it's warm outside. He gets so dirty it doesn't all come off. His hands look like those of a laborer, not the gentleman's hands he used to be so proud of. But he seems happy. This AM he put on a prissy air, picked up his coffee cup & crooked his little finger. In a haughty voice, he said, "What maavelous coffee." Then he started laughing & we all cracked up.

3/20 M. I just realized I'm scared. Of what? I'm not sure. Of the future? Of having a future? All my life & non-life I never really had a future. Oh, I had hopes & dreams when I was a kid, but most of them were never realized, or never lead me anywhere. When I was a teenager, I wanted my own place & a car. When I finally got my apt, it was a disappointment. I was free from dependence on my mother but had to slave for money to keep it. It wasn't the freedom I'd envisioned. Now my car—that was a dream come true. I could escape my apt. & go just about anywhere. The problem is, once I got there I wasn't happy. It'd be too hot at the beach, or the movie didn't meet my expectations. It wasn't the beach or the movie that was a disappointment. It was me. But that's where I was at the time. Things never turned out as I imagined.

When I was in college my hopes & dreams never panned out. So I lived a life w/ no future. Then I came here. For so long, trapped in non-time, there really was no future. Then I started the clock & time began to move. To where? Or when? What is my future? Will I get out someday? The thought terrifies me.

It's not that I worry about ending up on that slum street. In some sense, I've always dwelt there. If I were to escape w/ just the clothes on my back, I'd face the problem of getting food & shelter & money, finding a job, contacting my mother (if she's still alive). How could I explain where I've been all this time? Would I find myself back the day after the night of the party? If I went back to November 1st, I'd be starting a new life, wouldn't I? B/c I won't go back to my old ways. I can't. That thought is scary, but there's more—something else, something bigger frightens me. I don't know what it is.

* * *

That's probably why I stopped reading, Rick thought—Red's anxiety, too much gloom and doom. Why? He felt sorry for her, but why should these fictional emotions affect him? He kept reading only because he was curious to find out what happened next. Would they all get out of the house? Then what? In a way, he didn't want the story to end.

He set the notebook down and leaned back. What would Red think if she saw the Wilson House now? Would she be surprised to see it renovated? Would she be pleased by what they'd done? He had to admit that her imagination, her insight into what the place might have looked like when new, had inspired him and guided many of his choices. He wished he could talk to her, but what could he say? What would she say?

3/21 N. I had the same dream as the other night, but this time it was different. I went out the gate onto the same street, the same grime &

graffiti, the smell of garbage & gas fumes, but this time it didn't seem so dark.

The same people were there, the prostitutes & pimps & drug dealers. That scrawny man reeking of cheap booze approached me again & asked for money. I tried to get away from him, but I fell. He grabbed my arm & began dragging me. I tried to fight back but his grip was too strong. Before I could scream, I heard a car horn & felt a blast of air as a car shot by. Then he let me go.

Another man came down the street. His clothes were flashy but worn & dirty. "Here, you shouldn't scare her like that," he said. The derelict whined, "I was just trying to help. She almost got run over." The flashy man grabbed the old man's collar & said, "Well, if you hadn't frightened her, she wouldn't 'a been in the street, now would she?" The drunk turned to me & said, "I'm sorry, miss. I didn't mean you no harm." All I could think to say was, "I really don't have any money." The younger man gave the bum a little shove. "Aargh! If you gave him any, he'd just buy booze w/ it. Get away from here, Artie." The old drunk limped away.

Then 2 of the hookers came over. One stood on either side of me & held my arms. "Are you ok, honey?" one asked. I managed to nod. "You don't belong here, do you," the other said. I just looked at her. I didn't know what to say. She went on, "Should we call someone? To come get you?" The 1st said, "We can pay for a taxi, to take you home." I tried to smile. I was able to say, "No, thank you. It won't be necessary. I'll be ok." Then I stepped back & found myself in the fenced yard, where the sun was shining and flowers were blooming. Then I woke up.

3/21 M. At dinner, I told everyone about my dreams. "They're just dreams," Julio said. "Dreams are the result of brain cells firing. At most, they're your subconscious' way of sorting things out. There's nothing psychic or prophetic about them."

Doreen looked hard at him. "Hasn't our experience here shown that your science doesn't have all the answers?" Then she looked at me. "But it sounds to me like your mind IS sorting things out. We all have misgivings about going back to that world."

I couldn't help crying. "But one of those women said, 'You don't belong here.' What does that mean? That I don't belong out there?"

Louie chimed in, "It all depends on 'where' your dream pertains to. The slum street? You don't belong there. It's true some of the world is like that, ugly & full of crime. But it's more than that."

Rhoda put in, "But what about our world in here? If it had been up to us, this house would be as trashy as that street. Or worse." She gestured around at the fine furnishings. "We can't give ourselves credit for this."

Doreen added, "That's right. And what about us? Are we any better than the people on that street? Whores, beggars, panderers, druggies, drunks?"

I lowered my head. Was I the drunk in my dream? Or one of the prostitutes? I've probably committed the same sins as the people in my dreams. When I looked up, everyone had their heads down. I put mine back down & said, "But like the people in my 2nd dream, all of you have your good sides. You don't intentionally harm anyone, & you'll help somebody who's in trouble."

Rhoda broke the ensuing silence. "No, most of us HAVE intentionally hurt others. I know I have. But I think we've pretty much come out of that." She looked at me. "When we were 1st here, you wouldn't lift a finger to help anybody. But you started the clock, & that started changes, good changes. And now you are about the most generous of us all. You'd do anything for us." That really made me cry.

THE MEDALLION

3/22 N. Rhoda took up drawing again. While I play music, she sketches. I never suspected she had any artistic talent. Actually, I didn't know she had a talent for anything but meanness. When she stopped being mean, I guess she had to do something. I need to stop being so snarky. She's really quite good. This AM, she reclined on the settee & kept looking up at the ceiling while she drew. I glanced at her work. She was sketching that fancy plaster decoration that the chandelier hangs from. Then she ripped the page out & started to throw it in the fire. I rescued it. She said, "I'm not Michelangelo. I just can't draw lying down." I thought it looked nice, so I kept it.

* * *

Rick turned the page. A loose sheet fell out and fluttered to the floor. He picked it up. It wasn't a page from the notebook. A larger, heavier paper had been folded and inserted in the journal—a pencil sketch of a ceiling medallion. Had Red drawn it? Why?

When he began working on the house, most of the plaster trim was broken and lay on the floor. When he'd tried to put pieces together, many fragments were missing. By memory, he wasn't certain how closely this sketch matched the original medallions.

The following day, Rick took the sketch to the Wilson House and compared it to the one he'd pieced together. They weren't quite identical. When he compared details, some elements differed and the scrollwork didn't quite match. Perhaps the journal writer had obtained a sketch someone had drawn in a different house.

That afternoon, one of the workers called to Rick, "You have a package at the front door."

A man in a brown uniform stood on the porch with an electronic clipboard. At his feet lay a large box—the ceiling medallions Rick had ordered. As he signed for it, Rick asked, "How heavy is it?"

"Not as heavy as it looks. Mostly, it's awkward." With a, "Have a good day," the UPS man returned to his truck and drove off.

Rick wrestled the box into the parlor. He was glad he'd ordered urethane medallions instead of plaster. Not only were they less expensive, they'd be less strain on the old ceilings. Once painted, no one would know the difference. He opened the box and removed packing to look at a medallion. It was beautiful. He compared it to the one he'd pieced together. Pretty close.

Then he compared the new medallions to the sketch Rhoda had presumably drawn. His heart skipped a beat. The design in the sketch matched the new medallions. Perfectly. Rick's hands shook. He dropped the sketch and sat down on the box.

Hold on, he told himself. The new medallions were not identical to what was originally in the house. Rhoda didn't draw the one on the "parlour" ceiling. But how could she, or Red, or whoever made the sketch, anticipate what pattern he would order? They didn't. It must be a popular design. Probably if he looked at the ceilings of The Inn and other restored Victorians, he'd find the same pattern. But he couldn't help feeling like someone was messing with his head.

That evening, he took the sketch home and replaced it in the notebook.

3/22 M. At supper we had fresh green beans that Louie picked & prepared. They were cooked lightly & dressed w/ a butter & herb sauce. (He had a French name for them.) I asked him to write down the recipe for me. We had a pleasant meal w/ conversation. Louie started talking about some theory he'd heard once, that we create our world ourselves, that our troubles are of our own making. I told him about a psychologist who tried to tell me that we write the script of our lives & we're capable of rewriting that script. At the time I considered her idea pure nonsense. She was trying to blame me for my problems.

Julio said, "We are masters of our own fate." That's a sobering thought. Doreen asked, "You mean, that we created this situation? That we chose to be here? That maybe this isn't real, we can change it at will?" Rhoda added, "So if we created it, & we can change it, why don't we?"

I remembered Wendel's old theories & wished he were here to join the discussion. "Maybe that's how Linda and Wendel got out of here," I said. "Maybe they changed their script." I'm not sure I buy that idea.

Everyone was quiet for awhile. Finally, Hugh spoke up, "Whether we can create our own world or not, or write the script, I know we can change the direction of our lives if we choose to." I looked at his now trim body and had to agree.

3/23 N. This morning when I went down to the kitchen, I found it piled w/ produce. Julio didn't have to tell me. "Louie & Rhoda are gone." He had a stack of envelopes. Two were addressed to me, one in Rhoda's hand & one in Louie's. I took them back to my room. I didn't want anyone to see me cry. I never expected either of them to describe me as kind.

* * *

Rick found two notes folded up in the journal. How did he keep missing these things? Did they just materialize when he got to that part of the story?

The notes were written in different hands. The first had spots where tears may have fallen. It said:

We found a gate. If it's still there when we go back out, we'll leave. I'll miss you. I know I was very cruel to you for a long time. You weren't exactly easy to get along with either, but you were only trying to protect yourself. I went out of my way to be mean. Please accept my apology, and also my gratitude that you have become a real friend to me. I was always too possessive in the past to

have friends, and now I value your friendship. I hate to leave all of you, but I hope to meet you again in the outside world. You will come, I know. Thank you again for your forgiveness and your friendship.
    Rhoda

The other was more succinct:

Before you changed my life, I was a conceited prick. I was mean to you on more occasions than I care to remember. But you taught me how to love. You taught me how to make love to a woman, how to please her. I will miss you, for now, but I look forward to us reuniting on the outside.
    Louie

Rick rifled through the notebook until he found the first letter, from Linda. That handwriting was different, too. Who did the writer get to pen these notes? Why go to all the trouble of this subterfuge in what was obviously a first draft of a story? Was it possible that these were actual notes from friends? That made no sense.

3/23 M. Things have been somber today. Not that Rhoda & Louie really made things cheerful, until lately, that is, but we now look at one another & wonder who's next? There used to be such a gang of us & now only 4. A few weeks ago, I would have expected Julio or Doreen or both to leave before Louie & Rhoda. It seemed they had earned their escape more than Louie, & especially Rhoda. Both stayed on their high horses for so long, but when they came down, they came down hard. Especially Louie. Is that what we need to do? Have a nervous breakdown? What am I talking about? I'm not sure I want to go out there. But it's starting to get lonely in here.

3/24 N. Doreen's moving into Louie's room. She asked me & Julio if it was ok, but we're both comfortable where we are, so we gave her the go-ahead. She's happy to have her own bathroom. I wonder if we have to move into the attic, like Rhoda did, to escape?

3/24 **M.** Doreen is ecstatic. She was cutting thru the parlour door to the dining room & found herself on a porch instead. I'd noticed her absence but assumed she was sleeping. When at last she buzzed into the dining room, for a split second I imagined I saw the red glow of a sunset behind her. Coincidentally, it was dinnertime. She said she'd spent a lovely afternoon in the yard. First, she explored the porch, the one with the wicker furniture. When she went out into the yard, she was able to get all the way around the house. She didn't come in until sundown, but she found no gate, & no yard swing. "Why didn't you bring us some fresh vegetables?" Julio asked. She looked stunned for a moment. "I was so excited I didn't even think about it!"

3/25 **N.** Since those last 2 dreams, my windows have remained closed & I seem no closer to getting fresh air. Whenever I cut through an outside door, I hold my breath. Will I find myself in the next room or somewhere else? It's always the next room. Doreen has the run of the house & the yard. I'm happy for her, but also envious. We gave her an order for vegs & she brought them in, happy as a pig & covered w/ dirt.

3/25 **M.** 12 weeks. Despite my misgivings & thoughts about not winding the clock, I couldn't do that to the others. Would time stop again? If it did, would I be able to restart it? What if I couldn't, if this was my only chance? Would one of the others be able to? If I was the only one affected, I might see what would happen, but I can't compromise other people's lives. So I wound it. Everyone joined me. Hugh proposed a toast & Julio found some nice champagne. Even tho I didn't feel like celebrating, I joined them. As we drank, I remembered our first champagne toast, in the cellar, w/ Virgil, that last night of our lives. I remember I didn't drink with them. At the time I told myself I knew better than to mix wine w/ Scotch. Now I suspect there was more to my refusal. Maybe I just didn't want to participate. "To friendship" was the toast that night, right? I certainly wasn't looking for friendship, certainly not with this bunch. The funny thing is, I've found it, but it's taken me a long non-time & time.

3/26 **N.** Doreen's packing a bag in case she can get out. She said she probably won't write letters, but it's obvious she's trying to clear the air w/ the rest of us. She & I sat down to tea & a nice chat, just small talk at 1ˢᵗ. I don't think either of us wanted to dredge up our sordid past. I know I didn't. We were quiet for awhile. I was thinking about all the mean things I'd done to her. To my surprise, she suddenly smiled and said, "I wish we could get out together." That made me feel good. I thanked her for being a friend & told her how sorry I was for being so unkind. She returned the apology. I hate to see her leave. That will leave me without another female to talk to. Not that Julio & Hugh are bad company. They're not, but they're guys. What happened to the bitch who couldn't get along with other women?

* * *

On Monday, Rick went to his bank to cash a check. While he waited in line, he heard two other customers chat about that new virus in China. One said, "The death toll is climbing over there, and it's spreading to other countries. They say it's worse than SARS."

Rick vaguely recalled the SARS scare. It didn't amount to much in the long run. *People just need something to worry about.*

The line moved. His teller was a young Asian woman identified on her name plate as Rhonda. His pulse pounded in his ears, almost deafening him. Rhonda—Rhoda? As they completed the transaction, trying to act casual, he asked, "Do I know you from somewhere, Rhonda?"

The woman looked up, startled, then peeped at the name plate. "Oh, sorry. I'm Michelle. I guess we neglected to change this when we switched stations." She removed the name plate and said, "Have a nice day."

"You, too." The girl must have thought he was coming onto her. Just because Rhoda used to work in a bank didn't mean that she'd take the same job after she left the Wilson House. He shook his head—was he beginning to believe the journal was a true account?

3/26 **M.** Hugh now has a weight bench in his room & has been work-ing out. I'd noticed changes in his appearance, slimmer waist & bulkier shoulders, but I'd attributed it to more activity & better food. Doreen took over Linda's exercise class after she left, but what motivation will I have when she's gone?

3/27 **N.** Since the last entry, I've had a night's sleep & a nap. Each time, I've dreamed about my windows being open. In the dreams, I get up & look out. I remember the weather & positions of the sun, the flowers & birds & trees, but I never seem to look over the fence. It's weird—why don't we look over the fence when we dream? Julio said we should make auto-suggestions before we fall asleep. I try to. I can recall the yard & the sky in detail, but I never look across the fence.

3/27 **M.** I dreamed about my window again & now Hugh is dreaming about his. He said he can hear Doreen out in the yard. She talks to the birds & sings. When he told her this, she was embarrassed. "Don't stop," he said. "You have a nice voice." Doreen is packed & ready to go, but she confided to me that she has misgivings about going alone. I don't blame her. The others had companions. I wouldn't want to walk out into the street from my dreams by myself, even if the people are more harmless than they appear. Julio said it would be up to me or Hugh to go w/ her. Not him, in case whoever is left needs medical care. Hugh pulled a muscle in his shoulder. Julio examined him & said he was ok, but he advised him to rest & stop overdoing it.

3/28 **N.** I used Doreen's bathroom today. When I went thru her room, it was a mess. Her bed was unmade & dirty clothes were strewn all over. I couldn't hide my surprise. Doreen laughed. "I told it to stop cleaning itself. I used to be a slob. The other day, my room reminded me of a motel room after the maid's been there. It didn't seem like home. So I told it to stop. I won't leave it messy forever, but I want to be the one to clean it. I've been trying to see how long this will go on, to make sure it won't clean itself."

This got me thinking. I've been cleaning the kitchen behind myself lately, but I never thought to tell it to stop cleaning itself. Maybe I want to leave my options open in case sometimes I don't feel like it. I've been making my bed, but little else. When I went back to my room, I took a good look. Yes, it reminded me of a motel room. Even the bed was neater than I'd left it. So out loud I said, "Stop cleaning yourself." Let's see what happens.

3/28 M. Doreen brought in a load of vegs when nobody was looking, & then was nowhere to be found. We thought we knew what that meant, but a while later she came through the front door! She said she found a gate in the front fence & went back to stock up on vegs, but the gate was gone. She didn't seem terribly disappointed or even worried that she'd missed what might be her only opportunity. We all urged her to just go next time. She promised she would.

3/29 N. Hugh said he dreamed about his windows again & this time he woke up. He swore he was awake. He saw Doreen out in the garden & called to her. She came over & they carried on a conversation about what vegs she should bring in. He decided to join her, but he couldn't get out the door. He tried all four doors before giving up. So he went back to his window & enjoyed the view until he felt sleepy again. After she came in, Doreen verified all this. I asked him why he didn't just climb out his window. After all, he's on the ground floor. The thought never occurred to him.

3/29 M. Doreen said she found the gate again but came back in for her stuff. The gate disappeared while she was inside. "Forget about your stuff," we told her. Now she takes her bag w/ her when she goes outside. I suspect her failure to leave is b/c she's not ready to go. Is she waiting for one of us to go with her? Hugh seems to be the most ready but he can't get out the doors yet. Julio still says he won't leave any of us alone. I don't seem to be anywhere near getting out. What if some of us can't leave? What if only one of us is left? We can't let that happen.

3/30 N. My room has stopped cleaning itself. I pick up behind myself, even empty the ashtray. Thank goodness the cigs still get replenished. Doreen & I told the guys about our rooms & w/ their permission we told the kitchen to stop cleaning itself. I thought about telling the whole house to, but this is a big house. Let's see if I can keep up with the kitchen & bedroom. As for the bathrooms, well, I don't want to clean up behind other people.

3/30 **M.** I dreamed my windows were open & Doreen was out in the yard calling me. In my dream, I went down & out the front door. There was a gate in the fence. Doreen was standing by it with her bag. "Tell the others goodbye for me," she said & hugged me. When she opened the gate, I couldn't see anything beyond it, & after she went thru, the gate disappeared. Only the fence remained. I woke up in my bed, & Doreen was gone.

3/31 **N.** Playing piano is the most satisfying thing in my life. With little else to do, I spend hours playing. The constant practice has helped me improve beyond my imagination. Making music has become almost 2nd nature, like I breathe music. Sometimes I improvise & it doesn't sound ½ bad. Even my left hand seems to have a life of its own, finding & playing the right keys.

3/31 **M.** Hugh said his windows are open all the time. He tried climbing out one but it "closed" up on him. This scared him b/c he had a leg ½ way out when that happened, but he was ok. Thank goodness it didn't cut his leg off, but he has no idea how he got it back inside. He's afraid to try again. He took me & Julio into his room to show us his windows. He said they were open & he could see thru them, but we couldn't.

4/1 **N.** I miss Doreen. Julio & Hugh are good company, but I need female companionship. If wishing would bring me some—but I wouldn't want anyone else to be trapped here.

4/1 **M.** 13 weeks. When we wound the clock this time, it wasn't as festive b/c most of us are missing. Maybe they're no longer missing, we're the ones who are. Dust bunnies are starting to collect in the corners of my room. I spilled my ashtray & had to find a broom to clean it up. I may have to look for a vacuum cleaner. Otherwise, things have been unremarkable. Cleaning up behind myself is a chore but it gives me a sense of accomplishment.

* * *

On Friday, Kyle called. "Dad, have you been following the news?"

"I try not to. What's going on?"

"The world is going crazy."

"That's news?"

"You've heard about that new coronavirus? Well, some of the professors are pretty worried. If kids come to class sick, they send them home and tell them to go get tested. Now the administration is telling the profs they can't do that, and a few of them are so upset they're threatening to strike."

"Do you think it's that serious? There've been only a few cases so far. None here."

"One of our virologists said it's already here, and the way this bug is acting, it's likely to become a worldwide pandemic. There's even talk about quarantines and economic collapse."

"Relax, Kyle. I've lived through these scares more times than I can remember. In a few weeks the hype will die down and there'll be something else to occupy everyone's attention."

"Well, the reason I called is, Allison wanted me to remind you to go get a flu shot. This flu season is nothing to laugh at."

"I thought the new virus isn't the flu."

"It's not, but they don't have anything for it yet."

THE AZALEA FESTIVAL

Rick was pleased with the new ceiling medallions and how they dressed up the house. One by one, as rooms neared completion, they were affixed to the ceilings and Barry installed the light fixtures. Rick thumbed through the remaining notebooks to see if he could find any more drawings. No. As the story went, Rhoda had drawn the one sketch and she'd left shortly after.

He found himself compulsively walking through the house, over and over, looking for anything left undone. When he glanced in the closet of the turret room, he was almost disappointed that the loose boards covering the hiding place had been replaced and painted over. No way to hide anything there now.

The exterior of the house was pressure washed and Cecil affixed new gingerbread. The painter began to apply its original colors, white with green trim. Cecil's crew repaired the privacy fence and built a more inviting picket fence across the front. When they finished the new porch steps, they poured concrete sidewalks. The house, now attached to the rest of the world, shone like a sunrise when Rick drove up the street. He wished Amy could see it.

Bob dropped by. "It's starting to look nice."

Rick proposed finishing touches. Bob's eyes lit up with each detail. "Yes, I can envision it." His change of attitude pleased Rick but didn't prepare him for Bob's next statement. "You know, this is a good location for a real estate business. I've had an offer on my office building and maybe I'll take it. That would help pay for these renovations. With the Balrush lot next door for parking, I'd have more room to spread out."

They stood in the foyer. Rick looked at his nearly finished walls, the gentle curve of the staircase banister, the chandelier hanging above. "Does that mean that you want to alter the floor plan? Make it more business-like?"

"Oh, no. I wouldn't change a thing. An antique desk for my receptionist would fit perfectly here. The parlor would make a good conference room, and the library a comfortable waiting room. I'd use that back room with the private bath for my office and there's plenty of space for my associates. With this house to showcase, maybe I could specialize in vintage houses. Or…" He paused. "How about a sideline—a renovation business for historical buildings. Are you interested?"

Rick shook his head.

In late February, Kristie called. "Hey, Dad, when's the last time you went to the Azalea Festival in Palatka?"

"Not since you and Kyle were kids. Why do you ask?"

"It's next weekend. One of the teachers at school is involved and I thought I'd take the kids. It'd be nice if you could go with us."

Rick had fond memories of taking his family to the Azalea Festival. He couldn't remember why he and Amy stopped going after the children were grown. In early March, the weather could be a factor, so he checked the forecast. That weekend was supposed to be nice, so he looked forward to accompanying his grandchildren.

On the way to Palatka, all Kristie seemed to have on her mind was the new disease. "They're calling it COVID-19."

"That's a funny name."

"It's short for "coronavirus" something. The "19" is because it was discovered last year. You know the governor has declared a public health emergency."

"No. I didn't. I don't put much stock in what that politician does. He's stumping for votes."

"Well, there've already been a few cases in Florida and several deaths in the US."

"That's hardly what I call an emergency."

"FSU is talking about closing their campus and going to distance learning. Even some churches are discussing what to do if it gets bad. I worry about Spring Break. We'll have kids from all over the country flocking to the beaches. A few events have already been cancelled. This may be one of the last festivals we'll be able to go to for a while."

Rick gave her a patronizing smile. "It's a lot of hype. Something to sell newspapers."

"On the side of caution, don't shake hands with anyone. That's what they're advising. They recommend elbow bumps instead."

Elbow bumps? Rick chuckled.

At first, Rick was disappointed by the children's attitudes. Sandy complained that parades were for little kids. Michael resisted touring Ravine Gardens. After Kristie scolded them—they were ruining the day for Grandpa—they settled down and let him enjoy himself. Walking through the ravine, where the azaleas were in full bloom, he and Kristie reminisced about their previous outings here. He imagined Amy beside him, holding his hand, but he didn't mention this to Kristie. By the time they returned downtown to the arts and crafts show, the children admitted they were having a good time, and that they had enjoyed exploring the ravine.

They went in separate directions. Sandy wanted to look at jewelry, Michael was interested in knives and leather goods, and Kristie chatted with her friend who was exhibiting stained glass art. Rick wandered around, drifting from booth to booth. Some photographs of architectural features—columns, arches, gingerbread, and such—caught his attention. He remembered Rhoda and paid more attention to the artists themselves. He saw no Asian women but found a young man in a booth of Oriental-style pencil sketches.

After studying drawings of pagodas, bamboo, and river scenes, Rick glanced around to be sure no one who knew him was within ear shot. "Did you draw these?"

The young man sat up in his chair. "Yeah. See anything you like?"

"Nice work, but I'm looking for a particular artist. I'm not sure of her name, but she's Chinese-American. Are you familiar with her?"

The artist shrugged his shoulders. "I'm sure there are many Chinese-American artists."

"Yeah. Maybe someday I'll remember her name." Rick moved along.

He bumped into Michael at the car show. "I didn't know you were interested in antiques," Rick said.

"But these cars are cool."

A 1968 Mustang convertible caught Rick's eye. He thought about the journal, about Red and the car she'd left behind when she was trapped in the house. He wondered if the journal writer actually had a car like this.

He asked Michael, "If you could own one of these, which would you choose?"

Michael settled on the 1966 Corvette Stingray. "When I'm old enough to drive, will you get me one?"

Rick laughed. "I'd have to win the lottery first. These babies probably cost ten times what they did when they were new. Besides, for your first car, you need something cheap. It builds character."

On the way home, he told Kristie, "I managed not to shake hands with anyone. I also didn't elbow bump."

That night, Rick was glad to be home. It had been a long day.

4/2 N. I've been thinking. If I get out of here, what will I do with the rest of my life? I thought about going back to college, but what would I major in? I'd like to take up Humanities again, but what kind of job could I get with that, other than teaching? Do I really want to teach? I don't like high school kids. Teaching in a college would be ok, but that would take a graduate degree & I'm not sure I'm up for that. I don't know why I'm worried. It would take some time before I could get back into college. Unless I went back to Nov 1st, right after the party, I'd likely have no job, no apt, no car. I'd have to start from scratch. My mother, bless her heart, wouldn't be an option. I had no friends I could count on, unless I could find Linda & Wendel or Rhoda & Louie or Doreen. Or Julio & Hugh, if they get out. But depending on when they arrived compared to when I did, they might be struggling & not able to help. Maybe that's why I'm not so anxious to get out.

4/2 M. This afternoon, Julio & Hugh came in to listen to me play piano. When I stopped, Hugh asked if I was a professional musician. I laughed & said no, that I hadn't touched a piano since I was a child & only started playing again after I wound the clock. He shook his head & said I was a natural. His dad was a professional musician & tried to get Hugh into music, but Hugh wasn't interested.

His abusive father? I guess there's good in everyone. That got me thinking. Could I make a few dollars playing in bars or something until I could study music? Maybe even a church? Imagine that! People might come just to watch me play one handed. Maybe I could give piano lessons. I taught Doreen & she didn't do too badly. I'd never thought about going into music as a career, but why not?

* * *

Finally, Rick had a clue to the diarist's possible identity. He surprised Kristie by accompanying her to church the next day. During the service, when it came time to pass the peace, the minister said, "In light of recent health concerns, please refrain from shaking hands or hugging one another. Smiles and kind words will suffice."

After the service, he spoke with the pianist, Clare. "I enjoyed the music today."

"Thank you."

"You probably know a lot of the musicians in town, don't you?"

"Not all of them, but I know quite a few."

"Do you know a red haired piano player?"

"Yes," Clare said. "We had a college student with red hair a few years ago. He filled in for me on my weeks off."

"This one is a woman."

"Oh. What's her name?"

She would have to ask. "I don't know, but I heard about her and wanted to track her down if I could."

Clare shook her head. "I can't think of anyone like that. Do you know what kind of music? Or where she plays?"

"No. That's what I'm trying to find out. If you come across anyone with that description, will you let me know?"

"Sure."

Clare probably assumed, mistakenly, that Rick was looking for a new woman. He pondered his options. He could go church hopping, but this hunt for Red was even more bizarre that his search for her published book. Where else could he look? She mentioned playing in bars. Did bars still hire piano players? He couldn't ask a music teacher the color of her hair over the phone. Maybe she would give more clues to herself in her journal.

When he resumed reading that evening, Rick was nearing the end of the third notebook. One more to go.

4/3 N. I got outside! I really got outside! Words can't describe it. It didn't happen when I took a short cut from one room to another, like the others. I was simply playing the piano & looked up at the parlour curtains. Light was coming thru! I just sat there enjoying the sun shining thru those curtains while I continued to play. I remember—how long ago?—something similar happened. I was playing piano & saw light thru the curtains, but only for a moment, then it went away.

This time it stayed. Finally, I got up & opened a curtain. I could see out the window! I could see a porch w/ wicker furniture & plants, & beyond that a green lawn & flowers. I thought it was a dream, that I'd fallen asleep at the piano. I pinched myself—I was awake. I didn't want to break the spell, but finally went over to the door & opened it. It took a minute for my eyes to adjust to the bright light, then I stepped out onto the porch. It was morning & everything was still wet with dew. I sat on the porch for awhile & just enjoyed the sun & the scent of flowers. Finally, I left the porch & walked around the yard. All the way around. There was no opening in the high board fence. I looked up, but all I could see was sky.

It was like the others had described. Azalea bushes around the house, flower beds along the fence. The dogwood tree by my front window. The magnolia tree by Julio's. No swing in the yard, only on the other porch. I sat there, swinging for a long time, enjoying the bougainvillea in the hanging basket—hot pink—my favorite.

I didn't try to go back in the house. I went to the veg garden & learned why the others got so dirty. The garden may have planted itself, but it hadn't weeded itself. There was a pile of rotting weeds by the fence that my escaped friends must have pulled, so I added to it. I pulled up some onions & picked yellow squash to fry for supper. I was afraid to go inside, afraid I wouldn't get back out, but it was quite warm & I didn't want the vegs to wilt, so I took the chance.

4/3 M. I was cleaning the vegs when Hugh came into the kitchen. I told him what happened and he was happy for me. He told me to go back out if I could. He & Julio would cook supper. To my delight, I was able to get back out. Hugh came to his window & talked to me. I saw Julio at his window & tried to talk to him, but he seemed to be in a daze. I went around to the side of the house away from their windows, stripped off all my clothes & lay in the sun. My skin's so fair, I was careful not to overdo it. I went in for dinner. Hugh had fixed the squash & I have never tasted anything more delicious. After dinner, I went outside to enjoy the stars. Mosquitoes bit me, but I didn't care. I fell asleep on the dining room porch & came in only after it got a little chilly outside.

4/4 N. When I woke up this AM, I got a cup of coffee & went right outside. For everyone else, the days & nights in the yard didn't exactly correlate with the hours of the clock, but when I went out at 8:00, it was

early morning. The sun was shining on the parlour side of the house—
the east. As I remember, the house was on the south side of University
Ave, facing north, so that would have been the east side in the real world.
I wonder why time was all askew for everyone else, but not for me? And
what about direction? Could they tell N, E, S, & W? I wish I'd asked
them before they left.

Last night I asked for another notebook since I was running out of
room. This AM, it was waiting for me on my bedside stand. Thank
goodness! Since my room no longer cleans itself, I was a little worried
that the house might not continue to give us what we want.

I asked Hugh what he could see from his window, about the dir. of
the sun & how day & night compare to the clock. This is weird, but that
shouldn't

* * *

Shouldn't what? The last page ended mid-sentence. Rick picked up the
fourth notebook. That volume had been on top of the stack when he
found them, and unfortunately, it had suffered a little water damage.
The cover was stuck to the first page and when he tried to ease them
apart, the page was destroyed. His heart sank. The writer was about to
tell about something interesting. Unless he could find her and ask, he'd
never know what it was.

The next few pages were also fused together. He tried to separate
them without further damage, but most of the words were illegible. He
thought about calling Troy at the museum, but decided not to disgrace
himself. Ink on the first halfway readable page was smeared. He could
only guess at the date of that entry. Had he missed important clues to
the writer's identity? Flipping through intact pages, he saw there were
only a few more entries.

He closed the notebook with a sigh. He'd finish it another time.

On Monday, the yard of the Wilson House was full of activity. Carlos's
truck and trailer were full of shrubs and bedding plants. Bob, who must

have taken the day off, was supervising the crew, setting azaleas around the house and flowers near the fence, just as the journal had described. Rick felt numb.

"What d'ya think?" Bob gestured around the yard. "These azaleas will really set the place off when they get bigger. In the meantime, the annuals will provide some color."

Rick nodded.

"Come around back," Bob said. "There's something I want to show you."

The wild mustard was blooming in the weedy area near the back fence, and there was more. Rick recognized a struggling potato plant and stalks of onion going to seed. Looking more closely, he found seedlings that could be squash or melons.

"What do you make of this?" Bob asked. "It looks like somebody grew a garden here and a few plants went to seed and sprouted when the weather warmed up. I never knew of vagrants growing vegetables."

"Neither have I."

"I don't know who else would have, though."

"Yeah." Rick looked at the Wilson House. Despite the warmth of the day, he shivered.

When he got home, Rick found a message from Kristie on his voice mail. "Dad, I thought I'd let you know. Someone gave me a hanging plant for my house, but there're no hooks on the porch to hang it on and my landlord doesn't want me making holes, so I took it over to the Wilson House. There was a hook on one of the porches, just right for a plant, so I put it there. I wanted to give you heads up so you'd know where it came from."

Although the notebooks sat invitingly on a corner of his desk, Rick had been too busy to read further. Or was he sorry to see the story come to a close? His disappointment over the damage to the last volume had eased. After supper, he picked it up.

Fourth Notebook

4/10 **M.** Julio is gone. Hugh & I are alone. I was outside talking to them thru their windows. At 1st, Julio seemed to be in a daze, then all of a sudden he answered me. He looked around at the yard like he could see it in detail & began asking if I saw what he did. I asked if he could see over the fence. He lifted his head & looked off into the distance. He didn't answer but a change came over his face. "What do you see?" I asked.

"I see…" but he just kept looking around. Finally he said, "I'm coming down." The next thing I knew, he was walking thru the back door! I ran up to him. "What did you see?"

He cleared his throat. "Houses, & trees, & a radio tower, off that way." He pointed to the SE. "And an apartment building, that way." He indicated the SW.

* * *

Rick paused a moment. It was true, what Julio described. The houses and trees and radio tower to the southeast of the house may have been there many years, but the apartment building to the southwest was built recently. Of course, anyone looking out an upstairs window would know that, but they weren't there in the seventies. Once again he wondered, when was this written? He continued with the entry.

I walked around w/ Julio. He acted like he'd never seen a flower or butterfly before. When we got to the front yard, he ran like a little boy down the walk to where it ended at the fence. He grabbed something I couldn't see & said, "Let's go!" I asked, "Where?" He stepped back a little & said, "No, we can't leave Hugh. You go. I'll stay with him." "Go where?" He gave me a funny look & said, "Out the gate."

I looked at his hand. It was holding thin air. "I see no gate." My heart was heavy, but I said, "You go. You must." Before he could say anything else, I pushed him. He stumbled. Then he disappeared. Just like that. Only the fence was left. I went inside & cried in Hugh's arms for what seemed like forever.

4/11 N. I'm very unsure about our future, but I'll be ok. I won't leave w/out Hugh. I won't leave him here by himself. I don't know how long it will take. It doesn't really matter. It's not really so bad here, as long as I can go outside.

4/11 M. I've been trying to stay upbeat but it's hard. I played piano for hours, but the day was still too long. I think about nothing but Julio. I miss him, but I'm not sorry I made him go. He needed to get out. They all did. What about me & Hugh? I try to stay cheerful, for Hugh's sake, but it's hard. What will I do if he leaves & I'm here alone? Will I be able to cope? Will I drink myself to death? Would I be able to die? I won't leave him here by himself, no matter what. Would I push him out a gate like I did Julio? Even if it meant that I'd be trapped in here alone? A fate worse than death! Would High leave w/out me? I'm scared.

* * *

Rick shivered. That would be a horrible fate, to be trapped for eternity all alone. For the hundredth time, he reminded himself, it's only a story. He resisted peeking ahead to see how the writer would end it.

4/12 N. As far as I know, Hugh is the only one who could ever see out his windows when he was awake. Now he tells me he can see out of all the downstairs windows. We walked around together, looking at windows. He described things in the yard, detail for detail. I asked him to look for a yard swing, even tho I haven't found one. Only the one on the porch. And he can't look beyond the fence.

We went upstairs, but all he could see from those windows was the other bedrooms, just like I do. I still can't see out my bedroom windows unless I'm dreaming. I told Hugh if he finds a gate, he must leave. What if he does?

4/12 M. Hugh & I continue to live day by day. I gather vegs, he cooks, I play piano, he lifts weights. We are friends but not lovers. There's nothing to stop us but I think sex would ruin our friendship, so we live like sister & brother. He hasn't been able to get outdoors & I haven't found a gate. He's content to look out windows. He's good company but I still get lonely. Will we be stuck here forever? Will we grow old here & die? Will we decide not to wind the clock & be stuck in some timeless oblivion? I'd rather die.

4/13 N. Hugh & I talked about packing bags, just in case. We found a couple of gym bags & packed them with a few things. I put them on the front porch where they'd be handy to grab if we find a gate.

4/13 M. I can see out the ground floor windows now! I wouldn't have tried again if Hugh hadn't encouraged me to. I've avoided windows for so long. Come to think of it, none of the others, once they were able to get outside, mentioned looking out windows. Was it just habit or were they unable to see anything? Today Hugh opened a curtain in the dining room & made me look. I could see the porch & the bougainvillea, & the yard beyond. Then I went thru' the whole house, opening curtains & looking outside. I see the same things as when I'm out there, just like this was a real house. I don't know why that should surprise me but it does. I only went outside today to pick some beans & okra. I spent most of the day looking out windows. But I still can't see beyond the fence or out of any of the upstairs windows when I'm awake.

4/14 N. I keep all the downstairs curtains open & can see day & night, sun & rain. I can't open any of the windows, tho. Hugh can open his, but no others. He still doesn't try to go thru them. I'd be afraid to try to climb thru windows, too.

* * *

The following morning, when Rick pulled into the yard of the Wilson House, he noticed a splash of hot pink hanging from the west porch. Was this what Kristie was talking about? He got out of his truck, walked over, and touched it as if to assure himself it was real. Bougainvillea. Hanging from the west porch. Hot pink. Just like the journal.

How did Kristie become complicit in these manifestations? He examined the hook. It looked new. How did it conveniently appear in the right place? It was unlikely one of the workers put it there. He shook his head, trying to clear it. There was no answer.

He called the building inspector to make an appointment for the final inspection.

"I'll come by Friday morning. Can't give you a good time. I'm trying to get as much done as possible this week. There's talk of closing the office for a few weeks because of this pandemic. I don't know why I'm in such a rush, no one else will be able to do business, either."

Rick couldn't get azaleas, bedding plants, and especially hot pink bougainvillea out of his mind. He was afraid to read more of the journal and chose to watch TV that evening. He was disappointed when the news came on. There seemed to be nothing but hype about that coronavirus.

No sooner had he turned it off than Kyle called. "Dad, how are you feeling?"

"I'm fine. How should I feel?"

"Allison's worried about you. A lot of elderly people are starting to quarantine themselves, and she thinks you should, too."

"Since when did I become elderly?"

"You were old enough to retire."

"Kyle, I'm perfectly capable of handling my own life, even if the rest of the country is going crazy."

"You need to take this seriously! UF is switching to online classes and the governor has declared a state of emergency."

"Okay, okay. Tell Allison I'll get a flu shot. But I'm not going to quarantine myself. I don't have leprosy."

Wednesday evening, Bob called. "I took Melody over to the Wilson House today. She loves it."

"Enough to move in?"

"No, I can't pry her out of our house, but she approves of it as my new office. And she wants one of the bedrooms for her quilting club. I need to think about furnishings. I have plenty of office furniture, but that house calls for something more elegant."

"Check out the antique shop at the flea market."

"Yeah, I will."

Rick thought about the journal. Red didn't put a lot of description into the furnishings, but there were clues. Should he share the notebooks with Bob? The muscles in his neck and back contracted. No. Red's story was too intimate to share.

The next day, Rick went to the grocery store. The parking lot was full and there was a line at the entrance. Why? The store hadn't been this crowded at holiday time. He queued behind a woman who turned and said, "You're too close. Stand on that tape."

He looked at the ground and backed up. Other customers stood obediently with their toes on lines of tape, six feet apart. "What's going on?"

"Haven't you been following the news? We have to socially distance so we don't spread the virus." The line advanced. The woman stepped forward and Rick moved onto the strip of tape she'd vacated. When he reached the door, an employee stood guard with a dispenser of hand sanitizer. Rick followed the lead of the people ahead of him and dutifully cleansed his hands.

In the store, some items on his list had sold out. *What's going on? It's not even hurricane season.* He was able to find paper towels, but toilet paper had been stripped from the shelves. He located an employee. "Do you have more toilet paper in the back?"

"Sorry, it's all gone. We have more on backorder."

Rick returned to the sanity of his own home.

About midafternoon, Kyle called. "Dad, I'm in mourning."

"What?"

"I took the afternoon off to watch the basketball game, but it's been cancelled."

"Why? What happened?"

"They're afraid of spreading COVID. The whole SEC Tournament has been called off."

"This is nuts. Why are people so afraid? There haven't been that many cases."

"I know, but apparently this bug is acting like the kind that become major pandemics."

"There hasn't been a major pandemic in a hundred years. Surely medicine has progressed enough by now to handle it."

"Let's hope so. Allison wants to talk to you."

Before Allison had a chance to ask, Rick said, "No I don't have my flu shot yet."

"That's not what I want to talk about. They're saying people your age should stay home, stay away from crowds. If you need anything from the store, let one of us know and we'll pick it up for you."

"I went to Publix this morning, so I'm good. You wouldn't believe what I had to go through just to get into the store."

"Yes, I do know. I just want you to be careful. Maybe forget the flu shot. A doctor's office isn't a safe place to be right now."

"Okay. I bow to your expertise. Oh, if you come across any toilet paper, pick me up a pack."

At six o'clock, he turned on the news. The panic seemed to have ratcheted up several notches. As he reached for the remote to switch it off, the local newsman announced, "There are a lot of disappointed NHRA fans this weekend. Gatornationals has been postponed due to concerns about the coronavirus…"

Rick heard no more. Although he wasn't a hot rod fan, this was un-heard of. What would be called off next? That evening, he decided to trade one madness for another and read the last few pages of the journal:

4/14 M. When I watered my little pothos plant today, I realized I'd made plans for me & Hugh, but not for the plant. If we left, there'd be no one to take care of it & it would die. I may not be able to take it with me, so I put it outside where it can get rain & have a chance to live. I hung it on a limb of that nice live oak in the back yard, where it can get rain & still be in the shade like Louie said it needs to be. I'll take care of it as long as I'm here.

* * *

Rick sighed. He thought about the pothos he'd found under that tree, brought home, and repotted. He tended it all winter and, with spring, hung it in the carport with Amy's plants. If he ever found Red, would she want her plant back?

4/15 N. Tonight it will be 16 weeks & time to wind the clock, if we choose to. We've talked about little else. At first, Hugh was non-committal. He said it was up to me. He's happy with the way things are & doesn't even think about leaving. Then he got quiet & I could see the wheels turning in his head. Finally he said, "I'm satisfied with life here for the time being, but that might change. I'm enjoying the moment, but maybe we should keep our options open. We need a progression of time or we may fall back into depression. Let's wind it." Well, that's 12 hours away. Let's see if we change our minds between now & then.

4/16—3:45 AM! I overslept! I've never done that before. When the clock strikes midnight it always wakes me. Hugh must not have heard the clock, either. I don't know what to do. It's still going, but will I mess things up if I wind it now? Why did I oversleep? Do I unconsciously not want to wind it?

4/16 N. Last night Hugh heard me pacing the floor & crying. When I told him what I'd done (or hadn't done) he stayed calm. "It's still running. It's not too late to wind it, but I don't think it'll make any difference either way. We'll continue to move forward."

"But we were trapped so long in a timeless void. It's the only way I can keep track of days."

He actually laughed at me! "Have you forgotten you can go outside now? You can see day & night. So can I. All I have to do is look out my windows." So we decided to let it rest. We didn't wind it. It's an 8 day clock, so it's still going.

I was so nervous, I didn't try to go back to sleep. Instead, I went out to the screened porch—the east side of the house—& stayed until daybreak. I was so relieved when the sky started to get light & the sun rose. I went down the steps & walked around the yard. When I passed Hugh's window, he waved. So, he stayed up to see if morning came, too.

4/16 A little after midnight. Did I think the clock was magical? That it'd keep going w/out being wound? Well, it ran down. When it struck 12, it sounded very tired, barely able to get out those last few bongs. I went outdoors to be sure I still could, & the stars were shining, just like they did last night. But when I went back in the house, it was so quiet w/out the clock ticking. Too quiet. My life the past 4 ½ months has centered around the clock sounding the hours. We decided to wind it & I advanced the hands a little.

4/17 N. Apparently, letting the clock run down didn't mess anything up. Things are rocking along like they did before. I can still see out the downstairs windows and go outside. But still no gate.

4/17 M. We seem to have settled back into our routine. I play piano, Hugh lifts weights. I harvest vegs, Hugh cooks them. He always chooses a delectable meat dish to accompany them. He's actually a good cook, maybe better than Wendel. I think even Louie would approve of his cuisine. In some ways, the past few days seem like no time at all (as opposed to non-time) yet they also seem like eternity.

4/18 A little after 1pm. I was reading in my room & must have fallen asleep. I dreamed my windows were open & this time I could look out beyond the fence. There were trees on the street & they were fully leafed out. I could see a yellow house across the street & a blue one next to it. In the front yard of the house next door is some sort of sign, but I can't read the words, b/c the branches of the dogwood are in the way. When I woke up, I was standing at my windows, but they were closed up again. Then I heard the clock strike one. I missed noon, so I wrote this quickly. I don't know why I was standing up while I was sleeping.

* * *

Rick searched his memory. Yes, the house across from the Wilson House was yellow, the next one blue, and the law firm's sign was in their front yard. Of course, she knew this, but how long ago did she write it? Rick turned the page. The entry continued for two more lines. There was a little scribble, as if the pen had been drawn accidentally across the paper:

Whoops. I thought I heard the front door open. Hugh's calling me. I'd better go see what's going on. It sounds like ~~~~

* * *

That was it. Rick flipped through the rest of the notebook. Nothing more. Did she get out? Why didn't she take the notebooks with her? Was she in too great a hurry? On his first visit to the Wilson House, he'd found them in her hiding place in the closet. Why did she take the time to put the journal back in her hidey hole?

Or did she?

FRIDAY THE 13TH

On Friday, Rick arrived at the Wilson House for his meeting with the building inspector. He parked in the now-vacant lot next door and walked around the white picket fence to the front gate. The house seemed to smile at him.

His mind conjured the image it had presented on his first visit, when he came to check out the place for Bob. The old Queen Anne style home had lurked behind a tall privacy fence and scrub trees, concealing decades of neglect. The weathered siding, broken gingerbread, and boarded-over windows made it the perfect setting for a ghost story.

Rick's thoughts wandered to the journal. String up Halloween lights on the porch, add a scarecrow with a pumpkin head, and he would be looking at the scene Red had witnessed when she first arrived so long ago. As his admiring eyes roamed over the product of his labor, the spell was broken by the large green W in the gable window—backlit by a light in the attic! *Now, who left that light on?*

Leaving the front door unlocked, he made one last walk-through, alert for minor things he may have overlooked. Every light switch and outlet had its cover, every blemish repaired. Even scraps and stray tools had been removed. Finding the downstairs in good shape, Rick proceeded to the second floor.

He opened the door to the attic staircase, intending to turn off the light, but to his surprise, the switch was off and the attic was dark. He turned the light on and climbed the steps to investigate. All seemed in order. Rick shook his head. It must have been his imagination. Perhaps the stained glass had somehow captured the sun's light.

He heard the front door open and close. *The building inspector's here.* Rick descended to the landing and turned off the attic light. As he crossed toward the main staircase, an incongruity captured his attention. The open bedroom doors admitted light from their windows, but the turret room, which had the most windows, was dim, as though lit by a single lamp.

Someone called from below. From the turret room came sounds of paper rustling, a chair scraping across the floor, an answering shout, "I'm coming."

Suddenly, daylight filled the turret room, and the doorway framed the figure of a woman. A woman with red hair. She appeared not to notice Rick, but paused to adjust her glasses with her left hand.

Her left hand! Suddenly, things fell into place. That hand was not fully formed—an almost baby-like fist with a nub of a thumb and two vestigial fingers. Yet she played piano.

Rick could neither move nor speak. The woman crossed the landing and hurried down the staircase. The sound of the front door jolted him into action. "Wait! I want to talk to you!" Before he was halfway down the stairs, the door closed behind her.

When Rick snatched the door open, his jaw dropped. A weathered board fence confronted him. The gate stood open.

"Wait! I have your notebooks!"

The world was eerily quiet. No traffic noises, no children playing. Even the birds were silent. The woman disappeared through the gate. It closed behind her and dissolved.

Rick was left looking at the white picket fence and the brightly painted houses of the neighborhood. He ran to the street and searched in both directions. There was no trace of her.

"I only want to talk to you!" he shouted to the empty air. "What is your name?"

When the building inspector arrived, Rick was almost too distracted to follow what the man said. *He must think I'm a blithering idiot. Or on something*. After the inspector left, Rick had to study the papers to assure himself that the house had, indeed, passed inspection.

Before he left, he searched the building and grounds thoroughly but found no evidence of Red's existence.

Back at home, Rick flipped through a couple of the notebooks, as if looking for—for what? He reread the last entry: "I thought I heard the front door open. Hugh's calling me."

He had come to the end of the journal, but not the end of the story. Red had finally escaped from the Wilson House, Hugh with her.

The image of her emerging from the turret room and fleeing from the house was burned into his brain. What exactly had he witnessed? All those months of denial, of ignoring bizarre things... Objects that appeared: wicker furniture, remains of a piano, a half-mask, the sledge-hammer, the notebooks themselves. Elements of the story that bled into his reality: a scorched floor, cigarette smoke, the ceiling medallions, pink bougainvillea.

Neighbors thought the Wilson House was haunted. Several workers had sensed an uncanny presence. Something had spooked Kyle and his friends. The policeman, Tony, claimed the house was "sure haunted." At first, even Bob acted reluctant to go inside.

A different kind of haunting—eight people trapped in a *Twilight Zone* scenario, their lives playing out through the journal while the rest of the world went on around them: curious teenagers exploring the house, vagrants trying to live there, Rick and his workmen wreaking havoc and eventually restoring it to the pristine beauty Red and her friends knew.

A few of the characters even turned out to exist: Virgil, Louie/Calvin, a woman with a biracial child named Wendell, a seamstress resembling Doreen.

And then Red shows up at the last minute, vacating the house just as it begins a new life. But what had he actually seen? She'd acted as though he didn't exist, ignoring his plea to wait, to talk to him. And that impossible fence, the disappearing gate. Suddenly, he understood why

Red dared not wait. The gate was open, perhaps her only opportunity to escape.

Rick could no longer think of the journal as fiction. But what was it?

Red's unformed left hand—like Amy's right hand. So much in common, yet polar opposites. Red had poured her heart and soul into her journal, disclosing secrets few would confess to another. With regret, he realized he'd been privy to Red's inner thoughts in ways he had never been with Amy.

A one-handed piano player shouldn't be hard to find. He could call the University, even if the people in the music department thought he was crazy. Where else could he look? Churches and any venue with a piano player. Scan the want ads and call piano teachers? Talk to "Doreen" at Amber's Alterations? Kristie said he should get out more—he could visit the Mall. If he spotted a woman with red hair, how would she react if he tried to get a closer look at her hands?

The phone jangled him back to reality.

"Hey, Rick." Bob sounded funny.

"Are you okay?"

"Depends on what you mean by okay."

"Are you sick?"

"Not physically."

"I'm sorry, Bob, I meant to call you. The house passed inspection. You can move in any time now."

Bob cleared his throat. "No, I can't."

"Why?"

"Cause they're shutting me down."

"Shutting you down?"

"It's that blasted coronavirus. They're shutting down everything—restaurants, schools, sports—they want everybody to stay home, no contact with anyone outside their household. I can't do business! I don't know what I'm going to do." Bob sighed. "Rick, it's not your fault, it's mine, but I poured a ton of money into that house. I dug myself into a hole so deep, if the economy tanks, I don't know that I'll ever get out of it."

"Well, once they get a handle on this virus, it should ease up."

"I hope you're right. They say everything's closed until March 30th, at least. Maybe longer." He grunted. "When I'm home all day, I grate on Melody's nerves. One reason I haven't retired. She's gonna end up killing me."

Rick wanted to laugh, but Bob's distress was too real.

After they got off the phone, he called Kristie. "What's this I hear about schools closing?"

"Yes. They told us today. Until the end of the month, at least. Next week is spring break, anyway, so that's not so bad, but I talked to Allison and she thinks this is going to be a long drawn-out affair. Maybe until summer, if not longer."

"They're overreacting."

"I don't think so. Every day there are more and more cases. It's deadly, and they don't have a cure. Dad, you need to stay home. Don't go anywhere, even to my house or Kyle's. Older people are more susceptible. Even the church is closed Sunday. If you need anything from the store, let me know. I'll pick it up for you and leave it in the carport."

The irony was not lost on Rick—Red gains her freedom, and he is sentenced to solitary confinement.

He managed to stay home all weekend. Yard work was a welcome diversion, but he couldn't do that forever. By Monday, he could stand no more. He jumped into his truck and drove to the Wilson House. Ben Whitehead stood in front of his law firm, watering a newly planted shrub. "Rick, what'er you doin' here?"

"Going stir crazy."

"Don't I know it. I had to close up shop. Even the courthouse is closed. Never thought I'd see the day.... I figure I'm safe enough as long as nobody else is around, but you better keep your distance from me. One of my guys was coughing so bad last week I sent him home. Hope he doesn't have it."

"I'm just going to check on the house, make sure nobody's been bothering anything. See you around."

"Yeah. Stay healthy."

After walking through the Wilson House and around the yard, Rick went home. The next day, after he checked on the house, he drove through town. The streets were empty, like a ghost town. A police car cruised by. The officer seemed to frown at him. How was he going to cope with this? He thought about Red. All the places he'd planned to look for her were closed.

At home, he idly paged through the newspaper. Yes—place an ad! He labored over the wording and settled on "Piano player wanted. Looking for red hair and a distinguishing characteristic. I have your notebooks and your plant. If you'd like them back, please reply." *Do people even read these?*

March 30th came and went. Rick drove to the Wilson House every day. When he needed gas, he used his credit card at the pump for the first time since it had been hacked last year. Why not? He had all the time in the world to sit on hold with the card company to get it straightened out.

No one answered his ad.

His imagination ran away with him. Driving through the empty town, he'd mistake a mailbox, or a sign, or a shrub for a human being. In his mind's eye, it was a tall blond man, an Asian woman, a Hispanic man, an aging hippy, a biracial couple, or a body builder. As the image morphed back to its true form, he'd open his window and whisper, "Tell her to meet me at the Wilson House."

If instead, he thought he saw a woman with red hair, he'd shout, "I will gladly return your notebooks to you. All I want is—please tell me the rest of the story!"

Finis

ABOUT THE AUTHOR

Marie Q Rogers lives and writes in the woods of North Florida. An avid reader, her favorites include classical literature, especially Charles Dickens; science fiction, including Robert Heinlein; the masterpieces of J. R. R. Tolkien; and just about anything that catches her fancy. In addition to fiction, she irregularly publishes creative non-fiction on her weblog marieqrogers.com.

Other Novels by Marie Q Rogers:

Trials by Fire

Quest for Namai

Season of the Dove